Richard Pike

Railway Adventures and Anecdotes

Extending over More than Fifty Years

Richard Pike

Railway Adventures and Anecdotes
Extending over More than Fifty Years

ISBN/EAN: 9783337178956

Printed in Europe, USA, Canada, Australia, Japan

Cover: Foto ©Andreas Hilbeck / pixelio.de

More available books at **www.hansebooks.com**

RAILWAY ADVENTURES

AND ANECDOTES:

Extending over more than Fifty Years.

EDITED BY RICHARD PIKE.

"Soon shall thy arm, unconquer'd steam, afar
Drag the slow barge, or drive the rapid car."
— *Dr. Darwin's Botanic Garden*, 1789.

LONDON: HAMILTON, ADAMS, AND CO.
NOTTINGHAM: J. DERRY.

1884.

PREFACE.

ALTHOUGH railways are comparatively of recent date we are so accustomed to them that it is difficult to realize the condition of the country before their introduction. How different are the present day ideas as to speed in travelling to those entertained in the good old times. The celebrated historian, Niebuhr, who was in England in 1798, thus describes the rapid travelling of that period:—"Four horses drawing a coach with six persons inside, four on the roof, a sort of conductor besides the coachman, and overladen with luggage, have to get over seven English miles in the hour; and as the coach goes on without ever stopping except at the principal stages, it is not surprising that you can traverse the whole extent of the country in so few days. But for any length of time this rapid motion is quite too unnatural. You can only get a very piece-meal view of the country from the windows, and with the tremendous speed at which you go can keep no object long in sight; you are unable also to stop at any place." Near the same time the late Lord Campbell, travelling for the first time by coach from Scotland to London, was seriously advised to stay a day at York, as the rapidity of motion (eight miles per hour) had caused several through-going passengers to die of apoplexy.

It is stated in the year 1825, there was in the whole world, only one railway carriage, built to convey passengers. It was on the first railway between Stockton and Darlington, and bore on its panels the motto—"Periculum privatum,

publica utilitas" At the opening of this line the people's
ideas of railway speed were scarcely ahead of the canal boat.
For we are told, "Strange to say, a man on horseback
carrying a flag headed the procession. It was not thought
so dangerous a place after all. The locomotive was only
supposed to go at the rate of from four to six miles an hour;
an ordinary horse could easily keep ahead of that. A great
concourse of people stood along the line. Many of them
tried to accompany the procession by running, and some
gentlemen on horseback galloped across the fields to keep
up with the engine. At a favourable part of the road
Stephenson determined to try the speed of the engine, and
he called upon the horseman with the flag to get out of his
way! The speed was at once raised to twelve miles an
hour, and soon after to fifteen, causing much excitement
among the passengers."

George Stephenson was greatly impressed with the vast
possibilities belonging to the future of railway travelling.
When battling for the locomotive he seemed to see with
true prescience what it was destined to accomplish. "I will
do something in course of time," he said, "which will
astonish all England." Years afterwards when asked to
what he alluded, he replied, "I meant to make the mail
run between London and Edinburgh by the locomotive
before I died, and I have done it." Thus was a similar
prediction fulfilled, which at the time he uttered it was
doubtless considered a very wild prophecy, "Men shall
take supper in London and breakfast in Edinburgh."

From a small beginning railways have spread over the
four quarters of the globe. Thousands of millions of pounds
have been spent upon their construction. Railway con-

tractors such as Peto and Brassey at one time employed
armies of workmen, more numerous than the contending
hosts engaged in many a battle celebrated in history.
Considering the mighty revolutions that have been wrought
in social affairs and in the commerce of the world by railways, John Bright was not far wrong when he said in the
House of Commons "Who are the greatest men of the
present age? Not your warriors, not your statesmen.
They are your engineers."

Tho Railway era, although of modern date, has been rich
in adventures and incidents. Numerous works have been
written upon Railways, also memoirs of Railway Engineers,
relating their struggles and triumphs, which have charmed
multitudes of readers. Yet no volume has been published
consisting exclusively of Railway Adventures and Anecdotes.
Books having the heading of Railway Anecdotes, or similar
titles, containing few of such anecdotes but many of a
miscellaneous character, have from time to time appeared.
Anecdotes, racy of the Railway calling and circumstances
connected with it are very numerous: they are to be
found scattered in Parliamentary Blue Books, Journals,
Biographies, and many out-of-the-way channels. Many of
them are highly instructive, diverting, and mirth-provoking,
having reference to persons in all conditions. The "Railway
Adventures and Anecdotes," illustrating many a quaint
and picturesque scene of railway life, have been drawn
from a great variety of sources. I have for a long time
been collecting them, and am willing to believe they may
prove entertaining and profitable to the railway traveller
and the general reader, relieving the tedium of hours when
the mind is not disposed to grapple with profounder
subjects.

The romance of railways is in the past and not in the future. How desirable then it is that a well written history of British Railways should speedily be produced, before their traditions, interesting associations, and early workers shall be forgotten. A work of such magnitude would need to be entrusted to a band of expert writers. With an able man like Mr. Williams, the author of *Our Iron Roads*, and the *History of the Midland Railway*, presiding over the enterprise, a history might be produced which would be interesting to the present and to future generations. The history although somewhat voluminous would be a necessity to every public and private library. Many of our railway companies might do worse than contribute £500 or £1000 each to encourage such an important literary undertaking. It would give an impetus to the study of railway matters and it is not at all unlikely in the course of a short time the companies would be recouped for their outlay.

Before concluding, it is only right I should express my grateful acknowledgments to the numerous body of subscribers to this work. Among them are noblemen of the highest rank and distinction, cabinet ministers, members of Parliament, magistrates, ministers of all sections of the Christian church, merchants, farmers, tradesmen, and artisans. Through their helpful kindness my responsibility has been considerably lightened, and I trust they will have no reason to regret that their confidence has been misplaced.

CONTENTS.

10 CONTENTS.

RAILWAY ADVENTURES AND ANECDOTES.

ORIGIN OF RAILWAYS

The immediate parent of the railway was the wooden tram-road, which existed at an early period in colliery districts. Mr. Beaumont, of Newcastle, is said to have been the first to lay down wooden rails as long ago as 1630. More than one hundred and forty years elapsed before the invention was greatly improved. Mr. John Carr, in 1776 (although not the first to use iron rails), was the first to lay down a cast-iron railway, nailed to wooden sleepers, for the Duke of Newcastle's colliery near Sheffield. This innovation was regarded with great disfavour by the workpeople as an interference with the vested rights of labour. Mr. Carr's life, as a consequence, was in much jeopardy and for four days he had to conceal himself in a wood to avoid the violence of an indignant and vindictive populace.

WAY-LEAVES.

Roger North, referring to a visit paid to Newcastle by his brother, the Lord Keeper Guildford, in 1676, writes:— "Another remarkable thing is their *way-leaves*; for when men have pieces of ground between the colliery and the river, they sell the leave to lead coal over the ground, and so dear that the owner of a rood of ground will expect £20 per annum for this leave. The manner of the carriage is by laying rails of timber from the colliery down to the river exactly straight and parallel, and bulky carts are made with four rowlets fitting these rails, whereby the carriage is so easy that one horse will draw four or five chaldron of coals, and is an immense benefit to the coal merchants."

B

SIR ISAAC NEWTON'S PREDICTION OF RAILWAY SPEED.

In a tract by the Rev. Mr. Craig, Vicar of Leamington, entitled "Astral Wonders," is to be found the following remarkable passage:—"Let me narrate to you an anecdote concerning Sir Isaac Newton and Voltaire. Sir Isaac wrote a book on the Prophet Daniel, and another on the Revelations; and he said, in order to fulfil certain prophecies before a certain date terminated, namely 1260 years, there would be a certain mode of travelling of which the men in his time had no conception; nay, that the knowledge of mankind would be so increased that they would be able to travel at the rate of fifty miles an hour. Voltaire, who did not believe in the Holy Scriptures, got hold of this, and said, "Now look at that mighty mind of Newton, who discovered Gravity, and told us such marvels for us all to admire, when he became an old man and got into his dotage, he began to study that book called the Bible; and it appears that in order to credit its fabulous nonsense, we must believe that mankind's knowledge will be so much increased that we shall be able to travel fifty miles an hour. The poor 'dotard!' exclaimed the philosophic infidel, Voltaire, in the complaisancy of his pity. But who is the dotard now?"

THE ATMOSPHERIC RAILROAD ANTICIPATED.

First Voice.
" But why drives on that ship so fast,
   Without or wave or wind?"

Second Voice.
" The air is cut away before,
   And closes from behind."
—*The Ancient Mariner.*

This is the exact principle of the atmospheric railroad, and it is, perhaps, worthy of note as a curious fact that such a means of locomotion should have occurred to Coleridge so long ago.

W. Y. Bernhard Smith, in *Notes and Queries.*

EARLY STEAM CARRIAGES.

Stuart in his "Historical and Descriptive Anecdotes of Steam Engines and of their Inventors and Improvers," gives a description of what was supposed to be the first model of a steam carriage. The constructor was a Frenchman named Cuguot, who exhibited it before the Marshal de Saxe in 1763. He afterwards built an engine on the same model at the cost of the French monarch But when set in motion it projected itself onward with such force that it knocked down a wall which stood in its way, and—its power being considered too great for ordinary use—it was put aside as being a dangerous machine, and was stowed away in the Arsenal Museum at Paris. It is now to be seen in the Conservatoire des Arts et Métiers.

Mr. Smiles also remarks that "An American inventor, named Oliver Evans, was also occupied with the same idea, for, in 1772, he invented a steam carriage to travel on common roads; and, in 1787, he obtained from the State of Maryland the exclusive right to make and use steam carriages. The invention, however, never came into practical use.

It also appears that, in 1784, William Symington, the inventor of the steamboat, conceived the idea of employing steam power in the propulsion of carriages; and, in 1786, he had a working model of a steam carriage constructed which he submitted to the professors and other scientific gentlemen of Edinburgh. But the state of the Scotch roads was at that time so horrible that he considered it impracticable to proceed further with his scheme, and he shortly gave it up in favour of his project of steam navigation.

The first English model of a steam carriage was made in 1784 by William Murdoch, the friend and assistant of Watt. It was on the high-pressure principle and ran on three wheels. The boiler was heated by a spirit lamp, and the whole machine was of very diminutive dimensions, standing little more than a foot high. Yet, on one occasion, the little engine went so fast that it outran the speed of the inventor. Mr. Buckle says that one night after returning from his duties in the mine at Redruth, in Cornwall, Murdoch determined to try the working of his model locomotive.

For this purpose he had recourse to the walk leading to the church, about a mile from the town. The walk was rather narrow and was bounded on either side by high hedges. It was a dark night, and Murdoch set out alone to try his experiment. Having lit his lamp, the water shortly began to boil, and off started the engine with the inventor after it. He soon heard distant shouts of despair. It was too dark to perceive objects, but he shortly found, on following up the machine, that the cries for assistance proceeded from the worthy pastor of the parish, who, going towards the town on business, was met on this lonely road by the hissing and fiery little monster, which he subsequently declared he had taken to be the Evil One in *propriâ personâ*. No further steps, however, were taken by Murdoch to embody his idea of a locomotive carriage in a more practical form.

FIRST RAILWAY BILL.

The first Railway Bill passed by Parliament was for a line from Wandsworth to Croydon, in 1801, but a quarter of a century elapsed before the first line was actually constructed for carrying passengers between Stockton and Darlington. People still living can remember the mail coaches that plied once a month between Edinburgh and London, making the journey in twelve or fourteen days. The *Annual Register* of 1820 boasts that "English mail coaches run 7 miles an hour; French only $4\frac{1}{2}$ miles; the former travelling, in the year, forty times the length of miles that the French accomplish." These coaches were a great improvement on the previous method of sending the mails. In 1783 a petition to Parliament stated that "the mails are generally entrusted to some idle boy, without character, mounted on a worn-out hack."

"*Progress of the World*" by M. G. Mulhall.

RAILWAY FROM MERSTHAM TO WANDSWORTH.

Charles Knight thus describes this old line:—"The earliest railway for public traffic in England was one passing from Merstham to Wandsworth, through Croydon; a small, single line, on which a miserable team of donkeys, some thirty years ago, might be seen crawling at the rate

of four miles an hour, with several trucks of stone and lime
behind them. It was commenced in 1801, opened in 1803;
and the men of science of that day—we cannot say that the
respectable name of Stephenson was not among them,
(Stephenson was then a brakesman at Killingworth)—
tested its capabilities and found that one horse could draw
some thirty-five tons at six miles an hour, and then, with
prophetic wisdom, declared that railways could never be
worked profitably. The old Croydon railway is no longer
used. The genius loci must look with wonder on the
gigantic offspring of the little railway, which has swallowed
up its own sire. Lean mules no longer crawl leisurely
along the little rails with trucks of stone through Croydon,
once perchance during the day, but the whistle and the
rush of the locomotive are now heard all day long. Not a
few loads of lime, but all London and its contents, by com-
parison—men, women, children, horses, dogs, oxen, sheep,
pigs, carriages, merchandise, food,—would seem to be now-
a-days passing through Croydon ; for day after day, more
than 100 journeys are made by the great railroads which
pass the place."

RAILWAY ANNOUNCEMENT.

The following announcement was published in a London
periodical, dated August 1, 1802 :—"The Surrey Iron
Railway is now completed over the high road through
Wandsworth town. On Wednesday, June 8, several
carriages of all descriptions passed over the iron rails without meeting with the least obstacle. Among these, the
Portsmouth wagon, drawn by eight horses and weighing
from eight to ten tons, passed over the rails, and did not
appear to make the slightest impression upon them."

MERTHYR TYDVIL RAILWAY.

An Act of Parliament was granted for a railway to
Merthyr Tydvil in 1803, and the following year the first
locomotive which ran on a railway is described in a racy
manner by the *Western Mail*, as follows : — "Quaint, rattling,
puffing, asthmatic, and wheezy, the pioneer of ten thousand
gilding creations of beauty and strength made its way
between the white-washed houses of the old tramway at

Merthyr. It has a dwarf body placed on a high framework, constructed by the hedge carpenter of the place in the roughest possible fashion. The wheels were equally rough and large, and surmounting all was a huge stack, ugly enough when it was new, but in after times made uglier by whitewash and rust. Every movement was made with a hideous uproar, snorting and clanking, and this, aided by the noise of the escaping steam, formed a tableau from which, met in the byeway, every old woman would run with affright. The Merthyr locomotive was made jointly by Trevithick, a Cornishman, and Rees Jones, of Penydarran. The day fixed for the trial was the 12th of February, 1804, and the track a tramway, lately formed from Penydarran, at the back of Plymouth Works, by the side of the Troedyrhiw, and so down to the navigation. Great was the concourse assembled; villagers of all ages and sizes thronged the spot; and the rumour of the day's doings even penetrated up the defiles of Taff Vawr and Taff Vach, bringing down old apple-faced farmers and their wives, who were told of a power and a speed that would alter everything, and do away with horses altogether. Prim, cosy, apple-faced people, innocent and primitive, little thought ye then of the changes which the clanking monster was to yield; how Grey Dobbin would see flying by a mass of wood and iron, thousands of tons of weight, bearing not only the commerce of the country, but hundreds of people as well; how rivers and mountains would afford no obstacle, as the mighty azure waves leap the one and dash through the other. On the first engine and trains that started on the memorable day in February, twenty persons clustered like bees, anxious, we learn in the 'History of Merthyr,' to win immortality by being thus distinguished above all their fellows; the trains were six in number, laden with iron, and amidst a concourse of villagers, including the constable, the 'druggister,' and the class generally dubbed 'shopwors' by the natives, were Richard Crawshay and Mr. Samuel Homfray. The driver was one William Richards, and on the engine were perched Trevithick and Rees Jones, their faces black, but their eyes bright with the anticipation of victory. Soon the signal was given, and amidst a mighty roar from the people, the wheels turned and the mass moved forward, going steadily at the rate of five miles an hour until a bridge was reached a little below the town that did not admit of the stack going under, and as this was built of bricks, there was a great crash and instant stoppage. Trevithick and Jones were of the old-fashioned school of men who did not believe in impossibilities. The fickle crowd, too, who had hurrahed like mad, hung back and said 'It won't do'; but these heroes, the advance-guard of a race who had done more to make England famous than battles by land or sea, sprang to the ground and worked like Britons, never ceasing until they had repaired the mishap, and then they rattled on, and finally reached their journey's end. The return journey was a failure, on account of gradients and curves, but the possibility of success was demonstrated; and from this run on the Merthyr tramway the railway age—marked with throes and suspense, delays, accidents, and misadventures—finally began."

AN AFFRIGHTED TOLL-KEEPER.

There is a story told by Coleridge about the steam engine which Trevithick exhibited at work on a temporary railroad in London. Trevithick and his partner Captain Vivian, prior to this exhibition were riding on the carriage on the turnpike road near to Plymouth. It had committed sundry damage in its course, knocking down the rails of a gentleman's garden, when Vivian saw the toll-bar in front of them closed he called to Trevithick to slacken speed which he did just in time to save the gate. The affrighted toll-keeper instantly opened it. "What have us got to pay?" asked Captain Vivian, careful as to honesty if reckless as to grammar.

"Na-na-na-na!" stammered the poor man, trembling in every limb, with his teeth chattering as if he had got the ague.

"What have us got to pay, I ask?"

"Na-noth-nothing to pay! My de-dear Mr. Devil, do drive as fast as you can! Nothing to pay!"

AN EARLY RAILWAY.

More than twenty years before the opening of the Liverpool and Manchester Railway, the celebrated engineer Trevithick constructed, not only a locomotive engine, but also a railway, that the London public might see with their own eyes what the new high pressure steam engine could effect, and how greatly superior a railway was to a common road for locomotion. The sister of Davies Gilbert named this engine "Catch me who can." The following interesting account in a letter to a correspondent was given by John Isaac Hawkins, an engineer well known in his day.

"Sir,—Observing that it is stated in your last number (No. 1232, dated the 20th instant, page 269), under the head of 'Twenty-one Years' Retrospect of the Railway System,' that the greatest speed of Trevithick's engine was five miles an hour, I think it due to the memory of that extraordinary man to declare that about the year 1808 he laid down a circular railway in a field adjoining the New Road, near or at the spot now forming the southern half of Euston Square; that he placed a locomotive engine, weighing about ten tons, on that railway—on which I rode, with my watch in hand—at the rate of twelve miles an hour; that Mr. Trevithick then gave his opinion that it would go twenty miles an hour, or more, on a straight railway; that the engine was exhibited at one shilling admittance, including a ride for the few who were not too timid; that it ran for some weeks, when a rail broke and occasioned the engine to fly off in a tangent and overturn, the ground being very soft at the time. Mr. Trevithick having expended all his means in erecting the works and enclosure, and the shillings not having come in fast enough to pay current expenses, the engine was not again set on the rail."

SHREWD OBSERVERS.

Sir Richard Phillips was a man of foresight, for, in the year 1813, he wrote the following words in his "Morning Walk to Kew," a book of some popularity in its day :— "I found delight in witnessing at Wandsworth the economy of horse labour on the iron railway. Yet a heavy sigh escaped me as I thought of the inconceivable millions of money which had been spent about Malta, four or five of which might have been the means of extending double lines of iron railway from London to Edinburgh, Glasgow, Holyhead, Milford, Falmouth, Yarmouth, Dover, and Portsmouth. A reward of a single thousand would have supplied coaches and other vehicles of various degrees of speed, with the best tackle for readily turning out; and we might ere this have witnessed our mail coaches running at the rate of ten miles an hour, drawn by a single horse, or impelled fifteen miles an hour by Blenkinsop's steam engine. Such would have been a legitimate motive for overstepping the income of a nation; and the completion of so great and useful a work would have afforded rational ground for public triumph in general jubilee." Mr. Edgeworth, writing to James Watt on the 7th of August, 1813, remarks, "I have always thought that steam would become the universal lord, and that we should in time scorn post-horses. An iron railroad would be a cheaper thing than a road on the common construction."

CUVIER'S DESCRIPTION OF THE LOCOMOTIVE.

The celebrated Cuvier, in an address delivered by him before the French Institute in the year 1816, thus referred to the nascent locomotive:—"A steam engine, mounted upon a carriage whose wheels indent themselves along a road specially prepared for it, is attached to a line of loaded vehicles. A fire is lit underneath the boiler, by which the engine is speedily set in motion, and in a short time the whole are brought to their journey's end. The traveller who, from a distance, first sees this strange spectacle of a train of loaded carriages traversing the country by the simple force of steam, can with difficulty believe his eyes."

The locomotive thus described by Cuvier was the first engine of the kind regularly employed in the working of railway traffic. It was impelled by means of a cogged wheel, which worked into a cogged rail, after the method adopted by Mr. Blenkinsop, upon the Middleton Coal Railway, near Leeds; and the speed of the train which it dragged behind it was only from three to four miles an hour.

Ten years later, the same power and speed of the locomotive were still matters of wonderment. for. in 1825, we
find Mr. Mackenzie, in his " History of Northumberland."
thus describing the performances on the Wylam Coal Railroad :—" A stranger." said he, " is struck with surprise
and astonishment on seeing a locomotive engine moving
majestically along the road at the rate of four or five miles
an hour, drawing along from ten to fourteen loaded wagons.
weighing about twenty-one-and-a-half tons; and his surprise
is increased on witnessing the extraordinary facility with
which the engine is managed.   This invention is indeed a
noble triumph of science."

In the same year, the first attempt was made to carry
passengers by railway between Stockton and Darlington.
A machine resembling the yellow caravan still seen at
country fairs was built and fitted up with seats all round
it, and set upon the rails, along which it was drawn by a
horse.   It was found exceedingly convenient to travel by,
and the number of passengers between the two towns so
much increased that several bodies of old stage coaches were
bought up, mounted upon railway wheels, and added to
the carrying stock of the Stockton and Darlington Company.
At length the horse was finally discarded in favour of the
locomotive, and not only coals and merchandise, but passengers of all classes, were drawn by steam.

—*Railway News.*

A RAILWAY PROJECTOR.

In the year 1819, Thomas Gray—a deep thinker with a
mind of comprehensive grasp—was travelling in the North
of England when he saw a train of coal-wagons drawn by
steam along a colliery tramroad.   " Why," he questioned
the engineer, " are not these tramroads laid down all over
England, so as to supersede our common roads, and steam
engines employed to convey goods and passengers along
them. so as to supersede horse power ? "   The engineer
replied, " Just propose you that to the nation, sir, and see
what you will get by it !   Why, sir, you will be worried to
death for your pains."   Nothing daunted by this reply,
Thomas Gray could scarcely think or talk upon any other
subject.   In vision he saw the country covered with a net-

work of tramroads. Before his time the famous Duke of
Bridgewater might have some misgivings about his canals.
It is related on a certain occasion some one said to him,
"You must be making handsomely out of your canals."
"Oh, yes," grumbled he in reply, "they will last my time,
but I don't like the look of these tramroads; there's mischief in them." Mr. Gray, with prophetic eye, saw the
great changes which the iron railway would make in the
means of transit throughout the civilized world. In 1820
he brought out his now famous work, entitled "Observations
on a General Iron Railway, or Land Steam Conveyance, to
supersede the necessity of horses in all public vehicles;
showing its vast superiority in every respect over all the
present pitiful methods of conveyance by Turnpike-roads,
Canals, and Coasting Traders: containing every species of
information relative to Railroads and Locomotive Engines."
The book is illustrated by a plate exhibiting different kinds
of carriages drawn on the railway by locomotives. He
evidently anticipated that the locomotive of the future
would be capable of going at a considerable speed, for on
the plate is engraved these lines :—

> "No speed with this can fleetest horse compare;
> No weight like this canal or vessel bear.
> As this will commerce every way promote,
> To this let sons of commerce grant their vote."

Mr. Gray in his book exhibits a marvellous insight into
the wants and requirements of the country. He remarks,
"The plan might be commenced between the towns of
Manchester and Liverpool, where a trial could soon be
made, as the distance is not very great, and the commercial
part of England would thereby be better able to appreciate
its many excellent properties and prove its efficacy. All
the great trading towns of Lancashire and Yorkshire would
then eagerly embrace the opportunity to secure so commodious and easy a conveyance, and cause branch railways
to be laid down in every possible direction. The convenience
and economy in the carriage of the raw material to the
numerous manufactories established in these counties, the
expeditious and cheap delivery of piece goods bought by
the merchants every week at the various markets, and the
despatch in forwarding bales and packages to the outposts

cannot fail to strike the merchant and manufacturer as
points of the first importance. Nothing, for example, would
be so likely to raise the ports of Hull, Liverpool, and Bristol
to an unprecedented pitch of prosperity as the establishment
of railways to those ports, thereby rendering the communication from the east to the west seas, and all intermediate
places, rapid, cheap, and effectual. Anyone at all conversant
with commerce must feel the vast importance of such an
undertaking in forwarding the produce of America, Brazils,
the East and West Indies, etc., from Liverpool and Bristol,
via Hull, to the opposite shores of Germany and Holland,
and, *rice versa*, the produce of the Baltic, *via* Hull, to Liverpool and Bristol. Again, by the establishment of morning
and evening mail steam carriages, the commercial interest
would derive considerable advantage ; the inland mails
might be forwarded with greater despatch and the letters
delivered much earlier than by the extra post ; the opportunity of correspondence between London and all mercantile
places would be much improved, and the rate of postage
might be generally diminished without injuring the receipts
of the post office, because any deficiency occasioned by a
reduction in the postage would be made good by the
increased number of journeys which mail steam carriages
might make.   The London and Edinburgh mail steam
carriages might take all the mails and parcels on the line
of road between these two cities, which would exceedingly
reduce the expense occasioned by mail coaches on the present
footing.   The ordinary stage coaches, caravans, or wagons,
running any considerable distance along the main railway,
might also be conducted on peculiarly favourable terms to
the public ; for instance, one steam engine of superior
power would enable its proprietors to convey several coaches,
caravans, or wagons, linked together until they arrive at
their respective branches, when other engines might proceed
on with them to their destination.   By a due regulation of
the departure and arrival of coaches, caravans, and wagons
along these branches the whole communication throughout
the country would be so simple and so complete as to enable
every individual to partake of the various productions of
particular situations, and to enjoy, at a moderate expense
every improvement introduced into society.   The great

economy of such a measure must be obvious to everyone, seeing that, instead of each coach changing horses between London and Edinburgh, say twenty-five times, requiring a hundred horses, besides the supernumary ones kept at every stage in case of accidents, the whole journey of several coaches would be performed with the simple expense of one steam engine. No animal strength will be able to give that uniform and regular acceleration to our commercial intercourse which may be accomplished by railways; however great animal speed, there cannot be a doubt that it would be considerably surpassed by mail steam carriages, and that the expense would be infinitely less. The exorbitant charge now made for small parcels prevents that natural intercourse of friendship between families resident in different parts of the kingdom, in the same manner as the heavy postage of letters prevents free communication, and consequently diminishes very considerably the consumption of paper which would take place under a less burdensome taxation."

Mr. Gray's book would no doubt excite ridicule and amazement when published sixty years ago. The farmers of that day might well be excused for incredulity when perusing a passage like the following:—"The present system of conveyance," says Mr. Gray, "affords but tolerable accommodation to farmers, and the common way in which they attend markets must always confine them within very limited distances. It is, however, expected that the railway will present a suitable conveyance for attending market-towns thirty or forty miles off, as also for forwarding considerable supplies of grain, hay, straw, vegetables, and every description of live stock to the metropolis at a very easy expense, and with the greatest celerity, from all parts of the kingdom."

A writer in Chambers's Journal, 1847, remarks:—"It was not until after four or five years of agitation, and several editions of Mr. Gray's work had been published and successively commented upon by many newspapers, that commercial men were roused to give the proposed scheme its first great trial on the road between Liverpool and Manchester. The success of that experiment, insured by the engineering skill of Stephenson, was the signal for all that

has since been done both in this island and in other parts
of the world.   Unfortunately, the public has been too busy
these many years in making railways to inquire to whom it
owes its gratitude for having first expounded and advocated
their claims; and probably there are few men now living
who have served the public as effectually, with so little
return in the way of thanks or applause, as Mr. Thomas
Gray, the proposer in 1820 of a general system of transit
by railways."

Poor Gray! He was far ahead of his times.   Public men
called him a bore, and people in Nottingham, where he
resided, said he was cracked.   The *Quarterly Review*
declared such persons are not worth our notice, and the
Edinburgh Review said "Put him in a straight jacket."
Thus the world is often ignorant of its greatest benefactors.
Gray died in poverty.   His widow and daughters earned
their living by teaching a small school at Exeter.

OPENING OF THE DARLINGTON AND STOCKTON RAILWAY.

In the autumn of 1825 the *Times* gave an account of the
origin of one of the most gigantic enterprises of modern
times.   In that year the Darlington and Stockton Railway
was formally opened by the proprietors for the use of the
public.   It was a single railway, and the object of its promoters was to open the London market to the Durham
Collieries, as well as to facilitate the obtaining of fuel to
the country along its line and certain parts of Yorkshire.
The account of the opening says :—

A train of carriages was attached to a locomotive engine
of the most improved construction, and built by Mr. George
Stephenson, in the following order :—(1) Locomotive
engine, with the engineer and assistants; (2) tender with
coals and water; next six wagons loaded with coals and
flour; then an elegant covered coach, with the committee
and other proprietors of the railway; then 21 wagons fitted
up on the occasion for passengers; and, last of all, six
wagons loaded with coals, making altogether a train of 38
carriages, exclusive of the engine and tender.   Tickets were
distributed to the number of nearly 300 for those whom it
was intended should occupy the coach and wagons; but
such was the pressure and crowd that both loaded and

empty carriages were instantly filled with passengers. The signal being given, the engine started off with this immense train of carriages. In some parts the speed was frequently 12 miles per hour, and in one place, for a short distance, near Darlington, 15 miles per hour, and at that time the number of passengers was counted to 450, which, together with the coals, merchandise, and carriages, would amount to nearly 90 tons. After some little delay in arranging the procession, the engine, with her load, arrived at Darlington a distance of eight miles and three-quarters, in 65 minutes, exclusive of stops, averaging about eight miles an hour. The engine arrived at Stockton in three hours and seven minutes after leaving Darlington, including stops, the distance being nearly 12 miles, which is at the rate of four miles an hour, and upon the level part of the railway the number of passengers in the wagons was counted about 550, and several more clung to the carriages on each side, so that the whole number could not be less than 600.

EARLY RAILWAY COMPETITION.

The first Stockton and Darlington Act gave permission to all parties to use the line on payment of certain rates. Thus private individuals might work their own horses and carriages upon the railway and be their own carriers. Mr. Clepham, in the *Gateshead Observer*, gives an interesting account of the competition induced by the system :—"There were two separate coach companies in Stockton, and amusing collisions sometimes occurred between the drivers—who found on the rail a novel element for contention. Coaches cannot pass each other on the rail as on the road; and at the more westward public-house in Stockton (the Bay Horse, kept by Joe Buckton), the coach was always on the line betimes, reducing its eastward rival to the necessity of waiting patiently (or impatiently) in the rear. The line was single, with four sidings in the mile; and when two coaches met, or two trains, or coach and train, the question arose which of the drivers must go back? This was not always settled in silence. As to trains, it came to be a sort of understanding that light wagons should give way to loaded; as to trains and coaches, that the passengers should have preference over coals; while coaches, when they met, must quarrel it out. At length, midway between sidings a post was erected, and a rule was laid down that he who had passed the pillar must go on, and the 'coming man' go back. At the Goose Pool and Early Nook, it was common for these coaches to stop; and there, as Jonathan would say, passengers and coachmen 'liquored.' One coach, introduced by an innkeeper, was a compound of two mourning coaches, an approximation to the real railway coach, which still adheres, with multiplying exceptions, to the stage coach type. One Dixon, who drove the 'Experiment' between Darlington and Shildon, is the inventor of carriage lighting on the rail. On a dark winter night, having compassion on his passengers, he would buy a penny candle, and place it lighted amongst them, on the table of the 'Experiment'—the first railway coach (which, by the way, ended its days at Shildon, as a railway cabin), being also the first coach on the rail (first, second, and third class jammed all into one) that indulged its customers with light in darkness."

CALCULATION AS TO RAILWAY SPEED,

The Editor of *The Scotsman*, having engaged in researches into the laws of friction established by Vince and Coloumb, published the results in a series of articles in his journal in 1824 showing how twenty miles an hour was, on theoretic grounds, within the limits of possibility; and it was to his writings on this point that Mr. Nicholas Wood alluded when he spoke of the ridiculous expectation that engines would ever travel at the rate of twenty, or even twelve miles an hour.

ALARMIST VIEWS.

A writer in the *Quarterly Review*, in 1825, was quite prophetical as to the dangers connected with railway travelling. He observes:—"It is certainly some consolation to those who are to be whirled at the rate of 18 or 20 miles an hour by means of a high-pressure engine, to be told that there is no danger of being sea-sick while on shore, that they are not to be scalded to death, nor drowned, nor dashed to pieces by the bursting of a boiler; and that they need not mind being struck by the flying off or breaking of a wheel What can be more palpably absurd or ridiculous than the prospect held out of locomotives travelling *twice as fast* as stage coaches! We should as soon expect the people of Woolwich to suffer themselves to be fired off upon one of Congreve's Ricochet Rockets, as trust themselves to the mercy of such a machine going at such a rate. We will back old Father Thames against the Woolwich Railway for any sum. We trust that Parliament will, in all railways it may sanction, limit the speed to *eight or nine miles an hour*, which we entirely agree with Mr. Sylvester is as great as can be ventured on with safety."

PARLIAMENTARY OPPOSITION.

On the third reading of the Liverpool and Manchester Railway Bill in the House of Commons, The Hon. Edward Stanley moved that the bill be read that day six months, assigning, among other reasons, that the railway trains worked by horses would take *ten hours* to do the distance, and that they could not be worked by locomotive engines. Sir Isaac Coffin seconded the motion, indignantly denouncing the project as fraught with fraud and imposition. He would not consent to see widows' premises invaded, and "how," he asked, "would any person like to have a railroad under his parlour window? . . . What, he would like to know, was to be done with all those who had advanced money in making and repairing turnpike-roads? What with those who may still wish to travel in their own or hired carriages, after the fashion of their forefathers? What was to become of coach-makers and harness-makers, coach-masters and coachmen, innkeepers, horse-breeders, and horse-dealers? Was the House aware of the smoke and noise, the hiss and whirl, which locomotive engines, passing at the rate of ten or twelve miles an hour, would occasion? Neither the cattle ploughing in the fields or grazing in the meadows could behold them without dismay. . . . Iron would be raised in price 100 per cent., or, more probably, exhausted altogether! It would be the greatest nuisance, the most complete disturbance of quiet and comfort in all parts of the kingdom, that the ingenuity of man could invent!"

c

SPEED OF RAILWAY ENGINES.

At the present day it is amusing to read the speeches of the counsel employed against an act of Parliament being passed in favour of the railway between Liverpool and Manchester. Mr. Harrison, who appeared on behalf of certain landowners against the scheme, thus spoke with regard to the powers of the locomotive engine :—" When we set out with the original prospectus—I am sorry I have not got the paper with me—we were to gallop, I know not at what rate, I believe it was at the rate of twelve miles an hour. My learned friend, Mr. Adam, contemplated, possibly in alluding to Ireland, that some of the Irish members would arrive in wagons to a division. My learned friend says, that they would go at the rate of twelve miles an hour, with the aid of a devil in the form of a locomotive, sitting as a postillion upon the fore-horse, and an Honourable Member, whom I do not see here, sitting behind him to stir up the fire, and to keep it up at full speed. But the speed at which these locomotive engines are to go has slackened; Mr. Adam does not now go faster than five miles per hour. The learned Sergeant says, he should like to have seven, but he would be content to go six. I will show you he cannot go six; and probably, for any practical purposes, I may be able to show, that I can keep up with him by the canal. Now the real evidence to which you alone can pay attention shows, that practically, and for useful purposes, upon the average, and to keep up the rate of speed continually, they may go at something more than four miles an hour. In one of the collieries, there is a small engine with wheels four feet in diameter, which, with moderate weights has gone six; but I will not admit, because, in an experiment or two, they may have been driven at the rate of seven or eight miles an hour—because a small engine has been driven at the rate of six, that this is the average rate at which they can carry goods upon a railroad for the purpose of commerce, for that is the point to which the Committee ought to direct their attention, and to which the evidence is to be applied. It is quite idle to suppose, that an experiment made to ascertain the speed, when the power is worked up to the greatest extent, can afford a fair criterion of that which an engine will do in

all states of the weather. In the first place, locomotive
engines are liable to be operated upon by the weather.
You are told that they are affected by rain, and an attempt
has been made to cover them; but the wind will affect
them, and any gale of wind which would affect the traffic
on the Mersey, would render it impossible to set off a locomotive engine. either by poking up the fire, or keeping up
the pressure of the steam till the boiler is ready to burst.
I say so, for a scientific person happened to see a locomotive
engine coming down an inclined plane, with a tolerable
weight behind it, and he found that the strokes were reduced
from fifty to twelve, as soon as the wind acted upon it ; so
that every gale that would produce an interruption to the
intercourse by the canals, would prevent the progress of a
locomotive engine, so that they have no advantage in that
respect."

DIFFICULTIES ENCOUNTERED IN MAKING RAILWAY SURVEYS.

Difficulties connected with making surveys of land were
encountered from the very commencement of railway
enterprise. The following dialogue on the subject took
place in the Committee of the House of Commons, April 27,
1825. Mr. Sergeant Spankie was the questioner and
George Stephenson was the respondent.

Q. "You were asked about the quality of the soil through
which you were to bore in order to ascertain the strata, and
you were rather taunted because you had not ascertained
the precise strata ; had you any opportunity of boring ?"

A. "I had none ; I was threatened to be driven off the
ground,and severely used if I were found upon the ground."

Q. "You were right, then, not to attempt to bore ?"

A. "Of course, I durst not attempt to bore, after those
threats "

Q. "Were you exposed to any inconvenience in taking
your surveys in consequence of these interruptions ?"

A. "We were."

Q. "On whose property ?"

A. "On my Lord Sefton's, Lord Derby's, and particularly
Mr. Bradshaw's part."

Q. "I believe you came near the coping of some of the
canals ?"

A. " I believe I was threatened to be ducked in the pond if I proceeded; and, of course we had a great deal of the survey to make by stealth, at the time the persons were at dinner; we could not get it by night, and guns were discharged over the grounds belonging to Captain Bradshaw, to prevent us; I can state further, I was twice turned off the ground myself (Mr. Bradshaw's) by his men; and they said, if I did not go instantly they would take me up, and carry me off to Worsley."

Committee.   *Q.* " Had you ever asked leave? "

A. "I did, of all the gentlemen to whom I have alluded; at least, if I did not ask leave of all myself, I did of my Lord Derby, but I did not of Lord Sefton, but the Committee had—at least I was so informed; and I last year asked leave of Mr. Bradshaw's tenants to pass there, and they denied me; they stated that damage had been done, and I said if they would tell me what it was, I would pay them, and they said it was two pounds, and I paid it, though I do not believe it amounted to one shilling."

Q. " Do you suppose it is a likely thing to obtain leave from any gentleman to survey his land, when he knew that your men had gone upon his land to take levels without his leave, and he himself found them going through the corn, and through the gardens of his tenants, and trampling down the strawberry beds, which they were cultivating for the Liverpool market? "

A. "I have found it sometimes very difficult to get through places of that kind."

In some cases, Mr. Williams remarks, large bodies of navvies were collected for the defence of the surveyors; and being liberally provided with liquor, and paid well for the task, they intimidated the rightful owners, who were obliged to be satisfied with warrants of committal and charges of assault.   The navvies were the more willing to engage in such undertakings, because the project, if carried out, afforded them the prospect of increased labour.

LIVERPOOL AND MANCHESTER RAILWAY.

Mr. C. F. Adams, jun., remarks :—" It was this element of spontaneity, therefore,—the instant and dramatic recognition of success, which gave a peculiar interest to everything connected with the Manchester and Liverpool railroad. The whole world was looking at it, with a full realizing sense that something great and momentous was impending. Every day people watched the gradual development of the thing, and actually took part in it. In doing so they had sensations and those sensations they have described. There is consequently an element of human nature surrounding it. To their descriptions time has only lent a new freshness. They are full of honest wonder. They are much better and more valuable and more interesting now than they were fifty years ago, and for that reason are well worth exhuming.

"To introduce the contemporaneous story of the day, however, it is not necessary even to briefly review the long series of events which had slowly led up to it. The world is tolerably familiar with the early life of George Stephenson, and with the vexatious obstacles he had to overcome before he could even secure a trial for his invention. The man himself, however, is an object of a good deal more curiosity to us, than he was to those among whom he lived and moved. A living glimpse at him now is worth dwelling upon, and is the best possible preface to any account of his great day of life triumph. Just such a glimpse of the man has been given to us at the moment when at last all difficulties had been overcome—when the Manchester and Liverpool railroad was completed; and, literally, not only the eyes of Great Britain but those of all civilized countries were directed to it and to him who had originated it. At just that time it chanced that the celebrated actor, John Kemble, was fulfilling an engagement at Liverpool with his daughter, since known as Mrs. Frances Kemble Butler. The extraordinary social advantages the Kemble family enjoyed gave both father and daughter opportunities such as seldom come in the way of ordinary mortals, For the time being they were, in fact, the lions of the stage, just as George Stephenson was the lion of the new railroad. As was most natural the three lions were brought together. The young actress has since published her impressions, jotted down at the time, of the old engineer. Her account of a ride side by side with George Stephenson, on the seat of his locomotive, over the as yet unopened road, is one of the most interesting and life-like records we have of the man and the enterprise. Perhaps it is the most interesting. The introduction is Mrs. Kemble's own, and written forty-six years after the experience :—

"While we were acting at Liverpool, an experimental trip was proposed upon the line of railway which was being constructed between Liverpool and Manchester, the first mesh of that amazing iron net which now covers the whole surface of England, and all civilized portions of the earth. The Liverpool merchants, whose far-sighted self-interest prompted to wise liberality, had accepted the risk of George Stephenson's magnificent experiment, which the committee of inquiry of the House of Commons had rejected for the Government. These men, of less intellectual culture than the Parliament members, had the adventurous imagination proper to great speculators, which is the poetry of the counting house and wharf, and were better able to receive the enthusiastic infection of the great projector's sanguine hope than the Westminster committee. They were exultant and triumphant at the near completion of the work, though, of course, not without some misgivings as to the eventual success of the stupendous enterprise. My father knew several of the gentlemen most deeply interested in the undertaking, and Stephenson having proposed a trial trip as far as the fifteen-mile viaduct, they, with infinite kindness, invited him and permitted me to accompany them: allowing me, moreover, the place which I felt to be one of supreme honour, by the side of Stephenson. All that wonderful history, as much more interesting than a romance as truth is stranger than fiction, which Mr. Smiles's biography of the projector has given in so attractive a form to the world, I then heard from his own lips. He was rather a stern-featured man, with a dark and deeply marked countenance : his speech was strongly inflected with his native Northumbrian accent, but the fascination of that story told by himself, while his tame dragon flew panting along his iron pathway with us, passed the first reading of the Arabian Nights, the incidents of which it almost seemed to recall. He was wonderfully condescending and kind, in answering all the questions of my eager ignorance, and I listened to him with eyes brimful of warm tears of sympathy and enthusiasm, as he told me of all his alternations of hope and fear, of his many trials and disappointments, related with fine scorn, how the " Parliament men " had badgered and baffled 'him with their book-knowledge, and how, when at last they had smothered the irrepressible prophecy of his genius in the quaking depths of Chat Moss, he had exclaimed, ' Did ye ever see a boat float on water ? I will make my road float upon Chat Moss!' The well-read Parliament men (some of whom, perhaps, wished for no railways near their parks and pleasure-grounds) could not believe the miracle, but the shrewd Liverpool merchants, helped to their faith by a great vision of immense gain, did ; and so the railroad was made, and I took this memorable ride by the side of its maker, and would not have exchanged the honour and pleasure of it for one of the shares in the speculation."

"LIVERPOOL, August 26th, 1830.

" MY DEAR H——: A common sheet of paper is enough for love, but a foolscap extra can only contain a railroad and my ecstasies. There was once a man born at Newcastle-upon-Tyne, who was a common coal-digger; this man had an immense constructiveness, which displayed itself in pulling his watch to pieces and putting it together again ; in making a pair of shoes when he happened to be some days without occupation ; finally—here there is a great gap in my story—it brought him in the capacity of an engineer before a Committee of the House of Commons, with his head full of plans for constructing a railroad from Liverpool to Manchester. It so happened that to the quickest and most powerful perceptions and conceptions, to the most indefatigable industry and perseverance, and the most accurate knowledge of the phenomena of nature as they affect his peculiar labours, this man joined an utter want of the ' gift of gab ; ' he could no more explain to others what he meant to do and how he meant to do it, than he could fly, and therefore the members of the House of Commons, after saying ' There is a rock to be excavated to a depth of more than sixty feet, there are embankments to be made nearly to the same height, there is a swamp of five miles in length to be traversed, in which if you drop an iron rod it sinks and disappears; how will you do all this?' and receiving no answer but a broad Northumbrian, 'I can't tell you how I'll do it, but I can tell you I *will* do it,' dismissed Stephenson as a visionary. Having prevailed upon a company of Liverpool gentlemen to be less incredulous, and having raised funds for his great undertaking, in December of 1826 the first spade was struck in the ground. And now I will give you an account of my yesterday's excursion. A party of sixteen persons was ushered into a large court-yard, where, under cover, stood several carriages of a peculiar construction, one of which was prepared for our reception. It was a long-bodied vehicle with seats placed across it back to back; the one we were in had six of these benches, and was a sort of uncovered *char à banc*. The wheels were placed upon two iron bands, which formed the road, and to which they are fitted, being so constructed as to slide along without any danger of hitching or becoming displaced, on the same principle as a thing sliding on a concave groove. The carriage was set in motion by a mere push, and, having received this impetus, rolled with us down an inclined plane into a tunnel, which forms the entrance to the railroad. This tunnel is four hundred yards long (I believe), and will be lighted by gas. At the end of it we emerged from darkness, and, the ground becoming level, we stopped. There is another tunnel parallel with this, only much wider and longer, for it extends from the place we had now reached, and where the steam carriages start, and which is quite out of Liverpool, the whole way under the town, to the docks. This tunnel is for wagons and other heavy carriages; and as the engines which are to draw the trains along the railroad do not enter these tunnels, there is a large building at this entrance which is to be inhabited by steam engines of a stationary turn of mind, and different constitution from the travelling ones, which are to propel the trains through the tunnels to the terminus in the town, without going out of their houses themselves. The length of the tunnel parallel to the one we passed through is (I believe) two thousand two hundred yards. I wonder if you are understanding one word I am saying all this while? We were introduced to the little engine which was to drag us along the rails. She (for they make these curious little fire horses all mares) consisted of a boiler, a stove, a platform, a bench, and behind the bench a barrel containing enough water to prevent her being thirsty for fifteen miles,—the whole machine not bigger than a common fire engine. She goes upon two wheels, which are her feet, and are moved by bright steel legs called pistons; these are propelled by steam, and in proportion as more steam is applied to the upper extremities (the hip-joints, I suppose) of these pistons, the faster they move the wheels; and when it is desirable to diminish the speed, the steam, which unless suffered to escape would burst the boiler, evaporates through a safety valve into the air. The reins, bit, and bridle of this wonderful beast, is a small steel handle, which applies or withdraws the steam from its legs or pistons, so that a child might manage it.

"The coals, which are its oats, were under the bench, and there was a small glass tube affixed to the boiler, with water in it, which indicates by its fullness or emptiness when the creature wants water, which is immediately conveyed to it from its reservoirs. There is a chimney to the stove, but as they burn coke there is none of the dreadful black smoke which accompanies the progress of a ,steam vessel. This snorting little animal, which I felt rather inclined to pat, was then harnessed to our carriage, and Mr. Stephenson having taken me on the bench of the engine with him, we started at about ten miles an hour. The steam horse being ill adapted for going up and down hill, the road was kept at a certain level, and appeared sometimes to sink below the surface of the earth and sometimes to rise above it. Almost at starting it was cut through the solid rock, which formed a wall on either side of it, about sixty feet high. You can't imagine how strange it seemed to be journeying on thus, without any visible cause of progress other than the magical machine, with its flying white breath and rhythmical, unvarying pace, between these rocky walls, which are already clothed with moss and ferns and grasses; and when I reflected that these great masses of stone had been cut asunder to allow our passage thus far below the surface of the earth, I felt as if no fairy tale was ever half so wonderful as what I saw. Bridges were thrown from side to side across the top of these cliffs, and the people looking down upon us from them seemed like pigmies standing in the sky. I must be more concise, though, or I shall want room. We were to go only fifteen miles, that distance being sufficient to show the speed of the engine, and to take us to the most beautiful and wonderful object on the road. After proceeding through this rocky defile, we presently found ourselves raised upon embankments ten or twelve feet high; we then came to a moss or swamp, of considerable extent, on which no human foot could tread without sinking, and yet it bore the road which bore us. This had been the great stumbling-block in the minds of the committee of the House of Commons; but Mr. Stephenson has succeeded in overcoming it. A foundation of hurdles, or, as he called it, basket-work, was thrown over the morass, and the interstices were filled with moss and other elastic matter.

"Upon this the clay and soil were laid down, and the road does float, for we passed over it at the rate of five and twenty miles an hour, and saw the stagnant swamp water trembling on the surface of the soil on either side of us. I hope you understand me. The embankment had gradually been rising higher and higher, and in one place where the soil was not settled enough to form banks, Stephenson had constructed artificial ones of woodwork, over which the mounds of earth were heaped, for he said that though the woodwork would rot, before it did so the banks of earth which covered it would have been sufficiently consolidated to support the road. We had now come fifteen miles, and stopped where the road traversed a wide and deep valley. Stephenson made me alight and led me down to the bottom of this ravine, over which, in order to keep his road level, he has thrown a magnificent viaduct of nine arches, the middle one of which is seventy feet high, through which we saw the whole of this beautiful little valley. It was lovely and wonderful beyond all words. He here told me many curious things respecting this ravine; how he believed the Mersey had once rolled through it; how the soil had proved so unfavorable for the foundation of his bridge that it was built upon piles, which had been driven into the earth to an enormous depth; how while digging for a foundation he had come to a tree bedded in the earth, fourteen feet below the surface of the ground; how tides are caused, and how another flood might be caused; all of which I have remembered and noted down at much greater length than I can enter upon here. He explained to me the whole construction of the steam engine, and said he could soon make a famous engineer of me, which, considering the wonderful things he has achieved, I dare not say is impossible. His way of explaining himself is peculiar, but very striking, and I understood, without difficulty, all that he said to me. We then rejoined the rest of the party, and the engine having received its supply of water, the carriage was placed behind it, for it cannot turn, and was set off at its utmost speed, thirty-five miles an hour, swifter than a bird flies (for they tried the experiment with a snipe). You cannot conceive what that sensation of cutting the air was; the motion is as smooth as possible, too. I could either have read or written; and as it was, I stood up, and with my bonnet off 'drank the air before me.' The wind, which was strong, or perhaps the force of our own thrusting against it, absolutely weighed my eyelids down.

"When I closed my eyes this sensation of flying was quite delightful, and strange beyond description; yet strange as it was, I had a perfect sense of security, and not the slightest fear. At one time, to exhibit the power of the engine, having met another steam-carriage which was unsupplied with water, Mr. Stephenson caused it to be fastened in front of ours; moreover, a wagon laden with timber was also chained to us, and thus propelling the idle steam-engine, and dragging the loaded wagon which was beside it, and our own carriage full of people behind, this brave little she-dragon of ours flew on. Farther on she met three carts, which, being fastened in front of her, she pushed on before her without the slightest delay or difficulty; when I add that this pretty little creature can run with equal facility either backwards or forwards, I believe I have given you an account of all her capacities. Now for a word or two about the master of all these marvels, with whom I am most horribly in love. He is a man from fifty to fifty-five years of age; his face is fine, though careworn, and bears an expression of deep thoughtfulness; his mode of explaining his ideas is peculiar and very original, striking, and forcible; and although his accents indicates strongly his north country birth, his language has not the slightest touch of vulgarity or coarseness. He has certainly turned my head. Four years have sufficed to bring this great undertaking to an end. The railroad will be opened upon the fifteenth of next month. The Duke of Wellington is coming down to be present on the occasion, and, I suppose, what with the thousands of spectators and the novelty of the spectacle, there will never have been a scene of more striking interest. The whole cost of the work (including the engines and carriages) will have been eight hundred and thirty thousand pounds; and it is already worth double that sum. The directors have kindly offered us three places for the opening, which is a great favour, for people are bidding almost anything for a place, I understand."

Even while Miss Kemble was writing this letter, certainly before it had reached her correspondent, the official programme of that opening to which she was so eagerly looking forward was thus referred to in the Liverpool papers:

"The day of opening still remains fixed for Wednesday the fifteenth instant. The company by whom the ceremony is to be performed. is expected to amount to eight or nine hundred persons, including the Duke of Wellington and several others of the nobility. They will leave Liverpool at an early hour in the forenoon, probably ten o'clock, in carriages drawn by eight or nine engines, including the new engine of Messrs. Braithwaite and Ericsson, if it be ready in time. The other engines will be those constructed by Mr. Stephenson, and each of them will draw about a hundred persons. On their arrival at Manchester, the company will enter the upper stories of the warehouses by means of a spacious outside wooden staircase, which is in course of erection for the purpose by Mr. Bellhouse. The upper storey of the range of warehouses is divided into five apartments, each measuring sixty-six feet by fifty-six. In four of these a number of tables (which Mr. Bellhouse is also preparing) will be placed, and the company will partake of a splendid cold collation which is to be provided by Mr. Lynn, of the Waterloo Hotel, Liverpool. A large apartment at the east end of the warehouses will be reserved as a withdrawing room for the ladies, and is partitioned off for that purpose. After partaking of the hospitality of the directors, the company will return to Liverpool in the same order in which they arrive. We understand that each shareholder in the railway will be entitled to a seat (transferable) in one of the carriages, on this interesting and important occasion. It may be proper to state, for the information of the public, that no one will be permitted to go upon the railway between Ordsall lane and the warehouses, and parties of the military and police will be placed to preserve order, and prevent intrusion. Beyond Ordsall lane, however, the public will be freely admitted to view the procession as it passes : and no restriction will be laid upon them farther than may be requisite to prevent them from approaching too close to the rails, lest accidents should occur. By extending themselves along either side of the road towards Eccles any number of people, however great may be easily accommodated "

Of the carrying out on the 15th the programme thus carefully laid down, a contemporaneous reporter has left the following account :—

"The town itself [Liverpool] was never so full of strangers; they poured in during the last and the beginning of the present week from almost all parts of the three kingdoms, and we believe that through Chester alone, which is by no means a principal road to Liverpool. four hundred extra passengers were forwarded on Tuesday. All the inns in the town were crowded to overflowing, and carriages stood in the streets at night, for want of room in the stable yards.

"On the morning of Wednesday the population of the town and of the country began very early to assemble near the railway. The weather was favourable, and the Company's station at the boundary of the town was the rendezvous of the nobility and gentry who attended, to form the procession at Manchester. Never was there such an assemblage of rank, wealth, beauty, and fashion in this neighbourhood. From before nine o'clock until ten the entrance in Crown street was thronged by the splendid equipages from which the company was alighting, and the area in which the railway carriages were placed was gradually filling with gay groups eagerly searching for their respective places, as indicated by numbers corresponding with those on their tickets. The large and elegant car constructed for the nobility, and the accompanying cars for the Directors and the musicians were seen through the lesser tunnel, where persons moving about at the far end appeared as diminutive as if viewed through a concave glass. The effect was singular and striking. In a short time all those cars were brought along the tunnel into the yard which then contained all the carriages, which were to be attached to the eight locomotive engines which were in readiness beyond the tunnel in the great excavation at Edge-hill. By this time the area presented a beautiful spectacle, thirty-three carriages being filled by elegantly dressed persons, each train of carriages being distinguished by silk flags of different colours; the band of the fourth King's Own Regiment, stationed in the adjoining area, playing military airs, the Wellington Harmonic Band, in a Grecian car for the procession, performing many beautiful miscellaneous pieces; and a third band occupying a stage above Mr. Harding's Grand Stand, at William the Fourth's Hotel, spiritedly adding to the liveliness of the hour whenever the other bands ceased.

"A few minutes before ten, the discharge of a gun and the cheers of the assembly announced the arrival of the Duke of Wellington, who entered the area with the Marquis and Marchioness of Salisbury and a number of friends, the band playing 'See the conquering hero comes.' He returned the congratulations of the company, and in a few moments the grand car, which he and the nobility and the principal gentry occupied, and the cars attached to it, were permitted to proceed; we say permitted, because no applied power, except a slight impulse at first, is requisite to propel carriages along the tunnel, the slope being just sufficient to call into effect the principle of gravitation. The tunnel was lighted with gas, and the motion in passing through it must have been as pleasing as it was novel to all the party. On arriving at the engine station, the cars were attached to the *Northumbrian*, locomotive engine, on the southern of the two lines of rail; and immediately the other trains of carriages started through the tunnel and were attached to their respective engines on the northern of the lines.

"We had the good fortune to have a place in the first train after the grand cars, which train, drawn by the *Phœnix*, consisted of three open and two close carriages, each carrying twenty-six ladies and gentlemen. The lofty banks of the engine station were crowded with thousands of spectators, whose enthusiastic cheering seemed to rend the air. From this point to Wavertree-lane, while the procession was forming, the grand cars passed and repassed the other trains of carriages several times, running as they did in the same direction on the two parallel tracks, which gave the assembled thousands and tens of thousands the opportunity of seeing distinctly the illustrious strangers, whose presence gave extraordinary interest to the scene. Some soldiers of the 4th Regiment assisted the railway police in keeping the way clear and preserving order, and they discharged their duty in a very proper manner. A few minutes before eleven all was ready for the journey, and certainly a journey upon a railway is one of the most delightful that can be imagined. Our first thoughts it might be supposed, from the road being so level, were that it must be monotonous and uninteresting. It is precisely the contrary ; for as the road does not rise and fall like the ground over which we pass, but proceeds nearly at a level, whether the land be high or low, we are at one moment drawn through a hill, and find ourselves seventy feet below the surface, in an Alpine chasm, and at another we are as many feet above the green fields, traversing a raised path, from which we look down upon the roofs of farm houses, and see the distant hills and woods. These variations give an interest to such a journey which cannot be appreciated until they are witnessed. The signal gun being fired, we started in beautiful style, amidst the deafening plaudits of the well dressed people who thronged the numerous booths, and all the walls and eminences on both sides the line. Our speed was gradually increased till, entering the Olive Mountain excavation, we rushed into the awful chasm at the rate of twenty-four miles an hour. The banks, the bridges over our heads, and the rude projecting corners along the sides, were covered with masses of human beings past whom we glided as if upon the wings of the wind. We soon came into the open country of Broad Green, having fine views of Huyton and Prescot on the left, and the hilly grounds of Cheshire on the right. Vehicles of every description stood in the fields on both sides, and thousands of spectators still lined the margin of the road; some horses seemed alarmed, but after trotting with their carriages to the farther hedges, they stood still as if their fears had subsided. After passing Whiston, sometimes going slowly, sometimes swiftly, we observed that a vista formed by several bridges crossing the road gave a pleasing effect to the view. Under Rainhill Bridge, which, like all the others, was crowded with spectators, the Duke's car stopped until we passed, and on this, as on similar occasions, we had excellent opportunities of seeing the whole of the noble party, distinguishing the Marquis and Marchioness of Salisbury, the Earl and Countess of Wilton, Lord Stanley, and others, in the fore part of the car; alongside of the latter part was Mr. Huskisson, standing with his face always toward us; and further behind was Lord Hill, and others, among whom the Mayor of Liverpool took his station. At this place Mr. Bretherton had a large party of friends in a field, overlooking the road. As we approached the Sutton inclined plane the Duke's car passed us again at a most rapid rate—it appeared rapid even to us who were travelling then at, probably, fifteen miles an hour. We had a fine view of Billings Hill from this neighbourhood, and of a thousand various coloured fields. A grand stand was here erected, beautifully decorated, and crowded with ladies and gentlemen from St. Helen's and the neighbourhood. Entering upon Parr Moss we had a good view of Newton Race Course and the stands, and at this time the Duke was far ahead of us; the grand cars appeared actually of diminutive dimensions, and in a short time we saw them gliding beautifully over the Sankey Viaduct, from which a scene truly magnificent lay before us.

"The fields below us were occupied by thousands who cheered us as we passed over the stupendous edifice; carriages filled the narrow lanes, and vessels in the water had been detained in order that their crews might gaze up at the gorgeous pageant passing far above their masts heads. Here again was a grand stand, and here again enthusiastic plaudits almost deafened us. Shortly, we passed the borough of Newton, crossing a fine bridge over the Warrington road, and reached Parkside, seventeen miles from Liverpool, in about four minutes under the hour. At this place the engines were ranged under different watering stations to receive fresh water, the whole extending along nearly half a mile of road. Our train and two others passed the Duke's car, and we in the first train had had our engine supplied with water, and were ready to start, some time before we were aware of the melancholy cause of our apparently great delay. We had. most of us, alighted, and were walking about, congratulating each other generally, and the ladies particularly, on the truly delightful treat we were enjoying, all hearts bounding with joyous excitement, and every tongue eloquent in the praise of the gigantic work now completed, and the advantages and pleasures it afforded. A murmur and an agitation at a little distance betokened something alarming and we too soon learned the nature of that lamentable event, which we cannot record without the most agonized feelings. On inquiring, we learnt the dreadful particulars. After three of the engines with their trains had passed the Duke's carriage, although the others had to follow, the company began to alight from all the carriages which had arrived. The Duke of Wellington and Mr. Huskisson had just shaken hands, and Mr. Huskisson, Prince Esterhazy, Mr. Birch, Mr. H. Earle, Mr. William Holmes, M.P., and others were standing in the road, when the other carriages were approaching. An alarm being given, most of the gentlemen sprang into the carriage, but Mr. Huskisson seemed flurried, and from some cause, not clearly ascertained, he fell under the engine of the approaching carriages, the wheel of which shattered his leg in the most dreadful manner. On being raised from the ground by the Earl of Wilton, Mr. Holmes, and other gentlemen, his only exclamations were:—"Where is Mrs. Huskisson? I have met my death. God forgive me." Immediately after he swooned. Dr. Brandreth, and Dr. Southey, of London, immediately applied bandages to the limb. In a short time the engine was detached from the Duke's carriage, and the musician's car being prepared for the purpose, the Right Honorable gentleman was placed in it, accompanied by his afflicted lady, with Dr. Brandreth, Dr. Southey, Earl of Wilton, and Mr. Stephenson, who set off in the direction of Manchester.

D

"The whole of the procession remained at least another hour uncertain what course to adopt. A consultation was held on the open part of the road, and the Duke of Wellington was soon surrounded by the Directors, and a mournful group of gentlemen. At first it was thought advisable to return to Liverpool, merely despatching one engine and a set of carriages, to convey home Lady Wilton, and others who did not wish to return to Liverpool. The Duke of Wellington and Sir Robert Peel seemed to favour this course; others thought it best to proceed as originally intended: but no decision was made till the Boroughreeve of Manchester stated, that if the procession did not reach Manchester, where an unprecedented concourse of people would be assembled, and would wait for it, he should be fearful of the consequences to the peace of the town. This turned the scale, and his Grace then proposed that the whole party should proceed, and return as soon as possible, all festivity at Manchester being avoided. The *Phænix*, with its train, was then attached to the *North Star* and its train, and from the two united a long chain was affixed to his Grace's car, and although it was on the other line of rail, it was found to draw the whole along exceedingly well. About half-past one, we resumed our journey; and we should here mention that the Wigan Branch Railway Company had erected near Parkside bridge a grand stand, which they and their friends occupied, and from which they enthusiastically cheered the procession. On reaching the twentieth mile post we had a beautiful view of Rivington Pike and Blackstone Edge, and at the twenty-first the smoke of Manchester appeared to be directly at the termination of our view. Groups of people continued to cheer us, but we could not reply; our enjoyment was over. Tyldesley Church, and a vast region of smiling fields here met the eye, as we traversed the flat surface of Chat Moss, in the midst of which a vast crowd was assembled to greet us with their plaudits; and from the twenty-fourth mile post we began to find ourselves flanked on both sides by spectators extending in a continuous and thickening body all the way to Manchester. At the twenty-fifth mile post we met Mr. Stephenson returning with the *Northumbrian* engine. In answer to innumerable and eager inquiries,

Mr. Stephenson said he had left Mr. Huskisson at the house
of the Rev. Mr. Blackburne, Vicar of Eccles, and had then
proceeded to Manchester, whence he brought back medical
assistance, and that the surgeons, after seeing Mr. Huskisson,
had expressed a hope that there was no danger.
Mr. Stephenson's speed had been at the rate of thirty-four
miles an hour during this painful errand.   The engine
being then again attached to the Duke's car, the procession
dashed forward, passing countless thousands of people upon
house tops, booths, high ground, bridges, etc., and our
readers must imagine, for we cannot describe, such a movement through an avenue of living beings, and extending
six miles in length.   Upon one bridge a tri-colored flag
was displayed; near another the motto of "Vote by ballot"
was seen; in a field near Eccles, a poor and wretchedly
dressed man had his loom close to the roadside, and was
weaving with all his might; cries of "No Corn Laws,"
were occasionally heard, and for about two miles the cheer-
ings of the crowd were interspersed with a continual hissing
and hooting from the minority.   On approaching the bridge
which crosses the Irwell, the 59th regiment was drawn up,
flanking the road on each side, and presenting arms as his
Grace passed along.   We reached the warehouses at a
quarter before three, and those who alighted were shown
into the large upper rooms where a most elegant cold
collation had been prepared by Mr. Lynn, for more than
one thousand persons.   The greater portion of the company,
as the carriages continued to arrive, visited the rooms and
partook in silence of some refreshment.   They then returned to their carriages which had been properly placed
for returning.   His Grace and the principal party did not
alight; but he went through a most fatiguing office for
more than an hour and a half, in shaking hands with
thousands of people, to whom he stooped over the hand rail
of the carriage, and who seemed insatiable in their desire
to join hands with him.   Many women brought their
children to him, lifting them up that he might bless them,
which he did, and during the whole time he had scarcely a
minute's respite.   At half-past four the Duke's car began
to move away for Liverpool.

"They would have been detained a little longer, in order that three of the engines, which had been to Eccles for water, might have dropped into the rear to take their places; but Mr. Lavender represented that the crowd was so thickening in upon all sides, and becoming so clamorous for admission into the area, that he would not answer for the peace of the town, if further delay took place. The three engines were on the same line of rail as the Duke, and they could not cross to the other line without getting to a turning place, and as the Duke could not be delayed on account of his keeping the crowd together, there was no alternative but to send the engines forward. One of the other engines was then attached to our train, and we followed the Duke rapidly, while the six trains behind had only three engines left to bring them back. Of course, we kept pace with the Duke, who stopped at Eccles to inquire after Mr. Huskisson. The answer received was that there was now no hope of his life being saved : and this intelligence plunged the whole party into still deeper distress. We proceeded without meeting any fresh incident until we passed Prescot, where we found two of the three engines at the 6½ mile post, where a turning had been effected. but the third had gone on to Liverpool; we then detached the one we had borrowed, and the three set out to meet the six remaining trains of carriages. Our carriages were then connected with the grand cars, the engine of which now drew the whole number of nine carriages, containing nearly three hundred persons, at a very smart rate. We were now getting into vast crowds of people, most of them ignorant of the dreadful event which had taken place, and all of them giving us enthusiastic cheers which we could not return.

"At Roby, his Grace and the Childwalls alighted and proceeded home; our carriages then moved forward to Liverpool, where we arrived about seven o'clock, and went down the great tunnel, under the town, a part of the work which, more than any other, astonished the numerous strangers present. It is, indeed, a wonderful work, and makes an impression never to be effaced from the memory. The Company's yard, from St. James's Street to Wapping, was filled with carriages waiting for the returning parties, who separated with feelings of mingled gratification and distress, to which we shall not attempt to give utterance. We afterwards learnt that the parties we left at Manchester placed the three remaining engines together, and all the carriages together, so as to form one grand procession, including twenty-four carriages, and were coming home at a steady pace, when they were met near Newton, by the other three engines, which were then attached to the rest, and they arrived in Liverpool about ten o'clock.

"Thus ended a pageant which, for importance as to its object and grandeur in its details, is admitted to have exceeded anything ever witnessed. We conversed with many gentlemen of great experience in public life, who spoke of the scene as surpassing anything they had ever beheld, and who computed, upon data which they considered to be satisfactory, that not fewer than 500,000 persons must have been spectators of the procession."

So far from being a success, the occasion was, after the accident to Mr. Huskisson, such a series of mortifying disappointments and the Duke of Wellington's experience at Manchester had been so very far removed from gratifying that the directors of the company felt moved to exonerate themselves from the load of censure by an official explanation. This they did in the following language :—

"On the subject of delay which took place in the starting from Manchester, and consequently in the arrival at Liverpool, of the last three engines, with twenty-four carriages and six hundred passengers, being the train allotted to six of the engines, we are authorized to state that the directors think it due to the proprietors and others constituting the large assemblage of company in the above trains to make known the following particulars :

"Three out of the six locomotive engines which belonged to the above trains had proceeded on the south road from Manchester to Eccles, to take in water, with the intention of returning to Manchester, and so getting out of that line of road before any of the trains should start on their return home. Before this, however, was accomplished, the following circumstances seemed to render it imperative for the train of carriages containing the Duke of Wellington and a great many of the distinguished visitors to leave Manchester. The eagerness on the part of the crowd to see the Duke,

and to shake hands with him, was very great, so much so
that his Grace held out both his hands to the pressing
multitude at the same time; the assembling crowd becoming
more dense every minute, closely surrounded the carriages,
as the principal attraction was this particular train. The
difficulty of proceeding at all increased every moment and
consequently the danger of accident upon the attempt being
made to force a way through the throng also increased.
At this juncture Mr. Lavender, the head of the police
establishment of Manchester, interfered, and entreated that
the Duke's train should move on, or he could not answer
for the consequences. Under these circumstances, and the
day being well advanced, it was thought expedient at all
events to move forward while it was still practicable to do
so. The order was accordingly given, and the train passed
along out of the immediate neighbourhood of Manchester
without accident to anyone. When they had proceeded a
few miles they fell in with the engines belonging to the
trains left at Manchester, and these engines being on the
same line as the carriages of the procession, there was no
alternative but bringing the Duke's train back through the
dense multitude to Manchester, or proceeding with three
extra engines to the neighbourhood of Liverpool (all passing
places from one road to the other being removed, with a
view to safety, on the occasion), and afterwards sending
them back to the assistance of the trains unfortunately left
behind. It was determined to proceed towards Liverpool,
as being decidedly the most advisable course under the
circumstances of the case ; and it may be mentioned for the
satisfaction of any party who may have considered that he
was in some measure left in the lurch, that Mr. Moss, the
Deputy Chairman, had left Mrs. Moss and several of his
family to come with the trains which had been so left
behind. Three engines having to draw a load calculated
for six, their progress was of course much retarded, besides
a considerable delay which took place before the starting
of the last trains, owing to the uncertainty which existed
as to what had become of the three missing engines. These
engines, after proceeding to within a few miles of Liverpool,
were enabled to return to Park-side, in the neighbourhood
of Newton, where they were attached to the other three
and the whole proceeding safely to Liverpool, where they
arrived at ten in the evening."

The case was, however, here stated, to say the least, in the mildest possible manner. The fact was that the authorities at Manchester had, and not without reason, passed a very panic-stricken hour on account of the Duke of Wellington. That personage had been in a position of no inconsiderable peril. Though the reporter preserved a decorous silence on that point, the ministerial car had on the way been pelted, as well as hooted; and at Manchester a vast mass of not particularly well disposed persons had fairly overwhelmed both police and soldiery, and had taken complete possession of the tracks. They were not riotous, but they were very rough; and they insisted on climbing upon the carriages and pressing their attentions on the distinguished inmates in a manner somewhat at variance with English ideas of propriety. The Duke's efforts at conciliatory manners, as evinced through much hand-shaking, were not without significance. It was small matter for wonder, therefore, that the terrified authorities, before they got him out of their town, heartily regretted that they had not allowed him to have his own way after the accident to Mr. Huskisson, when he proposed to turn back without coming to it. Having once got him safely started back to Liverpool, therefore, they preferred to leave the other guests to take care of themselves, rather than have the Duke face the crowd again. As there were no sidings on that early road, and the connections between the tracks had, as a measure of safety, been temporarily removed, the ministerial train in moving towards Liverpool had necessarily pushed before it the engines belonging to the other trains. The unfortunate guests on those other trains, thus left to their fate, had for the rest of the day a very dreary time of it. To avoid accidents, the six trains abandoned at Manchester were united into one, to which were attached the three locomotives remaining. In this form they started. Presently the strain broke the couplings. Pieces of rope were then put in requisition, and again they got in motion. In due time the three other engines came along, but they could only be used by putting them on in front of the three already attached to the train. Two of them were used in that way, and the eleven cars thus drawn by five locomotives, and preceded at a short distance by one other, went on towards Liverpool. It was dark, and to meet the exigencies of the occasion the first germ of the present elaborate system of railroad night signals was improvised on the spot From the foremost and pioneer locomotive obstacles were signalled to the train locomotives by the very primitive expedient of swinging the lighted end of a tar-rope. At Rainhill the weight of the train proved too much for the combined motive-power, and the thoroughly wearied passengers had to leave their carriages and walk up the incline. When they got to the summit and, resuming their seats, were again in motion, fresh delay was occasioned by the leading locomotive running into a wheel-barrow, maliciously placed on the track to obstruct it. Not until ten o'clock did they enter the tunnel at Liverpool. Meanwhile all sorts of rumours of general disaster had for hours been circulating among the vast concourse of spectators who were assembled waiting for their friends, and whose relief expressed itself in hearty cheers as the train at last rolled safely into the station.

We have also Miss Kemble's story of this day, to which in her letter of August 25th she had looked forward with such eager interest. With her father and mother she had been staying at a country place in Lancashire, and in her account of the affair, written in 1876, she says :—

"The whole gay party assembled at Heaton, my mother and myself included, went to Liverpool for the opening of the railroad. The throng of strangers gathered there for the same purpose made it almost impossible to obtain a night's lodging for love or money ; and glad and thankful were we to put up with and be put up in a tiny garret by an old friend, Mr. Radley, of the Adelphi, which many would have given twice what we paid to obtain. The day opened gloriously, and never was an innumerable concourse of sight-seers in better humour than the surging, swaying crowd that lined the railroad with living faces. . . . . After this disastrous event [the accident to Mr. Huskisson] the day became overcast, and as we neared Manchester the sky grew cloudy and dark, and it began to rain. The vast concourse of people who had assembled to witness the triumphant arrival of the succesful travellers was of the lowest order of mechanics and artisans, among whom great distress and a dangerous spirit of discontent with the government at that time prevailed. Groans and hisses greeted the carriage, full of influential personages, in which the Duke of Wellington sat. High above the grim and grimy crowd of scowling faces a loom had been erected, at which sat a tattered, starved-looking weaver, evidently set there as a *representative man*, to protest against this triumph of machinery, and the gain and glory which the wealthy Liverpool and Manchester men were likely to derive from it. The contrast between our departure from Liverpool and our arrival at Manchester was one of the most striking things I ever witnessed.

MANCHESTER, *September 20th*, 1830.

MY DEAREST H—:

❀   ❀   ❀   ❀   ❀   ❀   ❀   ❀   ❀

" You probably have by this time heard and read accounts of the opening of the railroad, and the fearful accident which occurred at it, for the papers are full of nothing else. The accident you mention did occur, but though the unfortunate man who was killed bore Mr. Stephenson's name, he was not related to him. [Besides Mr. Huskisson, another man named Stephenson had about this time been killed on the railroad]. I will tell you something of the events on the fifteenth, as, though you may be acquainted with the circumstances of poor Mr. Huskisson's death, none but an eye-witness of the whole scene can form a conception of it. I told you that we had had places given to us, and it was the main purpose of our returning from Birmingham to Manchester to be present at what promised to be one of the most striking events in the scientific annals of our country. We started on Wednesday last, to the number of about eight hundred people, in carriages constructed as I before described to you. The most intense curiosity and excitement prevailed, and though the weather was uncertain, enormous masses of densely packed people lined the road, shouting and waving hats and handkerchiefs as we flew by them. What with the sight and sound of these cheering multitudes and the tremendous velocity with which we were borne past them, my spirits rose to the true champagne height. and I never enjoyed anything so much as the first hour of our progress. I had been unluckily separated from my mother in the first distribution of places, but by an exchange of seats which she was enabled to make she rejoined me, when I was at the height of my ecstasy, which was considerably damped by finding that she was frightened to death, and intent upon nothing but devising means of escaping from a situation which appeared to her to threaten with instant annihilation herself and all her travelling companions. While I was chewing the cud of this disappointment, which was rather bitter, as I expected her to be as delighted as myself with our excursion, a man flew by us, calling out through a speaking trumpet to stop the engine, for that somebody in the directors' car had sustained an injury. We were all stopped accordingly and presently a hundred voices were heard exclaiming that Mr. Huskisson was killed. The confusion that ensued is indescribable; the calling out from carriage to carriage to ascertain the truth, the contrary reports which were sent back to us, the hundred questions eagerly uttered at once, and the repeated and urgent demands for surgical assistance, created a sudden turmoil that was quite sickening. At last we distinctly ascertained that the unfortunate man's thigh was broken.

"From Lady W—, who was in the duke's carriage, and within three yards of the spot where the accident happened, I had the following details, the horror of witnessing which we were spared through our situation behind the great carriage. The engine had stopped to take in a supply of water, and several of the gentlemen in the directors' carriage had jumped out to look about them. Lord W—, Count Batthyany, Count Matuscenitz, and Mr. Huskisson among the rest were standing talking in the middle of the road, when an engine on the other line, which was parading up and down merely to show its speed, was seen coming down upon them like lightning. The most active of those in peril sprang back into their seats; Lord W— saved his life only by rushing behind the duke's carriage, Count Matuscenitz had but just leaped into it, with the engine all but touching his heels as he did so; while poor Mr. Huskisson, less active from the effects of age and ill health, bewildered too by the frantic cries of 'Stop the engine! Clear the track!'

that resounded on all sides, completely lost his head, looked helplessly to the right and left, and was instantaneously prostrated by the fatal machine, which dashed down like a thunderbolt upon him, and passed over his leg, smashing and mangling it in the most horrible way. (Lady W— said she distinctly heard the crushing of the bone). So terrible was the effect of the appalling accident that except that ghastly 'crushing' and poor Mrs. Huskisson's piercing shriek, not a sound was heard or a word uttered among the immediate spectators of the catastrophe. Lord W— was the first to raise the poor sufferer, and calling to his aid his surgical skill, which is considerable, he tied up the severed artery, and for a time at least, prevented death by a loss of blood. Mr. Huskisson was then placed in a carriage with his wife and Lord W—, and the engine having been detached from the directors' carriage, conveyed them to Manchester. So great was the shock produced on the whole party by this event that the Duke of Wellington declared his intention not to proceed, but to return immediately to Liverpool. However, upon its being represented to him that the whole population of Manchester had turned out to witness the procession, and that a disappointment might give rise to riots and disturbances, he consented to go on, and gloomily enough the rest of the journey was accomplished. We had intended returning to Liverpool by the railroad, but Lady W—, who seized upon me in the midst of the crowd, persuaded us to accompany her home, which we gladly did. Lord W—, did not return till past ten o'clock, at which hour he brought the intelligence of Mr. Huskisson's death. I need not tell you of the sort of whispering awe which this event threw over our circle; and yet great as was the horror excited by it, I could not help feeling how evanescent the effect of it was, after all. The shuddering terror of seeing our fellow-creature thus struck down by our side, and the breathless thankfulness for our own preservation, rendered the first evening of our party at Heaton almost solemn; but the next day the occurrence became a subject of earnest, it is true, but free discussion; and after that was alluded to with almost as little apparent feeling as if it had not passed under our eyes, and within the space of a few hours."

MRS. BLACKBURNE'S PRESENTIMENT.

Miss Kemble was mistaken in stating Mr. Huskisson after his accident was removed to Manchester. He was conveyed to the vicarage, at Eccles, near Manchester. Of the vicar's wife, Dean Stanley's mother thus writes, (January 17, 1832,):—"There is one person who interests me very much, Mrs. Tom Blackburne, the Vicaress of Eccles, who received poor Mr. Huskisson, and immortalised herself by her activity, sense, and conduct throughout." A writer in the *Cornhill Magazine*, for March, 1884, referring to the opening of the Liverpool and Manchester Railway, remarks:—" In celebration of this experiment, for even then most people only looked upon it as a doubtful thing, the houses of the adjacent parts of Lancashire were filled with guests. Mr. John Blackburne, M.P., asked his brother and sister-in-law, Mr. and Mrs. Thomas Blackburne, to stay at Hale Hall, near Liverpool, (which his ancestors in the direct line had possessed since 1199,) and to go with his party to the ceremony and fetes of the day.

The invitation was accepted, and Mr. and Mrs. Blackburne went to Hale. Now, however, occurred one of those strange circumstances utterly condemned by critics of fiction as 'unreal,' 'unnatural,' or 'impossible;' only in this case it happened to be true, in spite of all these epithets. Mrs. Blackburne, rather strong-minded than otherwise, at all events one of the last women in the world to be affected by imagination. became possessed by an unmistakable presentiment, which made her feel quite sure *that her presence was required at home; and she went home at once.* There were difficulties in her way; every carriage was required, but she would go. She drove to Warrington, and from thence 'took boat' up the Irwell to Eccles. Canal boats were then regular conveyances, divided into first and second classes. There were no mobs or excitement anywhere on the 14th, and Mrs. Blackburne got quickly to Eccles without any adventures. When there, except that one of her children was unwell, she could find nothing wrong, or in the least likely to account for the presentiment which had driven her home in spite of all the natural enough, ridicule of her husband and friends at Hale.

Early on the morning of the 15th, an incident occurred, the narration of which may throw some light on the temper of the times. Mr. Barton, of Swinton, came to say that a mob was expected to come from Oldham to attack the Duke of Wellington, then at the height of his unpopularity among the masses; for just by Eccles three miles of the line was left unguarded, 'Could Mr. Blackburne say what was to be done?'

'My husband is away.' said the Vicaress, 'but I know that about fifty special constables were out last year, the very men for this work, if their licenses have not expired.'

'Never mind licenses,' replied Mr. Barton, with a superb indifference to form, quite natural under the circumstances. 'Where can I find the men?'

'Oh,' replied Mrs. Blackburne, 'I can get the men for you.'

Mr Barton hesitated, but soon with gratitude accepted the offer, and with the help of the churchwardens and constables 'a guard for the Duke' was soon collected on the bridge of Eccles, armed with staves and clubs to be dispersed along the line.

This done, she had a tent put up for herself and children, with whom were Lord Wilton's little daughters, the Ladies Elizabeth and Katherine Egerton, and their governess. The tent was just above the cutting and looked down on to it, and they would have a good view of the first train, expected to pass about eleven o'clock. The morning wore on, the crowds were increasing, and low murmurs of wonder were heard. It was thought that the experiment had failed. A few of the villagers came into the field, but none troubled the little band of watchers. The bright sunshine had passed away, and it had become dark, with large hot drops of rain, forerunners of a coming thunderstorm. The people lined the whole of the way from Manchester to Liverpool, and, as far as the eye could reach, faces were seen anxiously looking towards Liverpool. Suddenly a strange roar was heard from the crowd, not a cheer of triumph, but a prolonged wail, beginning at the furthest point of travelling along the swarming banks like the incoming swirl of a breaker as it runs upon a gravelled beach.

Like a true woman, her first thought was for her husband, as Mrs. Blackburne heard the words repeated on all sides, 'An accident!' 'The Vicarage!' She flew across the field to the gate and met a sad procession bringing in a sorely-wounded yet quite conscious man. She saw in a moment that he had medals on his coat, and had been very tall, so that it could not be as she feared. The relief of that moment may be imagined. Then the quiet presence of mind, by practice habitual to her, and the ready flow of sympathy left her no time to think of anything but the sufferer, who said to her pathetically, 'I shall not trouble you long!' She had not only the will but the power to help, even to supplying from her own medicine chest and stores, kept for the poor, everything that the surgeons required.

It was Lord Wilton who suggested the removal of Mr. Huskisson to Eccles Vicarage and improvised a tourniquet on the spot, while soon the medical men who were in the train did what they could for him. Mr. Blackburne, as will be remembered, was not with his wife, and only the pre-sentiment which had brought Mrs. Blackburne home had given the means of so readily and quickly obtaining surgical necessaries and rest. Mr. Blackburne, writing to his mother-in-law the day after this accident, referring to Mr. Huskisson, remarks:—" To the last he retained his senses. Lord Granville says when the dying man heard Wilton propose to take him to this house he exclaimed, ' Pray take me there; there I shall indeed be taken care of.'

But fancy my horror! *Not one word did I know of his being here till I had passed the place, and was literally eating my luncheon at Manchester!* In vain did I try to get a con-veyance, till at last the Duke of Wellington sent to me and ordered his car to start, and I came with him back, he intending to come here; but the crowd was so *immense* that the police dared not let him get out. To be sure, when my people on the bridge saw me standing with him, they did shout, 'That's as it should be—Vicar for us!' He said, ' These people seem to know you well.'

Entre nous, at the door I met my love, and after a good cry (I don't know which was the greatest fool!) set to work. The poor fellow was glad to see me, and never shall I forget the scene, his poor wife holding his head, and the great men weeping, for they all wept! He then received the Sacrament, added some codocils to his will, and seemed perfectly resigned. But his agonies were dreadful! Ransome says they must have been so. He expired at nine. We never left him till he breathed his last. Poor woman! How she lamented his loss; yet her struggles to bear with fortitude are wonderful. I wish you could have heard him exclaim, after my petition 'Forgive us our trespasses as we forgive . . .' 'I have not the smallest ill-will to any one person in the whole world.' They stay here until Saturday, when they begin the sad journey to convey him to Sussex. They wanted to bury him at Liverpool, but she refused. I forgot to tell you that he told Lawrence before starting that he *wished he were safe back*."

Mr. Huskisson was not buried at Chichester, for at last Mrs. Huskisson consented to the popular wish that his body might have a public funeral at Liverpool, where a statue of him by Gibson now stands in the cemetery."

ELEVATED SIGHT-SEERS WISHING TO DESCEND.

Sir J. A. Picton, in his *Memorials of Liverpool*, relates an amusing incident connected with the opening of the railway at that town. "On the opening of the railway," he remarks, "of course, every point and 'coin of vantage' from whence the procession could be best seen was eagerly availed of. A tolerably high chimney had recently been built upon the railway ground, affording a sufficient platform on the scaffolding at the top for the accommodation of two or three persons, Two gentlemen connected with the engineer's department took advantage of this crowning eminence to obtain a really 'bird's eye view' of the whole proceedings. They were wound up by the tackle used in hoisting the bricks, and enjoyed the perspective from their airy height to their hearts' content. When all was over they, of course, wished to descend, and gave the signal to be let down again, but alas! there was no response. The man in charge, excited by the events of the day, confused by the sorrowful news by which it was closed, and, it may be, oblivious from other causes, had utterly forgotten his engagement and gone home. Here was a prospect! The shades of evening were gathering, the multitudes departing, and every probability of being obliged to act the part of St. Simeon of Stylites very involuntarily. Despair added force and strength to their lungs, and at length—their condition and difficulty having attracted attention—they were relieved from their unpleasant predicament."

THE DUKE'S CARRIAGE.

A correspondent of the *Athenæum*, in 1830, speaking of the carriage prepared for the Duke of Wellington at the opening of the Liverpool and Manchester Railway, remarks: "It rather resembled an eastern pavilion than anything our northern idea considers a carriage. The floor is 32 feet long by 8 wide, gilt pillars support a crimson canopy 24 feet long, and it might for magnitude be likened to the car of Juggernaut; yet this huge machine, with the preceding steam engine, moved along at its own fiery will even more swimmingly, a 'thing of heart and mind,' than a ship on the ocean."

LORD BROUGHAM'S SPEECH.

At a dinner given at Liverpool in celebration of the opening of the Liverpool and Manchester Railway, Lord Brougham thus discourses upon the memorable event and the death of Mr. Huskisson:—"When I saw the difficulties of space, as it were, overcome; when I beheld a kind of miracle exhibited before my astonished eyes; when I saw the rocks excavated and the gigantic power of man penetrating through miles of the solid mass, and gaining a great, a lasting, an almost perennial conquest over the powers of nature by his skill and industry; when I contemplated all this, was it possible for me to avoid the reflections which crowded into my mind, not in praise of man's great success, not in admiration of the genius and perseverance he had displayed, or even of the courage he had shown in setting himself against the obstacles that matter afforded to his course—no! but the melancholy reflection that these prodigious efforts of the human race, so fruitful of praise but so much more fruitful of lasting blessing to mankind, have forced a tear from my eye by that unhappy casualty which deprived me of a friend and you of a representative!"

AN EARLY RIDE ON THE LIVERPOOL AND MANCHESTER RAILWAY.

No account of its first beginnings would, however, be complete for our time, which did not also give an idea of the impressions produced on one travelling over it before yet the novelty of the thing had quite worn away. It was a long time, comparatively, after September, 1830, before the men who had made a trip over the railroad ceased to be objects of deep curiosity. Here is the account of his experience by one of these far-travelled men, with all its freshness still lingering about it :—

"Although the whole passage between Liverpool and Manchester is a series of enchantments, surpassing any in the Arabian Nights, because they are realities, not fictions, yet there are epochs in the transit which are peculiarly exciting. These are the startings, the ascents, the descents, the tunnels, the Chat Moss, the meetings. At the instant of starting, or rather before, the automaton belches forth an explosion of steam, and seems for a second or two quiescent. But quickly the explosions are reiterated, with shorter and shorter intervals, till they become too rapid to be counted, though still distinct. These belchings or explosions more nearly resemble the pantings of a lion or tiger, than any sound that has ever vibrated on my ear. During the ascent they become slower and slower, till the automaton actually labours like an animal out of breath, from the tremendous efforts to gain the highest point of elevation. The progression is proportionate; and before the said point is gained, the train is not moving faster than a horse can pace. With the slow motion of the mighty and animated machine, the breathing becomes more laborious, the growl more distinct, till at length the animal appears exhausted and groans like the tiger, when overpowered in combat by the buffalo.

"The moment that the height is reached and the descent commences, the pantings rapidly increase; the engine with its train starts off with augmenting velocity; and in a few seconds it is flying down the declivity like lightning, and with a uniform growl or roar, like a continuous discharge of distant artillery.

"At this period, the whole train is going at the rate of thirty-five or forty miles an hour! I was on the outside,

E.

and in front of the first carriage, just over the engine. The scene was magnificent, I had almost said terrific. Although it was a dead calm the wind appeared to be blowing a hurricane, such was the velocity with which we darted through the air. Yet all was steady; and there was something in the precision of the machinery that inspired a degree of confidence over fear—of safety over danger. A man may travel from the Pole to the Equator, from the Straits of Malacca to the Isthmus of Darien, and he will see nothing so astonishing as this. The pangs of Etna and Vesuvius excite feelings of horror as well as of terror; the convulsion of the elements during a thunderstorm carries with it nothing but pride, much less of pleasure, to counteract the awe inspired by the fearful workings of perturbed nature; but the scene which is here presented, and which I cannot adequately describe, engenders a proud consciousness of superiority in human ingenuity, more intense and convincing than any effort or product of the poet, the painter, the philosopher, or the divine. The projections or transits of the train through the tunnels or arches are very electrifying. The deafening peal of thunder, the sudden immersion in gloom, and the clash of reverberated sounds in confined space combine to produce a momentary shudder or idea of destruction—a thrill of annihilation, which is instantly dispelled on emerging into the cheerful light.

"The meetings or crossings of the steam trains flying in opposite directions are scarcely less agitating to the nerves than their transits through the tunnels. The velocity of their course, the propinquity or apparent identity of the iron orbits along which these meteors move, call forth the involuntary but fearful thought of a possible collision, with all its horrible consequences. The period of suspense, however, though exquisitely painful, is but momentary; and in a few seconds the object of terror is far out of sight behind.

"Nor is the rapid passage across Chat Moss unworthy of notice. The ingenuity with which two narrow rods of iron are made to bear whole trains of wagons, laden with many hundred tons of commerce, and bounding across a wide, semi-fluid morass, previously impassable by man or beast, is beyond all praise and deserving of eternal record.

Only conceive a slender bridge of two minute iron rails, several miles in length, level as Waterloo, elastic as whalebone, yet firm as adamant! Along this splendid triumph of human genius—this veritable *via triumphalis*—the train of carriages bounds with the velocity of the stricken deer ; the vibrations of the resilient moss causing the ponderous engine and its enormous suite to glide along the surface of an extensive quagmire as safely as a practiced skater skims the icy mirror of a frozen lake.

" The first class or train is the most fashionable, but the second or third are the most amusing. I travelled one day from Liverpool to Manchester in the lumber train. Many of the carriages were occupied by the swinish multitude, and others by a multitude of swine. These last were naturally vociferous if not eloquent. It is evident that the other passengers would have been considerably annoyed by the orators of this last group, had there not been stationed in each carriage an officer somewhat analogous to the Usher of the Black Rod, but whose designation on the railroad I found to be 'Comptroller of the Gammon.' No sooner did one of the long-faced gentlemen raise his note too high, or wag his jaw too long, than the 'Comptroller of the Gammon' gave him a whack over the snout with the butt end of his shillelagh ; a snubber which never failed to stop his oratory for the remainder of the journey."

To one familiar with the history of railroad legislation the last paragraph is peculiarly significant. For years after the railroad system was inaugurated, and until legislation was invoked to compel something better, the companies persisted in carrying passengers of the third class in uncovered carriages, exposed to all weather, and with no more decencies or comforts than were accorded to swine.

EARLY RAILWAY TRAVELLING.

A writer in *Notes and Queries* remarks :—" On looking over a diary kept by my father during two journeys northward in 1830-31, I thought the readers might be amused with his account of what he saw of railway travelling, then in its infancy :—

"Monday, Oct. 11, 1830, Darlington.—Walked to the railroad, which comes within half-a-mile of the town. Saw a steam engine drawing about twenty-five wagons, each containing about two tons and a half of coals. A single horse draws four such wagons. I went to Stockton at four o'clock by coach on the railroad; one horse draws about twenty-four passengers. I did not like it at all, for the road is very ugly in appearance, and, being only one line with occasional turns for passing, we were sometimes obliged to wait, and at other times to be drawn back, so that we were full two hours going eleven miles, and they are often more than three hours. There is no other conveyance, as the cheapness has driven the stage-coaches off the road. I only paid 1s. for eleven miles. The motion was very unpleasant—a continual jolting and disagreeable noise."

On Sept. 1, 1831, he remarks :—"The railroad to Stockton has been improved since I was here, as they are now laying down a second line."

"Wednesday, Oct. 27, 1830.—Left Manchester at ten o'clock by the railroad for Liverpool. We enter upon it by a staircase through the office from the street at present, but there will, I suppose, be an open entrance, by-and-bye; they have built extensive warehouses adjoining. We were two hours and a half going to Liverpool (about thirty-two miles), and I must think the advantages have been a good deal overrated, for, prejudice apart, I think most people will allow that expedition is the only real advantage gained; the road itself is ugly, though curious and wonderful as a work of art. Near Liverpool it is cut very deeply through rock, and there is a long tunnel which leads into a yard where omnibusses wait to convey passengers to the inns. The tunnel is too low for the engines at present in use, and the carriages are drawn through it by donkeys. The engines are calculated to draw fifty tons. . . . . I cannot say that I at all liked it; the speed was too great to be pleasant, and makes you rather giddy, and certainly it is not smoother and easier than a good turnpike road. When the carriages stop or go on, a very violent jolting takes place, from the ends of the carriages jostling together. I have heard many say they prefer a horse-coach, but the majority are in favour of the railroad, and they will, no doubt, knock up the coaches."

" Monday, Sept. 12, 1831.—Left Manchester by coach at ten o'clock, and arrived in Liverpool at half-past two. . . The railroad is not supposed to answer vastly well, but they are making a branch to Warrington, which will hurt the Sankey Navigation, and throw 1,500 men out of employment ; these people are said to be loud in their execrations of it, and to threaten revenge. It is certain the proprietors do not all feel easy about it, as one living at Warrington has determined never to go by it, and was coming to Liverpool by our coach if there had been room. He would gladly sell his shares. A dividend of 4 per cent. had been paid for six months, but money had been borrowed. . . . Charge for tonnage of goods, 10s. for thirty-two miles, which appears very dear to me."

CRABB ROBINSON'S FIRST RAILWAY JOURNEY.

" June 9th, 1833.—(Liverpool). At twelve o'clock I got upon an omnibus, and was driven up a steep hill to the place where the steam carriages start. We travelled in the second class of carriages. There were five carriages linked together, in each of which were placed open seats for the travellers, four or five facing each other ; but not all were full ; and, besides, there was a close carriage, and also a machine for luggage. The fare was four shillings for the thirty-one miles. Everything went on so rapidly that I had scarcely the power of observation. The road begins at an excavation through a rock, and is to a certain extent insulated from the adjacent country. It is occasionally placed on bridges, and frequently intersected by ordinary roads. Not quite a perfect level is preserved. On setting off there is a slight jolt. arising from the chain catching each carriage, but, once in motion, we proceeded as smoothly as possible. For a minute or two the pace is gentle, and is constantly varying. The machine produces little smoke or steam. First in order is the tall chimney ; then the boiler, a barrel-like vessel ; then an oblong reservoir of water ; then a vehicle for coals ; and then comes, of a length infinitely extendible, the train of carriages. If all the seats had been filled, our train would have carried about 150 passengers ; but a gentleman assured me at Chester that he went with a thousand persons to Newton fair. There must have

been two engines then.   I have heard since that two
thousand persons or more went to and from the fair that
day.   But two thousand only, at three shillings each way,
would have produced £600!   But, after all, the expense is
so great that it is considered uncertain whether the
establishment will ultimately remunerate the proprietors.
Yet I have heard that it already yields the shareholders a
dividend of nine per cent.   And Bills have passed for
making railroads between London and Birmingham, and
Birmingham and Liverpool.   What a change it will produce
in the intercourse!   One conveyance will take between 100
and 200 passengers, and the journey will be made in a forenoon!   Of the rapidity of the journey I had better experience on my return; but I may say now that, stoppages
included, it may certainly be made at the rate of twenty
miles an hour!

"I should have observed before that the most remarkable
movements of the journey are those in which trains pass
one another.   The rapidity is such that there is no recognizing the features of a traveller.   On several occasions, the
noise of the passing engine was like the whizzing of a
rocket.   Guards are stationed in the road, holding flags,
to give notice to the drivers when to stop.   Near Newton
I noticed an inscription recording the memorable death of
Huskisson."

—Crabb Robinson's Diary.

EARLY AMERICAN RAILWAY ENTERPRISE.

Mr. C. F. Adams, in his work on *Railroads: Their Origin
and Problems,* remarks:—"There is, indeed, some reason
for believing that the South Carolina Railroad was the first
ever constructed in any country with a definite plan of
operating it exclusively by locomotive steam power.   But
in America there was not—indeed, from the very circumstances of the case, there could not have been—any such
dramatic occasions and surprises as those witnessed at
Liverpool in 1829 and 1830.   Nevertheless, the people of
Charleston were pressing close on the heels of those at
Liverpool, for on the 15th of January, 1831—exactly four
months after the formal opening of the Manchester and
Liverpool road—the first anniversary of the South Carolina

Railroad was celebrated with due honor. A queer-looking machine, the outline of which was sufficient in itself to prove that the inventor owed nothing to Stephenson, had been constructed at the West Point Foundry Works in New York during the summer of 1830—a first attempt to supply that locomotive power which the Board had, with sublime confidence in possibilities, unanimously voted on the 14th of the preceding January should alone be used on the road. The name of *Best Friend* was given to this very simple product of native genius. The idea of the multitubular boiler had not yet suggested itself in America. The *Best Friend*, therefore, was supplied with a common vertical boiler, 'in form of an old-fashioned porter-bottle, the furnace at the bottom surrounded with water, and all filled inside of what we call teats running out from the sides and tops.' By means of the projections or 'teats' a portion at least of the necessary heating surface was provided. The cylinder was at the front of the platform, the rear end of which was occupied by the boiler, and it was fed by means of a connecting pipe. Thanks to the indefatigable researches of an enthusiast on railroad construction, we have an account of the performances of this and all the other pioneers among American locomotives, and the pictures with which Mr. W. H. Brown has enriched his book would alone render it both curious and valuable. Prior to the stockholders' anniversary of January 15th, 1831, it seems that the *Best Friend* had made several trips 'running at the rate of sixteen to twenty-one miles an hour, with forty or fifty passengers in some four or five cars, and without the cars, thirty to thirty-five miles an hour.' The stockholders' day was, however, a special occasion, and the papers of the following Monday, for it happened on a Saturday, gave the following account of it :—

"Notice having been previously given, inviting the stockholders, about one hundred and fifty assembled in the course of the morning at the company's buildings in Line Street, together with a number of invited guests. The weather the day and night previous had been stormy, and the morning was cold and cloudy. Anticipating a postponement of the ceremonies, the locomotive engine had been taken to pieces for cleaning, but upon the assembling of the company she was put in order, the cylinders new packed and at the word the apparatus was ready for movement. The first trip was performed with two pleasure cars attached, and a small carriage, fitted for the occasion, upon which was a detachment of United States troops and a field-piece which had been politely granted by Major Belton for the occasion. . . . , . The number of passengers brought down, which was performed in two trips, was estimated at upward of two hundred. A band of music enlivened the scene, and great hilarity and good humour prevailed throughout the day."

It was not long, however, before the *Best Friend* came to serious grief. Naturally, and even necessarily, inasmuch as it was a South Carolina institution, it was provided with a negro fireman. It so happened that this functionary while in the discharge of his duties was much annoyed by the escape of steam from the safety valve, and, not having made himself complete master of the principles underlying the use of steam as a source of power, he took advantage of a temporary absence of the engineer in charge to effect a radical remedy of this cause of annoyance. He not only fastened down the valve lever, but further made the thing perfectly sure by sitting upon it. The consequences were hardly less disastrous to the *Best Friend* than to the chattel fireman. Neither were of much further practical use. Before this mishap chanced, however in June, 1831, a second locomotive, called the *West Point*, had arrived in Charleston, and this last was constructed on the principle of Stephenson's *Rocket*. In its general aspect, indeed, it greatly resembled that already famous prototype. There is a very characteristic and suggestive cut representing a trial trip made with this locomotive on March 5th, 1831. The nerves of the Charleston people had been a good deal disturbed and their confidence in steam as a safe motor shaken by the disaster which had befallen the *Best Friend*. Mindful of this fact, and very properly solicitous for the safety of their guests, the directors now had recourse to a very simple and ingenious expedient. They put what they called a 'barrier car' between the locomotive and passenger coaches of the train. This barrier car consisted of a platform on wheels upon which were piled six bales of cotton. A fortification was thus provided between the passengers and any future negro sitting on the safety valve. We are also assured that 'the safety valve being out of the reach of any person but the engineer, will contribute to the prevention of accidents in the future, such as befel the *Best Friend*.' Judging by the cut which represents the train, this occasion must have been even more marked for its 'hilarity' than the earlier one which has already been described. Besides the locomotive and the barrier car there are four passenger coaches. In the first of these was a negro band, in general appearance very closely resembling the minstrels of a later day, the members of which are energetically performing on musical instruments of various familiar descriptions. Then follow three cars full of the saddest looking white passengers, who were present as we were informed to the number of one hundred and seventeen. The excursion was, however, highly successful, and two-and-a-quarter miles of road were passed over in the short space of eight minutes—about the speed at which a good horse would trot for the same distance.

This was in March, 1831. About six months before, however, there had actually been a trial of speed between a horse and one of the pioneer locomotives, which had not resulted in favour of the locomotive. It took place on the present Baltimore and Ohio road upon the 28th of August, 1830. The engine in this case was contrived by no other than Mr. Peter Cooper. And it affords a striking illustration of how recent those events which now seem so remote really were, that here is a man until very recently living, and amongst the most familiar to the eyes of the present generation, who was a contemporary of Stephenson, and himself invented a locomotive during the Rainhill year, being then nearly forty years of ago. The Cooper engine, however, was scarcely more than a working model. Its active-minded inventor hardly seems to have aimed at anything more than a demonstration of possibilities. The whole thing weighed only a ton, and was of one horse power; in fact it was not larger than those handcars now in common use with railroad section-men. The boiler, about the size of a modern kitchen boiler, stood upright and was fitted above the furnace—which occupied the lower section—with vertical tubes. The cylinder was but three-and-a-half inches in diameter, and the wheels were moved by gearing. In order to secure the requisite pressure of steam in so small a boiler, a sort of bellows was provided which was kept in action by means of a drum attached to one of the car-wheels over which passed a cord which worked a pulley, which in turn worked the bellows. Thus, of Stephenson's two great devices, without either of which his success at Rainhill would have been impossible—the waste steam blast and the multitubular boiler—Peter Cooper had only got hold of the last. He owed his defeat in the race between his engine and a horse to the fact that he had not got hold of the first. It happened in this wise. Several experimental trips had been made with the little engine on the Baltimore and Ohio road, the first sections of which had recently been completed and were then operated upon by means of horses. The success of these trips was such that at last, just seventeen days before the formal opening of the Manchester and Liverpool road on the other side of the Atlantic, a small open car was attached to the engine—the name of which, by the way, was *Tom Thumb*—and upon this a party of directors and their friends were carried from Baltimore to Ellicott's Mills and back, a distance of some twenty-six miles.

The trip out was made in an hour, and was very successful. The return was less so, and for the following reason:—

"The great stage proprietors of the day were Stockton and Stokes; and on that occasion a gallant grey, of great beauty and power, was driven by them from town. attached to another car on the second track—for the company had begun by making two tracks to the Mills—and met the engine at the Relay House, on its way back. From this point it was determined to have a race home, and the start being even, away went horse and engine, the snort of the one and the puff of the other keeping tune and time.

"At first the grey had the best of it, for his *steam* would be applied to the greatest advantage on the instant, while the engine had to wait until the rotation of the wheels set the blower to work. The horse was perhaps a quarter of a mile ahead when the safety valve of the engine lifted, and the thin blue vapour issuing from it showed an excess of steam. The blower whistled, the steam blew off in vapoury clouds, the pace increased, the passengers shouted, the engine gained on the horse, soon it lapped him—the silk was plied—the race was neck and neck, nose and nose—then the engine passed the horse, and a great hurrah hailed the victory. But it was not repeated,. for, just at this time, when the grey's master was about giving up, the band which draws the pulley which moved the blower slipped from the drum, the safety valve ceased to scream, and the engine—for want of breath—began to wheeze and pant. In vain Mr. Cooper, who was his own engineer and fireman, lacerated his hands in attempting to replace the band upon the wheel; the horse gained upon the machine and passed it, and although the band was presently replaced, and the steam again did its best, the horse was too far ahead to be over-taken, and came in the winner of the race."

ENGLISH AND AMERICAN OPPOSITION.

What wonder that such an innovation as railways was strenuously opposed, threatening, as it did, the coaching interest, and the posting interest, the canal interest, and the sporting interest, and private interests of every variety. "Gentlemen, as an individual," said a sporting M.P. for Cheltenham, "I hate your railways; I detest them alto-gether; I wish the concoctors of the Cheltenham and Oxford, and the concoctors of every other scheme, including the solicitors and engineers, were at rest in Paradise. Gentle-men, I detest railroads; nothing is more distasteful to me than to hear the echo of our hills reverberating with the noise of hissing railroad engines, running through the heart of our hunting country, and destroying that noble sport to which I have been accustomed from my childhood." And at Tewkesbury, one speaker contended that "any railway would be injurious;" compared engines to "war-horses and fiery meteors;" and affirmed that "the evils contained in Pandora's box were but trifles compared with those that would be consequent on railways." Even in go-aheadative America, some steady jog-trotting opponents raised their voices against the nascent system; one of whom (a canal stockholder, by the way) chronicled the following objective arguments. "He saw what would be the effect of it; that it would set the whole world a-gadding. Twenty miles an hour, sir! Why you will not be able to keep an apprentice-boy at his work; every Saturday evening he must take a trip to Ohio, to spend the Sabbath with his sweetheart. Grave plodding citizens will be flying about like comets. All local attachments must be at an end. It will encourage flightiness of intellect. Veracious people will turn into the most immeasurable liars; all their conceptions will be exaggerated by their magnificent notions of distance. 'Only a hundred miles off! Tut, nonsense, I'll step, across, madam, and bring your fan!' 'Pray, sir, will you dine with me to-day at my little box at Alleghany?' 'Why, indeed, I don't know. I shall be in town until twelve. Well, I shall be there; but you must let me off in time for the theatre.' And then, sir, there will be barrels of pork, and cargoes of flour, and chaldrons of coals, and even lead and whiskey, and such-like sober things, that have always been used to sober travelling, whisking away like a set of sky-rockets. It will upset all the gravity of the nation. If two gentlemen have an affair of honour, they have only to steal off to the Rocky Mountains, and there no jurisdiction can touch them. And then, sir, think of flying for debt! A set of bailiffs, mounted on bomb-shells, would not over-take an absconded debtor, only give him a fair start. Upon the whole, sir, it is a pestilential, topsy-turvy, harum-scarum whirligig. Give me the old, solemn, straightforward, regular Dutch canal—three miles an hour for expresses, and two for ordinary journeys, with a yoke of oxen for a heavy load! I go for beasts of burthen: it is more primitive and scriptural, and suits a moral and religious people better. None of your hop-skip-and-jump whimsies for me."

—*Sharpe's London Journal.*

AN UNPLEASANT TRIAL TRIP.

Mr. C. F. Adams remarks:—"A famous trial trip with a new locomotive engine was that made on the 9th of August, 1831, on the new line from Albany to Schenectady over the Mohawk Valley road. The train was made up of a loco-motive, the *De Witt Clinton*, its tender, and five or six passenger coaches—which were, indeed, nothing but the bodies of stage coaches placed upon trucks. The first two of these coaches were set aside for distinguished visitors; the others were surmounted with seats of plank to accommodate as many as possible of the great throng of persons who were anxious to participate in the trip. Inside and out the coaches were crowded; every seat was full. What followed the starting of the train has thus been described by one who took part in the affair:—

" ' The trucks were coupled together with chains or chain-links, leaving from two to three feet slack, and when the locomotive started it took up the slack by jerks, with sufficient force to jerk the passengers who sat on seats across the tops of the coaches, out from under their hats, and in stopping they came together with such force as to send them flying from their seats.

" They used dry pitch-pine for fuel, and, there being no smoke or spark-catcher to the chimney or smoke-stack, a volume of black smoke, strongly impregnated with sparks, coal, and cinders, came pouring back the whole length of the train. Each of the outside passengers who had an umbrella raised it as a protection against the smoke and fire. They were found to be but a momentary protection, for I think in the first mile the last one went overboard, all having their covers burnt off from the frames, when a general mêlée took place among the deck passengers, each whipping his neighbour to put out the fire. They presented a very motley appearance on arriving at the first station." Here, "a short stop was made, and a successful experiment tried to remedy the unpleasant jerks. A plan was soon hit upon and put into execution. The three links in the couplings of the cars were stretched to their utmost tension, a rail from a fence in the neighbourhood was placed between each pair of cars and made fast by means of the packing yarn from the cylinders. This arrangement improved the order of things, and it was found to answer the purpose when the signal was again given and the engine started.' "

PROGNOSTICATIONS OF FAILURE.

In the year 1831, the writer of a pamphlet, who styled himself *Investigator*, essayed the task of " proving by facts and arguments" that a railway between London and

Birmingham would be a "burden upon the trade of the country and would never pay." The difficulties and dangers of the enterprise he thus sets forth :—

"The causes of greater danger on the railway are several. A velocity of fifteen miles an hour is in itself a great source of danger, as the smallest obstacle might produce the most serious consequences. If, at that rate, the engine or any forward part of the train should suddenly stop, the whole would be cracked by the collision like nutshells. At all turnings there is a danger that the latter part of the train may swing off the rails; and, if that takes place, the most serious consequences must ensue before the whole train can be stopped. The line, too, upon which the train must be steered admits of little lateral deviation, while a stage coach has a choice of the whole roadway. Independently of the velocity, which in coaches is the chief source of danger, there are many perils on the railway, the rails stand up like so many thick knives, and any one alighting on them would have but a slight chance of his life . . . Another consideration which would deter travellers, more especially invalids, ladies, and children, from making use of the railways, would be want of accommodation along the line, unless the directors of the railway choose to build inns as commodious as those on the present line of road. But those inns the directors would have in part to support also, because they would be out of the way of any business except that arising from the railway, and that would be so trifling and so accidental that the landlords could not afford to keep either a cellar or a larder.

"Commercial travellers, who stop and do business in all the towns and by so doing render commerce much cheaper than it otherwise would be, and who give that constant support to the houses of entertainment which makes them able to supply the occasional traveller well and at a cheap rate, would, as a matter of course, never by any chance go by the railroad; and the occasional traveller, who went the same route for pleasure, would go by the coach road also, because of the cheerful company and comfortable dinner. Not one of the nobility, the gentry, or those who travel in their own carriages, would by any chance go by the railway. A nobleman would really not like to be drawn at the tail of a train of wagons, in which some hundreds of bars of iron were jingling with a noise that would drown all the bells of the district, and in the momentary apprehension of having his vehicle broke to pieces, and himself killed or crippled by the collision of those thirty-ton masses."

SIR ASTLEY COOPER'S OPPOSITION TO THE LONDON AND BIRMINGHAM RAILWAY.

Robert Stephenson, while engaged in the survey of the above line, encountered much opposition from landed proprietors. Many years after its completion, when recalling the past, he said :—"I remember that we called one day on Sir Astley Cooper, the eminent surgeon, in the hope of overcoming his aversion to the railway. He was one of our most inveterate and influential opponents. His country house at Berkhampstead was situated near the intended line, which passed through part of his property. · We found a courtly, fine-looking old gentleman, of very stately manners, who received us kindly and heard all we had to say in favour of the project. But he was quite inflexible in his opposition to it. No deviation or improvement that we could suggest had any effect in conciliating him. He was opposed to railways generally, and to this in particular. 'Your scheme,' said he, 'is preposterous in the extreme. It is of so extravagant a character as to be positively absurd. Then look at the recklessness of your proceedings! You are proposing to cut up our estates in all directions for the purpose of making an unnecessary road. Do you think, for one moment, of the destruction of property involved by it? Why, gentlemen, if this sort of thing be permitted to go on you will in a very few years *destroy the nobility !*'"

OPPOSITION TO MAKING SURVEYS.

A great deal of opposition was encountered in making the surveys for the London and Birmingham Railway, and although, in every case, as little damage was done as possible, simply because it was the interest of those concerned to conciliate all parties along the line, yet, in several instances, the opposition was of a most violent nature; in one case no skill or ingenuity could evade the watchfulness and determination of the lords of the soil, and the survey was at last accomplished at night by means of dark lanterns.

On another occasion, when Mr. Gooch was taking levels through some of the large tracts of grazing land, a few miles from London, two brothers, occupying the land came to him in a great rage, and insisted on his leaving their property immediately. He contrived to learn from them that the adjoining field was not theirs and he therefore remonstrated but very slightly with them, and then walked quietly through the gap in the hedge into the next field, and planted his level on the highest ground he could find— his assistant remaining at the last level station, distant about a hundred and sixty yards, apparently quite unconscious of what had taken place, although one of the brothers was moving very quickly towards him, for the purpose of sending him off. Now, if the assistant had moved his staff before Mr. Gooch had got his sight at it through the telescope of his level, all his previous work would have been completely lost, and the survey must have been completed in whatever manner it could have been done—the great object, however, was to prevent this serious inconvenience. The moment Mr. Gooch commenced looking through his telescope at the staff held by his assistant, the grazier nearest him, spreading out the tails of his coat, tried to place himself between the staff and the telescope, in order to intercept all vision, and at the same time commenced shouting violently to his comrade, desiring him to make haste and knock down the staff. Fortunately for Mr. Gooch, although nature had made this amiable being's ears longer than usual, yet they performed their office very badly, and as he could not see distinctly what Mr. Gooch was about —the hedge being between them—he very simply asked the man at the staff what his (the enquirer's) brother said. " Oh," replied the man, " he is calling to you to stop that horse there which is galloping out of the fold yard." Away went Clodpole, as fast as he could run, to restrain the unruly energies of Smolensko the Ninth, or whatever other name the unlucky quadruped might be called, and Mr. Gooch in the meanwhile quietly took the sight required—he having, with great judgment, planted his level on ground sufficiently high to enable him to see over the head of any grazier in the land; but his clever assistant, as soon as he perceived that all was right, had to take to his heels and make the shortest cut to the high road.

In another instance, a reverend gentleman of the Church of England made such alarming demonstrations of his opposition that the extraordinary expedient was resorted to of surveying his property during the time he was engaged in the pulpit, preaching to his flock. This was accomplished by having a strong force of surveyors all in readiness to commence their operations, by entering the clergyman's grounds on the one side at the same moment that they saw him fairly off them on the other, and, by a well organised and systematic arrangement, each man coming to a conclusion with his allotted task just as the reverend gentleman came to a conclusion with his sermon; and before he left the church to return to his home, the deed was done.

—Roscoe's *London and Birmingham Railway.*

SANITARY OBJECTIONS.

Mr. Smiles, in his *Life of George Stephenson*, remarks:—" Sanitary objections were also urged in opposition to railways, and many wise doctors strongly inveighed against tunnels. Sir Anthony Carlisle insisted that "tunnels would expose healthy people to colds, catarrhs, and consumption." The noise, the darkness, and the dangers of tunnel travelling were depicted in all their horrors. Worst of all, however, was 'the destruction of the atmospheric air,' as Dr. Lardner termed it. Elaborate calculations were made by that gentleman to prove that the provision of ventilating shafts would be altogether insufficient to prevent the dangers arising from the combustion of coke, producing carbonic acid gas, which in large quantities was fatal to life. He showed, for instance, that in the proposed Box tunnel, on the Great Western Railway, the passage of 100 tons would deposit about 3090lbs. of noxious gases, incapable of supporting life! Here was an uncomfortable prospect of suffocation for passengers between London and Bristol. But steps were adopted to allay these formidable sources of terror. Solemn documents, in the form of certificates, were got up and published, signed by several of the most dis-

F

tinguished physicians of the day, attesting the perfect wholesomeness of tunnels, and the purity of the air in them. Perhaps they went further than was necessary in alleging, what certainly subsequent experience has not verified, that the atmosphere of the tunnel was 'dry, of an agreeable temperature, and free from smell.' Mr. Stephenson declared his conviction that a tunnel twenty miles long could be worked safely and without more danger to life than a railway in the open air; but, at the same time, he admits that tunnels were nuisances, which he endeavoured to avoid wherever practicable."

ELEVATED RAILWAYS.

In the *Gentleman's Magazine* for June, 1830, it is stated:— "There are at present exhibiting in Edinburgh three large models, accompanied with drawings of railways and their carriages, invented by Mr. Dick, who has a patent. These railways are of a different nature from those hitherto in use, inasmuch as they are not laid along the surface of the ground, but elevated to such a height as, when necessary, to pass over the tops of houses and trees. The principal supports are of stone, and, being placed at considerable distances, have cast-iron pillars between them. The carriages are to be dragged along with a velocity hitherto unparalleled, by means of a rope drawn by a steam engine or other prime mover, a series being placed at intervals along the railway. From the construction of the railway and carriages the friction is very small."

EVIDENCE OF A GENERAL SALESMAN.

The advantages London derives from railways, in regard to its supply of good meat, may be gathered from the evidence given by Mr. George Bowley in 1834, on behalf of the Great Western Railway Company.

"You have been a general salesman of live and dead stock of all descriptions in Newgate Market 32 years?"—"Yes."

"What is about the annual amount of your sales?"— "I turn over £300,000 in a year."

"Would a railway that facilitated the communication between London and Bristol be an advantage to your business?"—"I think it would be a special advantage to London altogether."

"In what way?"—"The facility of having goods brought in reference to live stock is very important; I have been in the habit of paying Mr. Bowman, of Bristol, £1,000 a-week for many weeks; that has been for sending live hogs to me to be sold, to be slaughtered in London; and I have, out of that £1,000 a-week as many as 40 or 50 pigs die on the road, and they have sold for little or nothing. The exertion of the pigs kills them."

"The means of conveying pigs on a railway would be a great advantage?"—"Yes, as far as having the pigs come good to market, without being subject to a distemper that creates fever, and they die as red as that bag before you, and when they are killed in good health they die a natural colour."

"Then do I understand you that those who are fortunate enough to survive the journey are the worse for it?"—"Yes, in weight."

"And in quality?"—"Yes! All meat killed in the country, and delivered in the London market dead, in a good state, will make from 6d. to 8d. a stone more than what is slaughtered in London."

THE ANXIOUS HAIR-DRESSER.

"Clanwilliam mentioned this evening an incident which proves the wonderful celerity of the railroads. Mr. Isidore, the Queen's coiffeur, who receives £2,000 a year for dressing Her Majesty's hair twice-a-day, had gone to London in the morning to return to Windsor in time for her toilet; but on arriving at the station he was just five minutes too late, and saw the train depart without him. His horror was great, as he knew that his want of punctuality would deprive him of his place, as no train would start for the next two hours. The only resource was to order a special train, for which he was obliged to pay £18; but the establishment feeling the importance of his business, ordered extra steam to be put on, and conveyed the anxious hair-dresser 18 miles in 18 minutes, which extricated him from all his difficulties.
—*Raike's Diary from* 1831 *to* 1847.

SHARP PRACTICE.

Sir Francis Head, Bart., in his *Stokers and Pokers*, remarks :—" During the construction of the present London and North Western Railway, a landlady at Hillmorton, near Rugby, of very sharp practice, which she had imbibed in dealings for many years with canal boatmen, was constantly remarking aloud that no navvy should ever "do" her; and although the railway was in her immediate neighbourhood, and although the navvies were her principal customers, she took pleasure on every opportunity in repeating the invidious remark.

" It had, however, one fine morning scarcely left her large, full-blown, rosy lips, when a fine-looking young fellow, walking up to her, carrying in both hands a huge stone bottle, commonly called a 'grey-neck,' briefly asked her for 'half a gallon of gin;' which was no sooner measured and poured in than the money was rudely demanded before it could be taken away.

"On the navvy declining to pay the exorbitant price asked, the landlady, with a face like a peony, angrily told him he must either pay for the gin or *instantly* return it.

" He silently chose the latter, and accordingly, while the eyes of his antagonist were wrathfully fixed upon his, he returned into her measure the half gallon, and then quietly walked off; but having previously put into his grey-neck half a gallon of water, each party eventually found themselves in possession of half a gallon of gin and water; and, however either may have enjoyed the mixture, it is historically recorded at Hillmorton that the landlady was never again heard unnecessarily to boast 'that no navvy could *do* her.'"

A NAVVY'S REASON FOR NOT GOING TO CHURCH.

A navvy at Kilsby, being asked why he did not go to church? duly answered in geological language—" *Why, Soonday hasn't cropped out here yet!* " By which he meant that the clergyman appointed to the new village had not yet arrived.

SNAKES' HEADS.

One of the earliest forms of rails used by the Americans consisted of a flat bar half-an-inch thick spiked down to longitudinal timbers. In the process of running the train, the iron was curved, the spikes loosened, and the ends of the bars turned up, and were known by the name of snakes' heads. Occasionally they pierced the bottoms of the carriages and injured passengers, and it was no uncommon thing to hear passengers speculate as to which line they would go by, as showing fewest snakes' heads.

PREJUDICE REMOVED.

Mr. William Reed. a land agent, was called, in 1834, to give evidence in favour of the Great Western Railway. He was questioned as to the benefits conferred upon the localities passed through by the Manchester and Liverpool Railway. He was asked, "From your knowledge of the property in the neighbourhood, can you say that the houses have not decreased in value?" "Yes; I know an instance of a gentleman who had a house very near, and, though he quarrelled very much with the Company when they came there, and said, 'Very well, if you will come let me have a high wall to keep you out of sight,' and a year-and-a-half ago he petitioned the Company to take down the wall, and he has put up an iron railing, so that he may see them."

A RIDE FROM BOSTON TO PROVIDENCE IN 1835.

The early railway enterprise in America was not regarded by all persons with feelings of unmixed satisfaction. Thus we read of the railway journey taken by a gentleman of the old school, whose experience and sensations—if not very satisfactory to himself—are worth recording:—"July 22, 1835.—This morning at nine o'clock I took passage in a railroad car (from Boston) for Providence. Five or six other cars were attached to the locomotive, and uglier boxes I do not wish to travel in. They were made to stow away some thirty human beings, who sit cheek by jowl as best they can. Two poor fellows who were not much in the habit of making their toilet squeezed me into a corner, while the hot sun drew from their garments a villanous compound

of smells made up of salt fish, tar, and molasses. By and bye, just twelve—only twelve—bouncing factory girls were introduced, who were going on a party of pleasure to Newport. 'Make room for the ladies!' bawled out the superintendent, 'Come, gentlemen, jump up on the top; plenty of room there.' 'I'm afraid of the bridge knocking my brains out,' said a passenger. Some made one excuse and some another. For my part, I flatly told him that since I had belonged to the corps of Silver Greys I had lost my gallantry, and did not intend to move. The whole twelve were, however, introduced, and soon made themselves at home, sucking lemons and eating green apples. . . . .
The rich and the poor, the educated and the ignorant, the polite and the vulgar, all herd together in this modern improvement of travelling. The consequence is a complete amalgamation. Master and servant sleep heads and points on the cabin floor of the steamer, feed at the same table, sit in each other's laps, as it were, in the cars; and all this for the sake of doing very uncomfortably in two days what would be done delightfully in eight or ten. Shall we be much longer kept by this toilsome fashion of hurrying, hurrying, from starting (those who can afford it) on a journey with our own horses, and moving slowly, surely, and profitably through the country, with the power of enjoying its beauty, and be the means of creating good inns. Undoubtedly, a line of post-horses and post-chaises would long ago have been established along our great roads had not steam monopolized everything. . . . Talk of ladies on board a steamboat or in a railroad car. There are none! I never feel like a gentleman there, and I cannot perceive a semblance of gentility in any one who makes part of the travelling mob. When I see women whom, in their drawing rooms or elsewhere, I have been accustomed to respect and treat with every suitable deference—when I see them, I say, elbowing their way through a crowd of dirty emigrants or lowbred homespun fellows in petticoats or breeches in our country, in order to reach a table spread for a hundred or more, I lose sight of their pretensions to gentility and view them as belonging to the plebeian herd. To restore herself to her caste, let a lady move in select company at five miles an hour, and take her meals in comfort at a good inn, where

she may dine decently. . . . After all, the old-fashioned
way of five or six miles, with liberty to dine in a decent inn
and be master of one's movements, with the delight of seeing
the country and getting along rationally, is the mode to
which I cling, and which will be adopted again by the
generations of after times."

—*Recollections of Samuel Breck.*

APPEALING TO THE CLERGY.

Mr. C. F. Adams remarks:—" During the periods of dis-
couragement which, a few years later, marked certain
stages of the construction of the Western road, connecting
Worcester with Albany—when both money and courage
seemed almost exhausted—Mr. De Grand never for a
moment faltered. He might almost be said to have then
had Western railroad on the brain. Among other things,
he issued a circular which caused much amusement and
not improbably some scandal among the more precise. The
Rev. S. K. Lothrop, then a young man, had preached a
sermon in Brattle Street Church which attracted a good deal
of attention, on the subject of the moral and Christianizing
influence of railroads. Mr. De Grand thought he saw his
occasion, and he certainly availed himself of it. He at
once had a circular printed, a copy of which he sent to every
clergyman in Massachusetts, suggesting the propriety of a
discourse on 'The moral and Christianizing influence
of railroads in general and of the Western railroad in
particular.' "

AIR-WAYS INSTEAD OF RAILWAYS.

In the *Mechanics' Magazine* for July 22nd, 1837, is to be
found the following remarkable suggestion:—"In many
parts of the new railroads, where there has been some
objection to the locomotive engines, stationary ones are
resorted to, as everyone knows to draw the vehicles along.
Why might not these vehicles be balloons? Why, instead
of being dragged on the surface of the ground, along costly
viaducts or under disagreeable tunnels, might they not
travel two or three hundred feet high? By balloons, I
mean, of course, anything raised in the air by means of a
gas lighter than the air. They might be of all shapes and

sizes to suit convenience. The practicability of this plan does not seem to be doubtful. Its advantages are obvious. Instead of having to purchase, as for a railway, the whole line of track passed over, the company for a balloon-way would only have to procure those spots of ground on which they proposed to erect stationary engines; and these need in no case be of peculiar value, since their being a hundred yards one way or the other would make little difference. Viaducts of course would never be necessary, cuttings in very few occasions indeed, if at all. The chief expense of balloons is their inflation, which is renewed at every new ascent; but in these balloons the gas once in need never to be let out, and one inflation would be enough."

The same writer a few years later on observes:—"One feature of the air-way to supersede the railway would be, that besides preventing the destruction of the architectural beauties of the metropolis, now menaced by the multitudinous network of viaducts and subways at war with the existing thoroughfares, it would occasion the construction of numerous lofty towers as stations of arrival and departure, which would afford an opportunity of architectural effect hitherto undreamed of."

PREJUDICE AGAINST CARRYING COALS BY RAILWAYS.

Rev. F. S. Williams in an article upon "Railway Revolutions," remarks:—"When railways were first established it was never imagined that they would be so far degraded as to carry coals; but George Stephenson and others soon saw how great a service railways might render in developing and distributing the mineral wealth of the country. Prejudice had, however, to be timidly and vigorously overcome. When it was mentioned to a certain eminent railway authority that George Stephenson had spoken of sending coals by railway: 'Coals!' he exclaimed, 'they will want us to carry dung next.' The remark was reported to 'Old George,' who was not behind his critic in the energy of his expression. 'You tell B——,' he said, 'that when he travels by railway, they carry dung now!' The strength of the feeling against the traffic is sufficiently illustrated by the fact that, when the London and Birmingham Railway began to carry coal, the wagons that contained it were sheeted over that their contents might not be seen; and when a coal wharf was first made at Crick station, a screen was built to hide the work from the observation of passengers on the line. Even the possibility of carrying coal at a remunerative price was denied. 'I am very sorry,' said Lord Eldon, referring to this subject, 'to find the intelligent people of the north country gone mad on the subject of railways;' and another eminent authority declared: 'It is all very well to spend money; it will do some good; but I will eat all the coals your railway will carry.'

George Stephenson, however, and other friends of coal, held on their way; and he declared that the time would come when London would be supplied with coal by railway. 'The strength of Britain,' he said, 'is in her coal beds; and the locomotive is destined, above all other agencies, to bring it forth. The Lord Chancellor now sits upon a bag of wool; but wool has long ceased to be emblematical of the staple commodity of England. He ought rather to sit upon a bag of coals, though it might not prove quite so comfortable a seat. Then think of the Lord Chancellor being addressed as the noble and learned lord on the coal-sack? I'm afraid it wouldn't answer, after all.'"

AN EPITAPH ON THE VICTIM OF A RAILWAY ACCIDENT.

A correspondent writes to the *Pall Mall Gazette*:—"Our poetic literature, so rich in other respects, is entirely wanting in epitaphs on the victims of railway accidents. A specimen of what may be turned in this line is to be seen on a tombstone in the picturesque churchyard of Harrow-on-the-Hill. It was, I observe, written as long ago as 1838, so that it can be reproduced without much danger of hurting the feelings of those who may have known and loved the subject of this touching elegy. The name of the victim was Port, and the circumstances of his death are thus set forth:—

> Bright was the morn, and happy rose poor Port;
> Gay on the train he used his wonted sport.
> Ere noon arrived his mangled form they bore
> With pain distorted and overwhelmed with gore.
> When evening came and closed the fatal day,
> A mutilated corpse the sufferer lay."

AN ENGINE-DRIVER'S EPITAPH.

In the cemetery at Alton, Illinois, there is a tombstone
bearing the following inscription :—

> " My engine is now cold and still,
> No water does my boiler fill,
> My coke affords its flame no more,
> My days of usefulness are o'er ;
> My wheels deny their noted speed,
> No more my guiding hand they heed ;
> My whi·tle—it has lost its tone,
> Its shrill and thrilling sound is gone ;
> My valves are now thrown open wide,
> My flanges all refuse to glide ;
> My clacks—alas ! though once so strong,
> Refuse their aid in the busy throng ;
> No more I feel each urging breath,
> My steam is now condensed in death ;
> Life's railway o'er, each station past,
> In death I'm stopped, and rest at last."

This epitaph was written by an engineer on the old
Chicago and Mississippi Railroad, who was fatally injured
by an accident on the road; and while he lay awaiting the
death which he knew to be inevitable, he wrote the lines
which are engraved upon his tombstone.

TRAFFIC-TAKING.

Between the years 1836 and 1839, when there were many
railway acts applied for, traffic-taking became a lucrative
calling. It was necessary that some approximate estimate
should be made as to the income which the lines might be
expected to yield. Arithmeticians, who calculated traffic
receipts, were to be found to prove what promoters of railways required to satisfy shareholders and Parliamentary
Committees. The Eastern Counties Railway was estimated
to pay a dividend of $23\frac{1}{2}$ per cent.; the London and
Cambridge, $14\frac{1}{2}$ per cent.; the Sheffield and Manchester, $18\frac{1}{4}$
per cent. One shareholder of this company was so sanguine
as to the success of the line that in a letter to the *Railway
Magazine* he calculated on a dividend of 80 per cent. Bitter
indeed must have been the disappointment of those railway
shareholders who pinned their faith to the estimates of
traffic-takers, when instead of receiving large dividends,
little was received, and in some instances the lines paid no
dividend at all.

MONEY LOST AND FOUND.

On Friday night, a servant of the Birmingham Railway Company found in one of the first-class carriages, after the passengers had left, a pocket book containing a check on a London Bank for £2,000 and £2,500 in bank notes. He delivered the book and its contents to the principal officer, and it was forwarded to the gentleman to whom it belonged, his address being discovered from some letters in the pocket book. He had gone to bed, and risen and dressed himself next morning without discovering his loss, which was only made known by the restoration of the property. He immediately tendered £20 to the party who had found his money, but this being contrary to the regulations of the directors, the party, though a poor man, could not receive the reward. As the temptation, however, was so great to apply the money to his own use, the matter is to be brought before a meeting of the directors.

—*Aris's Gazette*, 1839.

ORIGIN OF COOK'S RAILWAY EXCURSIONS.

Mr. Thomas Cook, the celebrated excursionist, in an article in the *Leisure Hour* remarks:—"As a pioneer in a wide field of thought and action, my course can never be repeated. It has been mine to battle against inaugural difficulties, and to place the system on a basis of consolidated strength. It was mine to lay the foundations of a system on which others, both individuals and companies, have builded, and there is not a phase of the tourist plans of Europe and America that was not embodied in my plans or foreshadowed in my ideas. The whole thing seemed to come to me as by intuition, and my spirit recoiled at the idea of imitation.

"The beginning was very small, and was on this wise. I believe that the Midland Railway from Derby to Rugby *via* Leicester was opened in 1840. At that time I knew but little of railways, having only travelled over the Leicester and Swannington line from Leicester to Long Lane, a terminus near to the Leicestershire collieries. The reports in the papers of the opening of the new line created astonishment in Leicestershire, and I had read of an interchange of visits between the Leicester and Nottingham Mechanics' Institutes. I was an enthusiastic temperance man, and the secretary of a district association, which embraced parts of the two counties of Leicester and Northampton. A great meeting was to be held at Leicester, over which Lawrence Heyworth, Esq., of Liverpool—a great railway as well as temperance man—was advertised to preside. From my residence at Market Harborough I walked to Leicester (fifteen miles) to attend that meeting. About midway between Harborough and Leicester—my mind's eye has often reverted to the spot—a thought flashed through my brain, what a glorious thing it would be if the newly-developed powers of railways and locomotion could be made subservient to the promotion of temperance! That thought grew upon me as I travelled over the last six or eight miles. I carried it up to the platform, and, strong in the confidence of the sympathy of the chairman, I broached the idea of engaging a special train to carry the friends of temperance from Leicester to Loughborough and back to attend a quarterly delegate meeting appointed to be held there in two or three weeks following. The chairman approved, the meeting roared with excitement, and early next day I proposed my grand scheme to John Fox Bell, the resident secretary of the Midland Counties Railway Company. Mr. Paget, of Loughborough, opened his park for a gala, and on the day appointed about five hundred passengers filled some twenty or twenty-five open carriages—they were called 'tubs' in those days—and the party rode the enormous distance of eleven miles and back for a shilling, children half-price. We carried music with us, and music met us at the Loughborough station. The people crowded the streets, filled windows, covered the house-tops, and cheered us all along the line, with the heartiest welcome. All went off in the best style and in perfect safety we returned to Leicester; and thus was struck the keynote of my excursions, and the social idea grew upon me."

THE DEODAND.

It was a principle of English common law derived from the feudal period, that anything through the instrumentality of which death occurred was forfeited to the crown as a deodand; accordingly down to the year 1840, and even later, we find, in all cases where persons were killed, records of deodands levied by the coroners' juries upon locomotives. These appear to have been arbitrarily imposed and graduated in amount accordingly as circumstances seemed to excite in greater or less degree the sympathies or the indignation of the jury. In November, 1838, for instance, a locomotive exploded upon the Liverpool and Manchester line, killing its engineer and fireman; and for this escapade a deodand of twenty pounds was assessed upon it by the coroner's jury; while upon another occasion, in 1839, when the locomotive struck and killed a man and horse at a street crossing, the deodand was fixed at no less a sum than fourteen hundred pounds, the full value of the engine. Yet in this last case there did not appear to be any circumstances rendering the company liable in civil damages. The deodand seems to have been looked upon as a species of rude penalty imposed on the use of dangerous appliances, a sharp reminder to the companies to look sharply after their locomotives and employés. Thus upon the 24th of December, 1841, on the Great Western Railway, a train, while moving through a thick fog at a high rate of speed, came suddenly in contact with a mass of earth which had slid from the embankment at the side on to the track. Instantly the whole rear of the train was piled up on the top of the first carriage, which happened to be crowded with passengers, eight of whom were killed on the spot, while seventeen others were more or less injured. The coroner's jury returned a verdict of accidental death, and at the same time, as if to give the company a forcible hint to look closer to the condition of its embankment, a deodand of one hundred pounds was levied on the locomotive and tender.

AN UNFORTUNATE DISCUSSION.

Two gentlemen sitting opposite each other in a railway carriage got into a political argument; one was elderly and a staunch Conservative, the other was young and an ultra-Radical. It may be readily conceived that, as the argument went on, the abuse became fast and furious; all sorts of unpleasant phrases and epithets were bandied about, personalities were freely indulged in, and the other passengers were absolutely compelled to interfere to prevent a *fracas*. At the end of the journey the disputants parted in mutual disgust, and looking unutterable things. It so happened that the young man had a letter of introduction to an influential person in the neighbourhood respecting a legal appointment which was then vacant, which the young man desired to obtain, and which the elderly gentleman had the power to secure. The young petitioner, first going to his hotel and making himself presentable, sallied forth on his errand. He reached the noble mansion of the person to whom his letter of introduction was addressed, was ushered into an ante-room, and there awaited, with mingled hope and fear, the all-important interview. After a few minutes the door opened and, horrible to relate! he who entered was the young man's travelling opponent, and thus the opponents of an hour since stood face to face. The confusion and humiliation on the one side, and the hauteur and coldness on the other, may be readily imagined. Sir Edward C——, however—for such he was—although he instantly recognized his recent antagonist, was too well-bred to make any allusion to the transaction. He took the letter of introduction in silence, read it, folded it up, and returned it to the presenter with a bitter smile and the following speech : " Sir, I am infinitely obliged to my friend, Mr. ——, for recommending to my notice a gentleman whom he conceives to be so well fitted for the vacant post as yourself; but permit me to say that, inasmuch as the office you are desirous to fill exists upon a purely Conservative tenure, and can only be appropriately administered by a person of Conservative tendency, I could not think of doing such violence to your *well-known* political principles as to recommend you for the post in question." With these words and another smile more grim than before, Sir Edward C—— bowed the chapfallen petitioner out, and he quickly took his way to the railway station, secretly vowing never again to enter into political argument with an unknown railway traveller.

—*The Railway Traveller's Handy Book.*

DOG TICKET.

Shortly after telegraphs were laid alongside of railways, a principal officer of a railway company got into a compartment of a stopping train at an intermediate station. The train had hardly left, when an elderly gentleman, in terms of endearment, invited what turned out to be a little Skye terrier to come out of its concealment under the seat. The dog came out, jumped up, and appeared to enjoy his journey until the speed of the train slackened previous to stopping at a station, the dog then instinctively retreated to its hiding place, and came out again in due course after the train had started. The officer of the company left the train at a station or two afterwards. On its arrival at the London ticket platform the gentleman delivered up the tickets for his party. "Dog ticket, sir, please." "Dog ticket, what dog ticket?" "Ticket, sir, for Skye terrier, black and tan, with his ears nearly over his eyes; travelling, for comfort's sake, under the seat opposite to you, sir, in a large carpet bag, red ground with yellow cross-bars." The gentleman found resistance useless; he paid the fare demanded, when the ticket-collector—who throughout the scene had never changed a muscle—handed him a ticket that he had prepared beforehand. "Dog ticket, sir; gentlemen not allowed to travel with a dog without a dog ticket; you will have to give it up in London." "Yes, but how did you know I had a dog? That's what puzzles me!" "Ah, sir," said the ticket-collector, relaxing a little, but with an air of satisfaction, "the telegraph is laid on our railway. Them's the wires you see on the outside; we find them very useful in our business, etc. Thank you, sir, good morning." It is needless to tell what part the principal officer played in this little drama. On arrival in London the dog ticket was duly claimed, a little word to that effect having been sent up by a previous train to be sure to have it demanded, although, as a usual practice, dog tickets are collected at the same time as those of passengers.

—*Koney's Rambles on Railways.*

THE ELECTRIC CONSTABLE.

The first application of the telegraph to police purposes took place in 1844, on the Great Western Railway, and, as it was the first intimation thieves got of the electric constable being on duty, it is full of interest. The following extracts are from the telegraph book kept at the Paddington Station :—

"Eton Montem Day, August 28, 1844.—The Commissioners of Police having issued orders that several officers of the detective force shall be stationed at Paddington to watch the movements of suspicious persons, going by the down train, and give notice by the electric telegraph to the Slough station of the number of such suspected persons, and dress, their names (if known), also the carriages in which they are."

Now come the messages following one after the other, and influencing the fate of the marked individuals with all the celerity, certainty, and calmness of the Nemesis of the Greek drama :—

"Paddington, 10.20 a.m.—Mail train just started. It contains three thieves, named Sparrow, Burrell, and Spurgeon, in the first compartment of the fourth first-class carriage."

"Slough, 10.50 a.m.—Mail train arrived. *The officers have cautioned the three thieves.*"

"Paddington, 10.50 a.m.—Special train just left. It contained two thieves; one named Oliver Martin, who is dressed in black, *crape on his hat;* the other named Fiddler Dick, in black trousers and light blouse. Both in the third compartment of the first second-class carriage."

"Slough, 11.16 a.m.—Special train arrived. Officers have taken the two thieves into custody, a lady having lost her bag, containing a purse with two sovereigns and some silver in it; one of the sovereigns was sworn to by the lady as having been her property. It was found in Fiddler Dick's watch fob."

It appears that, on the arrival of the train, a policeman opened the door of the "third compartment of the first second-class carriage," and asked the passengers if they had missed anything? A search in pockets and bags accordingly ensued, until one lady called out that her purse was gone.

"Fiddler Dick, you are wanted," was the immediate demand of the police officer, beckoning to the culprit, who came out of the carriage thunder-struck at the discovery, and gave himself up, together with the booty, with the air of a completely beaten man. The effect of the capture so cleverly brought about is thus spoken of in the telegraph book :—

"Slough, 11.51 a.m.—Several of the suspected persons who came by the various down-trains are lurking about Slough, uttering bitter invectives against the telegraph. Not one of those cautioned has ventured to proceed to the Montem."

RUNAWAY MATCH.

Sir Francis Head in his account of the London and North-Western Railway remarks :—"During a marriage which very lately took place at ——, one of the bridesmaids was so deeply affected by the ceremony that she took the opportunity of the concentrated interest excited by the bride to elope from church with an admirer. The instant her parents discovered their sad loss, messengers were sent to all the railway stations to stop the fugitives. The telegraph also went to work, and with such effect that, before night, no less than four affectionate couples legitimately married that morning were interrupted on their several marriage jaunts and most seriously bothered, inconvenienced, and impeded by policemen and magistrates."

A RAILWAY ROMANCE.

An incident of an amusing though of a rather serious nature occurred some years ago on the London and South-Western Railway. A gentleman, whose place of residence was Maple Derwell, near Basingstoke, got into a first-class carriage at the Waterloo terminus, with the intention of proceeding home by one of the main line down trains. His only fellow-passengers in the compartment were a lady and an infant, and another gentleman, and thus things remained until the arrival of the train at Walton, where the other gentleman left the carriage, leaving the first gentleman with the lady and child. Shortly after this the train reached the Weybridge station, and on its stopping the lady, under the pretence of looking for her servant or carriage, requested her male fellow-passenger to hold the infant for a few minutes while she went to search for what she wanted. The bell rang for the starting of the train and the gentleman thus strangely left with the baby began to get rather fidgety, and anxious to return his charge to the mother. The lady, however, did not again put in any appearance, and the train went on without her, the child remaining with the gentleman, who, on arriving at his destination took the child home to his wife and explained the circumstance under which it came into his possession. No application has, at present, it is understood, been made for the "lost child," which has for the nonce been adopted by the gentleman and his wife, who, it is said, are without any family of their own.

GIGANTIC POWER OF LOCOMOTIVE ENGINES.

Sir Francis Head remarks:—"The gigantic power of the locomotive engines hourly committed to the charge of these drivers was lately strangely exemplified in the large engine stable at the Camden Station. A passenger engine, whose furnace-fire had but shortly been lighted, was standing in this huge building surrounded by a number of artificers, who, in presence of the chief superintendent. were working in various directions around it. While they were all busily occupied, the fire in the furnace—by burning up faster than was expected—suddenly imparted to the engine the breath of life; and no sooner had the minimum of steam necessary to move it been thus created, than this infant Hercules not only walked *off*, but without the smallest embarrassment walked *through* the 14-inch brick wall of the great building which contained it, to the terror of the superintendent and workmen, who expected every instant that the roof above their heads would fall in and extinguish them. In consequence of the spindle of the regulator having got out of its socket the very same accident occurred shortly afterwards with another engine, which, in like manner, walked through another portion of this 14-inch wall of the stable that contained it, just as a thorough-bred horse would have walked out of the door. And if such be the irresistible power of the locomotive engine when feebly walking in its new-born state, unattended or unassisted even by its tender, is it not appalling to reflect what must be its momentum when, in the full vigour of its life, it is flying down a steep gradient at the rate of 50 miles an hour, backed up by, say, 30 passenger carriages, each weighing on an average 5½ tons? If ordinary houses could suddenly be placed in its path, it would, passengers and all, run through them as a musket-ball goes through a keg of butter; but what would be the result if, at this full speed, the engine by any accident were to be diverted against a mass of solid rock, such as sometimes is to be seen at the entrance of a tunnel, it is impossible to calculate or even to conjecture. It is stated by the company's superintendent, who witnessed the occurrence, that some time ago an ordinary accident happening to a luggage train near Loughborough, the wagons overrode each other until the uppermost one was found piled 40 feet above the rails!"

NOVEL NOTICE TO DEFAULTING SHAREHOLDERS.

In the early days of railway enterprise there was often much difficulty in obtaining the punctual payment of calls from the shareholders. The Leicester and Swannington line was thus troubled. The Secretary, adopting a rather novel way to collect the calls, wrote to the defaulters:—
" I am therefore necessitated to inform you, that unless the sum of £2 is paid on or before the 22nd instant, your name will be furnished to one of the principal and most pressing creditors of the company." The missives of the Secretary generally had the desired effect.

A QUICK DECISION.

The elder Brunel was habitually absent in society, but no man was more remarkable for presence of mind in an emergency. Numerous instances are recorded of this latter quality, but none more striking than that of his adventure in the act of inspecting the Birmingham Railway. Suddenly in a confined part of the road a train was seen approaching from either end of the line, and at a speed which it was difficult to calculate. The spectators were horrified; there was not an instant to be lost; but an instant sufficed to the experienced engineer to determine the safest course under the circumstances. Without attempting to cross the road, which would have been almost certain destruction, he at once took his position exactly midway between the up and down lines, and drawing the skirts of his coat close around him, allowed the two trains to sweep past him; when to the great relief of those who witnessed the exciting scene, he was found untouched upon the road. Without the engineer's experience which enabled him to form so rapid a decision, there can be no doubt that he must have perished.

—*The Temple Anecdotes.*

THE VERSAILLES ACCIDENT IN 1842.

Mr. Charles F. Adams thus describes it :—" On the 8th of May, 1842, there happened in France one of the most famous and horrible railroad slaughters ever recorded. It was the birthday of the king, Louis Phillipe, and, in accordance with the usual practice, the occasion had been celebrated at Versailles by a great display of the fountains. At half-past five o'clock these had stopped playing, and a general rush ensued for the trains then about to leave for Paris. That which went by the road along the left bank of the Seine was densely crowded, and was so long that it required two locomotives to draw it. As it was moving at a high rate of speed between Bellevue and Mendon, the axle of the fore-most of these two locomotives broke, letting the body of the engine drop to the ground. It instantly stopped, and the second locomotive was then driven by its impetus on top of the first, crushing its engineer and fireman, while the contents of both the fire-boxes were scattered over the road-way and among the *debris*. Three carriages crowded with passengers were then piled on top of this burning mass, and there crushed together into each other. The doors of the train were all locked, as was then, and indeed is still, the custom in Europe, and it so chanced that the carriages had all been newly painted. They blazed up like pine kindlings. Some of the carriages were so shattered that a portion of those in them were enabled to extricate themselves, but no less than forty were held fast; and of these such as were not so fortunate as to be crushed to death in the first shock perished hopelessly in the flames before the eyes of a throng of impotent lookers-on. Some fifty-two or fifty-three persons were supposed to have lost their lives in this disaster, and more than forty others were injured; the exact number of the killed, however, could never be ascertained, as the telescoping of the carriages on top of the two locomotives had made of the destroyed portion of the train a visible holocaust of the most hideous description. Not only did whole families perish together—in one case no less than eleven members of the same family sharing a common fate—but the remains of such as were destroyed could neither be identified nor separated. In one case a female foot was alone recognisable, while in others the bodies were calcined and fused into an undistinguishable mass. The Academy of Sciences' appointed a committee to inquire whether Admiral D'Urville, a distinguished French navigator, was among the victims. His body was thought to be found, but it was so terribly mutilated that it could be recognized only by a sculptor, who chanced some time before to have taken a phrenological cast of his skull. His wife and only son had perished with him.

It is not easy now to conceive the excitement and dismay which this catastrophe caused throughout France. The new invention was at once associated in the minds of an excitable people with novel forms of imminent death. France had at best been laggard enough in its adoption of the new appliance, and now it seemed for a time as if the Versailles disaster was to operate as a barrier in the way of all further railroad development. Persons availed themselves of the steam roads already constructed as rarely as possible, and then in fear and trembling, while steps were taken to substitute horse for steam power on other roads then in process of construction."

AN AMATEUR SIGNALMAN.

Mr. Williams in his book, *Our Iron Roads*, gives an account of a foolish act of signalling to stop a train; he says:—"An Irishman, who appears to have been in some measure acquainted with the science of signalling, was on one occasion walking along the Great Western line without permission, when he thought he might reduce his information to practical use. Accordingly, on seeing an express train approach, he ran a short distance up the side of the cutting, and began to wave a handkerchief very energetically, which he had secured to a stick, as a signal to stop. The warning was not to be disregarded, and never was command obeyed with greater alacrity. The works of the engine were reversed—the tender and van breaks were applied—and soon, to the alarm of the passengers, the train came to a 'dead halt.' A hundred heads were thrust out of the carriage windows, and the guard had scarcely time to exclaim, 'What's the matter?' when Paddy, with a knowing touch of his 'brinks,' asked his 'honour if he would give him a bit of a ride?' So polite and ingenuous a request was not to be denied, and, though biting his lips with annoyance, the officer replied 'Oh, certainly; jump in here,' and the pilgrim was ensconced in the luggage van. But instead of having his ride 'for his thanks,' the functionary duly handed him over to the magisterial authorities, that he might be taught the important lesson, that railway companies did not keep express trains for Irish beggars, and that such costly machinery was not to be imperilled with impunity, either by their freaks or their ignorance."

STEAM WHISTLE.

In the early days of railways, the signal of alarm was given by the blowing of a horn. In the year, 1833, an accident occurred on the Leicester and Swannington railway near Thornton, at a level crossing, through an engine running against a horse and cart. Mr. Bagster, the manager, after narrating the circumstance to George Stephenson, asked "Is it not possible to have a whistle fitted on the engine, which the steam can blow?" "A very good thought," replied Stephenson. "You go to Mr. So-and-So, a musical instrument maker, and get a model made, and we will have a steam whistle, and put it on the next engine that comes on the line." When the model was made it was sent to the Newcastle factory and future engines had the whistle fitted on them.

EXEMPTION FROM ACCIDENTS.

Mr. C. F. Adams, remarks :—"Indeed, from the time of Mr. Huskisson's death, during the period of over eleven years, railroads enjoyed a remarkable and most fortunate exemption from accidents. During all that time there did not occur a single disaster resulting in any considerable loss of life. This happy exemption was probably due to a variety of causes. Those early roads were in the first place, remarkably well and thoroughly built, and were very cautiously operated under a light volume of traffic. The precautions then taken and the appliances in use would, it is true, strike the modern railroad superintendent as both primitive and comical; for instance, they involved the running of independent pilot locomotives in advance of all night passenger trains, and it was, by the way, on a pioneer locomotive of this description, on the return trip of the excursion party from Manchester after the accident to Mr. Huskisson, that the first recorded attempt was made in the direction of our present elaborate system of night signals. On that occasion obstacles were signalled to those in charge of the succeeding trains by a man on the pioneer locomotive, who used for that purpose a bit of lighted tarred rope. Through all the years between 1830 and 1841, nevertheless, not a single serious railroad disaster had to be recorded. Indeed, the luck—for it was nothing else —of these earlier times was truly amazing. Thus on this same Liverpool and Manchester road, as a first-class train on the morning of April 17, 1836, was moving at a speed of some thirty miles an hour, an axle broke under the first passenger carriage, causing the whole train to leave the rails and throwing it down the embankment, which at that point was twenty feet high. The carriages were rolled over, and the passengers in them turned topsy-turvy; nor, as they were securely locked in, could they even extricate themselves when at last the wreck of the train reached firm bearings. And yet no one was killed."

RIVAL CONTRACTORS AND THE BLOTTING PAD.

In rails, the same system has prevailed. Ironmasters have been pitted against each other, as to which should produce an apparent rail at the lowest price. At the outset of railways the rails were made of iron. Competition gradually produced rails in which a core, of what is technically called "cinder," is covered up with a skin of iron; and the cleverest foreman for an ironmaster was the man who could make rails with the maximum of cinder and the minimum of iron. In more than one instance has it been known in relaying an old line the worn-out rails have been sold at a higher price per ton than the new ones were bought for; yet this would hardly open the eyes of the buyers. The contrivances which are resorted to to get hold of one another's prices beforehand by competing contractors are manifold; and, when they attend in person, they commonly put off the filling up of their tender till the last moment. Once a shrewd contractor found himself at the same inn with a rival who always trod close on his heels. He was followed about and cross-questioned incessantly. and gave vague answers. Within half-an-hour of the last moment he went into the coffee room and sat himself down in a corner where his rival could not overlook him. There and then he filled up his tender, and, as he rose from the table, left behind him the paper on which he had blotted it. As he left the room his rival caught up the blotting paper, and, with the exulting glee of a consciously successful rival, read off the amount backwards. "Done this time!" was his mental thought, as he filled up his own tender a dollar lower, and hastened to deposit it. To his utter surprise, the next day he found that he had lost the contract, and complainingly asked his rival how it was, for he had tendered below him. "How did you know you were below me?" "Because I found your blotting paper." "I thought so. I left it on purpose for you, and wrote another tender in my bedroom. You had better make your own calculations next time!"

—*Roads and Rails*, by W. B. Adams.

RAILWAY LEGISLATION.

A writer in the *Encyclopædia Britannica* remarks:—"The expenses, direct and incidental, of obtaining an Act of Parliament have been in many cases enormous, and generally are excessive. The adherence to useless and expensive forms of Parliamentary Committees in what are called the standing orders, or general regulations for the observance of promoters of railway bills, on the one part, and the itching for opposition of railway companies, to resist fancied inroads on vested rights, supposed injurious competition, on the other part, have been amongst the sources of excessive expenditure. Mr. Stephenson mentioned an instance showing how Parliament has entailed expense upon railway companies by the system complained of. The Trent Valley Railway was under other titles originally proposed in 1836. It was, however, thrown out by the standing orders committee, in consequence of a barn of the value of £10, which was shown upon the general plan, not having been exhibited upon an enlarged sheet. In 1840, the line again went before Parliament. It was opposed by the Grand Junction Railway Company, now part of the London and North-Western. No less than 450 allegations were made against it before the standing orders sub-committee, which was engaged twenty-two days in considering those objections. They ultimately reported that four or five of the allegations were proved, but the committee nevertheless allowed the bill to proceed. It was read a second time and then went into committee, by whom it was under consideration for sixty-three days; and ultimately Parliament was prorogued before the report could be made. Such were the delays and consequent expenses which the forms of the House occasioned in this case, that it may be doubted if the ultimate cost of constructing the whole line was very much more than was expended in obtaining permission from Parliament to make it. This example serves to show the expensive formalities, the delays, and difficulties, with which Parliament surround railway legislation. Another instance, quoted by the same authority, will show not only the absurdity of the system of legislation, but also the afflicting spirit of competition and opposition with which railway bills are canvassed in Parliament, and the expensive outlay incurred by companies themselves.

In 1845, a bill for a line now existing went before Parliament with eighteen competitors, each party relying on the wisdom of Parliament to allow their bill at least to pass a second reading! Nineteen different parties condemned to one scene of contentious litigation! They each and all had to pay not only the costs of promoting their own line, but also the costs of opposing eighteen other bills. And yet conscious as government must have been of this fact, Parliament deliberately abandoned the only step it ever took on any occasion of subjecting railway projects to investigation by a preliminary tribunal. Parliamentary committees generally satisfied themselves with looking on and watching the ruinous game of competition for which the public are ultimately to pay. In fact, railway legislation became a mere scramble, conducted on no system or principle. Schemes of sound character were allowed to be defeated on merely technical grounds, and others of very inferior character were sanctioned by public act, after enormous Parliamentary expenses had been incurred. Competing lines were granted, sometimes parallel lines through the same district, and between the same towns,"

AN EXPENSIVE PARLIAMENTARY BILL.

A writer in the *Popular Encyclopædia* observes:—" But the most conspicuous example in recent times, which overshadowed all others, of excessive expenditure in Parliamentary litigation as well as in land and compensation, is supplied in the history of the Great Northern Company. The preliminary expenses of surveys, notices to landowners, etc., commenced in 1844, and the Bill was introduced into the House of Commons in 1845, when it was opposed by the London and North-Western, the Eastern Counties, and the Midland Railways. It was further opposed successively by two other schemes, called the London and York and the Direct Northern. The contest lasted eighty-two days before the House of Commons, more than half the time having been consumed by opposition to the Bill. The Bill was allowed to stand over till next year (1846), when it began, before the Committee of the House of Lords, where it left off in the Lower House in the year 1845 on account of the magnitude of the case. The Bill was before the Upper House between three and four weeks, and in the same year (1846) it was granted. The promoters of the rival projects were bought off, and all their expenses paid, including the costs of the opposition of the neighbouring lines already named, before the Great Northern bill was passed; and the 'preliminary expenses,' comprising the whole expenditure of every kind up to the passing of the bill was £590,355, or more than half-a-million sterling, incurred at the end of two years of litigation. Subsequently to the passing of the Act an additional sum of £172,722 was expended for law engineering expenses in Parliament to 31st December, 1857, which was spent almost wholly in obtaining leave from Parliament to make various alterations. Thus it would appear that a sum total of £763,077 was spent as Parliamentary charges for obtaining leave to construct 245 miles, being at the rate of £3,118 per mile."

THE RECTOR AND HIS PIG.

"I have been a rector for many years," writes a clergyman, "and have often heard and read of tithe-pigs, though I have never met with a specimen of them. But I had once a little pig given to me which was of a choice breed, and only just able to leave his mother. I had to convey him by carriage to the X station; from thence, twenty-three miles to Y station, and from thence, eighty-two miles to Z station, and from there, eight miles by carriage. I had a comfortable rabbit-hutch of a box made for him, with a supply of fresh cabbages for his dinner on the road. I started off with my wife, children, and nurse; and of these impediments piggy proved to be the most formidable. First, a council of war was held over him at X station by the railway officials, who finally decided that this small porker must travel as 'two dogs.' Two dog tickets were therefore procured for him; and so we journeyed on to Y station. There a second council of war was held, and the officials of Y said that the officials of X (another line) might be prosecuted for charging my piggy as two dogs, but that he must travel to Z as a horse, and that he must have a huge horse-box entirely to himself for the next eighty-two miles. I declined to pay for the horse-box—they refused to let me have my pig—officials swarmed around me—the station master advised me to pay for the horse-box and probably the company would return the extra charge. I scorned the probability, having no faith in the company—the train (it was a London express) was

already detained ten minutes by this wrangle; and finally
I whirled away bereft of my pig. I felt sure that he would
be forwarded by the next train, but as that would not reach
Z till a late hour in the evening, and it was Saturday, I
had to tell my pig tale to the officials; and not only so, but
to go to the adjacent hotel and hire a pig-stye till the
Monday, and fee a porter for seeing to the pig until I could
send a cart for him on that day. Of course the pig was
sent after me by the next train; and as the charge for him
was less than a halfpenny a mile, I presume he was not
considered to be a horse. Yet this fact remains—and it is
worth the attention of the Zoological Society, if not of
railway officials—that this small porker was never recognised as a pig, but began his railway journey as two dogs,
and was then changed into a horse."

SIR MORTON PETO'S RAILWAY MISSION.

Mr., afterwards Sir S. Morton Peto, having undertaken
the construction of certain railways in East Anglia, was at
this time in the habit of spending a considerable part of the
year in the neighbourhood of Norwich, and, with his family,
joined Mr. Brock's congregation. It will afterwards appear
how many important movements turned upon the friendship
which was thus formed; but it is only now to be noted that,
in the course of frequent conversations, the practicability
was discussed of attempting something which might serve
to interest and improve the large number of labourers employed on the works in progress. They were part of that
peculiar body of men which had been gradually formed
during a long course of years for employment in the construction, first of navigable canals, and then of railways,
and called, from their earlier occupation, "navvies." They
were drawn from diverse parts of the British Islands, and
professed, in some instances, hostile forms of religion, but
were distinguished chiefly by extreme ignorance and all but
total spiritual insensibility. They had, at the same time,
a common life and an unwritten law, affecting their relations
to each other, their employers, and the rest of the world.
That they were accessible to kind attentions—clearly disinterested—followed from their being men, but they required
to be approached with the greatest caution and patience.

Mr. Brock's wide and various sympathy, joined with his friend's steady support, led—under the divine blessing—to measures which proved very successful. Mr. Peto constructed commodious halls capable of being moved onward as the line of railway advanced, and affording comfortable shelter for the men in their leisure hours, and furnished with books and publications supplying amusement, useful information, and religious knowledge. To give life to this apparatus, Christian men, carefully selected, mingled familiarly with the rude but grateful toilers, helping them to read and write, encouraging them to acquire self-command, and above all, especially when they were convened on Sundays, presenting and pressing home upon them the words of eternal life.

Mr. Brock had liberty to draw on the "Railway Mission Account," at the Norwich Bank, to any extent that he found necessary, and in a short time he had a body of the best men, he was accustomed to say, that he ever knew at work upon all the chief points of the lines. No part of his now extended labours gave him greater delight than in superintending these missionaries, reading their weekly journals, arranging their periodical movements, counselling and comforting them in their difficulties, and visiting them, sometimes apart and at other times at conferences for united consultation and prayer, held at Yarmouth, Ely, or March.

Results of the best character, of which the record is on high, arose out of these operations.

—Birrell's *Life of the Rev. W. Brock, D.D.*

CLEVER CAPTURE.

A few days ago (1845), a gentleman left Glasgow in one of the day trains, with a large sum of money about his person. On the train arriving at the Edinburgh terminus, the gentleman left it, along with the other passengers, on foot for some distance. It was not long, however, before he discovered that his pocket book, containing £700, in bank notes was missing. He immediately returned to the terminus, where the first person he happened to find was the stoker of the train that had brought him to Edinburgh, who, on being spoken to, remembered seeing the gentleman leaving the terminus, and another person following close behind him, whom he supposed to be his servant; he further stated, that the supposed servant had started to return with the train which had just left for Glasgow. The gentleman immediately ordered an express train, but as some time elapsed before the steam could be got up, it was feared the gentleman and the stoker would not reach Glasgow in time to secure the culprit. However, having gone the distance in about an hour, they had the satisfaction of seeing the train before them close to the Cowlairs station, just about to descend the inclined plane and tunnel, and thus within a mile and a half of the end of their journey. The stoker immediately sounded his whistle, which induced the conductor of the passenger train to conclude that some danger was in the way, who had his train removed to the other line of rails, which left the road then quite clear for the express train, which drove past the other with great speed, and arrived at the terminus in sufficient time to get everything ready for the apprehension of the robber. The stoker, who thought he could identify the robber, assisted the police in searching the passenger train, when the person whom he had taken for the gentleman's servant was found with the pocket book and also the £700 safe and untouched. The gentleman then offered a handsome reward to the stoker, who refused it on the plea that he had only done his duty; not satisfied, however, with this answer, he left £100, with the manager, requesting him to pay the expenses of the express train, and particularly to reward the stoker for his activity, and to remit the remainder to his address. Shortly after he received the whole £100, accompanied with a polite note, declining any payment for the express train, and stating that it was the duty of the company to reward the stoker, which they would not omit to do.

—Stirling Journal.

COMPENSATION FOR LAND.

Mr. Williams, in *Our Iron Roads*, gives much interesting information upon the subject of compensation for land and buying off opposition to railway schemes. He says:—
" One noble lord had an estate near a proposed line of railway, and on this estate was a beautiful mansion. Naturally averse to the desecration of his home and its neighbourhood, he gave his most uncompromising opposition to the Bill,

and found, in the Committee of both Houses, sympathizing
listeners. Little did it aid the projectors that they urged
that the line did not pass within six miles of that princely
domain ; that the high road was much closer to his dwelling;
and that, as the spot nearest the house would be passed by
means of a tunnel, no unsightliness would arise. But no ;
no worldly consideration affected the decision of the proprietor ; and, arguments failing, it was found that an
appeal must be made to other means. His opposition was
ultimately bought off for twenty-eight thousand pounds, to
be paid when the railway reached his neighbourhood.
Time wore on, funds became scarce, and the company
found that it would be best to stop short at a particular
portion of their line, long before they reached the estate of
the noble lord who had so violently opposed their Bill, by
which they sought to be released from the obligation of
constructing the line which had been so obnoxious to him.
What was their suprise at finding this very man their chief
opponent, and then fresh means had to be adopted for
silencing his objections !

" A line had to be brought near to the property of a certain
Member of Parliament. It threatened no injury to the
estate, either by affecting its appearance or its intrinsic
worth ; and, on the other hand, it afforded him a cheap,
convenient, and expeditious means of communication with
the metropolis. But the proprietor, being a legislator, had
power at head-quarters, and by his influence he nearly turned
the line of railway aside ; and this deviation would have
cost the projectors the sum of *sixty thousand pounds*. Now
it so happened that the house of this honourable member,
who had thus insisted on such costly deference to his
peculiar feelings respecting his property, was afflicted with
the dry rot, and threatened every hour to fall upon
the head of its owner. To pull down and rebuild it,
would require the sum of *thirty thousand pounds*. The
idea of compromise, beneficial to both parties, suggested
itself. If the railway company rebuilt the house, or paid
£30,000 to the owner of the estate, and were allowed to
pursue their original line, it was clear that they would be
£30,000 the richer, as the enforced deviation would cost
£60,000 ; and, on the other hand, the owner of the estate

would obtain a secure house, or receive £30,000 in money. The proposed bargain was struck, and £30,000 was paid by the Company. 'How can you live in that house,' said some friend to him afterwards, 'with the railroad coming so near?' 'Had it not done so,' was the reply, 'I could not have lived in it at all.'

"One rather original character sold some land to the London and Birmingham Company, and was loud and long in his outcries for compensation, expatiating on the damages which the formation of the line would inevitably bring to his property. His complaints were only stopped by the payment of his demands. A few months afterwards, a little additional land was required from the same individual, when he actually demanded a much larger price for the new land than was given him before; and, on surprise being expressed at the charge for that which he had declared would inevitably be greatly deteriorated in value from the proximity of the railway, he coolly replied: 'Oh, I made a mistake *then*, in thinking the railway would injure my property; it has increased its value, and of course you must pay me an increased price for it.'

"On one occasion, a trial occurred in which an eminent land valuer was put into the witness box to swell the amount of damages, and he proceeded to expatiate on the . injury committed by railroads in general, and especially by the one in question, in *cutting up* the properties they invaded. When he had finished the delivery of this weighty piece of evidence, the counsel for the Company put a newspaper into his hand, and asked him whether he had not inserted a certain advertisement therein. The fact was undeniable, and on being read aloud, it proved to be a declaration by the land valuer himself, that the approach of the railway which he had come there to oppose, would prove exceedingly beneficial to some property in its immediate vicinity then on sale.

"An illustration of the difference between the exorbitant demands made by parties for compensation, and the real value of the property, may be mentioned. The first claim made by the Directors of the Glasgow Lunatic Asylum on the Edinburgh and Glasgow railway is stated to have been no less than £44,000. Before the trial came on, this sum was reduced to £10,000; the amount awarded by the jury was £873.

" The opposition thus made, whether feigned or real, it was always advisable to remove; and the money paid for this purpose, though ostensibly in the purchase of the ground, has been on many occasions immense. Sums of £35,000, £40,000, £50,000, £100,000, and £120,000, have thus been paid; while various ingenious plans have been adopted of removing the opposition of influential men. An honourable member is said to have received £30,000 to withdraw his opposition to a Bill before the House; and ' not far off the celebrated year 1845, a lady of title, so gossip talks, asked a certain nobleman to support a certain Bill, stating that, if he did, she had the authority of the secretary of a great company to inform him that fifty shares in a certain railway, then at a considerable premium, would be at his disposal.'

" One pleasing circumstance, however, highly honourable to the gentleman concerned, must not be omitted. The late Mr. Labouchere had made an agreement with the Eastern Counties Company for a passage through his estate near Chelmsford, for the price of £35,000; his son and successor, the Right Honourable Henry Labouchere, finding that the property was not deteriorated to the anticipated extent, voluntarily returned £15,000.

" The practice of buying off opposition has not been confined to the proprietors of land. We learn from one of the Parliamentary Reports that in a certain district a pen-and-ink warfare between two rival companies ran so high, and was, at least on one side, rewarded with such success, that the friends of the elder of the two projected lines thought it expedient to enter into treaty with their literary opponent, and its editor very soon retired on a fortune. It is also asserted, on good authority, that, in a midland county, the facts and arguments of an editor were wielded with such vigour that the opposing company found it necessary to adopt extraordinary means on the occasion. Bribes were offered, but refused; an opposition paper was started, but its conductors quailed before the energy of their opponent, and it produced little effect; every scheme that ingenuity could devise, and money carry out, was attempted, but they successively and utterly failed. At length a Director hit on a truly Machiavelian plan—he was introduced to the proprietor of

the journal, whom he cautiously informed that he wished
to risk a few thousands in newspaper property, and actually
induced his unconscious victim to sell the property, unknown
to the editor.   When the bargain was concluded, the plot
was discovered; but it was then too late, and the wily
Director took possession of the copyright of the paper and
the printing office on behalf of the company.   The services
of the editor, however, were not to be bought, he refused
to barter away his independence, and retired—taking with
him the respect of both friends and enemies."

A LANDOWNER'S OPPOSITION.

In *Herepath's Railway Journal* for 1845 we meet with the
following:—"A learned counsel, the other day, gave as a
reason for a wealthy and aristocratic landowner's opposition
to a great line of railway approaching his residence by
something more than a mile distance, that 'His Lordship
rode horses that would not bear the puff of a steam engine.'
Truly this was a most potent reason, and one that should
weigh heavily against the scheme in the minds of the Committee.   His Lordship has a wood some two miles off,
between which and his residence this railway is intended to
pass.   His lordship is fond of amusing himself there in
hunting down little animals called hares, and sometimes
treats himself to a stag hunt.   Not the slightest interference
is contemplated with his lordship's pastime, or rather
pursuit, for such it is, occupying nearly his whole time, and
exercising all the ability of which he is possessed; but still
he objects to the intrusion.   The bridge that is to be constructed by the Company to give access to the wood, or
forest, is in itself all that could be wished, forming, rather
than otherwise, an ornamental structure to his lordship's
grounds; but then he fears that should an engine chance
(of course, these chances are not within his control) to pass
under the bridge at the same moment as he is passing over,
his high blood horses would prance and rear, and suffer
injury therefrom.   His lordship is very careful and proud
of his horse-flesh, and thinks it hard, and what the legislature ought not to tolerate, that they (his horses) are to be
worried, or subjected to the chance of it, by making a railway to serve the public wants!

"This *noble* man is of opinion, too, that, should the railway be made, he is entitled to an enormous amount of compensation; and, through his agent, assigns as a reason for his extravagant demand—we do not exaggerate the fact—that he is averse to railways in general, and considers the system as an unjustifiable invasion of the province of horse-flesh. This horse jockey lord thereby excuses his conscience in opposing and endeavouring to plunder the railway company as far as he possibly can."

PICTURE EVIDENCE.

Amongst laughable occurrences that enlivened the committee rooms during the gauge contest, was a scene occasioned by a parliamentary counsel putting in as evidence, before the committee on the Southampton and Manchester line, a printed picture of troubles consequent on a break of gauge. The picture was a forcible sketch that had appeared a few days before in the pages of the *Illustrated London News*. Opposing counsel of course argued against the production of the work of art as testimony for the consideration of the committee. After much argument on both sides the chairman decided in favour of receiving the illustration, which was forthwith put, amidst much laughter, into the hands of a witness, who was asked if it was a fair picture of the evils that arose from a break of gauge. The witness replying in the affirmative, the engraving was then laid before the committee for inspection.

—*Railway Chronicle*, June 13, 1846.

EXTRAORDINARY USE OF THE ELECTRIC TELEGRAPH.

Oct. 7, 1847. An extraordinary instance has occurred of the application of the electric telegraph at the London Bridge terminus of the South Eastern Railway.

Hutchings, the man found guilty and sentenced to death for poisoning his wife, was to have been executed at Maidstone Goal at twelve o'clock. Shortly before the appointed hour for carrying the sentence into effect, a message was received at the London Bridge terminus, from the Home Office, requesting that an order should be sent by the electric telegraph instructing the Under-Sheriff at

Maidstone to stay the execution two hours. By the agency of the electric telegraph the communication was received in Maidstone with the usual rapidity, and the execution was for a time stayed. Shortly after the transmission of the order deferring the execution, a messenger from the Home Office conveyed to the railway the Secretary of State's order, that the law was to take its course, and that the culprit was to be at once executed. The telegraph clerk hesitated to sending such a message without instructions from his principals. The messenger from the Home Office could not be certain that the order for Hutchings's execution was signed by the Home Secretary, although it bore his name; and Mr. Macgregor, the chairman, with great judgment and humanity, instantly decided that it was not a sufficient authority in such a momentous matter.

An officer of confidence was immediately sent to the Secretary of State, to state their hesitation and its cause, as the message was, in fact, a death warrant, and that Mr. Walter must have undoubted evidence of its correctness. On Mr. Walter drawing the attention of the Secretary of State to the fact, that the transmission of such a message was, in effect, to make him the Sheriff, the conduct of the railway company, in requiring unquestionable evidence and authority, was warmly approved. The proper signature was affixed in Mr. Walter's presence; and the telegraph then conveyed to the criminal the sad news, that the suspension of the awful sentence was only temporary. Hutchings was executed soon after it reached Maidstone.

—*Annual Register*, 1847.

LOST LUGGAGE.

Sir Francis Head, giving an account of the contents of the Lost Luggage Office, at Euston Station, observes:— "But there were a few articles that certainly we were not prepared to meet with, and which but too clearly proved that the extraordinary terminus-excitement which had suddenly caused so many virtuous ladies to elope from their red shawls—in short, to be all of a sudden not only in 'a bustle' behind, but all over—had equally affected men of all sorts and conditions.

"One gentleman had left behind him a pair of leather hunting breeches! another his boot-jacks! A soldier of the 22nd regiment had left his knapsack containing his kit! Another soldier of the 10th, poor fellow, had left his scarlet regimental coat! Some cripple, probably overjoyed at the sight of his family, had left behind him his crutches!! But what astonished us above all was, that some honest Scotchman, probably in the ecstasy of suddenly seeing among the crowd the face of his faithful *Jeanie*, had actually left behind him the best portion of his bagpipes!!!

"Some little time ago the superintendent, on breaking open, previous to a general sale, a locked leather hat-box, which had lain in this dungeon two years, found in it, under the hat, £65 in Bank of England notes, with one or two private letters, which enabled him to restore the money to the owner, who, it turned out, had been so positive that he had left his hat-box at an hotel at Birmingham that he had made no inquiry for it at the railway office."

VERY NICE TO BE A RAILWAY ENGINEER.

A lady in conversation with a railway engineer observed, "It must be very nice to be a railway engineer, and be able to travel about anywhere you want to go to for nothing."

"Yes, madam." was the reply, "It would, as you say, be very nice to travel about for nothing, *if we were not paid for it.* But you see," he remarked, "railway engineers are like the cabman's horse. The cabman has a very thin horse, 'Doesn't your horse have enough to eat?' inquired a benevolent lady passenger. 'Oh yes, ma'am,' replied cabby, 'I give him lots o' victuals to eat, only, you see, he hasn't any time to eat 'em.' So it is with the railway engineer; he has lots of pleasure of all kinds, only he has not any time to take it."

AN ACCOMMODATING CONTRACTOR.

One railway of some scores of miles hung fire; the directors were congested with their fears of exceeding the estimates, and so a shrewd man of business, a contractor, *i.e.*, a man with a mind contracted to profit and a keen eye to discern the paths of profit, called on them. This man had made his way upward, and passing through the process of sub-contracting, had obtained a glimpse of the upper glories. And thus he relieved the directors from their difficulties, by proffering to make the railway complete in all its parts, buy the land at the commencement, and, if required, to engage the station-clerks at the conclusion, with all the staff complete, so that his patrons might have no trouble, but begin business off-hand. But the latter condition—the staff and clerks—being simply a matter of patronage, the directors kept that trouble in their own hands.

Our contractor loomed on the directors' minds as a guardian angel, a guarantee against responsibilities, backed by sufficient sureties, so the matter was without delay handed over to him, and he knew what to do with it.

—*Roads and Rails*, by W. B. Adams.

THE TWO DUKES AND THE TRAVELLER.

The following amusing anecdote is related of a commercial traveller who happened to get into the same railway carriage in which the Dukes of Argyle and Northumberland were travelling. The three chatted familiarly until the train stopped at Alnwick Junction, where the Duke of Northumberland got out, and was met by a train of flunkeys and servants. "That must be a great swell," said the "commercial," to his remaining companion. "Yes," responded the Duke of Argyle, "he is the Duke of Northumberland." "Bless my soul!" exclaimed the "commercial." "And to think that he should have been so condescending to two little snobs like us!"

THE GREAT RAILWAY MANIA DAY.

Never had there occurred, in the history of joint-stock enterprise, such another day as the 30th of November, 1845. It was the day on which a madness for speculation arrived at its height, to be followed by a collapse terrible to many thousand families. Railways had been gradually becoming successful, and the old companies had, in many cases, bought off, on very high terms, rival lines which threatened to interfere with their profits. Both of these circumstances tended to encourage the concoction of new schemes. There is always floating capital in England waiting for profitable employment; there are always professional men looking out for employment in great engineering works; and there are always scheming moneyless men ready to trade on the folly of others. Thus the bankers and capitalists were willing to supply the capital; the engineers, surveyors, architects, contractors, builders, solicitors, barristers, and Parliamentary agents were willing to supply the brains and fingers; while, too often, cunning schemers pulled the strings. This was especially the case in 1845, when plans for new railways were brought forward literally by hundreds, and with a recklessness perfectly marvellous.

By an enactment in force at that time, it was necessary, for the prosecution of any railway scheme in Parliament, that a mass of documents should be deposited with the Board of Trade, on or before the 30th of November in the preceding year. The multitude of these schemes in 1845 was so great that there could not be found surveyors enough to prepare the plans and sections in time. Advertisements were inserted in the newspapers offering enormous pay for even a smattering of this kind of skill. Surveyors and architects from abroad were attracted to England; young men at home were tempted to break the articles into which they had entered with their masters; and others were seduced from various professions into that of railway engineers. Sixty persons in the employment of the Ordnance Department left their situations to gain enormous earnings in this way. There were desperate fights in various parts of England between property-owners who were determined that their land should not be entered upon for the purpose of railway surveying, and surveyors who knew that the schemes of their companies would be frustrated unless the surveys were made and the plans deposited by the 30th of November. To attain this end, force, fraud, and bribery were freely made use of. The 30th of November, 1845, fell on a Sunday; but it was no Sunday at the office near the Board of Trade. Vehicles were driving up during the whole of the day, with agents and clerks bringing plans and sections. In country districts, as the day approached, and on the morning of the day, coaches-and-four were in greater request than even at race-time, galloping at full speed to the nearest railway station. On the Great Western Railway an express train was hired by the agents of one new scheme. The engine broke down; the train came to a stand-still at Maidenhead, and, in this state, was run into by another express train hired by the agents of a rival project; the opposite parties barely escaped with their lives, but contrived to reach London at the last moment. On this eventful Sunday there were no fewer than *ten* of these express trains on the Great Western Railway, and *eighteen* on the Eastern Counties! One railway company was unable to deposit its papers because another company surreptitiously bought, for a high sum, twenty of the necessary sheets from the lithographic printer, and horses were killed in madly running about in search of the missing documents before the fraud was discovered. In some cases the lithographic stones were stolen; and in one instance the printer was bribed, by a large sum, not to finish in proper time the plans for a rival line. One eminent house brought over four hundred lithographic printers from Belgium, and even then, and with these, all the work ordered could not be executed. Some of the plans were only two-thirds lithographed, the rest being filled up by hand. However executed, the problem was to get these documents to Whitehall before midnight on the 30th of November. Two guineas a mile were in one instance paid for post-horses. One express train steamed up to London 118 miles in an hour-and-a-half, nearly 80 miles an hour. An established company having refused an express train to the promoters of a rival scheme, the latter employed persons to get up a mock funeral cortege, and engage an express train to convey it to London; they did so, and the plans and sections came *in the hearse*, with solicitors and surveyors as mourners!

Copies of many of the documents had to be deposited with the clerks of the peace of the counties to which the schemes severally related, as well as with the Board of Trade; and at some of the offices of these clerks, strange scenes occurred on the Sunday. At Preston, the doors of the office were not opened, as the officials considered the orders which had been issued to keep open on that particular Sunday, to apply only to the Board of Trade; but a crowd of law agents and surveyors assembled, broke the

windows, and threw their plans and sections into the office.
At the Board of Trade, extra clerks were employed on that
day, and all went pretty smoothly until nine o'clock in the
evening. A rule was laid down for receiving the plans and
sections, hearing a few words of explanation from the
agents, and making certain entries in books. But at length
the work accumulated more rapidly than the clerks could
attend to it, and the agents arrived in greater number than
the entrance hall could hold. The anxiety was somewhat
allayed by an announcement, that whoever was inside the
building before the clock struck twelve should be deemed
in good time. Many of the agents bore the familiar name
of Smith; and when 'Mr. Smith' was summoned by the
messenger to enter and speak concerning some scheme, the
name of which was *not* announced, in rushed several persons,
of whom, of course, only one could be the right Mr. Smith
at that particular moment. One agent arrived while the
clock was striking twelve, and was admitted. Soon afterwards, a carriage with reeking horses drove up; three
agents rushed out, and finding the door closed, rang
furiously at the bell; no sooner did a policeman open the
door to say that the time was past, than the agents threw
their bundles of plans and sections through the half-opened
door into the hall; but this was not permitted, and the
policeman threw the documents out into the street. The
baffled agents were nearly maddened with vexation; for
they had arrived in London from Harwich in good time,
and had been driven about Pimlico hither and thither, by
a post-boy who did not, or would not, know the way to the
office of the Board of Trade.

The *Times* newspaper, in the same month, devoted three
whole pages to an elaborate analysis, by Mr. Spackman, of
the various railway schemes brought forward in 1845.
There were no less than 620 in number, involving an
(hypothetical) expenditure of 560 millions sterling; besides
643 other schemes which had not gone further than issuing
prospectuses. More than 500 of the schemes went through
all the stages necessary for being brought before Parliament;
and 272 of these became Acts of Parliament in 1846—to the
ruin of thousands who had afterwards to find the money to
fulfil the engagements into which they had so rashly entered.
—*Chambers's Book of Days.*

PARODY UPON THE RAILWAY MANIA.

About the time of the bursting of the railway bubble, or
the collapse of the mania of 1844-5, the following clever
lines appeared :—

> "There was a sound of revelry by night."—*Childe Harold*.

"There was a sound that ceased not day or night,
    Of speculation. London gathered then
Unwonted crowds, and moved by promise bright,
    To Capel-court rushed women, boys, and men,
    All seeking railway shares and scrip ; and when
The market rose, how many a lad could tell,
    With joyous glance, and eyes that spake again,
'Twas e'en more lucrative than marrying well ;—
When, hark ! that warning voice strikes like a rising knell.

Nay, it is nothing, empty as the wind,
    But a 'bear' whisper down Throgmorton-street ;
Wild enterprise shall still be unconfined ;
    No rest for us, when rising premiums greet
    The morn to pour their treasures at our feet ;
When, hark ! that solemn sound is heard once more,
    The gathering 'bears' its echoes yet repeat—
'Tis but too true, is now the general roar,
The Bank has raised her rate, as she has done before.

And then and there were hurryings to and fro,
    And anxious thoughts, and signs of sad distress
Faces all pale, that but an hour ago
    Smiled at the thoughts of their own craftiness.
    And there were sudden partings, such as press
The coin from hungry pockets—mutual sighs
    Of brokers and their clients.   Who can guess
How many a stag already panting flies,
When upon times so bright such awful panics rise ?"

RAILWAY FACILITIES FOR BUSINESS.

A gentleman went to Liverpool in the morning, purchased,
and took back with him to Manchester, 150 tons of cotton,
which he sold, and afterwards obtained an order for a
similar quantity.   He went again, and actually, that same
evening, delivered the second quantity in Manchester,
"having travelled 120 miles in four separate journeys, and
bought, sold, and delivered, 30 miles off, at two distinct
deliveries, 300 tons of goods, in about 12 hours."   The
occurrence is perfectly astounding ; and, had it been hinted
at fifty years ago, would have been deemed impossible.
                              —*Railway Magazine*, 1840.

RAILWAYS AND THE POST-OFFICE.

It might naturally be thought that the new and quicker means of transport afforded by the railway would be eagerly utilised by the Post-office. There were, however, difficulties on both sides. The railway companies objected to running trains during the night, and the old stage-coach offered the advantage of greater regularity. The railway was quicker, but was at least occasionally uncertain. Thus, in November, 1837, the four daily mail trains between Liverpool and Birmingham on ten occasions arrived before the specified time, on eight occasions were exact to time, and on 102 occasions varied in lateness of arrival from five minutes to five hours and five minutes. There were all sorts of mishaps and long delays by train. The mail guard, like the passenger guard, rode outside the train with a box before him called an "imperial," which contained the letters and papers entrusted to his charge. In very stormy weather the mail guard would prop up the lid of his imperial and get inside for shelter. On one occasion when the mail arrived at Liverpool the guard was found imprisoned in his letter-box. The lid had fallen and fastened in the male travesty of "Ginevra." Fortunately for him it was a burlesque and not a tragedy. Bags thrown to the guards at wayside stations not unfrequently got under the wheels of the train and the contents were cut to pieces. On one occasion, on the Grand Junction, an engine failed through the fire-bars coming out. The mails were removed from the train and run on a platelayer's "trolly," but unfortunately the contents of the bags took fire and were destroyed. But many of these mishaps were obviated by the invention of Mr. Nathaniel Worsdell, a Liverpool coachbuilder, in the service of the railway, who took out a patent in 1838 for an appliance for picking up and dropping mail bags while the train was at full speed. This is still used. The loads of railway vehicles, it may be mentioned, were limited by law to four tons until the passage of the 5 and 6 Vic., c. 55. In 1837, when the weight of the mails passing daily on the London and Birmingham line was only about 14cwt., the late Sir Hardman Earle suggested that a special compartment should be reserved for the mail guard in which he could sort the letters *en route*. The first vehicle specially set apart for mail purposes was put upon the Grand Junction in 1838. From this humble beginning has gradually developed the express mails, in which the chief consideration is the swift transit of correspondence, and which are therefore limited in the number of the passengers they are allowed to carry, The cost of carrying the mails in 1838 and 1839 between Manchester and Liverpool by rail, including the guard's fare, averaged about £1 a trip, or half of the cost of sending them by coach. The price paid to the Grand Junction for carriage of mails between Manchester and Liverpool and Birmingham was 1d. a mile for the guard and ¾d. per cwt. per mile for the mails. This brought a revenue of about £3,000 a year. When the Chancellor of the Exchequer proposed and carried the imposition of the passenger duty, in 1832, the company intimated to the Post-office that they should advance the mail guard's fare ½d. per mile. In 1840 an agreement was negotiated between the Post-office and railway authorities to convey the mails between Lancashire and Birmingham four times daily for £19 10s. a day, with a penalty of £500 on the railway company in case of bad time keeping. This agreement was not carried into effect.

—*Manchester Guardian.*

RAILWAY SIGNALS.

The history of railway signals is a curious page in the annals of practical science. For some years signals seem scarcely to have been dreamt of. Holding up a hat or an umbrella was at first sufficient to stop a train at an intermediate station. At level crossings the gates had to stand closed across the line of rails, and on the top bar hung a lamp to indicate to drivers that the way was blocked. In 1839, Colonel Landman, of the Croydon line, said that he should avoid the danger at a junction during a fog by going slowly, tolling a bell, beating a drum, or sounding a whistle. The first junction signal was denominated a lighthouse. The difficulties attending junctions may be judged of by the fact that when the Bolton and Preston line was ready for opening it was agreed that no train should attempt to enter or leave the North Union line at Euxton junction within fifteen minutes of a train being due on the main line which might interfere with it. The movable rails at junctions had to be removed by hand and fixed into position by hammer and pin. Mr. Watts, engineer to the Lancashire and Yorkshire Railway, is believed to have been one of the first to use the tapering movable switch. One of Mr. Watts's men invented the back weight, another designed the crank, while a third suggested the long rod. These improvements were all about the year 1846. The first fixed signal set up at stations was an ordinary round flag pole having a pulley on the top, upon which was hoisted a green flag to stop a train and a red one to indicate danger on the road. The night signal was a hand lamp hoisted in the same way. These were superseded by a signal on which an arm was worked at the end of a rod, and a square lamp with two sides, red and white, having blinkers working on hinges to shut out the light. These were used until 1848. The semaphores only came into practical use some 20 years ago, and it is remarkable that the first time they were used on the Liverpool and Manchester line they were the cause of a slight collision. The use of signal lights on trains was much advanced by two accidents which occurred on the North Union line on the 7th September, 1841. One of these happened at Farrington, where two passenger trains came into collision. The other happened at Euxton, where a coal train ran into a stage coach which was taking passengers to Southport. The Rev. Mr. Joy was killed, and several others, including the station master, who lost one leg, were injured. These were the first serious accidents investigated by the new Government Inspector of Railways, Sir Frederic Smith, who was appointed by the Board of Trade under Lord Seymour's Act.

—*Manchester Guardian.*

FOG-SIGNALS.

During the prevalence of fogs, when neither signal-posts nor lights are of any use, detonating signals are frequently employed, which are affixed to the rails, and exploded by the iron tread of the advancing locomotive. All guards, policemen, and pointsmen who are not appointed to stations, and all enginemen, gatemen, gangers and platelayers, and tunnel-men, are provided with packets of these signals, which they are required always to have ready for use whilst on duty; and every engine, on passing over one of these signals, is to be immediately stopped, and the guards are to protect their train by sending back and placing a similar signal on the line behind them every two hundred yards, to the distance of six hundred yards; the train may then proceed slowly to the place of obstruction. When these detonating signals were first invented, it was resolved to ascertain whether they acted efficiently, and especially whether the noise they produced was sufficient to be distinctly heard by the engine driver. One of them was accordingly fixed to the rails on a particular line by the authority of the company, and in due time the train having passed over it, reached its destination. Here the engine driver and his colleague were found to be in a state of great alarm, in consequence of a supposed attack being made on them by an assassin, who, they said, lay down beside the line of rails on which they had passed, and deliberately fired at them. The efficiency of the means having thus been tested, the apprehensions of the enginemen were removed, though there was at first evident mortification manifested that they had been made the subjects of such a successful experiment.

—F. S. Williams's *Our Iron Roads.*

"ALMOST DAR NOW."

The following anecdote, illustrative of railroad facility, is very pointed. A traveller inquired of a negro the distance to a certain point. "Dat 'pends on circumstances," replied darkey. "If you gwine afoot, it'll take you about a day; if you gwine in de stage or homneybus, you make it half a day; but if you get in one of *dese smoke wagons,* you be almost dar now."

WORDSWORTH'S PROTEST.

Lines written by Wordsworth as a protest against making a railway from Kendal to Windermere :—

"Is there no nook of English ground secure
From rash assault ? Schemes of retirement sown

In youth, and 'mid the world kept pure
As when their earliest flowers of hope were blown,
Must perish ; how can they this blight endure ?
And must he, too, his old delights disown,
Who scorns a false, utilitarian lure
'Mid his paternal fields at random thrown ?
Baffle the threat, bright scene, from Orrest-head,
Given to the pausing traveller's rapturous glance!
Plead for thy peace, thou beautiful romance
Of nature ; and if human hearts be dead,
Speak, passing winds ; ye torrents, with your strong
And constant voice, protest against the wrong ! "

THE HON. EDWARD EVERETT'S REPLY TO WORDSWORTH'S PROTEST.

The Hon. Edward Everett in the course of his speech at the Boston Railroad Jubilee in commemoration of the opening of railroad communication between Boston and Canada, observed, "But, sir, as I have already said, it is not the material results of this railroad system in which its happiest influences are seen. I recollect that seven or eight years ago there was a project to carry a railroad into the lake country in England—into the heart of Westmoreland and Cumberland. Mr. Wordsworth, the lately deceased poet, a resident in the centre of this region, opposed the project. He thought that the retirement and seclusion of this delightful region would be disturbed by the panting of the locomotive and the cry of the steam whistle. If I am not mistaken, he published one or two sonnets in deprecation of the enterprise. Mr. Wordsworth was a kind-hearted man, as well as a most distinguished poet, but he was entirely mistaken, as it seems to me, in this matter. The quiet of a few spots may be disturbed, but a hundred quiet spots are rendered accessible. The bustle of the station-house may take the place of the Druidical silence of some shady dell; but, Gracious Heavens, sir, how many of those verdant cathedral arches, entwined by the hand of God in our pathless woods, are opened to the grateful worship of man by these means of communication?

"How little of rural beauty you lose, even in a country of comparatively narrow dimensions like England—how less than little in a country so vast as this—by works of this description. You lose a little strip along the line of the road, which partially changes its character; while, as the compensation, you bring all this rural beauty,

'The warbling woodland the resounding shore,
The pomp of groves, the garniture of fields,'

within the reach, not of a score of luxurious, sauntering tourists, but of the great mass of the population, who have senses and tastes as keen as the keenest. You throw it open, with all its soothing and humanizing influences, to thousands who, but for your railways and steamers, would have lived and died without ever having breathed the life-giving air of the mountains; yes, sir, to tens of thousands who would have gone to their graves, and the sooner for the prevention, without ever having caught a glimpse of the most magnificent and beautiful spectacle which nature presents to the eye of man, that of a glorious curving wave, a quarter-of-a-mile long, as it comes swelling and breasting toward the shore, till its soft green ridge bursts into a crest of snow, and settles and dies along the whispering sands."

REMARKABLE ADVERTISEMENT.

The most astonishing kind of property to leave behind at a railway station is mentioned in an advertisement which appeared in the newspapers dated Swindon, April 27th, 1844. It gave notice "That a pair of bright bay horses, about sixteen hands high, with black switch tails and manes," had been left in the name of Hibbert; and notice was given that unless the horses were claimed on or before the 12th day of May, they would be sold to pay expenses. Accordingly on that day they were sold.

—*Household Words.*

RAILWAY EPIGRAM.

In 1845, during the discussions on the Midland lines before the Committee of the House of Commons, Mr. Hill, the Counsel, was addressing the Committee, when Sir John Rae Reid, who was a member of it, handed the following lines to the chairman:—

" Ye railway men, who mountains lower,
Who level rocks and valleys fill;
Who thro' the *hills* vast tunnels bore;
Must now in turn be *bored* by *Hill*."

SINGULAR CIRCUMSTANCE.

A certain gentleman of large property, and who had figured, if he does not now figure, as a Railway Director, applied for shares in a certain projected railway. Fifty, it seems were allotted to him. Whether that was the number he applied for or not, deponent saith not; but by some means nothing (0) got added to the 50 and made it 500. The deposit for the said 500 was paid into the bankers', the scrip obtained, and before the mistake could be detected and corrected—for no doubt it was only a mistake, or at most a *lapsus pennæ*—the shares were sold, and some £2000 profit by this very fortunate accident found its way into the pocket of the gentleman.

—Herepath's Journal, 1845.

LOUIS PHILIPPE AND THE ENGLISH NAVVIES.

Whittlesea Will, William Elthorpe, from Cambridgeshire, had a large railway experience; during the construction of Longton Tunnel, he told me the following story:—" Ye see, Mr. Smith (Samuel Smith, of Woodberry Down), I was a ganger for Mr. Price on the Marseilles and Avignon Line in France, and I'd gangs of all nations to deal with. Well, I could not manage 'em nohow mixed—there were the Jarman Gang, the French Gang, the English, Scotch, and Irish Gangs, of course; the Belgic Gang, the Spanish Gang, and the Peamounter Gang—that's a Gang, d'ye see, that comes off the mountains somewhere towards Italy." "Oh, the Piedmontese, you mean." "Well, you may call 'em Peedmanteeze if you like, but we call'd 'em Peamounters— and so at last I hit on the plan of putting each gang by itself; gangs 'o nations, the Peamounter gang here, the Jarman gang there, and the Belgic gang there, and so on, and it worked capital, each gang worked against the other gang like good 'uns."

"Well one day our master, Mr. Price, gave the English gang a great entertainment at a sort of Tea Garden place, near Paris, called Maison Lafitte, and we were coming home along the road before dark—it was a summer's evening—singing and shouting pretty loud, I dare say, when a fat, oldish gentleman rode into the midst of us, and

I

pulling up said, taking off his hat—'I think you are
English Navigators.'   'Well, and what if we are, old
fellow, what's that to you?' 'Why you are making a
very great noise, and I noticed you did not make way for
me, or salute me as we met, which is not polite—every one
in France salutes a gentleman. I've been in England, I
like the English,' by this time his military attendants rode
up, and seeing him alone in the midst of us were going to
ride us down at once but the old boy beckoned with his
hand for them to hold back, and continued his sarmont.
'I should wish you,' says he, quite pleasant, 'whilst you
remain in France to be orderly, obliging, civil, and polite;
it's always the best—now remember this: and here's something for you to remember Louis Philippe by: putting his
hand into his pocket, he pulled out what silver he had, I
suppose, threw it among us, and rode off—but, my eyes,
didn't we give him a cheer!"

ADVANTAGES OF RAILWAY-TUNNELS.

We cannot help repeating a narrative which we heard
on one occasion, told with infinite gravity by a clergyman
whose name we at once inquired about, and of whom we
shall only say, that he is one of the worthiest and best sons
of the kirk, and knows when to be serious as well as when
to jest. "Don't tell me," said he to a simple-looking Highland brother, who had apparently made his first trial of
railway travelling in coming up to the Assembly—"don't
tell me that tunnels on railways are an unmitigated evil:
they serve high moral and æsthetical purposes. Only the
other day I got into a railway carriage, and I had hardly
taken my seat, when the train started. On looking up, I
saw sitting opposite to me two of the most rabid dissenters
in Scotland. I felt at once that there could be no pleasure
for me in that journey, and with gloomy heart and countenance I leaned back in my corner. But all at once we
plunged into a deep tunnel, black as night, and when we
emerged at the other end, my brow was clear and my ill-
humour was entirely dissipated. Shall I tell you how this
came to be? All the way through the tunnel I was shaking

my fists in the dissenters' faces, and making horrible mouths at them, and *that* relieved me, and set me all right. Don't speak against tunnels again, my dear friend."

—*Fraser's Magazine.*

DAMAGES EASILY ADJUSTED.

It is related that the President of the Fitchburg Railroad, some thirty years ago, settled with a number of passengers who had been wet but not seriously injured by the running off of a train into the river, by paying them from $5 to $20 each. One of them, a sailor, when his terms were asked, said:— " Well, you see, mister, when I was down in the water, I looked up to the bridge and calculated that we had fallen fifteen feet, so if you will pay me a dollar a foot I will call it square."

LIABILITIES OF RAILWAY ENGINEERS FOR THEIR ERRORS.

An action was tried before Mr. Justice Maule, July 30, 1846—the first case of the kind—which established the liability of railway engineers for the consequences of any errors they commit.

The action was brought by the Dudley and Madeley Company against Mr. Giles, the engineer. They had paid him £4,000 for the preparation of the plans, etc., but when the time arrived for depositing them with the Board of Trade they were not completely ready. The scheme had consequently failed. This conduct of the defendant it was estimated had injured the company to the extent of £10,000. The counsel for the plaintiff did not claim damages to this amount, but would be content with such a sum as the jury should, under the circumstances, think the defendant ought to pay, as a penalty for the negligence of which he had been guilty. For Mr. Giles, it was contended, that the jury ought not, at the worst, to find a verdict for more than £1,700, alleging that the remainder £2,300 had been paid by him in wages for work done, and materials used.

The jury, however, returned a verdict to the tune of £4,500, or £500 beyond the full sum paid him.

But, what said the judge? That " it was clear that the defendant had undertaken more work than he could complete, and that he should not be allowed to gratify with impunity, and to the injury of the plaintiffs. his desire to realise in a few months a fortune which should only be the result of the labour of years."

EXTRAORDINARY ACCIDENT.

Yesterday afternoon, as the Leeds train, which left that terminus at a quarter-past one o'clock, was approaching Rugby, and within four miles of that station, an umbrella behind the private carriage of Earl Zetland took fire, in consequence of a spark from the engine falling on it, and presently the imperial on the roof and the upper part of the carriage were in a blaze. Seated within it were the Countess of Zetland and her maid. The train was proceeding at the rate of forty miles an hour. Under these circumstances, Her Ladyship and maid descended from the carriage to the truck, when—despite the caution to hold on given by a gentleman from a window of one of the railway carriages— the maid threw herself headlong on the rail, and was speedily lost sight of. On the arrival of the train at Rugby an engine was despatched along the line, when the young woman was found severely injured, and taken to the Infirmary at Leicester. Lady Zetland remained at Rugby, where she was joined by His Lordship and. the family physician last night, by an express train from Euston-square. How long will railway companies delay establishing a means of communication between passengers and the guard ?

—*Times*, Dec. 9th, 1847.

PROVIDENTIAL ESCAPE.

On Monday, at the New Bailey, two men, named William Hatfield and Mark Clegg, the former an engine-driver and the latter a fireman in the employ of the London and North-Western Railway, were brought up before Mr. Trafford, the stipendiary magistrate, and Captain Whittaker, charged with drunkenness and gross negligence in the discharge of their duty. Mr. Wagstaff, solicitor, of Warrington, appeared on behalf of the Company, and from his statement and the evidence of the witnesses it appeared that the prisoners had charge of the night mail train from

Liverpool to London, on Saturday, December 25, 1847. The number of carriages and passengers was not stated, but the pointsman at the Warrington junction being at his post, waiting for the train, was surprised to hear it coming at a very rapid rate. He had been preparing to turn the points in order to shunt the train on to the Warrington junction, but as the train did not diminish in speed, but rather increased as it approached, he, anticipating great danger if he should turn the points, determined on the instant upon letting the train take its course, and not turning them. Most fortunate was it that he exercised so much judgment and sagacity, for, in consequence of the acuteness of the curve at Warrington junction and the tremendous rate at which the train was proceeding—not less than forty miles an hour—it does not appear that anything could have otherwise prevented the train from being overturned, and a frightful sacrifice of human life ensuing. Meantime the train continued its frightful progress; but the mail guard seated at the end of the train, perceiving that it was going on towards Manchester, instead of staying at the junction, signalled to the engine-driver and fireman, but without effect, no notice whatever being taken of the signal. Finding this to be the case, he, at very considerable risk, passed over from carriage to carriage till he reached the engine, where he found both the prisoners lying drunk. At length, at Patricroft, however, he succeeded in stopping the train just before it reached that station, a distance of 14 miles from Warrington. This again appears to be almost a miraculous circumstance, for at the Patricroft station, on the same line as that on which the mail train was running was another train, containing a number of passengers, who thus escaped from the consequences of a dreadful collision. The prisoners were, of course, immediately given into custody, and conveyed to the New Bailey prison, while, other assistance being obtained, the train was taken back again to Warrington junction. The regulation is in consequence of the sharp curve at this junction, that the trains shall not run more than five miles an hour. The bench sentenced both prisoners to two months hard labour.

—*Manchester Examiner.*

HIS PORTMANTEAU.

An English traveller in Germany entered a first-class carriage in which there was only one seat vacant, a middle one. A corner seat was occupied by a German, who evidently had placed his portmanteau on the opposite one—at least the traveller suspected that this was the case. The latter asked, "Is this seat engaged?" "Yes," was the reply. When the time for the departure of the train had almost arrived, the Englishman said, "Your friend is going to miss the train, if he is not quick." "Oh, that is all right. I'll keep it for him." Soon the signal came and the train started, when the passenger seized the portmanteau, and threw it out of the window, exclaiming, "He's missed his train but he mustn't lose his baggage!" That portmanteau *was* the German's.

GROWTH OF STATION BOOKSHOPS.

The gradual rise of the railway book-trade is a singular feature of our marvellous railway era. In the first instance, when the scope and capabilities of the rail had yet to be ascertained, the privilege of selling books, newspapers, etc., at the several stations was freely granted to any who might think proper to claim it. Vendors came and went, when and how they chose, their trade was of the humblest, and their profits were as varying as their punctuality. By degrees the business assumed shape, the newspaper man found it his interest to maintain a *locus standi* in the establishment, and the establishment, in its turn, discerned a substantial means of helping the poor or the deserving among its servants. A cripple maimed in the company's service, or a married servant of a director or secretary, superseded the first batch of stragglers and assumed responsibility by express appointment. The responsibility, in truth, was not very great at starting. Railway travelling, at the time referred to, occupied but a very small portion of a man's time. The longest line reached only thirty miles, and no traveller required anything more solid than his newspaper for his hour's steaming. But as the iron lengthened, and as cities remote from each other were brought closer, the time spent in the railway carriage

extended, travellers multiplied, and the newspaper ceased
to be sufficient for the journey. At this period reading
matter for the rail sensibly increased; the tide of cheap
literature set in. French novels, unfortunately, of question-
able character were introduced by the newsman, simply
because he could buy them at one-third less than any other
publication selling at the same price. The public purchased
the wares they saw before them, and very soon the ingenious
caterers for railway readers flattered themselves that there
was a general demand amongst all classes for the peculiar
style of literature upon which it had been their good fortune
to hit. The more eminent booksellers and publishers stood
aloof, whilst others, less scrupulous, finding a market open
and ready-made to their hands were only too eager to supply
it. It was then that the *Parlour Library* was set on foot.
Immense numbers of this work were sold to travellers, and
every addition to the stock was positively made on the
assumption that persons of the better class, who constitute
the larger portion of railway readers, lose their accustomed
taste the moment they smell the engine and present themselves to the railway librarian.

--Preface to a Reprinted Article from the *Times*, 1851.

MESSRS. SMITHS' BOOKSTALLS.

The following appeared in the *Athenæum*, 27th Jan., 1849.
"The new business in bookselling which the farming of
the line of the North-Western Railway by Mr. Smith, of
the Strand, is likely to open up, engages a good deal of
attention in literary circles. This new shop for books will,
it is thought, seriously injure many of the country booksellers, and remove at the same time a portion of the
business transacted by London tradesmen. For instance, a
country gentleman wishing to purchase a new book will
give his order, not as heretofore, to the Lintot or Tonson
of his particular district, but to the agent of the bookseller
on the line of railway—the party most directly in his way.
Instead of waiting, as he was accustomed to do, till the
bookseller of his village or of the nearest town, can get his
usual monthly parcel down from his agent in ' the Row '—
he will find his book at the locomotive library, and so be
enabled to read the last new novel before it is a little flat

or the last new history in the same edition as the resident in London.   A London gentleman hurrying from town with little time to spare will buy the book he wants at the railway station where he takes his ticket—or perhaps at the next, or third, or fourth, or at the last station (just as the fancy takes him) on his journey.   It is quite possible to conceive such a final extension of this principle that the retail trade in books may end in a great monopoly :—nay, instead of seeing the *imprimatur* of the Row or of Albermarle Street upon a book, the great recommendation hereafter may be ' Euston Square,' 'Paddington,' 'The Nine Elms,' or even 'Shoreditch.'   Whatever may be the 'effect to the present race of booksellers of this change in their business—it is probable that this new mart for books will raise the profits of authors.   How many hours are wasted at railway stations by people well to do in the world, with a taste for books but no time to read advertisements or to drop in at a bookseller's to see what is new.   Already it is found that the sale at these places is not confined to cheap or even ephemeral publications ;—that it is not the novel or light work alone that is asked for and bought."

"The prophecy of progress contained in the above paragraph has been- fulfilled so far as the North-Western and Mr. Smith are concerned.   His example, however, was not infectious for other lines; and till within the last three months, when the Great Northern copied the good precedent, and entered into a contract with Mr. Smith and his son, the greenest literature in dress and in digestion was all that was offered to the wants of travellers by the directors of the South-Western, the Great Western, and other trunk and branch lines with which England is intersected.   A traveller in the eastern, western, and southern counties who does not bring his book with him can satisfy his love of reading only by the commonest and cheapest trash—for the pretences to the appearance of a bookseller's shop made at Waterloo, at Shoreditch, at Paddington, and at London Bridge, are something ridiculous.   This should not be.   It shows little for the public spirit of the directors of our railways that such a system should remain.   Mr. Smith has, we believe, as many as thirty-five shops at railway stations, extending from London to Liverpool, Chester and Edinburgh.   His

great stations are at Euston Square, Birmingham, Manchester Liverpool, and Edinburgh.   He has a rolling stock of books valued at £10,000.   We call his stock rolling, because he moves his wares with the inclinations of his readers.   If he finds a religious feeling on the rise at Bangor, he withdraws Dickens and sends down Henry of Exeter or Mr. Bennett, if a love for lighter reading is on the the increase at Rugby, he withdraws Hallam and sends down Thackeray and Jerrold.   He never undersells and he gives no credit.   His business is a ready-money one, and he finds it his interest to maintain the dignity of literature by resolutely refusing to admit pernicious publications among his stock.   He can well afford to pay the heavy fee he does for his privilege; for his novel speculation has been a decided hit—of solid advantage to himself and of permanent utility to the public."
—*Athenæum*, Sept. 5, 1851.

A RESIDENT ENGINEER AND SCIENTIFIC WITNESS.

Shortly after the first locomotives were placed on the London and Birmingham Railway, a scientific civilian, who had given very positive evidence before Parliament as to the injury to health and other intolerable evils that must arise from the construction of tunnels, paid a visit to the line.   The resident engineer accompanied him in a first-class carriage over the newly-finished portion of the works.   As they drew near Chalk Farm the engineer attracted the attention of his visitor to the lamp at the top of the carriage. "I should like to have your opinion on this," he said.   "The matter seems simple, but it requires a deal of thought. You see it is essential to keep the oil from dropping on the passengers. The cup shape effectually prevents this.   Then the lamps would not burn.   We had to arrange an up-cast and down-cast chimney, in order to ensure the circulation of air in the lamp.   Then there was the question of shadow;"—— and so he continued, to the great edification of his listener, for five or six minutes.   When a satisfactory conclusion as to the lamp had been arrived at, the learned man looked out of the window.   "What place is this?" said he.   "Kensal Green."   "But," said the other, "how is that?   I thought there was one of your great tunnels to

pass before we came to Kensal Green." "Oh," replied the
Resident, carelessly, "did you not observe? We came
through Chalk Farm Tunnel very steadily." The man of
science felt himself caught. He made no more reports
upon tunnels.

—*Personal Recollections of English Engineers.*

EXTRAORDINARY SCENE AT A RAILWAY JUNCTION.

A most extraordinary and unprecedented scene occurred
on Monday morning at the Clifton station, about five miles
from Manchester, where the East Lancashire line forms a
junction with the Lancashire and Yorkshire. The East
Lancashire are in the habit of running up-trains to
Manchester, past the Clifton junction, without stopping,
afterwards making a declaration to the Lancashire and
Yorkshire Company of the number of passengers the trains
contain, and for whom they will have to pay toll. The
Lancashire and Yorkshire Company object to this plan, and
demand that the trains shall stop at Clifton, so that the
number of passengers can be counted, and give up their
tickets. The East Lancashire Company say that in addition
to their declaration, the other parties have access to all
their books, and to the returns of their (the East Lancashire
Company's) servants; and that the demand to take tickets,
or to count, is only one of annoyance and detention, adopted
since the two companies have become competitors for the
traffic to Bradford. Towards the close of last week, the
dispute assumed a serious aspect, by one of the Lancashire
and Yorkshire Company's agents at Manchester
(Mr. Blackmore) threatening that he would blockade or stop
up the East Lancashire line, at the point of junction, with a
large balk of timber. The East Lancashire Company got
out a summons against Mr. Blackmore on Saturday; but,
notwithstanding this, the Lancashire and Yorkshire Company's
manager proceeded on Monday to carry the threat
into execution, despite the presence of a large body of the
county police. The East Lancashire early trains were
allowed to pass upon the Lancashire and Yorkshire line
without obstruction; but at half-past 10 o'clock in the
morning, as the next East Lancashire train to Manchester
was one which would not stop at Clifton, but attempt to

pass on to Manchester, a number of labourers, under the direction of Captain Laws, laid a large balk of timber, secured by two long iron crowbars, across the down rails to Manchester of the Lancashire and Yorkshire line, behind which was brought up a train of six empty carriages, with its engine at the Manchester end. When the East Lancashire train came in sight, it was signalled to stop, and the Lancashire and Yorkshire Company's servants went and demanded the tickets from the passengers. This demand, however, was fruitless, inasmuch as the East Lancashire parties had taken the tickets from the passengers at the previous station—Ringley. The first act of the East Lancashire Company's servants was to remove the balk of timber, and this they did without hindrance. They next attempted to force before them the Lancashire and Yorkshire blockading train. This they were not able to do. The East Lancashire Company then brought up a heavy train laden with stone, and took up a position on the top line to Manchester. Thus the Lancashire and Yorkshire Company's double line of rails was completely blocked up—one line by their own train, and the other by the stone train of the East Lancashire Company. In this position matters remained till near 12 o'clock. There were altogether eight trains on the double lines of rails of the two companies, extending more than half a mile. After which the blockade was broken up, and the various trains were allowed to pass onwards—fortunately without accident or injury to the passengers.

—*Manchester Examiner*, March 13th, 1849.

GOODS' COMPETITION.

Within the last fortnight, we understand, the London and North-Western, in conjunction with the Lancashire and Yorkshire, have commenced carrying goods between Liverpool and Manchester, a distance of 31 miles, at the ruinously low figure of 6d. per ton, where they used to have 8s. We further hear that the 6d. includes the expenses of collection and delivery. The cause is a competition with the East Lancashire and the canal. At a very low estimate it has been calculated that every ton costs 6s. 3d., so that they are losing 5s. 9d. on every 6d. earned, or 860 per cent.

How long this monstrous competition is to continue the directors only know, but the loss must be frightful on both sides. Chaplin and Horne had 10s. a ton for collecting and delivering the goods at the London end of the London and North-Western Railway, and, though the expense must be less in such comparatively small towns as Liverpool and Manchester, it can hardly be less than a half that, 5s. Therefore, allowing only 1s. 3d. for the bare railway carriage, which is under a halfpenny a ton a mile, we have 6s. 3d., the estimate showing the above-mentioned loss of 5s. 9d. on every 6d. earned.

—*Herepath's Journal*, Sept. 29th, 1849.

A POLITE REQUEST.

An amusing illustration of the formal politeness of a railway guard occurred some years ago at the Reigate station. He went to the window of a first-class carriage, and said: "If you please, sir, will you have the goodness to change your carriage here?" "What for?" was the gruff reply of Mr. Bull within. "Because, sir, if you please, the wheel has been on fire since half-way from the last station!" John looked out; the wheel was sending forth a cloud of smoke, and without waiting to require any further "persuasive influences," he lost no time in condescending to comply with the request.

A CHASE AFTER A RUNAWAY ENGINE.

Mr. Walker, the superintendent of the telegraphs of the South-Eastern Railway Company, remarks:—"On New Year's Day, 1850, a collision had occurred to an empty train at Gravesend, and the driver having leaped from his engine, the latter darted alone at full speed for London. Notice was immediately given by telegraph to London and other stations; and, while the line was kept clear, an engine and other arrangements were prepared as a buttress to receive the runaway, while all connected with the station awaited in awful suspense the expected shock. The superintendent of the railway also started down the line on an engine, and on passing the runaway he reversed his engine and had it transferred at the next crossing to the up-line, so as to be in the rear of the fugitive; he then started in chase, and on overtaking the other he ran into it at speed, and the driver of the engine took possession of the fugitive, and all danger was at an end. Twelve stations were passed in safety; it passed Woolwich at fifteen miles an hour; it was within a couple of miles of London when it was arrested. Had its approach been unknown, the money value of the damage it would have caused might have equalled the cost of the whole line of telegraph."

STEAM DEFINED.

At a railway station, an old lady said to a very pompous looking gentleman, who was talking about steam communication. "Pray, sir, what is steam?" "Steam, ma'am, is ah!—steam, is ah! ah! steam is—steam!" "I knew that chap couldn't tell ye," said a rough-looking fellow standing by; "but steam is a bucket of water in a tremendous perspiration."

IN A RAILWAY TUNNEL.

Mr. Osborne in the *Sunday at Home*, says, "I have heard from a friend a strange story of a tunnel, which I will try to tell you as it was told to me. A well-known engineer was walking one day through a tunnel, a narrow one, and as he was going along, supposing himself safe, he thought his ear caught the far-off rumble of a train *in the tunnel*. After stopping and listening for a moment, he became sure it was so, and that he was caught, and could not possibly get out in time. What was he to do? Should he draw himself up close to the side wall, making himself as small as possible, that the train might not touch him. Or should he lie down flat between the rails and let the train pass over him. Being an engineer, and knowing well the shape of things, he decided to lie down between the rails as his best chance. He had to make up his mind quickly, for in a minute or so the whole train came to where he lay, and went thundering over him, and—did him no harm whatever. But he afterwards told his friends, that in that brief moment of time, while the train was passing over, he saw his whole past life spread out like a map, like an illuminated transparency, with every particular circumstance standing out plain."

A QUICK WAY.

Some years ago, when a new railway was opened in the Highlands, a Highlander heard of it, and bought a ticket for the first excursion. The train was about half the distance to the next station when a collision took place, and poor Donald was thrown unceremoniously into an adjacent park. After recovering his senses, he made the best of his way home, when the neighbours asked him how he liked his ride. "Oh," replied Donald, "I liked it fine; but they have an awfu' nasty quick way in puttin' ane oot."

HIGHLANDER AND A RAILWAY ENGINE.

We remember hearing a story of an old Highland peasant who happened to see a railway engine for the first time. He was coming down from the Grampians into Perthshire, and he thus described the novel monster as it appeared in his astounded Celtic imagination:—"I was looking doon the glens, when I saw a funny beast blowing off his perspiration; an' I ran doon, an' I tried to stop him, but he just gave an awfu' skirl an' disappeared into a hole."—(meaning, of course, a tunnel).

—*Once a Week.*

EXTRACTS FROM MACREADY'S DIARIES.

"July 3rd, 1845.—Brewster called to cut my hair; he told me the tradesmen could not get paid in London, for all the money was employed in railroads."

"June 19th, 1850.—We were surprised by the entrance of Carlyle and Mrs. C—. I was delighted to see them. Carlyle inveighed against railroads—he was quite in one of his exceptious moods."

FREAKS OF CONCEALED BOGS.

Great difficulties have often been encountered by engineers in carrying earth embankments across low grounds, which, under a fair, green surface, concealed the remains of ancient bogs, sometimes of great depth. Thus, on the Leeds and Bradford Extension, about 600 tons of stone and earth were daily cast into an embankment near Bingley, and each morning the stuff thrown in on the preceding day was found to have disappeared. This went on for many weeks, the bank, however, gradually advancing. and forcing up on either side a spongy black ridge of moss. On the South-Western Railway a heavy embankment, about fifty feet high, crossed a piece of ground near Newham, the surface of which seemed to be perfectly sound and firm. Twenty feet, however, beneath the surface an old bog lay concealed; and the ground giving way, the fluid, pressed from beneath the embankment, raised the adjacent meadows in all directions like waves of the sea. A culvert, which permitted the flow of a brook under the bank, was forced down. the passage of the water entirely stopped, and several thousand acres of the finest land in Hampshire would have been flooded but for the exertions of the engineer, who completed a new culvert just as the other had become completely closed. The Newton-green embankment, on the Sheffield and Manchester line, gave way in like manner, and to such an extent as to spread out two or three times its original width. In this case it was found necessary to carry the line across the parts which yielded, under strong timber shores. On the Dundalk and Enniskillen line a heavy embankment twenty feet high suddenly disappeared one night in the bog of Meghernakill, nearly adjoining the river Fane. The bed of the river was forced up, and the flow of the water for the time was stopped, and the surrounding country heavily flooded. A concealed bog of even greater extent, on the Durham and Sunderland Railway, near Aycliff, was crossed by means of a double-planked road. about two miles in length. A few weeks after the line had been opened, part of the road sank one night entirely out of sight. The defect was made good merely by extending the floating surface of the road at this portion of the bog.

—Quarterly Review.

A RAILWAY MARRIAGE.

In Maine, a conductor—too busy, we suggest, saying "Go ahead!" to be particular about wedding formalities— invited his betrothed and a minister into a car, and while the train was in motion was married; leaving that station a bachelor, at this station he was a married man! It is but one of a thousand examples of life as it goes in this fast country.

—*New York Nation.*

ATTEMPTED FRAUDS.

Feb. 29, 1849, *Central Criminal Court.*—Robert Duncan. aged 47. staymaker, Mary Duncan, his wife, who surrendered to take her trial, and Pierce Wall O'Brien, aged 30, printer, were indicted for conspiring together to obtain money from the London and North-Western Railway Company by false pretences.

From the statement of Mr. Clarkson and the evidence, it appeared that the charges made against the prisoners involved a most impudent attempt at fraud. It appears that on the 5th of September last year an accident occurred to the up mail train from York, near the Leighton Buzzard station. but, although some injury was occasioned to the train, it seemed that none of the passengers received any personal injury. On the 26th of October following, however, the company received a communication from Mr. Harrison. requiring compensation on behalf of defendant. Robert Duncan, for an injury alleged to have been sustained by his wife upon the occasion of the collision referred to. it being represented. also, that her brother. the defendant O'Brien, who was travelling with her at the time from York, had likewise received serious injury by the same accident. The company immediately sent a medical gentleman to the place described as the residence of these persons, No. 59, George Street, Southwark, and he there saw the man Robert Duncan, who represented that his wife was dangerously ill, and that the result of the accident on the railway was a premature confinement, and that her life was in danger. Mr. Porter was then introduced to the female defendant, whom he found in bed, apparently in great pain, and she confirmed her husband's statement. In the same house the prisoner O'Brien was found in bed, and he also told the same story about the accident on the railway. It appeared that some suspicion was entertained by the company of the general character of the transaction, and they had been instituting inquiries. On the 2nd of November they received another letter from the prisoner Robert Duncan, in which he made an offer to accept £60 for the injury his wife had received, and also stating that Mr. O'Brien was willing to accept a similar amount for the damage he had sustained. At this it appeared Mr. Harrison resolved not to have anything further to do with the matter, unless he received satisfactory proof of the truth of the story told by the parties; and another solicitor was employed by the defendants, who brought an action against the company for damages for the alleged injury, and he proceeded so far as to give notice of trial. The case, however, never went before a jury in that shape, and by this time it was discovered that there was no truth in the story told by the defendants. It was proved at the period when the accident was alleged to have occurred to the female defendant, she was residing with her husband, and was in her usual health. With regard to O'Brien, there was no evidence to show that he was upon the train at the time the accident happened, but, according to the testimony of a witness named Darke, during the period when the negotiation was going on with the company, O'Brien requested him to write a letter to Mr. Harrison to the effect that he was riding in the same carriage with Mrs. Duncan and her brother at the time of the accident, and he was aware of her having been injured, and gave him a written statement to that effect, which he copied. This witness, in cross-examination, admitted that at the time he wrote the statement he was perfectly well aware it was false, and he also said that notwithstanding this, he made no difficulty in doing what O'Brien requested, and also that he should have been ready to make a solemn declaration of the truth of the statement if he had been required to do so.

A verdict of "Not Guilty" was taken as to the female prisoner, on the ground that she was acting under the control of her husband. The jury returned a verdict of "Guilty" against the two male defendants.

Mr. Clarkson said he was instructed to state that, at the period of the catastrophe on board the Cricket steam-boat, the prisoners obtained a sum of £70, from the company to which that vessel belonged, by the false pretence that they had received injury upon the occasion.

The Recorder sentenced Duncan to be imprisoned for twelve, and O'Brien for six months.

. *Annual Register.*

A BRIDE'S LOST LUGGAGE.

The trouble which is bestowed by railway companies to cause the restitution of lost property is incalculable. Some years ago, a young lady lost a portmanteau from the rest of her luggage—a pardonable oversight, for she was a bride starting on a honeymoon trip. The bridegroom—never on such occasions an accountable being—had not noticed the misfortune. When the loss was discovered, and application made respecting it, the lady spoke positively of having seen it at the station whence they started, then again at a station where they had to change carriages; she saw it also when they left the railway; it was all safe, she averred, at the hotel where they stopped for a few days. She was also certain that it was among the rest of the "things" when they again started for a watering-place; but, when they arrived there, it was missing. It contained a new riding habit, value fifteen pounds. The search that was instituted for this portmanteau recalled that of Telemachus for Ulysses; the railway officials sent one of their clerks with a *carte blanche* to trace the bride's journey to the end of the last mile. till some tidings of the strayed trunk could be traced. He went to every station, to every coach-office in connection with every station, to every town, to every hotel, and to every lodging that the happy couple had visited. His expenses actually amounted to fifteen pounds. He came back without success. At length the treasure was found; but where? At the by-station on another line, whence the bride had started from home a maiden. Yet she had positively declared, without doubt or reservation, that she had, "with her own eyes," seen the trunk on the various stages of her tour; this can only be accounted for by the peculiar flustration of a young lady just plunged into the vortex of matrimony. The husband paid the whole of the costs.

THIRD-CLASS PASSENGERS.

Tho conveyance of passengers at cheap fares was from the commencement of railways a great public concern, and it was soon found necessary that the legislature should take action in the matter. Accordingly, by the Regulation of Railways Act, 1844, all passenger railways were required to run one train every day from end to end of their line, carrying third-class passengers at a rate not exceeding one penny a mile, stopping at all stations, starting at hours approved by the Board of Trade, travelling at least twelve miles an hour, and with carriages protected from weather. This enactment greatly encouraged the poorer classes in railway travelling; but the companies were slow to carry out the new regulations cheerfully. The trains were timed at most inconvenient hours; to undertake a journey of any considerable length in one day at third-class fare was almost out of the question. In fact, a short-sighted policy of doing almost everything to discourage third-class travelling was adopted by the Companies.

A traveller having started on a long journey, thinking to be able to travel all the way third-class, would find at some stage of the route that he had arrived, only a few minutes perhaps, after the departure of the cheap train to his destination, with no alternative but to wait for hours or proceed by the express and pay accordingly. Moreover, the third-class carriages were provided with the very minimum of comfort. It was not seen by the railway executive of that time that the policy adopted was actually prejudicial to their own interests.

Our Railways, by Joseph Parsloe.

IMPROVEMENT IN THIRD-CLASS TRAVELLING.

The Rev. F. S. Williams, in an article in the *Contemporary Review*, entitled "Railway Revolutions," remarks:—"We need not go back so far as the time when third-class passengers had to stand in a sort of cattle-pen placed on wheels; it is only a few years since the Parliamentary trains were run in bare fulfilment of the obligations of Parliament, and when a journey by one of them could never be looked upon as anything better than a necessary evil. To start in the darkness of a winter's morning to catch the only third-class train that ran; to sit, after a slender breakfast, in a vehicle the windows of which were compounded of the largest amount of wood and the smallest amount of glass, and which were carefully adjusted to exactly those positions in which the fewest travellers could see out of them; to stop at every roadside station, however insignificant; and to accomplish a journey of 200 miles in about ten hours—such were the ordinary conditions which Parliament in its bounty provided for the people. Occasionally, moreover, the monotony of progress was interrupted by the shunting of the train into a siding, where it might wait for more respectable passenger trains and fast goods to pass."

"We remember," says a writer, " once standing on the platform at Darlington when the Parliamentary train arrived. It was detained for a considerable time to allow a more favoured train to pass, and, on the remonstrance of several of the passengers at the unexpected detention, they were coolly informed, " Ye mun bide till yer betters gaw past, ye are only the nigger train."

"If there is one part of my public life," recently said Mr. Allport (Midland Railway) to the writer, "in which I look back with more satisfaction than anything else, it is with reference to the boon we conferred on third-class passengers. When the rich man travels, or if he lies in bed all day, his capital remains undiminished, and perhaps his income flows in all the same. But when a poor man travels he has not only to pay his fare, but to sink his capital, for his time is his capital; and if he now consumes only five hours instead of ten in making a journey, he has saved five hours of time for useful labour—useful to himself, to his family, and to society. And I think with even more pleasure of the comfort in travelling we have been able to confer upon women and children. But it took," he added, "five-and-twenty years' work to get it done."

A GREAT DISCOVERY.

Confound that Pope Gregory who changed the style! He, or some one else, has robbed the month of February, in ordinary years, of no less than three days, for Mr. George Sutton, the solicitor, has discovered and established by the last Brighton Act of Parliament that February has *really thirty-one days*, while that good-for-nothing Pope led us to believe it had only twenty-eight. The language of the 45th clause of the Act or of the bill which went into the Lords is:—

"That so much of the said Consolidation Act as enacts that the ordinary meetings of the company, subsequent to the first ordinary meeting thereof, shall be held half-yearly on the 31st day of July, and *thirty-first day of February* in each year, or within one month before or after these days shall be, and the same is hereby repealed."

The next clause enacts, we suppose by reason of "the 31st of February" being an inconvenient day, that the meetings shall be held on the 31st of January and the 31st of July, a month before or a month after.

On account of the great value of an addition of three days to our years, and, therefore, an annual addition to our lives of three days, we beg to propose that a handsome testimonial be given to Mr. George Sutton, the eminent solicitor of the Brighton Railway Company, the author of the Act and the discoverer of the Pope's wicked conduct. We further propose that it be given him on "the 31st day of February" next year, and that his salary be paid on that day, and no other, every year.

—*Herepath's Journal*, June 24th, 1854.

A DREADED EVIL.

When the old Sheffield and Rotherham line was contemplated, "A hundred and twenty inhabitants of Rotherham, headed by their vicar, petitioned against the bill, because they thought the canal and turnpike furnished sufficient accommodation between the two towns, and because they dreaded an incursion of the idle, drunken, and dissolute portion of the Sheffield people as a consequence of increasing the facilities of transit." For a time the opposition was successful but eventually the Lord's Committee yielded to the perseverance of the promoters of the bill.

Sheffield and Rotherham Independent.

REMARKABLE ADVENTURE.

A young lady some years ago thus related an adventure she met with in travelling. "After I had taken my seat one morning at Paddington, in an empty carriage, I was joined, just as the train was moving off, by a strange-looking young man, with remarkably long flowing hair. He was, of course, a little hurried, but he seemed besides to be so disturbed and wild that I was quite alarmed, for fear of his not being in his right mind, nor did his subsequent conduct at all reassure me. Our train was an express, and he inquired eagerly, at once, which was the first station we were advertised to stop. I consulted my Bradshaw and furnished him with the required information. It was Reading. The young man looked at his watch.

"'Madam,' said he, 'I have but half-an-hour between me and, it may be, ruin. Excuse, therefore, my abruptness. You have, I perceive, a pair of scissors in your workbag. Oblige me, if you please, by cutting off all my hair.'

"'Sir,' said I, 'it is impossible.'

"'Madam,' he urged, and a look of severe determination crossed his features; 'I am a desperate man. Beware how you refuse me what I ask. Cut my hair off—short, close to the roots—immediately; and here is a newspaper to hold the ambrosial curls.'

"'I thought he was mad, of course; and believing that it would be dangerous to thwart him, I cut off all his hair to the last lock.'

"'Now, madam,' said he, unlocking a small portmanteau, 'you will further oblige me by looking out of the window, as I am about to change my clothes.'

"Of course I looked out of the window for a very considerable time, and when he observed, 'Madam, I need no longer put you to any inconvenience,' I did not recognise the young man in the least.

"Instead of his former rather gay costume, he was attired in black, and wore a grey wig and silver spectacles; he looked like a respectable divine of the Church of England, of about sixty-four years of age; to complete that character, he held a volume of sermons in his hand, which—they appeared so to absorb him—might have been his own.

" 'I do not wish to threaten you, young lady,' he resumed, 'and I think, besides, that I can trust your kind face. Will you promise me not to reveal this metamorphosis until your journey's end?'

" 'I will,' said I, 'most certainly.'

"At Reading, the guard and a person in plain clothes looked into our carriage.

" 'You have the ticket, my love,' said the young man, blandly, and looking to me as though he were my father.

" 'Never mind, sir; we don't want them,' said the official, as he withdrew his companion.

" 'I shall now leave you, madam,' observed my fellow-traveller, as soon as the coast was clear; 'by your kind and courageous conduct you have saved my life and, perhaps, even your own.'

"In another minute he was gone, and the train was in motion. Not till the next morning did I learn from the *Times* newspaper that the gentleman on whom I had operated as hair cutter had committed a forgery to an enormous amount, in London, a few hours before I met him, and that he had been tracked into the express train from Paddington; but that—although the telegraph had been put in motion and described him accurately—at Reading, when the train was searched, he was nowhere to be found."

SAFETY ON THE FLOOR.

Many concussions give no warning of their approach, while others do, the usual premonitory symptoms being a kind of bouncing or leaping of the train. It is well to know that the bottom of the carriage is the safest place, and, therefore, when a person has reason to anticipate a concussion, he should, without hesitation, throw himself on the floor of the carriage. It was by this means that Lord Guillamore saved his life and that of his fellow passengers some years since, when a concussion took place on one of the Irish railways. His Lordship feeling a shock, which he knew to be the forerunner of a concussion, without more ado sprang upon the two persons sitting opposite to him, and dragged them with him to the bottom of the carriage; the astonished persons at first imagined that they had been set upon by a maniac, and commenced struggling for their liberty, but in a few seconds they but too well understood the nature of the case; the concussion came, and the upper part of the carriage in which Lord Guillamore and the other two persons were was shattered to pieces, while the floor was untouched, and thus left them lying in safety; while the other carriages of the train presented nothing but a ghastly spectacle of dead and wounded.

—*The Railway Traveller's Handy Book.*

LIFE UPON THE RAILWAY, BY A CONDUCTOR.

The Western Division of our road runs through a very mountainous part of Virginia, and the stations are few and far between. About three miles from one of these stations, the road runs through a deep gorge of the Blue Ridge, and near the centre is a small valley, and there, hemmed in by the everlasting hills, stood a small one-and-a-half-story log cabin. The few acres that surrounded it were well cultivated as a garden, and upon the fruits thereof lived a widow and her three children, by the name of Graff. They were, indeed, untutored in the cold charities of an outside world—I doubt much if they ever saw the sun shine beyond their own native hills. In the summer time the children brought berries to the nearest station to sell, and with the money they bought a few of the necessities of the outside refinement.

The oldest of these children I should judge to be about twelve years, and the youngest about seven. They were all girls, and looked nice and clean, and their healthful appearance and natural delicacy gave them a ready welcome. They appeared as if they had been brought up to fear God and love their humble home and mother. I had often stopped my train and let them get off at their home, having found them at the station some three miles from home, after disposing of their berries.

I had children at home, and I knew their little feet would be tired in walking three miles, and therefore felt that it would be the same with these fatherless little ones. They seemed so pleased to ride, and thanked me with such hearty thanks, after letting them off near home. They frequently offered me nice, tempting baskets of fruit for my kindness ; yet I never accepted any without paying their full value.

Now, if you remember, the winter of '54 was very cold in that part of the State, and the snow was nearly three feet deep on the mountains.

On the night of the 26th of December, of that year, it turned around warm, and the rain fell in torrents. A terrible storm swept the mountain tops, and almost filled the valleys with water. Upon that night my train was winding its way, at its usual speed, around the hills and through the valleys, and as the road-bed was all solid rock, I had no fear of the banks giving out. The night was intensely dark, and the winds moaned piteously through the deep gorges of the mountains. Some of my passengers were trying to sleep, others were talking in a low voice, to relieve the monotony of the scene. Mothers had their children upon their knees, as if to shield them from some unknown danger without.

It was near midnight, when a sharp whistle from the engine brought me to my feet. I knew there was danger by that whistle, and sprang to the brakes at once, but the brakesmen were all at their posts, and soon brought the train to a stop. I seized my lantern and found my way forward as soon as possible, when, what a sight met my gaze ! A bright fire of pine logs illuminated the track for some distance, and not over forty rods ahead of our train a horrible gulf had opened its maw to receive us !

The snow, together with the rain, had torn the whole side of the mountain out, and eternity itself seemed spread out before us. The widow Graff and her children had found it out, and had brought light brush from their home below, and built a large fire to warn us of our danger. They had been there more than two hours watching beside that beacon of safety. As I went up where that old lady stood drenched through by the rain and sleet, she grasped my arm and cried :

"Thank God ! Mr. Sherbourn, we stopped you in time. I would have lost my life before one hair of your head should have been hurt. Oh, I prayed to heaven that we might stop the train, and, my God, I thank thee !"

The children were crying for joy. I confess I don't very often pray, but I did then and there. I kneeled down by the side of that good old woman, and offered up thanks to an All Wise Being for our safe deliverance from a most terrible death, and called down blessings without number upon that good old woman and her children. Near by stood the engineer, fireman, and brakesmen, the tears streaming down their bronzed cheeks.

I immediately prevailed upon Mrs. Graff and the children to go back into the cars out of the storm and cold. After reaching the cars I related our hair-breadth escape, and to whom we were indebted for our lives, and begged the men passengers to go forward and see for themselves. They needed no further urging, and a great many of the ladies went also, regardless of the storm. They soon returned, and their pale faces gave full evidence of the frightful death we had escaped. The ladies and gentlemen vied with each other in their thanks and heartfelt gratitude towards Mrs. Graff and her children, and assured her that they would never, never forget her, and before the widow left the train she was presented with a purse of four hundred and sixty dollars, the voluntary offering of a whole train of grateful passengers. She refused the proffered gift for some time, and said she had only done her duty, and the knowledge of having done so was all the reward she asked. However, she finally accepted the money, and said it should go to educate her children.

The railway company built her a new house, gave her and her children a life pass over the road, and ordered all trains to stop and let her get off at home when she wished, but the employés needed no such orders, they can appreciate all such kindness—more so than the directors themselves.

The old lady frequently visits my home at H ·—, and she is at all times a welcome visitor at my fireside. Two of the children are attending school at the same place.

—*Appleton's American Railway Anecdote Book.*

A COUNTY COURT JUDGE'S FEELING AGAINST RAILWAYS.

In a County Court case at Carlisle, reported in the *Carlisle Journal*, of October 31st, 1851, the judge (J. K. Knowles, Esq.) is represented to have said :—" You may depend upon it if

I could do anything for you, I would, for I detest all railways. If they get a verdict in this case it will be the first, and I hope it will be the last."

RAILWAY TICKETS.

A writer in that valuable miscellany *Household Words*, remarks:—"About thirteen years ago, a Quaker was walking in a field in Northumberland, when a thought struck him. The man who was walking was named Thomas Edmonson. He had been, though a Friend, not a very successful man in life. He was a man of integrity and honour, as he afterwards abundantly proved, but he had been a bankrupt, and was maintaining himself as a clerk at a small station on the Newcastle and Carlisle line. In the course of his duties in this situation, he found it irksome to have to write on every railway ticket that he delivered. He saw the clumsiness of the method of tearing the bit of paper off the printed sheet as it was wanted, and filling it up with pen and ink. He perceived how much time, trouble, and error might be saved by the process being done in a mechanical way; and it was when he set his foot down on a particular spot on the before mentioned field that the idea struck him how all that he wished might be done by a machine—how tickets might be printed with the names of stations, the class of carriage, the dates of the month, and all of them from end to end of the kingdom, on one uniform system. Most inventors accomplish their great deeds by degrees—one thought suggesting another from time to time; but, when Thomas Edmonson showed his family the spot in the field where his invention occurred to him, he used to say that it came to his mind complete, in its whole scope and all its details. Out of it has grown the mighty institution of the Railway Clearing House; and with it the grand organization by which the Railways of the United Kingdom act, in regard to the convenience of individuals, as a unity. We may see at a glance the difference to every one of us of the present organized system—by which we can take our tickets from almost any place to another, and get into a carriage on almost any of our great lines, to be conveyed without further care to the opposite end of the kingdom—

and the unorganized condition of affairs from which
Mr. Edmonson rescued us, whereby we should have been compelled to shift ourselves and our luggage from time to time,
buying new tickets, waiting while they were filled up,
waiting at almost every point of the journey, and having to
do it with divers companies who had nothing to do with
each other but to find fault and be jealous.

"On Mr. Edmonson's machines may be seen the name of
Blaycock; Blaycock was a watchmaker, and an acquaintance
of Edmonson's, and a man whom he knew to be capable of
working out his idea. He told him what he wanted; and
Blaycock understood him, and realized his thought. The
third machine that they made was nearly as good as those
now in use. The one we saw had scarcely wanted five
shillings worth of repairs in five years; and, when it needs
more, it will be from sheer wearing away of the brass-work,
by constant hard friction. The Manchester and Leeds
Railway Company were the first to avail themselves of
Mr. Edmonson's invention; and they secured his services
at their station at Oldham Road, for a time. He took out
a patent; and his invention became so widely known and
appreciated, that he soon withdrew himself from all other
engagements, to perfect its details and provide tickets to
meet the daily growing demand. He let out his patent on
profitable terms—ten shillings per mile per annum; that
is, a railway of thirty miles long paid him fifteen pounds a
year for a license to print its own tickets by his apparatus;
and a railway of sixty miles long paid him thirty pounds,
and so on. As his profits began to come in, he began to
spend them; and it is not the least interesting part of his
history to see how. It has been told that he was a bankrupt early in life. The very first use he made of his money
was to pay every shilling that he ever owed. He was
forty-six when he took that walk in the field in
Northumberland. He was fifty-eight when he died, on
the twenty-second of June last year."

TAKEN ABACK.

Four young cavalry officers, travelling by rail, from
Boulogne to Paris, were joined at Amiens by a quiet,
elderly gentleman, who shortly requested that a little of

one window might be opened—a not unreasonable demand, as both were shut, and all four gentlemen were smoking. But it was refused, and again refused on being preferred a second time, very civilly; whereupon the elderly gentleman put his umbrella through the glass. "Shall we stand the impertinence of this burgeois?" said the officers to one another. "Never." And they thrust four cards into his hand, which he received methodically, and looked carefully at all four; producing his own, one of which he tendered to each officer with a bow. Imagine their feelings when they read on each—"Marshal Randon, Ministre de Guerre."

FAITHFUL UNTO DEATH.

The engineer of a train near Montreal saw a large dog on the track. He was barking furiously. The engineer blew the whistle at him, but he did not stir, and crouching low, he was struck by the locomotive and killed. There was a bit of white muslin on the locomotive, and it attracted the attention of the engineer, who stopped the train and went back. There lay the dead dog, and a dead child, which had wandered upon the track and gone to sleep. The dog had given his signal to stop the train, and had died at his post.

NARROW ESCAPES FROM BEING LYNCHED.

A writer in *All the Year Round*, observes:—"A dreadful accident down in 'Illonoy,' had particularly struck me as a warning; for there, while the shattered bodies were still being drawn from under the piles of shivered carriages, the driver on being expostulated with, had replied:

'I suppose this ain't the first railway accident by long chalks!'

Upon which the indignant passengers were with difficulty prevented from lynching the wretch; but he fled into the woods, and there for a time escaped pursuit.

But, two other railway journeys pressed more peculiarly on my mind; one was that of eight or ten weeks ago, from Canandaigua to Antrim. It was there a gentleman from Baltimore, fresh from Chicago, told me of a railway accident he had himself been witness to, only two days before I met him. The 2.40 (night) train from Toledo to Chicago, in which he rode, was upset near Pocahontas by two logs that had evidently been wilfully laid across the rails. On inquiry at the next station, it was discovered that a farmer who had had, a week before, two stray calves killed near the same place, had been heard at a liquor store to say he would 'pay them out for his calves.' This was enough for the excited passengers, vexed at the detention, and enraged at the malice that had exposed them to danger and death. A posse of them instantly sallied out, beleagured the farmer's house, seized him after some resistance, put a rope round his neck, dragged him to the nearest tree, and would have then and there lynched him, had not two or three of the passengers rescued him, revolver in hand, and given him up to the nearest magistrate."

CURIOUS NOTICE.

The following notice, for the benefit of English travellers, was exhibited some years ago in the carriage of a Dutch railway:—"You are requested not to put no heads nor arms out of te windows."

OBTAINING INFORMATION.

But one of the most difficult things in the world is the levity with which people talk about "obtaining information." As if information were as easy to pick up as stones! "It ain't so hard to nuss the sick," said a hired nurse, "as some people might think; the most of 'em doesn't want nothing, and them as does doesn't get it." Parodying this, one might say, it is much harder to "obtain information" than some people think; the most don't know anything, and those who do don't say what they know. Here is a real episode from the history of an inquiry, which took place four or five years ago, into the desirability of making a new line of railway on the Border. A witness was giving what is called "traffic evidence," in justification of the alleged need of the railway, and this is what occurred:—

Mr. Brown (the cross-examining counsel for the opponents of the new line)—Do you mean to tell the committee that you ever saw an inhabited house in that valley?

Witness—Yes I do.

Mr. Brown—Did you ever see a vehicle there in your life?

Witness—Yes, I did.

Mr. Brown—Very good.

Some other questions were put, which led to nothing particular : but, just as the witness—a Scotchman—was leaving the box, the learned gentleman put one more question :—

Q.—I am instructed to ask you, if the vehicle you saw was not the hearse of the last inhabitant?

Answer—It was.

—*Cornhill Magazine.*

THE GOAT AND THE RAILWAY.

In Prussian Poland the goods and cattle trains are prohibited from carrying passengers under any conditions, and, however urgent their necessities, the only exception allowed being the herd-keepers in charge of cattle. So strictly is this regulation enforced that even medical men are not allowed to go by them when called for on an emergency, and where life and death may be the result of their quick transit. This is generally considered a great hardship, the more so as there are only two passenger trains daily on the above railroads. But the inventive genius of a small German innkeeper at Lissa has hit upon a clever plan of circumventing the government regulations in a perfectly legitimate manner. He keeps a goat, which he hires out to persons wanting to proceed in a hurry by a cattle train, at the rate of 6d. per station, the passenger then applying for a ticket as the person in charge of the goat, which he obtains without any difficulty. In this manner a well-known nobleman, residing a Lissa, is frequently seen travelling by the cattle train to Posen, in the passenger's carriage, and the goat is so tame that a very slender silk ribbon suffices to keep it from straying.

THE FIRST RAILWAY IN THE CRIMEA.

During the Russian War, in 1854, when the whole country was horror-struck with the report of the sufferings endured by our brave soldiers in the Crimea. Mr. Peto, in the most noble and disinterested manner, and at the cost of his seat in the House of Commons for Norwich—which city he had represented for several years—constructed for the Government a line of railway from Balaclava to the English camp before Sebastopol, which at the end of the war, with its various branches, was 37 English miles in length and had 10 locomotives on it. In recognition of this patriotic service the honour of a baronetcy was, in the following year, conferred upon him by Her Majesty.

—Old Jonathan.

THE BALACLAVA RAILWAY.

The following interesting extract from a communication to the *Times*, by Sir Morton Peto, Bart., respecting the construction of the railway from Balaclava to the British camp is worthy of preservation. Sir Morton remarks:—" It was in the midst of the dreary winter of 1854, when the British army was suffering unparalleled hardships before Sebastopol, that it was resolved to construct a railway from Balaclava to the British camp. Let honour be given where honour is due.—The idea emanated from the Duke of Newcastle. His Grace applied to our firm to assist in carrying out the design. The sympathies of all England were excited at the time by the sufferings of our troops. Every one was emulous to contribute all that could be contributed to their succour and support. The firm of which I am a partner was anxious to take its share in the good work, and, on the Duke of Newcastle's application, we cheerfully undertook to make all the arrangements for carrying his Grace's views into execution, on the understanding that the work should be considered National; and that we should be permitted to execute it without any charge for profit.

We accordingly placed at the disposal of Her Majesty's Government the whole of our resources. We fitted out transports with the stores necessary for the construction of the railway; employed and equipped hundreds of men to execute the works; provided a commissariat exclusively for their use; engaged medical officers to attend to their health, and placed the whole service under the direction of the most experienced agents on our staff. These important preliminaries were arranged so effectually, and with so much despatch, that the Emperor of the French sent an agent to this country to instruct himself as to the mode in which we equipped the expedition.

Every item shipped by us for the works was valued before shipment at its selling price; and for all these items of valuation, as well as for the payments which we made for labour, we received the certificate of the most eminent engineer of the day (the late lamented Mr. Robert Stephenson). We undertook the execution of the Balaclava Railway as a 'National' work, agreeing to execute it without profit. We performed our contract to the letter. We never profited by it to the extent of a single shilling.

The works (nearly seven miles of railway) were executed in less than a month; an incredibly short space of time, considering the season of the year, the severity of the climate, and the difficulties to which, considering the distance from home, we were all of us exposed. It is a matter of history that they eventuated in the taking of the great fortress of Sebastopol. Before the railway was made, all the shot, all the shell, and all the ammunition necessary for the siege, had to be carried from Balaclava to the camp, a distance of five miles up hill, through mud and sludge, upon the backs of the soldiers. An immense proportion of our troops was told off for this most laborious service; of whom no less than 25 per cent per month perished in its execution. On the day the railway was opened, it carried to the camp of the British army, in 24 hours, more shot and shell than had been brought from Balaclava for six weeks previously.

To our principal agent in the Crimea, the late Mr. Beattie, the greatest credit was due for the way in which the arrangements were made, and the work executed on that side. Mr. Beattie's labours were so arduous, and his efforts so untiring, that he died of fatigue within six weeks after the completion of the work—a victim, absolutely, to his unparalleled exertions. The only favour in connection

L.

with these works which the Duke of Newcastle ever granted at our request, he granted to the family of this lamented gentleman. Mr. Beattie left a widow and four children to deplore his loss, and through the favour of the Duke of Newcastle, the widow, who now resides with her father, an estimable clergyman in the North of Ireland, enjoys a pension as the widow of a colonel falling in the field."

PASSENGERS AND OTHER CATTLE.

At the Eastern Counties meeting (1854) the solicitor cut short a clause about passengers, animals, and cattle, by reading it "passengers and other cattle." We do not recollect passengers having been classed with cattle before. Perhaps the learned gentleman's eyesight was defective, or the print was not very clear.

EXPANSION OF RAILS.

Robert Routledge, in his article upon railways, remarks:— "It may easily be seen on looking at a line of rails that they are not laid with the ends quite touching each other, or, at least, they are not usually in contact. The reason of this is that space must must be allowed for the expansion which takes place when a rise in the temperature occurs. The neglect of this precaution has sometimes led to damage and accidents. A certain railway was opened in June, and, after an excursion train had in the morning passed over it, the midday heat so expanded the iron that the rails became, in some places, elevated to two feet above the level, and the sleepers were torn up; so that in order to admit the return of the train, the rails had to be fully relaid in a kind of zigzag. In June, 1856, a train was thrown off the metals of the North-Eastern Railway, in consequence of the rails rising up through expansion."

A SMART REJOINDER.

An American railway employé asked for a pass down to visit his family. "You are in the employ of the railway?" asked the gentleman applied to. "Yes." "You receive your pay regularly?" "Yes." "Well, now, suppose you were working for a farmer, instead of a railway, would you expect your employer to hitch up his team every Saturday night and carry you home?" This seemed a poser, but it wasn't. "No," said the man promptly, "I wouldn't expect that; but if the farmer had his team hitched up and was going my way, I should call him a contemptible fellow if he would not let me ride." Mr. Employé came out three minutes afterwards with a pass good for three months.

COURTING ON A RAILWAY THIRTY MILES AN HOUR.

An incident occurred on the Little Miami Railway which outstrips, in point of speed and enterprise, although in a somewhat different field, the lightning express, "fifty-cents-a-mile," special train achievement which attended the delivery of the recent famous "defalcation report" in this city. The facts are about thus: A lady, somewhat past that period of life which *the world* would term "young"—although she might differ from them—was on her way to this city, for purposes connected with active industry. At a point on the road a traveller took the train, who happened to enter the car in which the young lady occupied a seat. After walking up and down between the seats, the gentleman found no unoccupied seat, except the one-half of that upon which the lady had deposited her precious self and crinoline —the latter very modestly expansive. Making a virtue of necessity—a "stand-ee" berth or a little self-assurance— he modestly inquired if the lady had a fellow-traveller, and took a seat.

As the train flew along with express speed, the strangers entered into a cosy conversation, and mutual explanations. The gentleman was pleased, and the lady certainly did not pout. After other subjects had been discussed, and worn thread-bare, the lady made inquiries as to the price of a sewing machine, and where such an article could be purchased in this city. The gentleman ventured the opinion that she had "better secure a husband first." This opened the way for another branch of conversation, and the broken field was industriously cultivated.

By the time the train arrived at the depot in this city, the gentleman had proposed and been accepted (although the lady afterwards declared she regarded it all as a good joke). The party separated; the gentleman, all in good

earnest, started for a license, and the lady made her way to
a boarding-house on Broadway, above Third, for dinner.
At two o'clock the gentleman returned with a license and a
Justice, to the great astonishment of the fair one, and after
a few tears and half-remonstrative expressions, she submitted with becoming modesty, and the Squire performed
the little ceremony in a twinkling. If this is not a fast
country, a search-warrant would hardly succeed in finding
one.

—*Cincinnati Commercial.*

THE MERCHANT AND HIS CLERK.

A London merchant resided a few miles from the City,
in an elegant mansion, to and from which he journeyed
daily, and invariably by third class. It happened that one
of the clerks in his employ lived in a cottage accessible by
the same line of railway, but he always travelled first class;
the same train thus presenting the anomaly of the master
being in that place which one would naturally assign to the
man, and the man appearing to usurp the position of the
master. One day these two alighted at the terminus in full
view of each other. "Well," said Mr. B——, in that tone
of banter which a superior so frequently thinks it becoming
to adopt, "I don't know how you manage to ride first-class,
when in these hard times I find third-class fare as much as
I can afford." "Sir," replied the clerk, "you, who are
known to be a person of wealth and position, may adopt
the most economical mode of travelling at no more risk
than being thought eccentric, and even with the applause
of some for your manifest absence of pride. But, as for
myself, I cannot afford to indulge in such irregularities.
Among the persons I travel with I am reported to be a
well-paid *employé*, and am respected accordingly; to maintain this reputation I am compelled to travel in the same
manner as they do, and were I to adopt an inferior mode,
it would be attributed to some serious falling off of income;
a circumstance which would occasion me not only loss of
consideration among my *quondam* fellow-travellers, but one
which, upon coming to the ears of my butcher, baker, and
grocer, might seriously injure my credit with those highly

respectable, but certainly worldly-minded tradesmen."
Mr. B—— was not slow in recognizing the full force of the
argument, more particularly as the question of his own
liberality was involved, nor did he hesitate to give it a
practical application by immediately increasing the salary
of his clerk; not only to the amount of a first-class season
ticket, but something over.
—*The Railway Traveller's Handy Book.*

REMARKABLE WILL.

Some years ago an old gentleman of very eccentric habits,
Mr. John Younghusband, of Abbey Holme, Cumberland,
died, and his will has proved to be of the most eccentric
character. The Silloth Railway runs through part of his
property, an arrangement to which he was most passionately
averse; and though years have elapsed since then, his
bitterness was in no way assuaged. In his will he leaves
near £1000 to a solicitor who opposed the making of the
railway; the rest of his money he bequeathes to a compara-
tive stranger upon these conditions—that the legatee never
speaks to one of the directors of the railway, that he never
travels upon it, that he never sends cattle or other traffic
by it; and should he violate any of these conditions, the
estate reverts to the ordinary succession. To Mr. John Irving
and the other directors of the Silloth line Mr. Younghusband
has sarcastically bequeathed a *farthing*.

IMMENSE FRAUD ON THE GREAT-NORTHERN RAILWAY.

In the *Annual Register* for 1856, November 14th, we read,
" Another fraud connected with the transfer of shares and
stock, but on a far grander scale, and by a much more
pretentious criminal, has been discovered.

" Of late some strange discrepancies had been observed
in the accounts of the Great-Northern Railway Company,
and in particular that the amount paid for dividends considerably exceeded the rateable proportion to the capital
stock. An investigation was directed. The registrar of
shares, Mr. Leopold Redpath, expressed a decided opinion
that the investigation into his department would be useless,
and, on its being pressed, absconded. The investigation
developed a long-continued system of frauds of vast amount,
to the amount, it was said, of nearly £250,000.

' "Mr. Leopold Redpath passed in society as a gentleman of ample means, great taste, and possessed of the Christian virtue of charity in no common degree. He had a house in Chester Terrace, handsomely furnished, and a "place" at Weybridge complete with every luxury. that wealth could procure; gave good dinners with excellent wines; kept good horses and neat carriages. He was a governor of Christ's Hospital, the St. Ann's Schools, and subscribed freely to the most useful charities of London. His appointment on the Great-Northern was worth £300 per annum : but it was supposed that this was only of consequence to Mr. Redpath as affording him a regular occupation and an opportunity of operating in the share-market, in which he was known to have extensive dealings. The directors of the railway appear to have been perfectly aware that their servant was living far beyond his salary, but they considered him to be a very successful speculator. Upon this splendid bubble being blown up, Redpath fled to Paris; but, finding that the French authorities were not inclined to protect him, he returned to London and surrendered himself.

"The mode in which this gigantic swindler had committed his frauds is simple enough. Having charge of the books in which the stock of the company is registered, he altered the sum standing in the name of some *bonâ fide* stockholder to a much larger sum, generally by placing a figure before it, by which simple means £500 became £1,500, or £2,500, or any larger number of thousands. The surplus stock thus *created* Redpath sold in the stock-market, forging the name of the supposed transferer, transferring the sum to the account of the supposed transferree in the register, and either attesting it himself, or causing it to be attested by a young man, his protegé and tool, but who appears to have been free from guilty cognizance. In some instances the fraud was but the more direct course of making a fictitious entry of stock, and then selling it. By these processes the number of shareholders and the amount of stock on the company's register became greatly magnified, while. as the *bonâ fide* holders of stock remained credited with their proper. investments, there was no occasion for suspicion on their part. How Redpath dealt with subsequent transfers of the fictitious stock does not appear. The prisoner was subjected to repeated examination before the police magistrates, when this prodigious falsification was thoroughly sifted, and the prisoner was finally committed for trial at the Central Criminal Court in the following year. It is said that the value of the leases, furniture, and articles of taste in Redpath's house in Chester Terrace is estimated at £30,000, and at Weybridge at a still larger sum. It is also said that Redpath and Robson, whose forged transfer of Crystal Palace shares has been recorded in this chronicle, were formerly fellow clerks.

. "Lionel Redpath was tried, January 16th, 1857, at the Central Criminal Court, and, being found guilty, was sentenced to transportation for life. At the same time a junior clerk in his office, Charles Kent, was also charged as his partner in the crime. It appeared that Kent had acted on many occasions as attesting witness to the forged transfers which Redpath had employed to carry out his ends; but, as no guilty knowledge on the part of the former was shown, he was acquitted.

"The railway company at first attempted to repudiate the forged stock which Redpath had put into circulation, but pressing remonstrances, not unaccompanied by threats, having been made by the Committee of the Stock Exchange, they consented to acknowledge it. Then came the question by whom the loss was to be borne; a question which was not solved until after considerable litigation. The directors asserted that it ought to be paid out of the current income of the year, and so it was ultimately decided. This led to a further question between the guaranteed shareholders and the rest of the company. For the diminution of the year's earnings caused by taking up the fictitious stock being so great as to render it impossible to satisfy the guaranteed dividends out of the residue, it was contended on the part of the holders of those shares that, by the provisions of the deed of settlement, the deficiency ought to be made up out of the next year's profits, so that the guarantee that they should receive their specified dividends was not clogged with the condition in case a sufficient amount of earnings in each year was made to pay them. This dispute led to a Chancery suit, the decree in which was in favour of the holders of the guaranteed shares."

A LOST TICKET.

"Now, then, make haste there, will you, an' give up your ticket," exclaimed a railway guard to a bandsman in the Volunteers returning from a review. "Didna I tell ye I've lost it?" "Nonsense, man; feel in your pockets, you cannot hae lost it." "Can I no?" was the drunken reply; "man, that's naething, I've lost the big drum!"

MELANCHOLY ACCIDENT.—SINGULAR ACTION.

The *Annual Register* contains the following interesting case. July 25, 1857.—At the Maidstone Assizes an action arising out of a singular and melancholy accident was tried. The action, Shilling *v* The Accidental Insurance Company, was brought by Charlotte Shilling, widow and administratrix of Thomas Shilling, to recover from the defendants the sum of £2000, upon a policy effected by the deceased on the life of her father-in-law, James Shilling. The husband of the plaintiff, Thomas Shilling, carried on the business of a builder at Malling, a short distance from Maidstone. His father, James Shilling, lived with him; he was nearly 80 years old, and very infirm, and his son used to drive him about occasionally in his pony chaise. In the month of March, last year, an application was made to the defendants to effect two policies for £2000 each upon the lives of Thomas Shilling and James Shilling, and to secure that sum in the event of either of them dying from an accident, and the policies were completed and delivered in the following month of June. On the evening of the 11th of July, 1856, about half-past 7 o'clock, the father and son went from Malling with a pony and chaise, for the purpose of proceeding to a stone quarry at Aylesford, where Thomas Shilling had business to transact, and they never returned home again alive. There where two roads by which they could have got to the quarry from Malling, one of which was rather a dangerous one to be taken with a vehicle and horse, on account of a steep bank leading to the river Medway being on one side and the railway passing close to the other; but this route, it appears, was much shorter than the other, which was nearly two miles round, and it was consequently constantly used both by pedestrians and carriages. About 8 o'clock the pony and chaise and the father and son were seen on this road, and upon arriving at the gate leading to the quarry, Thomas Shilling got out, leaving the pony and chaise in charge of his father. Mr. Garnham, the owner of the quarry, was not at home, and while one of the labourers was conversing with Thomas Shilling, the sound of an approaching train was heard, and the men advised him to go back to his pony, for fear it should take fright at the train, and he said he would do so, as it had been frightened by a train on a previous occasion. He accordingly went towards the gate where he had left the pony and chaise, and from that time there was no evidence to show what took place. The family sat up the whole night awaiting the return of their relatives in the utmost possible alarm at their absence; but nothing was heard of them until the following morning, when a barge-man found the drowned pony and the chaise and the dead bodies of the father and son floating in the Medway, near the spot where the chaise had been last seen on the previous evening. They were taken home, and a coroner's inquest was held, and the only conclusion that could be arrived at was that the pony had taken fright at the noise of the train, which appeared to have passed about the time, and that he had jumped into the river, which at this spot was from 12 to 14 feet deep.

The policy on the life of the father had been assigned to the son, whose widow claimed the two sums insured from the defendants. That payable on the death of the son they paid : but they refused to pay that due on the father's policy, and pleaded to the action several pleas, alleging certain violations of the conditions; and singularly enough, considering that they had not disputed the son's policy on the same ground, they now pleaded that the death was not the result of accident, but arose from wanton and voluntary exposure to uunecessary danger.

The jury found a verdict for the plaintiff.

A CATASTROPHE.

An old lady was going from Brookfield to Stamford, and took a seat in the train for the first and last time in her life. During the ride the train was thrown down an embankment. Crawling from beneath the *débris* unhurt, she spied a man sitting down, but with his legs laid down by some heavy timber. "Is this Stamford?" she anxiously inquired. "No, madam," was the reply, "this is a catastrophe." "Oh!" she cried, "then I hadn't oughter got off here."

WEDDING AT A RAILWAY STATION.

Baltimore has had what it calls a romantic wedding at Camden Station. A few moments before the departure of the outbound Washington train, a gentleman accompanied by a lady and another gentleman, whose clerical appearance indicated his profession, alighted from a carriage and entered the depot. Upon the locks of the leader of the party the snows of fifty winters had evidently fallen, while the lady had apparently reached that age when she is supposed to have lain aside her matrimonial cap. Quietly approaching the officer on duty within the station, they asked for a room where a marriage ceremony might be privately performed. The request was readily granted, and under the leadership of the obliging officer, the party was conducted to the despatch room, a small lobby in the eastern part of the building, where in a few minutes the twain were made man and wife. With pleasant smiles, and a would-be-congratulated look upon their countenances, they mingled with the crowd in waiting; and when the gates were thrown open, arm in arm they boarded the train, their fellow-passengers all the while ignorant of the interesting ceremony.

—Illustrated World.

ENGINE FASCINATION.

The fascination which engines and their human satellites exercise over some minds is very great; and while speaking on the subject, I am reminded of a young man who haunted for years one of our chief termini : he was the son of a leading west end confectioner, so that his early training had in no way disposed him to an engineering life ; but he was the most remarkable accumulation of statistics in connection therewith I ever knew. The line employed several hundreds of engines, and ho not only knew the names of all of them, but when they were made, and who had made them ; when each one had last been supplied with a new set of tubes at the factory—this last, of course only referred to the engines employed on the main line, which ho had an opportunity of seeing, and would miss when they were laid up for repair—and how this had had the pressure on its safety-valve increased, and this had been diminished. He had such a retentive memory for these and kindred facts, that I have seen the foreman of the works appeal to him for information, which was never lacking. His penchant was so well known that he had special permission for access to the works.

—*Chambers's Journal.*

COMPETITION FOR PASSENGERS.

Mr Galt remarks :—"In the summer of 1857 the London and North-Western and Great Northern railways contended with each other for the passenger traffic from London to Manchester. First-class and second-class passengers were conveyed at fares, there and back, of seven and sixpence and five shillings respectively, the distance being 400 miles, and four clear days were allowed in Manchester. As might have been expected, trains were well filled, and, but for the fact that the other traffic was much interfered with, the fares would, it is said, have been remunerative. As it was, it is said the shareholders lost 1 per cent. dividend.

" Another memorable contest was carried on about the year 1853 between the Caledonian and the Edinburgh and Glasgow Companies. The latter suddenly reduced the fares between Edinburgh and Glasgow for the three classes from eight shillings, six shillings, and four shillings, to one shilling, ninepence, and sixpence. The contest was continued for a-year-and-a-half, and cost the Edinburgh and Glasgow Company nearly 1½ per cent. in their dividends."

ACCIDENT HOAX.

The following impudent hoax, contained in a letter which appeared in the *Times* in 1860, was most annoying to the officials of the Great Northern Company. It is headed :—

"Accident on the Great Northern Railway.
"To the Editor of the *Times*.

"Sir,—I beg to inform you of a serious accident, attended by severe injury, if not loss of life, which occured to-day to the 8 o'clock a.m. train from Wakefield, on the Great Northern railway, near Doncaster, by which I was a passenger. As the train approached Doncaster, about 9 o'clock, the passengers were suddenly alarmed by the vehement oscillation of the carriages. In a few seconds the engine had run off the line, dragging the greater part of the train with it across the opposite line of rails. By this time the concussion had become so vehement that the grappling chains connecting the engine, tender, and first carriage with the rest of the train providentially snapped. This circumstance saved the lives of many. But the engine, tender, and first carriage were hurled over the embankment, all three being together overturned, and the latter (a second-class one) nearly crushed. The stoker was severely injured on the head, and his recovery is more than doubtful; the engine driver contrived to leap off in time to save himself with a few bruises. The shrieks of the passengers in the overturned carriage (three women and five men) were fearful; and for some time their extrication was impossible. One middle-aged woman had her thigh broken, another her arm fractured. One old man had one, if not two of his ribs broken. The passengers in the other carriages, in one of which I was travelling, were less seriously injured, though sufficiently so to talk about compensation, instead of assisting in earnest those with broken limbs. The line of rails was torn up for a considerable distance. Owing to the telegraph being out of gear, some delay in communicating with Doncaster was experienced. A surgeon and various hands at length arrived with a special train for the injured passengers, who, after long delay, were removed to Doncaster. I, of course, as a medical man, rendered what assistance I could. Those worst injured were conveyed to the Railway Arms, the recovery of more than one being doubted by myself. At length a fresh train started from Doncaster, and we reached London nearly two hours after due.

The carelessness of the Company will, I hope, be the subject of your severest animadversion.   The accident was caused by the tire of one of the right wheels of the engine having flown off; and it is clear that the engine was not in a condition to ply between the stations of the Great Northern railway.

I have no objection to your use of my name if you think fit to publish it.

> Your obedient servant,
> Thomas Waddington, M.D., of Wakefield.
> Morley's Hotel, Charing Cross, March 26.

To the above letter the following reply was sent to the *Times*.

> "Alleged Accident on the Great Northern.
> "To the Editor of the *Times*.

"Sir,—The Directors of the Great Northern railway will feel much obliged by the insertion of the following statement in the *Times* to-morrow relative to a letter which appeared therein to-day, signed 'Thomas Waddington, M.D., of Wakefield,' and headed, 'Accident on the Great Northern railway.'

There was no accident whatever yesterday on the Great Northern railway.

The trains all reached King's Cross with punctuality, the most irregular in the whole day being only five minutes late.

No such person as Thomas Waddington is known at Morley's Hotel, whence the letter in question is dated.

> I am, Sir, yours faithfully,
> Seymour Clark, General Manager,
> King's Cross, March 27.

In the *Times* on the day following appeared a letter from the real Dr. Waddington, of Wakefield, (Edward not "Thomas") comfirmatory of the impudence of the hoax.

> "The alleged Accident on the Great Northern railway.
> "To the Editor of the *Times*.

"Sir,—My attention has been called to a letter in the *Times* of yesterday (signed 'Thomas Waddington, M.D., of Wakefield') the signature of which is as gross and impudent a fabrication as the circumstances which the writer professes to detail.   I need only say there is no 'M.D.' here named Waddington but myself, and that I was not on the Great Northern or any other Railway on the 26th inst, when the accident is alleged to have occured.

Having obtained possession of the original letter, I have handed it to my solicitors, in the hope that they may be enabled to discover and bring to justice the perpetrator of this very stupid hoax.

I am, Sir, your obedient servant,
Edward Waddington, M.D.

Wakefield, March 28.

A'PENNY A MILE.

Two costers were looking at a railway time-table.
" Say, Jem," said one of them, " vot's P.M. mean ? "
" Vy, penny a mile, to be sure."
" Vell, vot's A.M. ? "
" A'penny a mile, to be sure."

SINGULAR FREAK.

In October, 1857, Mr. Tindal Atkinson applied to Mr. Hammill, at Worship Street Police Court, to obtain a summons under the following strange circumstances :—

"Mr. Atkinson stated that he was instructed on behalf of the Directors of the Eastern Counties Railway Company to apply to the magistrate under the terms of their Act of Incorporation, for a summons against Mr. Henry Hunt, of Waltham-Cross, Essex, for having unlawfully used and worked a certain locomotive upon a portion of their line, without having previously obtained the permission or approval of the engineers or agents of the company, whereby he had rendered himself liable to a penalty of £20. He should confine himself to that by stating that in the dark, on the night of Thursday, the 1st instant, a locomotive engine belonging to Mr. Hunt was suddenly discovered by some of the company's servants to be running along the rails in close proximity to one of the regular passenger trains on the North Woolwich line. So great was the danger of a collision, that they were obliged to instantly stop the train till the stranger engine could get out of the way, to the great terror of the passengers by the train, and as he was instructed it was almost the result of a merciful interposition of Providence that a collision had not occurred between them, in which event it would probably have terminated fatally, to a greater or lesser extent. He now desired that summonses might be granted not only against the owner of the engine so used, but also against the driver and stoker of it, both of whom, it was obvious, must have been well aware of their committing an unlawful act, and of the perilous nature of the service in which they were engaged when they were running an engine at such a time and place.

"Mr. Hammill said it certainly was a most extraordinary proceeding for anyone to adopt, and after the learned gentleman's statement he had no hesitation whatever in granting summonses against the whole of the persons engaged in it."

A.B.C. AND D.E.F.

A gentleman travelling in a railway carriage was endeavouring, with considerable earnestness, to impress some argument upon a fellow-traveller who was seated opposite to him, and who appeared rather dull of apprehension. At length, being slightly irritated, he exclaimed in a louder tone. "Why, sir, it's as plain as A.B.C.!" "That may be," quietly replied the other, "but I am D.E.F.!"

NATIONAL CONTRAST.

The contrast which exists between the character of the French and English navvy may be briefly exemplified by the following trifling anecdote:—

"In excavating a portion of the first tunnel east of Rouen towards Paris, a French miner dressed in his blouse, and an English "navvy" in his white smock jacket, were suddenly buried alive together by the falling in of the earth behind them. Notwithstanding the violent commotion which the intelligence of the accident excited above ground, Mr. Meek, the English engineer who was constructing the work, after having quietly measured the distance from the shaft to the sunken ground, satisfied himself that if the men, at the moment of the accident, were at the head of "the drift" at which they were working, they would be safe.

Accordingly, getting together as many French and English labourers as he could collect, he instantly commenced sinking a shaft, which was accomplished to the depth of 50 feet in the extraordinary short space of eleven hours, and the men were thus brought up to the surface alive.

The Frenchman, on reaching the top, suddenly rushing forward, hugged and saluted on both cheeks his friends and acquaintances, many of whom had assembled, and then, almost instantly overpowered by conflicting feelings—by the recollection of the endless time he had been imprisoned and by the joy of his release—he sat down on a log of timber, and, putting both his hands before his face, he began to cry aloud most bitterly.

The English "navvy" sat himself down on the very same piece of timber—took his pit-cap off his head—slowly wiped with it the perspiration from his hair and face—and then, looking for some seconds into the hole or shaft close beside him through which he had been lifted, as if he were calculating the number of cubic yards that had been excavated, he quite coolly, in broad Lancashire dialect, said to the crowd of French and English who were staring at him, as children and nursery-maids in our London Zoological Gardens stand gazing half terrified at the white bear, "YAW'VE BEAN A DARMNATION SHORT TOIME ABAAOWT IT!"

Sir F. Head's *Stokers and Pokers.*

REMARKABLE ACCIDENT.

The most remarkable railway accident on record happened some years ago on the North-Western road between London and Liverpool. A gentleman and his wife were travelling in a compartment alone, when—the train going at the rate of forty miles an hour—an iron rail projecting from a car on a side-track cut into the carriage and took the head of the lady clear off, and rolled it into the husband's lap. He subsequently sued the company for damages, and created great surprise in court by giving his age at thirty-six years, although his hair was snow white. It had been turned from jet black by the horror of that event.

ENGINEERING LOAN, OR STAKING OUT A RAILWAY.

"Beau" Caldwell was a sporting genius of an extremely versatile character. Like all his fraternity, he was possessed of a pliancy of adaptation to circumstances that enabled him to succumb with true philosophy to misfortunes, and also to grace the more exalted sphere of prosperity with that natural ease attributed to gentlemen with bloated bank accounts.

Fertile in ingenuity and resources, Beau was rarely at his wit's end for that nest egg of the gambler, a stake. His providence, when in luck, was such as to keep him continually on the *qui vive* for a nucleus to build upon.

Beau, having exhausted the pockets and liberality of his contemporaries in Charleston, S.C., was constrained to "pitch his tent" in fresh pastures. He therefore selected Abbeville, whither he was immediately expedited by the agency of a "free pass."

Snugly ensconced in his hotel, Beau ruminated over the means to raise the "plate." The bar-keeper was assailed, but he was discovered to have scruples (anomalous bar-keeper!) The landlord was a "grum wretch," with no soul for speculation. The cornered "sport" was finally reduced to the alternative of "confidence of operation." Having arranged his scheme, he rented him a precious negro boy, and borrowed an old theodolite. Thus equipped, Beau betook himself to the abode of a neighbouring planter, notorious for his wealth, obstinacy, and ignorance. Operations were commenced by sending the nigger into the planter's barn-yard with a flagpole. Beau got himself up into a charming tableau, directly in front of the house. He now roared at the top of his voice, "72,000,000—51—8—11."

After which he went to driving small stakes, in a very promiscuous manner, about the premises.

The planter hearing the shouting, and curious to ascertain the cause, put his head out of the window.

"Now," said Beau, again assuming his civil engineering *pose*. "go to the right a little further—there, that'll do. 47,000—92—5."

"What the d—l are you doing in my barn-yard?" roared the planter.

Beau would not consent to answer this interrogation, but pursuing his business, hallooed out to his "nigger"—

"Now go to the house, place your pole against the kitchen door, higher—stop at that. 86—45—6."

M

"I say there," again vociferated the planter, "get out of my yard."

"I'm afraid we will have to go right through the house;" soliloquized Beau.

"I'm d——d if you do," exclaimed the planter.

Beau now looked up for the first time, accosting the planter with a courteous—

"Good day, sir."

"Good d—l, sir; you are committing a trespass."

"My dear friend," replied Beau, "public duty, imperative—no trespass—surveying railroad—State job—your house in the way. Must take off one corner, sir,—the kitchen part—least value—leave the parlour—delightful room to see the cars rush by twelve times a day—make you accessible to market."

Beau, turning to the nigger, cried out—

"Put the pole against the kitchen door again—so, 85."

"I say, stranger," interrupted the planter, "I guess you ain't dined. As dinner's up, suppose you come in, and we'll talk the matter over."

Beau, delighted with the proposition, immediately acceded, not having tasted cooked provisions that day.

"Now," said the planter, while Beau was paying marked attention to a young turkey, "it's mighty inconvenient to have one's homestead smashed up, without so much as asking the liberty. And more than that, if there's law to be had, it shan't be did either."

"Pooh! nonsense, my dear friend," replied Beau, "it's the law that says the railroad must be laid through kitchens. Why we have gone through seventeen kitchens and eight parlours in the last eight miles—people don't like it, but then it's law, and there's no alternative, except the party persuades the surveyor to move a little to the left, and as curves costs money most folks let it go through the kitchen."

"Cost something, eh?" said the planter, eagerly catching at the bait thrown out for him. "Would not mind a trifle. You see I don't oppose the road, but if you'll turn to the left and it won't be much expense, why I'll stand it."

"Let me see," said Beau, counting his fingers, "forty and forty is eighty, and one hundred. Yes, two hundred

dollars will do it." Unrolling a large map, intersected
with lines running in every direction, he continued—"There
is your house, and here's the road. Air line. You see to
move to the left we must excavate this hill. As we are
desirous of retaining the goodwill of parties residing on the
route, I'll agree on the part of the company to secure the
alteration, and prevent your house from being molested."

The planter revolved the matter in his mind for a moment
and exclaimed :—

" You'll guarantee the alteration ? "

" Give a written document."

" Then it's a bargain."

The planter without more delay gave Beau an order on
his city factor for the stipulated sum, and received in exchange a written document, guaranteeing the freedom of
the kitchen from any encroachment by the C. L. R. R. Co.

Before leaving, Beau took the planter on one side and
requested him not to disclose their bargain until after the
railroad was built.

" You see, it mightn't exactly suit the views of some
people—partiality, you know."

The last remark, accompanied by a suggestive wink, was
returned by the planter in a similar demonstration of
owlishness.

Beau resumed his theodolite, drove a few stakes on the
hill opposite, and proceeded onward in the fulfilment of his
duties. As his light figure receded into obscurity and the
distance, the planter caught a sound vastly like 40—40—
120—200.—And that was the last he ever heard of the
railroad.

Appleton's American Railway Anecdote Book.

MR. FRANK BUCKLAND'S FIRST RAILWAY JOURNEY.

Mr. Spencer Walpole remarks :—" Of Mr. Buckland's
Christ Church days many good stories are told. Almost
every one has heard of the bear which he kept at his rooms,
of its misdemeanours, and its rustication. Less familiar,
perhaps, is the story of his first journey by the Great
Western. The dons, alarmed at the possible consequences
of a railway to London, would not allow Brunel to bring
the line nearer than to Didcot. Dean Buckland in vain

protested against the folly of this decision, and the line was kept out of harm's way at Didcot. But, the very day on which it was opened, Mr. Frank Buckland, with one or two other undergraduates, drove over to Didcot, travelled up to London, and returned in time to fulfil all the regulations of the university. The Dean, who was probably not altogether displeased at the joke, told the story to his friends who had prided themselves in keeping the line from Oxford. 'Here,' he said, 'you have deprived us of the advantage of a railway, and my son has been up to London.'"

SCENE BEFORE A SUB-COMMITTEE ON STANDING ORDERS. PETITIONING AGAINST A RAILWAY BILL, 1846.

"Well, Snooks," began the Agent for the Promoters, in cross-examination, "You signed the petition against the Bill—aye?"

"Yees, zur. I zined summit, zur."

"But that petition—did you sign that petition?"

"I do'ant nar, zur; I zined zummit, zur."

"But don't you know the contents of the petition?"

"Tho what, zur?"

"The contents; what's in it."

"Oa! Noa, zur."

"You don't know what's in the petition!—Why, ain't you the petitioner himself?"

"Noa, zur, I doan't nar that I be, zur."

["Snooks! Snooks! Snooks!" issued a voice from a stout and benevolent-looking elderly gentleman from behind, "How can you say so, Snooks? It's your petition." The prompting, however, seemed to produce but little impression upon him for whom it was intended, whatever effect it may have had upon the minds of those whose ears it reached, but for whose service it was not intended].

"Really, Mr. Chairman," observed the Agent for the Bill, who appeared to have no idea of *Burking* the inquiry, "this is growing interesting."

"The interest is all on your side," remarked the Agent for the petition (against the Bill).

"Now, Snooks," continued the Agent for the Bill, "apply your mind to the questions I shall put to you, and let me caution you to reply to them truly and honestly.   Now, tell me—Who got you to sign this petition?"

"I object to the question," interposed the Agent for the petition, "The matter altogether is descending into mean, trivial, and unnecessary details, which I am surprised my friend opposite should attempt to trouble the Committee with."

"I can readily understand, sir," replied the other, "why my friend is so anxious to get rid of this inquiry—simple and short as it will be; but I trust, sir, that you will consider it of sufficient importance to allow it to proceed.   I purpose to put only a few questions more on this extraordinary petition against the Bill (the bare meaning of the name of which the petitioner does not seem to understand) for the purpose of eliciting some further information respecting it."

The Committee being thus appealed to by both parties, inclined their heads for a few moments in order to facilitate a communication in whispers, and then decided that the inquiry might proceed.   It was evident that the matter had excited an interest in the minds and breasts of the honourable members of the Committee; created as much perhaps by the extreme mean and poverty-stricken appearance of the witness—a miserable, dirty, and decrepit old man—as by the disclosures he had already made.

"Well, Snooks, I was about to ask you (when my friend interrupted me) who got you to sign the petition, or that zummit as you call it?"

"Some genelmen, zur."

"Who were they—do you know their names?"

"Noa, zur, co'ant say I do nar 'em a', zur."

"But do you know any of them, was that gentleman behind you one?"

[The gentleman referred to was the fine benevolent-looking individual who had previously kindly endeavoured to assist the witness in his answers, and who stood the present scrutiny with marked composure and complaisance].

"Yees, zur, he war one on 'em."

"Do you know his name?"

"Noa, zur, I doant; but he be one of the railway genelmen."

"What did he say to you, when he requested you to sign the petition?"

"He said I ware to zine (pointing to the petition) that zummit."

"When and where, pray, did you sign it?"

"A lot o' railway genelmen kum to me ou Sunday night last; and they wo' make me do it, zur."

"On Sunday night last, aye!"

"What, on Sunday night!" exclaimed one honourable member on the extreme right of the Chairman, with horror depicted on his countenance; "Are you sure, witness, that it was done in the evening of a Sabbath?"

"The honourable member asks you, whether you are certain that you were called upon by the railway gentlemen to sign the petition on a Sunday evening? I think you told me last Sunday evening."

"Oa, yees, zur; they kum just as we war a garing to chapel."

"Disgraceful, and wrong in the extreme!" ejaculated the honourable member.

"And did not that gentleman (continued the Agent for the Bill), nor any of the railway gentlemen, as you call them, when they requested you to sign, explain the nature and contents of the petition?"

"Noa, zur."

"Then you don't know at this moment what it's for?"

"Noa, zur."

"Of course, therefore, it's not your petition as set forth?"

"I doant nar, zur. I zined zummit."

"Now, answer me, do you object to this line of railway? Have you any dislike to it?"

"O, noa, zur. I shud loak to zee it kum."

"Exactly, you should like to see it made. So you have been led to petition against it, though you are favourable to it?"

The petitioner against the Bill did not appear to comprehend the precise drift of the remark, and his only reply to the wordy fix into which the learned agent had drawn him was made in the dumb-show of scratching with his one disengaged hand (the other being employed in holding his hat) his uncombed head—an operation that created much laughter, which was not damped by the Agent's putting, with a serious face, a concluding question or remark to him to the effect that he presumed he (the witness) had not paid, or engaged to pay, so many guineas a day to his friend on the other side for the prosecution of the opposition against the Bill—had he; yes, or no? The witness's appearance was the only and best answer.

The petition, of course, upon this exposé, was withdrawn.

This, the substance of what actually took place before one of the Sub-Committees on Standing orders will give some idea of the nature of many of the petitions against Railway Bills, especially on technical points. It will serve to show in some measure what heartless mockeries these petitions mostly are; the moral evils they give birth to— and that, even while complaining of errors, they are themselves made up of falsehood.

AN IDEA ON RAILWAYS.

A happy comment on the annihilation of time and space by locomotive agency, is as follows:—A little child who rode fifty miles in a railway train, and then took a coach to her uncle's house, some five miles further, was asked on her arrival if she came by the cars. "We came a little way in the cars, and all the rest of the way in a carriage."

BURNING THE ROAD CLEAR.

It is related of Colonel Thomas A. Scott, that on one occasion, when making one of his swift trips over the American lines under his control, his train was stopped by the wreck of a goods train. There was a dozen heavily loaded covered trucks piled up on the road, and it would take a long time to get help from the nearest accessible point, and probably hours more to get the track cleared by mere force of labour. He surveyed the difficulty, made a rough calculation of the cost of a total destruction of the freight, and promptly made up his mind to burn the road clear. By the time the relief train came the flames had done their work and nothing remained but to patch up a few injuries done to the track so as to enable him to pursue his way.

HARSH TREATMENT OF A MAN OF COLOUR.

My treatment in the use of public conveyances about these times was extremely rough, especially on "The Eastern Railroad," from Boston to Portland. On the road, as on many others, there was a mean, dirty, and uncomfortable car set apart for coloured travellers, called the "Jim Crow" car. Regarding this as the fruit of slaveholding prejudice, and being determined to fight the spirit of slavery wherever I might find it, I resolved to avoid this car, though it sometimes required some courage to do so. The coloured people generally accepted the situation, and complained of me as making matters worse rather than better, by refusing to submit to this proscription. I, however, persisted, and sometimes was soundly beaten by the conductor and brakeman. On one occasion, six of these "fellows of the baser sort," under the direction of the conductor, set out to eject me from my seat. As usual, I had purchased a first-class ticket, and paid the required sum for it, and on the requirement of the conductor to leave, refused to do so, when he called on these men "to snake me out." They attempted to obey with an air which plainly told me they relished the job. They, however, found me *much attached* to my seat, and in removing me tore away two or three of the surrounding ones, on which I held with a firm grasp, and did the car no service in some respects. I was strong and muscular, and the seats were not then so firmly attached or of as solid make as now. The result was that Stephen A. Chase, superintendent of the road, ordered all passenger trains to pass through Lynn, where I then lived, without stopping. This was a great inconvenience to the people, large numbers of whom did business in Boston, and at other points of the road. Led on, however, by James N. Buffum, Jonathon Buffum, Christopher Robinson, William Bassett, and others, the people of Lynn stood bravely by me, and denounced the railway management in emphatic terms. Mr. Chase made reply that a railroad corporation was neither a religious nor a reformatory body; and that the road was run for the accommodation of the public; and that it required the exclusion of the coloured people from its cars. With an air of triumph he told us that we ought not to expect a railroad company to be better than the Evangelical Church, and that until the churches abolished the "negro pew," we ought not to expect the railroad company to abolish the negro car. This argument was certainly good enough as against the Church, but good for nothing as against the demands of justice and equity. My old and dear friend, J. N. Buffum, made a point against the company that they "often allowed dogs and monkeys to ride in first-class cars, and yet excluded a man like Frederick Douglass!" In a very few years this barbarous practice was put away, and I think there have been no instances of such exclusion during the past thirty years; and coloured people now, everywhere in New England, ride upon equal terms with other passengers.

—Life and Times of Frederick Douglass.

QUITE TOO CLEVER

The elder Dumas was at the railway station, just starting to join his yacht at Marseilles. Several friends had accompanied him, to say good-bye. Suddenly he was informed that he had a hundred and fifty kilogrammes excess of luggage. "Ho, ho!" cried Dumas. "How many kilogrammes are allowed?" "Thirty for each person," was the reply. Silently he made a mental calculation, and then in a tone of triumph bade his secretary take places for five. "In that way," he explained, "we shall have no excess."

A DIFFICULTY · SOLVED.

Among the improvements that have been carried out at Windsor during the autumn, has been an entire alteration in the draining of the Home Park about Frogmore. New drains have been laid, and the waste earth has been used to level the ground. This portion of the Royal domain was almost wild at the beginning of the present reign. It consisted of fields, with low hedges and deep ditches, and was intersected by a road, on which stood several cottages and a public-house. It was quite an eyesore, and Prince Albert was at his wit's end to know how to convert it into a park and exclude the public, as before this could be done, it was necessary to make a new road in place of the one it was desired to abolish, and altogether a large outlay was inevitable; and even in those days, it was out of the question to apply to Parliament for the amount required, which, I believe, was about £80,000.

The difficulty, however, was solved in rather a strange way. In the early days of railroads they were looked upon as nuisances, and the authorities at Windsor Castle were firmly resolved that no line should approach the Royal borough, in which resolution they were warmly supported by the equally stupid and short-sighted managers of Eton College. Although the inhabitants sighed for a railway, none was brought nearer than Slough. At this moment, when the park question was being agitated, the South Western Directors brought forward a proposition that they should make a line into Windsor, running along one side of the Home Park, and right under the Castle. This audacious idea was regarded with indignation at the Castle, until a hint was received that possibly, if Royal interest were forthcoming to support the plan, the Company might be able to facilitate the proposed alterations; and it then came out, strangely enough, they had fixed the precise sum needed (£80,000) as compensation for the disturbance of the Royal property. No more was heard of the objections to the scheme, which had been so vehemently denounced a few days before, but, no sooner did it transpire that the South-Western plan was not opposed by the Castle interest than down came the Great-Western authorities in a fever of indignation, for it appeared they had received an explicit promise that, if Windsor was ever desecrated by a railway, they should have the preference. So resolute was their attitude, that so far as I remember, the sitting of Parliament was actually protracted in order that their Bill might be passed; not that they got it without paying, for they gave £20,000 for an old stable and yard which were required for their station, and which happened to stand on Crown property. Things were sometimes managed strangely enough in those days.

—*Truth*, Dec. 29, 1881.

AN EXACTING LADY.

A lady of fashion with a pugdog and a husband entered the train at Paddington the other day. There were in the carriage but two persons, a well-known Professor and his wife; yet the lady of fashion coveted, not indeed his chair, but his seat. "I wish to sit by the window, sir," she said imperiously, and he had to move accordingly. "No, sir, that won't do," she said, as he meekly took the next place. "I can't have a stranger sitting close to me. My husband must sit where you are."

Gentleman's Magazine.

AMERICAN PATIENCE AND IMPERTURBABILITY.

About an hour after midnight, on our journey from Boston to Albany, we came to a sudden pause where no station was visible; and immediately, very much to my surprise, the engine-driver, conductor, and several passengers were seen sallying forth with lanterns, and hastening down the embankment on our right. "What are they going to do now?" said I to a gentleman, who, like myself, kept his seat. "Only to take a look at some cars that were smashed this morning," was the reply. On opening the window to observe the state of affairs, as well as the darkness would allow, there, to be sure, at the bottom and along the side of the high bank, lay an unhappy train, just as it had been upset. The locomotive on its side was partly buried in the earth; and the cars which had followed it in its descent lay in a confused heap behind. On the top of the bank, near to us, the last car of all stood obliquely on end, with its hind wheels in the air in a somewhat grotesque and threatening attitude. All was now still and silent. The killed and wounded, if there were any, had been removed. No living thing was visible but the errant engineer and others from our train clambering with lanterns in their hands over a prostrate wreck, and with heedless levity passing critical remarks on the catastrophe. Curiosity being satisfied all resumed their places, and the train moved on without a murmur of complaint as to the unnecessary, and, considering the hour, very undesirable delay. I allude to the circumstance, as one of a variety of facts that fell

within my observation, illustrative of the singular degree
of patience and imperturbability with which railway travellers in America submit uncomplainingly to all sorts of
detentions on their journey.

Things as they are in America, by W. Chambers, 1853.

A WIDE-AWAKE CONDUCTOR.

Dana Krum, one of the conductors on the Erie Railway,
was approached before train time by an unknown man, who
spoke to him as if he had known him for years. "I say,
Dana," said he, "I have forgotten my pass, and I want to
go to Susquehanna; I am a fireman on the road, you
know." But the conductor told him he ought to have a
pass with him. It was the safest way. Pretty soon, Dana
came along to collect tickets. Seeing his man, he spoke
when he reached him. "Say, my friend, have you got the
time with you?" "Yes," said he, as he pulled out a watch.
"It is twenty minutes past nine." "Oh, it is, is it? Now,
if you don't show me your pass or fare, I will stop the train.
There is no railway man that I ever saw who would say
'Twenty minutes past nine.' He would say, 'Nine-twenty.'"
He settled.

A KID-GLOVED SAMSON.

A correspondent of the *Chicago Journal* relates the following
feat of strength, to which he was witness:—

"On Sunday, about nine o'clock A.M., as the train westward
was within three or four miles of Chicago, on the Fort
Wayne road, a horse was discovered on the stilt-work
between the rails. The train was stopped, and workmen were
sent to clear the track. It was then discovered that the
body of the horse was resting on the sleepers. His legs
having passed through the open spaces, were too short to
reach the ground. Boards and rails were brought, and the
open space in front of the horse filled up, making a plank
road for him in case he should be got up, and by means of
ropes one of his fore feet was raised, and there matters came
to a halt. It seemed that no strength or stratagem could
avail to release the animal. Levers of boards were splintered,
and the men tugged at the ropes in vain, when a passenger,

who was looking quietly on, stepped forward, leisurely slipped off a pair of tinted kids, seized the horse by the tail, and with tremendous force hurled him forward on the plank road. No one assisted, and, indeed, the whole thing was done so quickly that assistance was impossible. The horse walked away looking foolish, and casting suspicious side-glances towards his caudal extremity. The lookers-on laughed and shouted, while the stranger resumed his kids, muttering something about the inconvenience of railway delays, lit a cigar, and walked slowly into the smoking car. He was finely formed, of muscular appearance, was very fashionably dressed, wore a moustache and whiskers of an auburn or reddish colour, and to all questions as to who he was, only answered that he was a Pennsylvanian travelling westward for his health. The horse would certainly weigh at least twelve hundred."

A RAILWAY TRAIN TURNED INTO A MAN-TRAP.

A branch of the Bombay presidency runs through a wild region, the inhabitants of which are unsophisticated savages, addicted to thievery. The first day the line was opened a number of these Arcadians conspired to intercept the train, and have a glorious loot. To accomplish their object they placed some trunks of trees across the rails; but the engine driver, keeping a very sharp look out, as it happened to be his first trip on the line in question, descried the trunks while yet they were at a considerable distance from him. The breaks were then put on, and when the locomotive had approached within a couple of feet of the trunks it was brought to a standstill. Then, instantaneously, like Roderick Dhu's clansmen starting from the heather, natives, previously invisible, swarmed up on all sides, and, crowding into the carriages, began to pillage and plunder everything they could lay their hands upon. While they were thus engaged, the guard gave the signal to the driver, who at once reversed his engine and put it to the top of its speed. The reader may judge of the consternation of the robbers when they found themselves whirled backwards at a pace that rendered escape impossible. Some poor fellows that attempted it were killed on the spot.

—*Central India Times*, June 22, 1867.

THE RULING OCCUPATION STRONG ON SUNDAY.

In an Episcopal church in the north, not one hundred miles from Keith, a porter employed during the week at the railway station, does duty on Sunday by blowing the bellows of the organ. The other Sunday, wearied by the long hours of railway attendance, combined, it may be, with the soporific effects of a dull sermon, he fell sound asleep during the service, and so remained when the pealing of the organ was required. He was suddenly and rather rudely awakened by another official when apparently dreaming of an approaching train, as he started to his feet and roared out, with all the force and shrillness of stentorian lungs and habit, "Change here for Elgin, Lossiemouth, and Burghead." The effect upon the congregation, sitting in expectation of a concord of sweet sounds, may be imagined—it is unnecessary to describe it.

—*Dumfries Courier*, 1866.

THE GOOD THINGS OF RAILWAY ACCIDENTS.

We have always thought that, except to lawyers and railway carriage and locomotive builders, railway accidents were great misfortunes, but it is evident we were wrong and we hasten to acknowledge our error. Speaking on Thursday with a respectable broker about the heavy damages (£2,000) given the day before on account of the Tottenham accident against the Eastern Counties Company in the Court of Exchequer, he observed, "it is rather good when these things happen as it moves the stock. I have had an order for some days to buy Eastern Counties at 56 and could not do it, but this verdict has sent them down one per cent., and enabled me now to buy it." With all our railway experience we never dreamt of such a benefit as this accruing from railway accidents, but it is evidently among the possibilities.

—*Herepath's Railway Journal*, June 7th, 1860.

BENEFICIAL EFFECT OF A RAILWAY ACCIDENT.

A gentleman who was in a railway collision in 1869, wrote to the *Times* in November of that year. After stating that he had been threatened with a violent attack of rheumatic fever; in fact, he observed, "my condition so alarmed me, and my dread of a sojourn in a Manchester hotel bed for two or three months was so great, that I resolved to make a bold sortie and, well wrapped up, start for London by the 3.30 p.m. Midland fast train. From the time of leaving that station to the time of the collision, my heart was going at express speed; my weak body was in a profuse perspiration; flashes of pain announced that the muscular fibres were under the tyrannical control of rheumatism, and I was almost beside myself with toothache. From the moment of the collision to the present hour no ache, pain, sweat, or tremor has troubled me in the slightest degree, and instead of being, as I expected, and indeed intended, in bed drinking *tinct. aurantii*, or absorbing through my pores oil of horse-chestnut, I am conscientiously bound to be at my office bodily sound. Don't print my name and address, or the Midland Company may come down upon me for compensation."

AN EARLY MORNING RIDE TO THE RAILWAY STATION.

In the course of his peregrinations, the railway traveller may find himself in some out-of-the-way place, where no regular vehicle can be obtained to convey him to the station, and this *contretemps* is aggravated when the time of departure happens to be early in the morning. Captain B——, a man of restless energy and adventurous spirit, emerged early one morning from a hovel in a distant village, where from stress of weather he had been compelled to pass the night. It was just dawn of day, and within an hour of the train he wished to go by would start from the station, about six miles distant. He had with him a portmanteau, which it would be impossible for him to carry within the prescribed time, but which he could not very well leave behind. Pondering on what he should do, his eye lighted on a likely looking horse grazing in a field hard by, while in the next field there was a line extended between two posts, for the purpose of drying clothes upon. The sight of these objects soon suggested the plan for him to adopt. In an instant he detached the line, and then taking a piece of bread from his pocket, coaxed the animal to approach him. Captain

B—— was an adept in the management of horses, and as a rough rider, perhaps, had no equal. In a few seconds he had, by the aid of a portion of the line, arranged his portmanteau pannier-wise across the horse's back, and forming a bridle with the remaining portion of the line; he led his steed into the lane, and sprang upon his back. The horse rather relished the trip than otherwise, and what with the unaccustomed burden, and the consciousness that he was being steered by a knowing hand, he sped onwards at a terrific pace. While in mid career, one of the mounted police espied the captain coming along the road at a distance; recognizing the horse, but not knowing the rider, and noticing also the portmanteau, and the uncouth equipment, this rural guardian of the peace came to the conclusion that this was a case of robbery and horse stealing; and as the captain neared him, he endeavoured to stop him, and stretched forth his hand to seize the improvised bridle, but the gallant equestrian laughed to scorn the impotent attempt, and shook him off, and shot by him. Thus foiled, the policeman had nothing to do than to give chase; so turning his horse's head he followed in full cry. The clatter and shouts of pursuer and pursued brought forth the inhabitants of the cottages as they passed, and many of these joined in the chaise. Never since Turpin's ride to York, or Johnny Gilpin's ride to Edmonton, had there been such a commotion caused by an equestrian performance. To make a long story short, the captain reached the station in ample time; an explanation ensued; a handsome apology was tendered to the patrol, and a present equally handsome was forwarded, together with the abstracted property, to the joint owner of the horse and the clothes-line.

CHEAP FARES.

In the year 1868. Mr. Raphael Brandon brought out a book called *Railways and the Public*. In it he proposes that the railways should be purchased and worked by the government; and that passengers, like letters, should travel any distance at a fixed charge. He calculates that a three-penny stamp for third-class, a sixpenny stamp for second-class, and a shilling stamp for first-class, should take a passenger any distance whether long or short. With the adoption of the scheme, he believes, such an impetus would be given to passenger traffic that the returns would amount to more than double what they are at present. There may be flaws in Mr. Brandon's theory, yet it may be within the bounds of possibility that some great innovator may rise up and do for the travelling public by way of organization what Sir Rowland Hill has done for the postage of the country by the penny stamp.

WHAT ARE YOU GOING TO DO?

The above question was asked by a man of his friend who had been injured in a railway accident, "I am first going in for repairs, and then for *damages*," was the answer.

REPROOF FOR SWEARING.

The manager of one of the great Indian railways, in addressing a European subordinate given to indulge in needless strong language, wrote as follows:—"Dear sir, it is with extreme regret that I have to bring to your notice that I observed very unprofessional conduct on your part this morning when making a trial trip. I allude to the abusive language you used to the drivers and others. This I consider an unwarrantable assumption of my duties and functions, and, I may say, rights and privileges. Should you wish to abuse any of our employés, I think it will be best in future to do so in regular form, and I beg to point out what I consider this to be. You will please to submit to me, in writing, the form of oath you wish to use, when, if it meets my approval, I shall at once sanction it; but if not, I shall refer the same to the directors; and, in the course of a few weeks, their decision will be known. Perhaps, to save time, it might be as well for you to submit a list of the expletives generally in use by you, and I can then at once refer those to which I object to the directors for their decision. But, pending that, you will please to understand that all cursing and swearing at drivers and others engaged on the traffic arrangements in which you may wish to indulge must be done in writing, and through me. By adopting this course you will perceive how much responsibility you will save yourself, and how very much the business of the company will be expedited, and its interests promoted."

N

THE BULLY RIGHTLY SERVED.

In the *Railway Traveller's Handy Book*, there is an account of an occurrence which took place on the Eastern Counties line :—"A big hulking fellow, with bully written on his face, took his seat in a second-class carriage, and forthwith commenced insulting everybody by his words and gestures. He was asked to desist, but only responded with language more abusive. The guard was then appealed to, who told him to mind what he was about, shut the door, and cried 'all right.' Thus encouraged the miscreant continued his disgraceful conduct, and became every moment more outrageous. In one part of the carriage were four farmers sitting who all came from the same neighbourhood, and to whom every part along the line was well known. One of these wrote on a slip of paper these words, 'Let us souse him in Chuckley Slough.' This paper was handed from one to the other, and each nodded assent. Now, Chuckley Slough was a pond near one of the railway stations, not very deep, but the waters of which were black, muddy, and somewhat repellant to the olfactory nerves. The station was neared and arrived at; in the meantime the bully's conduct became worse and worse. As they emerged from the station, one of the farmers, aforesaid, said to the fellow, 'Now, will you be quiet?' 'No, I won't,' was the answer. 'You won't won't you?' asked a second farmer. 'You're determined you won't?' inquired a third. 'You're certain you won't?' asked the fourth. To all of which queries the response was in negatives, with certain inelegant expletives added thereto. 'Then,' said the four farmers speaking as one man, and rising in a body, 'out you go.' So saying, they seized the giant form of the wretch, who struggled hard to escape but to no purpose; they forced him to the window, and while the train was still travelling at a slow pace, and Chuckley Slough appeared to view, they without more ado thrust the huge carcass through the window, and propelling it forward with some force, landed it exactly in the centre of the black, filthy slough. The mingled cries and oaths of the man were something fearful to hear; his attempts at extrication and incessant slipping still deeper in the mire, something ludicrous to witness; all the passengers watched him with feelings of gratified revenge, and the last that was seen of him was a huge black mass, having no traces of humanity about it, crawling up the bank in a state of utter prostration. In this instance the remedy was rather a violent one; but less active measures had been found to fail, and there can be little doubt that this man took care ever afterwards not to run the risk of a similar punishment by indulging in conduct of a like nature."

LIABILITY OF COMPANIES FOR DELAY OF TRAINS.

There have been cases where claims have been made and recovered in courts of law for loss arising from delay in the arrival of trains, but the law does not render the company's liability unlimited. A remarkable case occurred not long since. A Mr. Le Blanche sued the London and North-Western Company for the cost of a special train to Scarborough, which he had ordered in consequence of his being brought from Liverpool to Leeds, too late for the ordinary train from Leeds to Scarborough. A judgment in the county court was given in favour of the applicant.

The railway company appealed to the superior court, and the points raised were argued by able counsel, when the decision of the county court judge was confirmed. The company was determined to put the case to the utmost possible test, and on appealing to the Supreme Court of Judicature the judgment was reversed, the decision being to the effect that, whilst there was some evidence of wilful delay, the measure of damage was wrong.

— *Our Railways*, by Joseph Parsloe.

THE DYING ENGINE DRIVER.

Doubts have been expressed whether our iron ships will ever be regarded in the same affectionate way as " liners " used to be regarded by our " old salts." It has been supposed that the latest creations of science will not nourish sentiment. The following anecdote shows, however, as romantic an attachment to iron as was ever manifested towards wood. On the Great Western Railway, the broad gauge and the narrow gauge are mixed; the former still existing to the delight of travellers by the " Flying

Dutchman," whatever economical shareholders may have to say to the contrary. The officials who have been longest on the staff also cling to the broad gauge, like faithful royalists to a fast disappearing dynasty. The other day an ancient guard on this line was knocked down and run over by an engine; and though good enough medical attendance was at hand, had skill been of any use, the dying man wished to see "the company's" doctor. The gentleman, a man much esteemed by all the employés, was accordingly sent for. "I am glad you came to see me start, doctor, (as I hope) by the up-train," said the poor man. "I am only sorry I can do nothing for you, my good fellow," answered the other. "I know that; it is all over with me. But there!—I'm glad it was *not one of them narrow-gauge engines that did it!*"   —*Gentleman's Magazine.*

"DOWN BRAKES," OR FORCE OF HABIT.

An Illinois captain, lately a railroad conductor, was drilling a squad, and while marching them by flank, turned to speak to a friend for a moment. On looking again toward his squad, he saw they were in the act of "butting up" against a fence. In his hurry to halt them, he cried, "Down brakes! Down Brakes!"

TRENT STATION.

This station on the Midland system is often a source of no little perplexity to strangers. Sir Edward Beckett thus humorously describes it:—"You arrive at Trent. Where that is I cannot tell. I suppose it is somewhere near the river Trent, but then the Trent is a very long river. You get out of your train to obtain refreshment, and having taken it, you endeavour to find your train and your carriage. But whether it is on this side or that, and whether it is going north or south, this way or that way, you cannot tell. Bewildered, you frantically rush into your carriage; the train moves off round a curve, and then you are horrified to see some lights glaring in front of you, and you are in immediate expectation of a collision, when your fellow-passenger calms your fears by telling you that they are only the tail lamps of your own train."

STEEL RAILS.

The first steel rail was made in 1857, by Mushet, at the Ebbw-Vale Iron Co.'s works in South Wales. It was rolled from cast blooms of Bessemer steel and laid down at Derby, England, and remained sixteen years, during which time 250 trains and at least 250 detatched engines and tenders passed over it daily. Taking 312 working days in each year, we have the total of 1,252,000 trains and 1,252,000 detached engines and tenders which passed over it from the time it was first laid before it was removed to be worked over.

The substitution of steel for iron, to an extent rendered possible by the Bessemer process, has worked a great and abiding change in the condition of our ways, giving greater endurance both in respect of wear and in resistance to breaking strains and jars.

Two steel rails of twenty-one feet in length were laid on the 2nd of May, 1862, at the Chalk Farm Bridge, side by side with two ordinary rails. After having outlasted sixteen faces of the ordinary rails, the steel ones were taken up and examined, and it was found that at the expiration of three years and three months, the surface was evenly worn to the extent of only a little more than a quarter of an inch, and to all appearance they were capable of enduring a great deal more work. The result of this trial was to induce the London and North Western to enter very extensively into the employment of steel rails."

Knight's Dictionary of Mechanics.

CURIOUS CASUALTY.

Out of three truck loads of cattle on the Great Western Railway two of the animals were struck dead by the lightning on Monday afternoon, July 5, 1852, not very far from Swindon. What renders it remarkable is, that one animal only in each of the two trucks was struck, and five or six animals in each escaped uninjured. · The animal killed in one of the trucks was a bull, the cows escaping injury, and in the other truck it was a bull or an ox that was killed.

GEORGE STEPHENSON'S WEDDING PRESENT.

A correspondent, writing to the *Derbyshire Courier* the week following the Stephenson Centenary celebration at Chesterfield, remarks:—"The other day I met a kindly and venerable gentleman who possesses quite a fund of anecdotes relating to the Stephensons, father and son. It appears we have, or had, relations of old George residing in Derby. Years ago, says my friend, an old gentleman, who by his appearance and carriage was stamped as a man distinguished among his fellow-men, was inquiring on Derby platform for a certain engine-driver in the North Midland or the Birmingham and Derby service, whose name he gave. On the driver being pointed out, the gentleman, with the rough but pleasing north-country burr in his voice, said, after asking his name, "Did you marry —— ?" "Yes, sir." "Then she's my niece, and I hope you'll make her a good husband. I have not had the chance of giving you a wedding present until now." Then slipping into his hand a bank note for £50, he talked of other matters. The joy of the engine-driver at receiving so welcome a present, was not greater than being recognised and kindly received by his wife's illustrious uncle, George Stephenson."

THE POLITE IRISHMAN.

It's a small matter, but a gentleman always feels angry at himself after he has given up his seat, in a railway car, to a female who lacks the good manners to acknowledge the favour. The following "hint" to the ladies will show that a trifle of politeness properly spread on, often has a happy effect.

The seats were all full, one of which was occupied by a rough-looking Irishman; and at one of the stations a couple of evidently well-bred and intelligent young ladies came in to procure seats, but seeing no vacant ones. were about to go into a back car, when Patrick rose hastily, and offered them his seat, with evident pleasure. "But you will have no seat yourself?" responded one of the young ladies with a smile, hesitating, with true politeness, as to accepting it. "Never ye mind *that!*" said the Hibernian, "ye'r welcome to 't! I'd ride upon the cow-catcher till New York, any time, for a smile from such *jintl-manly* ladies;" and retreated hastily to the next car, amid the cheers of those who had witnessed the affair.

AN ENTERTAINING COMPANION.

Once, during a tour in the Western States, writes Mr. Florence, the actor, an incident occurred in which I rather think I played the victim. We were *en route* from Cleveland to Cincinnati, an eight or ten-hour journey. After seeing my wife comfortably seated, I walked forward to the smoking car, and, taking the only unoccupied place, pulled out my cigar case, and offered a cigar to my next neighbour. He was about sixty years of age, gentlemanly in appearance, and of a somewhat reserved and bashful mien. He gracefully accepted the cigar, and in a few minutes we were engaged in conversation.

"Are you going far west?" I inquired.

"Merely so far as Columbus." (Columbus, I may explain is the capital of Ohio.) "And you, sir?" he added, interrogatively.

"I am journeying toward Cincinnati. I am a theatrical man, and play there to-morrow night." I was a young man then, and fond of avowing my profession.

"Oh, indeed! Your face seemed familiar to me as you entered the car. I am confident we have met before."

"I have acted in almost every State in the Union," said I. "Mrs. Florence and I are pretty generally known throughout the north-west."

"Bless me?" said the stranger in surprise. "I have seen you act many times, sir, and the recollection of Mrs. Florence's 'Yankee Girl,' with her quaint songs, is still fresh in my memory."

"Do you propose remaining long in Columbus?"

"Yes, for seven years," replied my companion.

Thus we chatted for an hour or two. At length my attention was attracted to a little, red-faced man, with small sharp eyes, who sat immediately opposite us and amused himself by sucking the knob of a large walking stick which he carried caressingly in his hand. He had more than once glanced at me in a knowing manner, and now and then gave a sly wink and shake of the head at me, as much as to say, "Ah, old fellow, I know you, too."

These attentions were so marked that I finally asked my companion if he had noticed them.

"That poor man acts like a lunatic," said I, *sotto voce*.

"A poor half-witted fellow, possibly," replied my fellow-traveller. "In your travels through the country, however, Mr. Florence, you must have often met such strange characters."

We had now reached Crestline, the dinner station, and, after thanking the stranger for the agreeable way in which he had enabled me to pass the journey up to this point, I asked him if he would join Mrs. Florence and myself at dinner. This produced an extraordinary series of grimaces and winks from the red-faced party aforesaid The invitation to dinner was politely declined.

The repast over, our train sped on toward Cincinnati. I told my wife that in the smoking car I had met a most entertaining gentleman, who was well posted in theatricals, and was on his way to Columbus. She suggested that I should bring him into our car, and present him to her. I returned to the smoking car and proposed that the gentleman should accompany me to see Mrs. Florence. The proposal made the red-faced man undergo a species of spasmodic convulsions which set the occupants of the car into roars of laughter.

"No, I thank you," said my friend, "I feel obliged to you for the courtesy, but I prefer the smoking car. Have you another cigar?"

"Yes," said I, producing another Partaga.

I again sat by his side, and once more our conversation began, and we were quite fraternal. We talked about theatres and theatricals, and then adverted to political economy, the state of the country, finance and commerce in turn, our intimacy evidently affording intense amusement to the foxy-faced party near us.

Finally the shrill sound of the whistle and the entrance of the conductor indicated that we had arrived at Columbus, and the train soon arrived at the station.

"Come," said the red-faced individual, now rising from his seat and tapping my companion on the shoulder, "This is your station, old man."

My friend rose with some difficulty, dragging his hitherto concealed feet from under the seat, when, for the first time, I discovered that he was shackled, and was a prisoner in charge of the Sheriff, going for seven years to the state prison at Columbus.

NOVEL ATTACK.

Auxerre, November 15th, 1851.—Last week, at the moment when a railway tender was passing along the line from Saint Florentin to Tonnerre, a wolf boldly leaped upon it and attacked the stoker. The man immediately seized his shovel and repulsed the aggressor, who fell upon the rail and was instantly crushed to pieces.

—*National.*

WOLVES ON A RAILWAY.

In 1867, "A cattle train on the Luxemburg Railway was stopped," says the *Nord*, "two nights back, between Libramont and Poix by the snow. The brakesman was sent forward for aid to clear the line, and while the guard, fireman, engine-driver, and a customs officer were engaged in getting the snow from under the engine they were alarmed by wolves, of which there were five, and which were attracted, no doubt, by the scent of the oxen and sheep cooped up in railed-in carriages. The men had no weapons save the fire utensils belonging to the engine. The wolves remained in a semicircle a few yards distant, looking keenly on. The engine-driver let off the steam and blew the whistle, and lanterns were waved to and fro, but the savage brutes did not move. The men then made their way, followed by the wolves, to the guard's carriage. Three got in safe; whilst the fourth was on the step one of the animals sprang on him, but succeeded only in tearing his coat. They all then made an attack, but were beaten off, one being killed by a blow on the head. Two hours elapsed before assistance arrived, and during that time the wolves made several attacks upon the sheep trucks, but failed to get in. None of the cattle were injured."

ARTEMUS WARD'S SUGGESTION.

"I was once," he remarks, "on a slow California train, and I went to the conductor and suggested that the cow-ketcher was on the wrong end of the train; for I said, 'You will never overtake a cow, you know; but if you'd put it on the other end it might be useful, for now there's nothin' on earth to hinder a cow from walkin' right in and bitin' the folks!'"

COACH VERSUS RAILWAY ACCIDENTS.

A coachman once remarked, "Why you see, sir, if a coach goes over and spills you in the road there you are; but if you are blown up by an engine, where are you?"

BAVARIAN GUARDS AND BAVARIAN BEER.

"In England," says Mr. Wilberforce, "the guard is content to be the servant of the train; in Germany he is in command of the passengers. 'When is the train going on?' asked an Englishman once of a foreign guard. 'Whenever I choose,' was the answer. To judge from the delays the trains make at some of the stations, one would suppose that the guard had uncontrolled power of causing stoppages. You see him chatting with the station-master for several minutes after all the carriages have been shut up, and at last, when the topics of conversation are exhausted, he gives a condescending whistle to the engine-driver. Time seems never to be considered by either guards or passengers. Bavarians always go to the station half-an-hour before the train is due, and their indifference to delay is so well known that the directors can put on their time book 'As the time of departure from small stations cannot be guaranteed, the travellers must be there twenty-five minutes beforehand.'" Mr. Wilberforce should not have omitted to mention the main cause of these delays, which appears at the same time to constitute the final cause of a Bavarian's existence—Beer. Guards and passengers alike require alcoholic refreshment at least at every other station. At Culmbach, the fountain of the choicest variety of Bavarian beer, the practice had risen to such a head that, as we found last summer, government had been forced to interfere. To prevent trains from dallying if there was beer to drink at Culmbach was obviously impossible. The temptation itself was removed; and no beer was any longer allowed to be sold at that fated railway station, by reason of its being so superlatively excellent.

—*Saturday Review*, 1864.

THE RAILWAY SWITCH-TENDER AND HIS CHILD.

On one of the railroads in Prussia, a few years ago, a switch-tender was just taking his place, in order to turn a coming train approaching in a contrary direction. Just at this moment, on turning his head, he discerned his little son playing on the track of the advancing engine. What could he do? Thought was quick at such a moment of peril! He might spring to his child and rescue him, but he could not do this and turn the switch in time, and for want of that hundreds of lives might be lost. Although in sore trouble, he could not neglect his greater duty, but exclaiming with a loud voice to his son, "Lie down," he laid hold of the switch, and saw the train safely turned on to its proper track. His boy, accustomed to obedience, did as his father commanded him, and the fearful heavy train thundered over him. Little did the passengers dream, as they found themselves quietly resting on that turnout, what terrible anguish their approach had that day caused to one noble heart. The father rushed to where his boy lay, fearful lest he should find only a mangled corpse, but to his great joy and thankful gratitude he found him alive and unharmed. Prompt obedience had saved him. Had he paused to argue, to reason whether it were best—death, and fearful mutilation of body, would have resulted. The circumstances connected with this event were made known to the King of Prussia, who the next day sent for the man and presented him with a medal of honour for his heroism.

VERY COOL.

Some years ago at a railway station a gentleman actually followed a person with a portmanteau, which he thought to be his, but the fellow, unabashed, maintaining it to be his own property, the gentleman returned to inquire after his, and found, when too late, that his first suspicions were correct.

THE BLACK REDSTART.

A railway carriage had been left for some weeks out of use in the station at Giessen, Hesse Darmstadt, in the month of May, 1852, and when the superintendent came to examine the carriage he found that a black redstart had built her nest upon the collision spring; he very humanely retained the carriage in its shed until its use was imperatively demanded, and at last attached it to the train which ran to Frankfort-on-the-Maine, a distance of nearly forty miles. It remained at Frankfort for thirty-six hours, and was then brought back to Giessen, and after one or two short journeys came back again to rest at Giessen, after a period of four days. The young birds were by this time partly fledged, and finding that the parent bird had not deserted her offspring, the superintendent carefully removed the nest to a place of safety, whither the parent soon followed. The young were, in process of time, full fledged and left the nest to shift for themselves. It is evident that one at least of the parent birds must have accompanied the nest in all its journeys, for, putting aside the difficulty which must have been experienced by the parents in watching for every carriage that arrived at Giessen, the nestlings would have perished from hunger during their stay at Frankfort, for everyone who has reared young birds is perfectly aware that they need food every two hours. Moreover, the guard of the train repeatedly saw a red-tailed bird flying about that part of the carriage on which the nest was placed.

STOPPING A RUNAWAY COUPLE.

Captain Galton who some years ago was the government railway inspector, in one of his reports relates the following singular circumstance. "A girl who was in love with the engine-driver of a train, had engaged to run away from her father's house in order to be married. She arranged to leave by a train this man was driving. Her father and brother got intelligence of her intended escape; and having missed catching her as she got into the train, they contrived, whether with or without the assistance of a porter is not very clear, to turn the train through facing points, as it left the station, into a bog." The captain does not pursue the subject further in his report, so that we are left in ignorance as to the success of the plan for stopping a contemplated runaway marriage.

A MADMAN IN A RAILWAY CARRIAGE.

We subjoin from the *Annual Register* for 1864 an account of an alarming occurrence which took place July 4th of that year:—"In one of the third class compartments of the express train leaving King's Cross Station at 9.15 p.m., a tall and strongly-built man, dressed as a sailor, and having a wild and haggard look, took his seat about three minutes before the train started. He was accompanied to the carriage by a woman, whom he afterwards referred to as his wife, and by a man, apparently a cab-driver, of both of whom he took leave when the train was about to start. It had scarcely done so, when, on putting his hand to his pocket, he called out that he had been robbed of his purse, containing £17, and at once began to shout and gesticulate in a manner which greatly alarmed his fellow-travellers, four in number, in the same compartment. He continued to roar and swear with increasing violence for some time, and then made an attempt to throw himself out of the window. He threw his arms and part of his body out of the window, and had just succeeded in placing one of his legs out, when the other occupants of the carriage, who had been endeavouring to keep him back, succeeded in dragging him from the window. Being foiled in this attempt, he turned round upon those who had been instrumental in keeping him back. After a long and severe struggle, which—notwithstanding the speed the train was running at—was heard in the adjoining compartments, the sailor was overcome by the united exertions of the party, and was held down in a prostrate position by two of their number. Though thus secured, he still continued to struggle and shout vehemently, and it was not till some time afterwards, when they managed to bind his hands and strap him to the seat, that the passengers in the compartment felt themselves secure. This train, it may be explained, makes the journey from London to Peterborough, a distance little short of eighty miles, without a single stoppage; and as the scene we have been describing began immediately after the train left London, the expectation of having to pass the time usually occupied between the two stations (one hour and fifty minutes) with such a companion must have been far from agreeable. While the struggle was going on, and even for some time afterwards, almost frantic attempts were made to get the train stopped. The attention of those in the adjoining compartment was readily gained by waving handkerchiefs out of the window, and by-and-by a full explanation of the circumstances was communicated through the aperture in which the lamp that lights both compartments is placed. A request to communicate with the guard was made from one carriage to another for a short distance, but it was found impossible to continue it, and so the occupants of the compartments beyond the one nearest the scene of the disturbance could learn nothing as to its nature, a vague feeling of alarm seized them, and all the way along to Peterborough a succession of shouts of 'Stop the train,' mixed with the frantic screams of female passengers, was kept up. On the arrival of the train at Peterborough the man was released by his captors and placed on the platform. No sooner was he there, however, than he rushed with a renewed outburst of fury on those who had taken the chief part in restraining his violence, and as he kept vociferating that they had robbed him of his money, it was some time before the railway officials could be got to interfere—indeed, it seemed likely for some time that he would be allowed to go on in the train. As remonstrances were made from all quarters to the station-master to take the fellow into custody, he at length agreed, after being furnished with the names and addresses of the other occupants of the carriage, to hand him over to the police. The general impression on those who witnessed the sailor's fury seemed to be that he was labouring under a violent attack of delirium tremens, and he had every appearance of having been drinking hard for some days. Had there been only one or even two occupants of the compartment besides himself, there seems every reason to believe that a much more deadly struggle would have ensued, as he displayed immense strength."

INSURED.

The engine of an ordinary railway train broke down midway between two stations. As an express train was momentarily expected to arrive at the spot, the passengers were urgently called upon to get out of the carriages. A countryman in leather breeches and top-boots, who sat in a corner of one of the carriages, comfortably swathed in a travelling blanket, obstinately refused to budge. In vain the porter begged him to come out, saying the express would reach the spot in a minute, and the train would in all probability be dashed to pieces. The traveller pulled an insurance ticket out of his breeches pocket, exclaiming, "Don't you see I've insured my life?" and with that he set up a horse laugh, and sunk back into his corner. They had to force him out of the train, and an instant afterwards the express ran into it.

A NEW TRICK.

A novel illustration of the ingenuity of thieves has been afforded by an incident reported from the continent. For some time past a North German railway company had been suffering from the repeated loss of goods which were sent by luggage train, and which, notwithstanding all research and precautions, continued to disappear in a very mysterious manner. The secret which the inquiries set on foot had failed to discover was at length revealed by a rather amusing accident. A long box, on one side of which were words equivalent to "This side up," had, in disregard of this caution, been set up on end in the goods shed. Some time afterwards the employés were not a little startled to hear a voice, apparently proceeding from the box in question, begging the hearers to let the speaker out. On opening the lid, the railway officials were surprised and amused to find a man inside standing on his head. In the explanation which followed, the fellow wanted to account for his appearance under such unusual circumstances as due to the result of a wager, but he was given into custody, and it was soon found that the thieves had adopted this method of conveying themselves on to the railway premises, and that during the absence of the employés they had let themselves out of the box which they at once filled with any articles they could lay their hands on, refastened the lid, and then decamped. But for the unfortunate inability of human nature to endure an inverted position for an indefinite period, the ingenious authors of the scheme might have flourished a long time without detection.

A TRAIN STOPPED BY CATERPILLARS.

Colonies and India quotes from a New Zealand paper the following story:—In the neighbourhood of Turakina an army of caterpillars, hundreds of thousands strong, was marching across the railway line, bound for a new field of oats, when the train came along. Thousands of the creeping vermin were crushed by the wheels of the engine, and suddenly the train came to a dead stop. On examination it was found that the wheels of the engine had become so greasy that they kept on revolving without advancing—they could not grip the rails. The guard and the engine driver procured sand and strewed it on the rails, and the train made a fresh start, but it was found that during the stoppage caterpillars in thousands had crawled all over the engine, and all over the carriages inside and out.

TRAVELLING IN RUSSIA.

Of course, travelling in Russia is no longer what it was. During the last quarter of a century a vast network of railways has been constructed and one can now travel in a comfortable first-class carriage from Berlin to St. Petersburg or Moscow, and thence to Odessa, Sebastopol, the Lower Volga, or even the foot of the Caucasus; and, on the whole, it must be admitted that the railways are tolerably comfortable. The carriages are decidedly better than in England, and in winter they are kept warm by small iron stoves, such as we sometimes see in steamers, assisted by double windows and double doors—a very necessary precaution in a land where the thermometer often descends to 30 degrees below zero. The trains never attain, it is true, a high rate of speed—so at least English and Americans think—but then we must remember that Russians are rarely in a hurry, and like to have frequent opportunities of eating and drinking. In Russia time is not money; if it were, nearly all the subjects of the Tsar would always have a large stock of ready money on hand, and would often have great difficulty in spending it. In reality, be it parenthetically remarked, a Russian with a superabundance of ready money is a phenomenon rarely met with in real life.

In conveying passengers at the rate of from fifteen to thirty miles an hour, the railway companies do at least all that they promise, but in one very important respect they do not always strictly fulfil their engagements. The traveller takes a ticket for a certain town, and on arriving at what he imagines to be his destination, he may merely find a railway station surrounded by fields. On making inquiries he finds to his disappointment, that the station is by no means identical with the town bearing the same name, and that the railway has fallen several miles short of fulfilling the bargain, as he understood the terms of the contract. Indeed, it might almost be said as a general rule railways in Russia like camel drivers in certain Eastern countries, studiously avoid the towns. This seems at first a strange fact. It is possible to conceive that the Bedouin is so enamoured of tent life and nomadic habits, that he shuns a town as he would a man-trap; but surely civil engineers and railway contractors have no such dread of brick and mortar. The true reason, I suspect, is that land within or immediately without the municipal barrier is relatively dear, and that the railways, being completely beyond the invigorating influence of healthy competition, can afford to look upon the comfort and convenience of passengers as a secondary consideration.

It is but fair to state that in one celebrated instance neither engineers nor railway contractors were to blame. From St. Petersburg to Moscow the locomotive runs for a distance of 400 miles, almost as "the crow" is supposed to fly, turning neither to the right hand nor to the left. For fifteen weary hours the passenger in the express train looks out on forest and morass and rarely catches sight of human habitation. Only once he perceives in the distance what may be called a town; it is Tver which has been thus favoured, not because it is a place of importance, but simply because it happened to be near the straight line. And why was the railway constructed in this extraordinary fashion? For the best of all reasons—because the Tsar so ordered it. When the preliminary survey was being made, Nicholas learned that the officers intrusted with the task—and the Minister of Ways and Roads in the number—were being influenced more by personal than by technical considerations,

O

and he determined to cut the Gordian knot in true Imperial style. When the Minister laid before him the map with the intention of explaining the proposed route, he took a ruler, drew a straight line from the one terminus to the other, and remarked in a tone that precluded all discussion, " You will construct the line so!" And the line was so constructed— remaining to all future ages, like St. Petersburg and the Pyramids, a magnificent monument of autocratic power.

Formerly this well-known incident was often cited in whispered philippics to illustrate the evils of the autocratic form of government. Imperial whims, it was said, override grave economic considerations. In recent years, however, a change seems to have taken place in public opinion, and some people now venture to assert that this so-called Imperial whim was an act of far-seeing policy. As by far the greater part of the goods and passengers are carried the whole length of the line, it is well that the line should be as short as possible, and that branch lines should be constructed to the towns lying to the right and left. Apart from political considerations, it must be admitted that a great deal may be said in support of this view.

In the development of the railway system there has been another disturbing cause, which is not likely to occur to the English mind. In England, individuals and companies habitually act according to their private interests, and the State interferes as little as possible; private initiative acts as it pleases, unless the authorities can prove that important bad consequences will necessarily result. In Russia, the *onus probandi* lies on the other side; private initiative is allowed to do nothing until it gives guarantees against all possible bad consequences. When any great enterprise is projected, the first question is—" How will this new scheme affect the interests of the State?" Thus, when the course of a new railway has to be determined, the military authorities are always consulted, and their opinion has a great influence on the ultimate decision. The consequence of this is that the railway map of Russia presents to the eye of the tactician much that is quite unintelligible to the ordinary observer—a fact that will become apparent to the uninitiated as soon as a war breaks out in Eastern Europe.

Russia is no longer what she was in the days of the Crimean war, when troops and stores had to be conveyed hundreds of miles by the most primitive means of transport. At that time she had only about 750 miles of railway; now she has more than 11,000 miles, and every year new lines are constructed.

Russia, by D. M. Wallace, M.A.

AN ARMY WITH BANNERS.

As giving an idea of the old way of signalling and precautions employed to ensure safety on the Hudson River Railroad nearly forty years ago, we append the following from the *Albany Journal*. It should be premised that this road extends from New York to East Albany, a distance of only 144 miles:—

"AN ARMY WITH BANNERS.—As you are whirled along over the Hudson River Railroad at the rate of 40 miles an hour, you catch a glimpse, every minute or two, of a man waving something like a white pocket handkerchief on the end of a stick, with a satisfactory sort of expression of countenance. If you take the trouble to count, you will find that it happens some two hundred times between East Albany and Thirty-first street. It looks like rather a useless ceremony, at first glance, but is a pretty important one, nevertheless.

"'There are 225 of these 'flagmen' stationed at intervals along the whole length of the line. Just before a train is to pass, each one walks over his "beat," and looks to see that every track and tie, every tunnel, switch, rail, clamp, and rivet, is in good order and free from obstruction. If so, he takes his stand with a white flag and waves it to the approaching train as a signal to 'come on'—and come on it does, at full speed. If there is anything wrong, he waves a red flag, or at night a red lamp, and the engineer, on seeing it, promptly shuts off the steam, and sounds the whistle to 'put down the brakes.' Every inch of the road is carefully examined after the passage of each train. Austrian espionage is hardly more strict.''

SEIZURE OF A RAILWAY TRAIN FOR DEBT.

The financial difficulties under which some railway companies have recently laboured were brought to a crisis lately
in the case of the Potteries, Shrewsbury, and North Wales
Railway, a line running from Llanymynech to Shrewsbury,
with a projected continuation to the Potteries.   A debenture
holder having obtained a judgment against the company, a
writ was forthwith issued, and a few days back the sheriff's
officers unexpectedly presented themselves at the company's
principal station in Shrewsbury, and formally entered upon
possession.   The down train immediately after entered the
station, and the bailiffs, without having given any previous
intimation to the manager, whose office adjoins the station,
seized the engines and carriages, and refused to permit the
outgoing train to start, although many passengers had
taken tickets.   Ultimately the manager obtained the
requisite permission, and it was arranged that the train
should make the journey, one of the bailiffs meanwhile
remaining in charge.   The acting-sheriff refused a similar
concession with regard to the further running of the trains,
and it being fair day at Shrewsbury, and a large number
of persons from various stations along the line having
taken return tickets, much inconvenience to the public
was likely to ensue.   The North Wales section of this line
was completed in August last at a cost of a little over
£1,100,000, and was opened for passenger and goods traffic
on the 13th of that month.   As has already been stated,
the ordinary traffic of the line was, after the enforcement
of the writ, permitted to be continued, with the proviso
that a bailiff should accompany each train.   This condition
was naturally very galling to the officials of the railway
company, but they nevertheless treated the representative
of the civil law with a marked politeness,   On the night of
his first becoming a constant passenger by the line he rode
in a first-class carriage to Llanymynech, and on the return
journey the attentive guard conducted him to a similar
compartment which was devoted to his sole occupation.
On arriving at Kennerly the bailiff became conscious of the
progress of an elaborate process of shunting, followed by
an entire stoppage of the train.   After sitting patiently
for some minutes it occurred to him to put his head out of

the window and inquire the reason for the delay, and in carrying out the idea he discovered that the train of which his carriage had lately formed a part was vanishing from sight round a distant curve in the line. He lost no time in getting out and making his way into the station, which he found locked up, according to custom, after the passage through of the last down train. Kennerly is a small road-side station about 12 miles from Shrewsbury, and offers no accommodation for chance guests; and, had it been otherwise, it was of course the first duty of the bailiff to look after the train, of which he at that moment was supposed to be in "possession." There being no alternative, he started on foot for Shrewsbury, where he arrived shortly after midnight, having accomplished a perilous passage ﹖﹖ ng the line. It appeared, on inquiry, that in the course ﹖ ﹖﹖ shunting the coupling-chain which connected the tail c﹖ ﹖ with the body of the train had by some means be ﹖ unlinked; hence the accident. The bailiff accepted th﹖ ﹖lanation, but on subsequent journeys he carefully avoi﹖﹖﹖ d the tail-coach.

Railway News, 1866.

A KANGAROO ATTACKING A TRAIN.

The latest marsupial freak is thus given by a thoroughly reliable correspondent of the *Courier* (an Australian paper) :—A rather exciting race took place between the train and a large kangaroo on Wednesday night last. When about nine miles from Dalby a special surprised the kangaroo, who was inside the fences. The animal ran for some distance in front, but getting exhausted he suddenly turned to face his opponent, and jumped savagely at the stoker on the engine, who, not being able to run, gamely faced the "old man" with a handful of coal. The kangaroo, however, only reached the side of the tender, when, the step striking him, he was "knocked clean out of it" in the one round. No harm happened beyond a bit of a scare to the stoker, as the kangaroo picked himself up quickly and cleared the fence.

SHE TAKES FITS.

Some time ago, an old lady and gentleman were coming from Devenport when the train was crowded. A young man got up and gave the old lady a seat, while his companion, another young gent, remained stedfast and let the old gent stand. This did not suit the old gentleman, so he concluded to get a seat in some way, and quickly turning to the young man on the seat beside his wife, he said :—"Will you be so kind as to watch that woman while I get a seat in another carriage? She takes fits!" This startled the young gent. He could not bear the idea of taking charge of a fitty woman, so the old gentleman got a seat, and his wife was never known to take a fit afterwards.

SNAGS' CORNERS.

The officials of a Michigan railroad that was being extended were waited upon the other day by a person from the pine woods and sand hills who announced himself as Mr. Snags, and who wanted to know if it could be possible that the proposed line was not to come any nearer than three miles to the hamlet named in his honour.

"Is Snags' Corners a place of much importance?" asked the President.

"Is it? Well, I should say it was! We made over a ton of maple sugar there last spring!"

"Does business flourish there?"

"Flourish! Why, business is on the gallop there every minute in the whole twenty-four hours. We had three false alarms of fire there in one week. How's that for a town which is to be left three miles off your railroad?"

Being asked to give the names of the business houses, he scratched his head for awhile, and then replied—

"Well, there's me, to start on. I run a big store, own eight yokes of oxen, and shall soon have a dam and a saw-mill. Then there's a blacksmith shop, a post-office, a doctor, and last week over a dozen patent-right men passed through there. In one brief year we've increased from a squatter and two dogs to our present standing. and we'll have a lawyer there before long."

"I'm afraid we won't be able to come any nearer the Corners than the present survey," finally remarked the President.

"You won't! It can't be possible that you mean to skip a growing place like Snags' Corners!"

"I think we'll have to."

"Wouldn't come if I'd clear you out a place in the store for a ticket office?"

"I don't see how we could."

"May be I'd subscribe 25 dols.," continued the delegate.

"No, we cannot change."

"Can't do it nohow?"

"No."

"Very well," said Mr. Snags as he put on his hat. "If this 'ere railroad thinks it can stunt or cripple Snags' Corners by leaving it out in the cold it has made a big mistake. Before I leave town to-day I'm going to buy a windmill and a melodeon, and your old locomotives may toot and be banged, sir—toot and be hanged!"

A NEWSPAPER WONDER.

The *Railway Journal*, an American newspaper, containing the latest intelligence with respect to home and foreign politics, the money market, Congress debates, and theatrical events, is now printed and published daily in the trains running between New York and San Francisco. All the news with which its columns are filled is telegraphed from different parts of the States to certain stations on the line, there collected by the editorial staff travelling in the train, and set up, printed, and circulated among the subscribing passengers, while the iron horse is persistently traversing plains and valleys, crossing rivers, and ascending mountain ranges. Every morning the traveller may have his newspaper served up with his coffee, and thus keep himself informed of all that is going on in the wide world during a seven days' journey covering over three thousand miles of ground. He who pays his subscription at New York, which he can do at the railway ticket-office, receives the last copy of his paper on the summit of the Sierra Nevada. The production of a news-sheet from a flying printing office

at an elevation of some ten thousand feet above the level
of the sea is most assuredly a performance worthy of conspicuous record in journalistic annals, and highly creditable
to American enterprise.

MONETARY DIFFICULTIES IN SPAIN.

Sir Arthur Helps, in his life of Mr. Brassey, remarks:—
"There were few, if any, of the great undertakings in which
Mr. Brassey embarked that gave him so much trouble in
respect of the financial arrangements as the Spanish railway
from Bilbao to Tudela. The secretary, Mr. Tapp, thus
recounts the difficulties which they had to encounter:—

"'The great difficulty in Spain was in getting money to
pay the men for doing the work—a very great difficulty.
The bank was not in the habit of having large cheques
drawn upon it to pay money; for nearly all the merchants
kept their cash in safes in their offices, and it was a very
debased kind of money, coins composed of half copper and
half silver, and very much defaced. You had to take a
good many of them on faith. I had to send down fifteen
days before the pay day came round, to commence getting
the money from the bank, obtaining perhaps £2,000 or
£3,000 a day. It was brought to the office, recounted, and
put into my safe. In that way I accumulated a ton-and-a-
half of money every month during our busy season. When
pay week came, I used to send a carriage or a large coach,
drawn by four or six mules, with a couple of civil guards,
one on each side, together with one of the clerks from the
office, a man to drive, and another—a sort of stableman—
who went to help them out of their difficulty in case the
mules gave any trouble up the hilly country. I was at the
office at six o'clock, and I was always in a state of anxiety
until I knew that the money had arrived safely at the end
of the journey. More than once the conveyance broke
down in the mountains. On one occasion the axle of our
carriage broke in half from the weight of the money, and
I had to send off two omnibuses to relieve them. I had
the load divided, and sent one to one section of the line and
one to the other.

"' Q.—Was any attempt made to rob the carriage?

" ' *A.*—Never; we always sent a clerk armed with a revolver as the principal guard. We heard once of a conspiracy to rob us; but, to avoid that, we went by another road. We were told that some men had been seen loitering about the mountain the night before.' "

A CARLIST CHIEF AS A SUB-CONTRACTOR.

The natural financial difficulties of constructing a railway in Spain were added to by the strange kind of people Mr. Brassey's agents were obliged to employ. One of the sub-contractors was a certain Carlist chief whom the government dared not arrest on account of his great influence. Mr. Tapp thus relates the Carlist chief's mode of settling a financial dispute :—

"When he got into difficulties, Mr. Small, the district agent, offered him the amount which was due to him according to his measured work. He had over 100 men to pay, and Mr. Small offered him the money that was coming to him, according to the measurement, but he would not have it, nor would he let the agent pay the men. He said he would have the money he demanded; and he brought all his men into the town of Orduna, and the men regularly bivouacked round Mr. Small's office. They slept in the streets and stayed there all night, and would not let Mr. Small come out of the office till he had paid them the money. He attempted to get on his horse to go out—his horses were kept in the house (that is the practice in the houses of Spain); but when he rode out they pulled him off his horse and pushed him back, and said that he should not go until he had paid them the money. He passed the night in terror, with loaded pistols and guns, expecting that he and his family would be massacred every minute, but he contrived eventually to send his staff-holder to Bilbao on horseback. The man galloped all the way to Bilbao, a distance of twenty-five miles, and went to Mr. Bartlett in the middle of the night, and told him what had happened. Mr. Bartlett immediately sent a detachment up to the place to disperse the men. This Carlist threatened that if Mr. Small did not pay the money he would kill every person in the house. When he was asked, 'Would you kill a man for that?' he replied, 'Yes, like a fly,' and this coming from a man who, as I was told, had already killed fourteen men with his own hand, was rather alarming. Mr. Brassey and his partners suffer a great amount of loss by their contracts for the Bilbao railway."

HOW TO BEAR LOSSES.

During the construction of the Bilbao line, shortly before the proposed opening, it set in to rain in such an exceptional manner that some of the works were destroyed. The agent telegraphed to Mr. Brassey to come immediately, as a certain bridge had been washed down. About three hours afterwards another telegram was sent, stating that a large bank was washed away; and next morning, another, stating the rain continued, and more damage had been done. Mr. Brassey, turning to a friend, said, laughingly: "I think I had better wait until I hear that the rain has ceased, so that when I do go, I may see what is *left* of the works, and estimate all the disasters at once, and so save a second journey."

No doubt Mr. Brassey felt these great losses that occasionally came upon him much as other men do; but he had an excellent way of bearing them, and, like a great general, never, if possible, gave way to despondency in the presence of his officers.

Helps' Life of Brassey.

RAILROAD INCIDENT.

An Englishwoman who travelled some years ago in America writes:—"I had found it necessary to study physiognomy since leaving England, and was horrified by the appearance of my next neighbour. His forehead was low, his deep-set and restless eyes significant of cunning, and I at once set him down as a swindler or a pickpocket. My conviction of the truth of my inference was so strong that I removed my purse—in which, however, acting by advice, I never carried more than five dollars—from my pocket, leaving in it only my handkerchief and the checks for my baggage, knowing that I could not possibly keep awake the whole morning. In spite of my endeavours to the contrary, I soon sunk into an oblivious state, from which I awoke to the consciousness that my companion was withdrawing his hand from my pocket. My first impulse was to make an exclamation; my second, which I carried into execution, to ascertain my loss, which I found to be the very alarming one of my baggage checks; my whole property being thereby placed at this vagabond's disposal, for I knew perfectly well that if I claimed my trunks without my checks the acute baggage-master would have set me down as a bold swindler. The keen-eyed conductor was not in the car, and, had he been there, the necessity for habitual suspicion incidental to his position would so far have removed his original sentiments of generosity as to make him turn a deaf ear to my request; and there was not one of my fellow-travellers whose physiognomy would have warranted me in appealing to him. So, recollecting that my checks were marked Chicago, and seeing that the thief's ticket bore the same name, I resolved to wait the chapter of accidents, or the reappearance of my friends. With a whoop like an Indian war-whoop the cars ran into a shed—they stopped—the pickpocket got up—I got up too—the baggage-master came to the door. 'This gentleman has the checks for my baggage,' said I, pointing to the thief. Bewildered, he took them from his waistcoat pocket, gave them to the baggage-master, and went hastily away. I had no inclination to cry 'stop thief!' and had barely time to congratulate myself on the fortunate impulse which had led me to say what I did, when my friends appeared from the next carriage. They were too highly amused with my recital to sympathize at all with my feelings of annoyance, and one of them, a gentleman filling a high situation in the cast, laughed heartily, saying, in a thoroughly American tone, 'The English ladies must be cute customers if they can outwit Yankee pickpockets.'"

NOVEL OBSTRUCTION.

On a certain railroad in Louisiana the alligators have the bad habit of crawling upon the track to sun themselves, and to such an extent have they pushed this practice that the drivers of the locomotives are frequently compelled to sound the engine whistle in order to scare the interlopers away. —*Railway News*, 1867.

BABY LAW.

The railways generously permit a baby to be carried without charge; but not, it seems, without incurring responsibility. It has been lately decided, in "Austin *v.* the Great Western Railway Company," 16 L. T. Rep., N. S., 320, that where a child in arms, not paid for as a passenger, is injured by an accident caused by negligence, the company is liable in damages under Lord Campbell's Act. Three of the judges were clearly of opinion that the company had, by permitting the mother to take the child in her arms, contracted to carry safely both mother and child; and Blackburn, J., went still further, and was of opinion that, independently of any such contract, express or implied, the law cast upon the company a duty to use proper and reasonable care in carrying the child, though unpaid for. It may appear somewhat hard upon railway companies to incur liabilities through an act of liberality, but they have chosen to do so. The law is against them, that is clear; but they have the remedy in their own hands. There was some reason for exempting a child in arms, for it occupies no place in the carriage, and is but a trifling addition of weight. But now it is established that the company is responsible for the consequences of accident to that child, the company is clearly entitled to make such a charge as will secure them against the risk. The right course would be to have a tariff, say one-fifth or one-fourth of the full fare, for a child in arms; and if strict justice was done, this would be deducted from the fares of the passengers who have the ill-luck to face and flank the squaller.

—*Law Times,* 1867.

RAILROAD TRACKLAYER.

The railroad tracklayer is now working along regularly at the rate of a mile a day. The machine is a car 60 feet long and 10 feet wide. It has a small engine on board for handling the ties and rails. The ties are carried on a common freight car behind, and conveyed by an endless chain over the top of the machinery, laid down in their places on the track, and, when enough are laid, a rail is put down on each side in proper position, and spiked down.

The tracklayer then advances, and keeps on its work until the load of ties and rails is exhausted, when other car loads are brought. The machine is driven ahead by a locomotive, and the work is done so rapidly that 60 men are required to wait on it, but they do more work than twice as many could do by the old system, and the work is done quite as well. The chief contractor of the road gives it as his opinion that when the machine is improved by making a few changes in the method of handling rails and ties it will be able to put down five or six miles per day. This will render it possible to lay down track twelve times as fast as the usual rate by hand, and it will do the work at less expense. The invention will be of immense importance to the country in connection with the Pacific railroad, which it was calculated could be built as fast as the track could be laid, and no faster; but hereafter the speed will be determined by the grading, which cannot advance more than five miles a day. Thirty millions of dollars have already been invested on the Pacific railroad, and if the time of completion is hastened one year by this tracklayer, as it will be if Central and Union Companies have money enough to grade each five miles a day, there will be a saving of three million dollars on interest alone on that one road.

—Alla California, 1868.

A GROWING LAD.

"This your boy, ma'am?" inquired a collector of a country woman, "he's too big for a 'alf ticket." "Oh, is he?" replied the mother. "Well, perhaps he is *now*, mister; but he wasn't when he started. The train is ever so much behind time—has been so long on the road—and he's a growing lad!"

FORGED TICKETS.

Attempts to defraud railway companies by means of forged tickets are seldom made, and still more seldom successful. In 1870, a man who lived in a toll-house near Dudley, and who rented a large number of tolls on the different turnpikes, in almost every part of the country, devised a plan for travelling cheaply. He set up a complete fount of type, composing stick, and every requisite for printing tickets, and provided himself with coloured papers, colours, and paints to paint them, and plain cards on which to paste them; and he prepared tickets for journeys of great length, and available to and from different stations on the London and North-Western, Great Western, and Midland lines. On arriving one day at the ticket platform at Derby, he presented a ticket from Masbro' to Smethwick. The collector, who had been many years in the service of the company, thought there was something unusual in the ticket. On examination he found it to be a forgery, and when the train arrived at the platform gave the passenger into custody. On searching his house, upwards of a thousand railway tickets were discovered in a drawer in his bedroom, and the apparatus with which the forgeries were accomplished was also secured. On the prisoner himself was the sum of £199 10s., and it appeared that he came to be present at the annual letting of the tolls on the different roads leading out of Derby. The punishment he received was sufficiently condign to serve as a warning to all who might be inclined to emulate such attempts after cheap locomotion.

—Williams's *Midland Railway*.

A YANKEE COMPENSATION CASE.

A horny-handed old farmer entered the offices of one of the railroad companies, and inquired for the man who settled for hosses which was killed by locomotives. They referred him to the company's counsel, whom, having found, he thus addressed:—

"Mister, I was driving home one evening last week—"

"Been drinking?" sententiously questioned the lawyer.

"I'm centre pole of the local Tent of Rechabites," said the farmer.

"That doesn't answer my question," replied the man of law; "I saw a man who was drunk vote for the prohibition ticket last year."

"Hadn't tasted liquor since the big flood of 1846," said the old man.

"Go ahead."

"I will, 'Squire. And when I came to the crossing of your line—it was pretty dark, and—zip! along came your train, no bells rung, no whistles tooted, contrary to the statutes in such cases made and provided, and—whoop! away went my off-hoss over the telegraph wires. When I had dug myself out'n a swamp some distance off and pacified the other critter, I found that thar off-hoss was dead, nothing valuable about him but his shoes, which mout have brought, say, a penny for old iron. Well—"

"Well, you want pay for that 'ere off-hoss?" said the lawyer, with a scarcely repressed sneer.

"I should, you see," replied the farmer, frankly; "and I don't care about going to law about it, though possibly I'd get a verdict, for juries out in our town is mostly made up of farmers, and they help each other as a matter of principle in these cases of stock killed by railroads."

"And this 'ere off-hoss," said the counsel, mockingly, "was well bred, wasn't he? He was rising four years, as he had been several seasons past. And you had been offered £500 for him the day he was killed, but wouldn't take it because you were going to win all the prizes in the next race with him? Oh, I've heard of that off-horse before."

"I guess there's a mistake somewhere," said the old farmer, with an air of surprise; "my hoss was got by old man Butt's roan-pacing hoss, Pride of Lemont, out'n a wall-eyed no account mare of my own, and, now that he's dead, I may say that he was twenty-nine next grass. Trot? Why, Fred Erby's hoss that he was fined for furious driving of was old Dexter alongside of him! Five hundred pounds! Bless your soul, do you think I'm a fool, or anyone else? It is true I was made an offer for him the last time I was in town, and, for the man looked kinder simple, and you know how it is yourself with hoss trading, I asked the cuss mor'n the animal might have been worth. I asked him forty pounds, but I'd have taken thirty.

"Forty?" gasped the lawyer; "forty?"

"Yes," replied the farmer, meekly and apologetically; "it kinder looks a big sum, I know, for an old hoss; but that 'ere off-hoss could pull a mighty good load, considering. Then I was kinder shook up, and the pole of my waggon was busted, and I had to get the harness fixed, and there's my loss of time, and all that counts. Say fifty pounds, and it's about square."

The lawyer whispered softly to himself, " Well, I'll be hanged!" and filled out a cheque for fifty pounds.

"Sir," said he, covering the old man's hand, " you are the first honest man I have met in the course of a legal experience of twenty-three years; the first farmer whose dead horse was worth less than a thousand pounds, and could trot better without training. Here, also, is a free pass for yourself and your male heirs in a direct line for three generations; and if you have a young boy to spare we will teach him telegraphing, and find him steady and lucrative employment."

The honest old farmer took the cheque, and departed, smiting his brawny leg with his horny hand in triumph as he did so, with the remark—

"I knew I'd ketch him on the honest tack! Last hoss I had killed I swore was a trotter, and all I got was thirty pounds and interest. Honesty is the best policy."

—*Once a Week.*

THE ABERGELE ACCIDENT.

The Irish mail leaving London at shortly after seven A.M., it was timed in 1868 to make the distance to Chester, one hundred and sixty-six miles, in four hours and eighteen minutes; from Chester to Holyhead is eighty-five miles, for running which the space of one hundred and twenty-five minutes was allowed. Abergele is a point on the sea-coast in North Wales, nearly midway between these two places. On the 20th of August, 1868, the Irish mail left Chester as usual. It was made up of thirteen carriages in all, which were occupied—as the carriages of that train usually were—by a large number of persons whose names, at least, were widely known. Among these, on this particular occasion, were the Duchess of Abercorn, wife of the then Lord Lieutenant of Ireland. with five children. Under the running arrangements of the London and North-Western line a goods train left Chester half-an-hour before the mail, and was placed upon the siding at Llanddulas, a station about a mile-and-a-half beyond Abergele, to allow the mail to pass. From Abergele to Llanddulas the track ascended by a gradient of some sixty feet to the mile. On the day of the accident it chanced that certain wagons between the engine and the rear end of the goods train had to be taken out to be left at Llanddulas, and, in doing this, it became necessary to separate the train and to leave five or six of the last wagons in it standing on the main line, while those which were to be left were backed on to a siding. The employé whose duty it was to have done so, neglected to set the brake on the wagons thus left standing, and consequently when the engine and the rest of the train returned for them, the moment they were touched, and before a coupling could be effected, the jar set them in motion down the incline toward Abergele. They started so slowly that a brakeman of the train ran after them, fully expecting to catch and stop them, but as they went down the grade they soon outstripped him, and it became clear that there was nothing to check them until they should meet the Irish mail, then almost due. It also chanced that the wagons thus loosened were oil wagons.

The mail train was coming up the line at a speed of about thirty miles an hour, when its engine-driver suddenly perceived the loose wagons coming down upon it around the curve, and then but a few yards off. Seeing that they were oil wagons, he almost instinctively sprang from his engine, and was thrown down by the impetus and rolled to the side of the road-bed. Picking himself up, bruised but not seriously hurt, he saw that the collision had already taken place, that the tender had ridden directly over the engine, that the colliding wagons were demolished, and that the front carriages of the train were already on fire. Running quickly to the rear of the train, he succeeded in uncoupling six carriages and a van, which were drawn away from the rest before the flames extended to them by an engine which most fortunately was following the train. All the other carriages were utterly destroyed, and every person in them perished.

The Abergele was probably a solitary instance, in the record of railway accidents, in which but one single survivor sustained any injury. There was no maiming. It was death or entire escape. The collision was not a particularly

P

severe one, and the engine driver of the mail train especially stated that at the moment it occurred the loose wagons were still moving so slowly that he would not have sprung from his engine had he not seen that they were loaded with oil. The very instant the collision took place, however, the fluid seemed to ignite and to flash along the train like lightning, so that it was impossible to approach a carriage when once it caught fire. The fact was that the oil in vast quantities was spilled upon the track and ignited by the fire of the locomotive, and then the impetus of the mail train forced all of its leading carriages into the dense mass of smoke and flame. All those who were present concurred in positively stating that not a cry, nor a moan, nor a sound of any description was heard from the burning carriages, nor did any one in them apparently make an effort to escape.

Though the collision took place before one o'clock, in spite of the efforts of a large gang of men who were kept throwing water on the line, the perfect sea of flame which covered the line for a distance of some forty or fifty yards could not be extinguished until nearly eight o'clock in the evening, for the petroleum had flowed down into the ballasting of the road, and the rails were red-hot. It was, therefore, small occasion for surprise that when the fire was at last gotten under, the remains of those who lost their lives were in some cases wholly undistinguishable, and in others almost so. Among the thirty-three victims of the disaster, the body of no single one retained any traces of individuality; the faces of all were wholly destroyed, and in no case were there found feet or legs or anything approaching to a perfect head. Ten corpses were finally identified as those of males, and thirteen as those of females, while the sex of ten others could not be determined. The body of one passenger, Lord Farnham, was identified by the crest on his watch, and, indeed, no better evidence of the wealth and social position of the victims of this accident could have been asked for than the collection of articles found on its site. It included diamonds of great size and singular brilliancy; rubies, opals, emeralds; gold tops of smelling bottles, twenty-four watches—of which but two or three were not gold—chains, clasps of bags, and very many bundles of keys. Of these, the diamonds alone had successfully resisted the intense heat of the flame; the settings were nearly all destroyed.

RAILWAY DESTROYERS IN THE FRANCO-GERMAN WAR.

One obvious means of hampering the military operations of the Germans was the cutting of railroads, so as to interrupt and overthrow on-coming trains. This method was resorted to by bands of volunteers, calling themselves "The Wild Boars of Ardennes," and "Railway Destroyers." Here again the invaders incurred great odium by announcing that, on the departure of a train in the disaffected districts, the mayor and principal inhabitants should be made to take their places on the engine, so that if the peasants chose to upset the conveyance, their surest victims would be their own compatriots. —*Annual Register*, 1870.

FRIGHTENED AT A RED LIGHT.

A driver, not on duty, had been drinking, and was, in company with his fireman, walking in the vicinity of the Edgware Road, when he suddenly started violently, and seizing his mate's arm, shouted—

"Hold hard, mate—hold hard!"

"What's the matter?" cried the fireman.

"Matter!" roared the driver, "why, you're a-running by the red light;" and he pointed to the crimson glare which streamed through a glass bottle in a chemist's window.

"Come along; that's nothing," said the fireman, trying to drag him on.

"What, run by the red light, and go afore Dannel in the morning?" retorted the driver, and no persuasion could or did get him to pass the shop. He was a Great Western man, and the "Dannel" whom he held in such wholesome awe was the celebrated engineer, now Sir Daniel Gooch, and chairman of that line. He was then the locomotive chief, and renowned above all other things for maintaining discipline among his staff, while they cherished a feeling for him very much akin to what we hear of the clannish enthusiasm of the ancient Scotch.

THE DECOY TRUNK.

August 27, 1875. The Metropolitan magistrates have had before them a case which seems likely to show how some, at least, of the robberies at railway stations are accomplished. Some ingenious persons, it appears, have devised a way by which a trunk can be made to steal a trunk, and a portmanteau to annex a portmanteau. The thieves lay a trunk artfully contrived on a smaller trunk; the latter clings to the former, and the owner of the larger carries both away. The decoy trunk is said to be fitted with a false bottom, which goes up when it is laid on a smaller trunk, and with mechanism inside which does for the innocent trunk what Polonius recommended Laertes to do for his friend, and grapples it to its heart with hooks of steel. In fact, the decoy duck—we do not know how better to describe it—is made to perform an office like that of certain flowers, which suddenly close at the pressure of a fly or other insect within their cup and imprison him there.

—*Annual Register*, 1875.

DRIVING A LAST SPIKE.

There are now two lines crossing the American continent. The western section of the new route goes through on the thirty-parallel—far enough south from the Rocky Mountains for the current of the train's own motion to be acceptable even in December, and to be a grateful relief in June. Beginning at San Francisco, the additional line runs south through California to Fort Yuma on the Colorado river; thence along the southern border of the territories of Arizona and New Mexico, and across the centre of Kansas, until it joins the lines connecting the Southern States with New York. The undertaking is a vast one, and has been one of some difficulty; but its completion has been the occasion of very little display. Never was a great project of any kind brought to a successful result with so much of active work and so little of actual talk. A cable message a line in length told the story a month ago to European readers, and none of the American papers appear to have dealt with the matter as anything out of the ordinary run of daily events.

Far otherwise was it with the finishing touch twelve years ago to the other Transcontinental line. The whole world heard of what was then done. All the bells in all the great cities of the United States rang out jubilant peals as the last stroke sent home the last spike on the last rail of the new highway of travel. The news was flashed by telegraph everywhere throughout the Union, and that there might be no delay in its transmission and no hindrance to its simultaneous reception, a certain pre-arranged signal was given and all the wires were for the time being kept free of other business. There were cases in which, to save time in ringing out the glad news, the message was conveyed on special wires right up to the bell towers; and everywhere there was a feeling that a great victory had been won. Preceding the consummation, there had been some wonderful feats in railroad construction. From the Missouri river on the one side and from the Sacramento on the other, the two companies—the Union Pacific and the Central Pacific—advanced against each other in friendly rivalry. The popular idea was that the length of the line of each company would be measured to the point at which it joined rails with the other. This was hardly the case; but an arrangement was come to after the completion of the work which has given this notion the strength of a tradition. The greater part of the Union Pacific route was over comparatively even ground, and it was not until the Salt Lake region was being approached that any serious constructive difficulties presented themselves. It was otherwise with the company advancing eastward. The line had to be carried over the Sierra Nevada, the ascent beginning almost from the starting point, and rising seven thousand feet in a hundred miles. On the other side of the mountain range, the descent was in turn formidable. Over this part of the road it was impossible to proceed rapidly. The work was surrounded with difficulties, and there were competent engineers who had no confidence that it could be carried out. Progress could only be made at the outset at the rate of about twenty miles each year; but in this slow work there was time to profit by experience, so that eventually, when it became a question simply of many hands, the platelayer went forward with the swing of an army on the march. Then it was that the two companies went vigorously into the race of construction. In one day, in 1868, the Union men were able to inform the Central men by telegraph that they had laid as many as six miles since morning. A few days afterwards the response came from the Central men that they had just finished as their day's work a stretch of seven miles. Spurred to fresh activity by this display, the Union men next reported to the other side a complete stretch for a day's work of seven and a half miles! The answer came back in the extraordinary announcement that the workers for the Central Company were prepared to lay ten miles in one day! The Union people were inclined to regard this as mere boasting, and the Vice-President of the company implied as much when he made an offer to bet ten thousand dollars that in one day such a stretch of railroad could not be well and truly laid. It is not on record that the bet was taken up. But the fact remains that it was made, that the Central army of workers heard of it, and that they determined to make good the pledge given in their name. So a day was fixed for the attempt. From the Union side men came to take note of the work and to measure it, and their verdict at the close of the day's toil was that not only had the promised ten miles been constructed, but that the measurement showed two hundred feet over! And this, on the words of an authority, is how it was done:—When the car loaded with rails came to the end of the track, the two outer rails on either side were seized with iron nippers, hauled forward off the car, and laid on the ties by four men who attended exclusively to this work. Over these rails the cars were pushed forward and the process repeated. Then came a gang of men who half-drove the spikes and screwed on the fish-plates on the dropped rails. At a short interval behind these came a gang of Chinamen, who drove home the spikes already inserted and added the rest. A second squad of Chinamen followed, two deep, on each side of the single track, the inner men carrying shovels and the outer men wielding picks, their duty being to ballast the track. Every movement was thus carefully arranged, and there was no loss of time. The average rate of speed at which the work was done was 1 min. 47½ secs. to every 240 feet of perfected track. There was, of course, an army of disciplined helpers, whose duty it was to bring up the materials. In this great feat of construction more than four thousand men found employment in various capacities. When they had carried their line four miles further east, the Central and the Union men met each other, the point of connection being known as Promontory. Afterwards the two companies made an arrangement whereby the Union Pacific relinquished fifty-three miles of road to the Central, thus fixing on Ogden as the western terminus of the one line and the eastern terminus of the other. The popular belief is that the fifty-three miles were obtained by the Central Pacific directors as an acknowledgement of the greater engineering difficulties they had to overcome in laying their part of the track, and that they served a handicapping purpose at the end of this wonderful railroad competition.

The placing of the final tie on the Pacific lines, as has been hinted, was a ceremonious undertaking. The event took place on Monday, March 10th, 1869. Representatives were present from almost every part of the Union, and the construction parties, not yet wholly dispersed, made up a greater crowd than had been seen at Promontory before or is likely ever to be seen there again—for, with the fixing of the termini at another point, the glory of the place has departed. The connecting tie had been made of California laurel. It was beautifully polished, and bore a series of inscribed silver plates. The tie was carefully placed, and over it the rails were laid by picked men on behalf of each company. The spikes were then inserted—one of gold, silver, and iron, from Arizona; another of silver, from Nevada; and a third of gold, from California. President Stanford, of the Central Pacific, armed with a hammer of solid silver, drove the last spike, the blow falling precisely at noon, and the news of the completion of the road being flashed abroad as it fell. Then the two locomotives, one from the west and the other from the east, drew up to each other on the single line, coming into gentle collision, that they in their way, in the pleasing conceit of their drivers, might symbolise the fraternisation that went on. It does not spoil the story of the ceremony to state that the laurel tie, with its inscriptions and its magnificent mountings, was only formally laid, and that it became from that day a relic to be officially cherished; and it should be added that the more serviceable tie which replaced it was cut into fragments by men eager to have some memento of the occasion. Other ties for a time shared the same fate, until splinters of what was claimed to be "the last tie laid" became as common as pieces of the Wellington boots the great commander is said to have left behind him at Waterloo.

With the junction of the two lines, it became possible to make safely in one week an overland journey that not many years before required months in its execution, and was attended by many hardships and dangers. It was, however, a route better known even in the days when the legend of the pilgrims over it was "Pike's Peak or bust!" than is the region crossed by the new southern line. This line opens up what is practically an undiscovered and an unsettled country, but the region traversed has been ascertained to be so rich in resources as to fully justify the heavy expenditure involved in the construction of the line. In another year the line will become a powerful agent in the development of the Union, for it will then be connected with the lines that run through Texas into Louisiana, and New Orleans and San Francisco will be brought into direct communication with each other. This, in fact, has been a prominent object in the undertaking. The effect of it will be to cheapen the tariff on goods from the Pacific Coast to Europe, and will, it is believed, have the effect of controlling a large share of the Asiatic trade.

—*Leeds Mercury*, April 23rd, 1881.

MARRIAGE AND RAILWAY DIVIDENDS.

Marriage would not seem to have any close connection with railroad traffic, but we find an officer of an East Indian railroad company explaining a falling off in the passenger receipts of the year (1874) by the fact that it was a "twelfth year," which is regarded by the Hindoos as so unfavourable to marriage that no one, or scarcely any one, is married. And, as weddings are the great occasions in Hindoo life when there is great pomp and a general gathering together of friends, they cause a great deal of travelling.

SECURITY FOR TRAVELLING.

A civil engineer, of long experience in connection with railways, gives some reassuring statements as to the precautions taken in keeping the lines in order. The majority of accidents occur, not from defects in the line, but from imperfections in the living agents who have charge of the signals and other arrangements of trains in transit. The engineer says:—"To begin at the bottom, we have the ganger of the 'beat,' a man selected from the waymen after several years' service for his aptitude and steadiness, whose duty it is to patrol his length of two or three miles every morning, and to make good fastenings, etc., afterwards superintending his gang in packing, replacing rails, sleepers, and other necessary repairs. Over the ganger is the inspector of permanent way, responsible for the gangers doing their duty, who generally goes over all his district once a day on the engine, and walks one or more gangers' beats. The inspectors, again, are under the district superintendent or engineer, who makes frequent inspections both by walking and on the engine. The ganger, if in want of men or materials, reports to his inspector, who, if they are required, sends a requisition to the engineer, keeping a small stock at his head-quarters to supply urgent demands. The engineer in his turn keeps the whole in harmony, sanctioning the employment of the necessary men, and ordering the materials, the only check upon the number of men or quantity of materials being the total half-yearly expenditure. Directors never within my experience grudge an outlay necessary to keep the line in good order; but, should they limit the expenditure from financial motives, it would then clearly be the duty of the engineer to recommend a reduction of speed to a safe point. Occasionally, idle gangers are met with, who are always asking for more men, and as naturally meeting with refusal.

THE NUMBER ONE HUNDRED AND TWENTY.

Lord Lymington, M.P., relates the following amusing tale of his experience with an inquiring and hospitable gentleman in Arkansas:—"He introduced himself to me very kindly on learning that I was a traveller and an Englishman, and offered me the hospitalities of the town. It was very obliging of him, but unfortunately I could not stay, so we had a chat while I was waiting for the train. During this chat his eye fell on a portmanteau of mine which I had caused to be marked, for convenience sake and easy identification, with the cabalistic figures 120. This he scanned for some time with ill-concealed curiosity, and finally, turning to me, said rather abruptly, 'If I am not mistaken, you are a nobleman, are you not?' I admitted that such was my unhappy lot. 'Then,' he said, 'I presume that number there on your valise is what they call in the nobility armorial bearings, is it not—in fact, your crest?' 'Hardly that,' I modestly replied. 'A number is only borne as a crest, I believe, by much more illustrious persons—for example, the Beast in the Apocalypse.' 'Oh!' he replied, and then, after meditating a moment or two, asked, 'Have your family been long in England?' 'Yes,' I said, 'they have been there for some time. But why do you ask?' 'Perhaps the number refers,' he replied, 'to the number of generations, just as they recite them in the Old Testament, you know?' 'Yes,' I unhesitatingly and with prompt mendacity replied, 'that is exactly it, and I don't see how you hit it so cleverly.' He smiled all over with delight as the train rushed up, and waved kind farewells to me as long as we were in sight."

ENGINE DRIVING.

But the regulator once in his hand, the engine-driver has only begun his experience. He goes through an apprenticeship with different varieties of engines. He must pick up what knowledge he can himself, and he must always be on the alert to benefit from the experience of others. The locomotive in its varying "moods" must be his constant study, and he must work it so that he shall not infringe more than an average share of a multiplicity of rules and regulations. The best position in the service, apart from that of superintendence, is in the driving of an express engine, and the greatest honour that can be conferred on an engine-driver is to select him to take charge of the locomotive on a Royal train. Only the best men are picked out to drive the Queen, and the best engine on the road is detailed for the Royal service; and although on these occasions railway officials, who are the superiors of the driver, get on the foot-boards, the latter is for the time being master of the situation.   Should the locomotive superintendent dictate to him, it would be to confess that the driver was unworthy of his high trust, and so the superintendent is content to look on; but it is the content-ment born of the conviction that he has chosen for the task a driver whose experience is great, and whose watchfulness and care and knowledge of enginery have given him a claim to the chief service his company has for him.   Not that there is any more risk in running the Queen's train than in running an ordinary passenger express.   In fact, the risk is reduced to a minimum.   A pilot engine has gone before to keep the way clear.   The pilot engine is fifteen minutes in advance of the Royal carriages at every station, and the space travelled over in that fifteen minutes is kept free and unobstructed.   The speed of the train is carefully regulated, and amongst other provisions for security the siding points are for the moment spiked.   Every crossing gate is guarded from the time of the passage of the advance engine until the train follows in its wake.   Everything is done to make the Royal journey over a railroad a safe one. Such arrangements, however, if they add to the responsi-bility, heighten also the pride a man feels in being the Queen's driver.

So far as the companies are concerned, it may be said that there is a fair field and no favour all the way from the fire-box in the cleaning-shed up to the footboard on the locomotive that takes Her Majesty from Windsor to Ballater.   Promotion comes practically as a result of com-petitive examination.   The mistake of a weak appointment is soon rectified, and the precautions taken to test a man's capacity in one grade before raising him to another are an absolute barrier to incompetence.   But there are circum-stances under which a man's chances are weakened.   His responsibilities make him liable for the faults of others, and mistakes of this kind go to his discredit.   Then if he is not companionable, or is over-confident, tricks may be played which will prevent his going forward as rapidly as he otherwise would.   Mr. Reynolds tells the story of a driver who had come to a dead stop on a journey because he was short of steam. The cause was a mystery. There appeared to be nothing wrong with the engine or the fire, and apparently the boiler was also in trim. It was eventually found that some one had put soft soap in the tender, and the water there being hot, the soap was gradually dissolved and introduced into the boiler, with the result that the grease covered the tubes, and together with the suds prevented the transmission of heat to the water. An enemy had done this, but under the rules the driver was responsible for his engine, and he was suspended; only, however, to be reinstated when once the mischief was traced to the perpetrator. Even an act which to the ordinary spectator is a marvellous example of presence of mind may, interpreted by the company's rules, be an offence on the part of the engine-driver. An engine attached to a train broke from the tender in the course of its journey, and became separated. Noticing the mishap, the driver slackened speed, allowed the tender and carriages to come up, and while the train was still in motion he and the fireman adroitly secured the runaway, and no harm was done. The men interested did not think it advisable to report the occurrence. But the clever management of the engine had been noticed by a peasant in a field, and Hodge, in his wonderment, began to talk about the affair all round the country-side. Then the story found its way to a station master, and thence to head quarters, and an inquiry brought the matter to light, and ended in the two men being advised not to do the same thing again. It was held that under the circumstances the train should have been stopped.

ENGINE DRIVERS' PRESENCE OF MIND.

An able writer upon railway topics remarks:—"I have alluded to a driver's coolness and resolution in an accident, but no chronicle ever has or ever will be written which will tell one tithe of the accidents which the courage and presence of mind of these men have averted. A railway ran over a river—indeed, it might be called an arm of the sea: as it was the inlet to an important harbour, provision was obliged to be made for the shipping, and so the piece of line which crossed the water, at a height of seventy feet, was, in fact, a bridge which swung round when large vessels had to pass. I need hardly say that such a point was carefully guarded. At each end, at a fitting distance, a man was placed specially to indicate whether the bridge was open or shut. One day, as the express was tearing along on its up journey, the driver received the usual 'all right' signal; but to his horror, on coming in full sight of the bridge, he found it was wide open, and a gulf of fatal depth yawning before him. He sounded his brake-whistle, that deep-toned scream which signals the guard, and he and his fireman held on, as before described, to the brake and regulator. The speed of the train was, of course, checked; but so short was the interval, so great had been the impetus, that it seemed almost impossible to prevent the whole train from going over into the chasm. Had the rails been in the least degree slippery, any of the brakes out of order, or the driver less determined, there would then have occurred the most fearful railway accident ever known in England; but by dint of quick decision and cool courage the danger was averted; the train was brought to a stand-still when the buffers of the engine absolutely and literally overhung the chasm. Three yards more, and a different result might have had to be chronicled.

Some of my readers may remember an incident in railway history which dates back to our first great Exhibition. I mention it here for its singularity, and for my having known the driver whose coolness was so marked. In ascending a very long gradient, the hindmost carriages of the train snapped their couplings when at the top; the engine rattled on with the remainder, while these ran down the slope, which was several miles in length, with a velocity which, of course, increased every moment. To make matters worse, the next train on the same line was comparatively close behind, and, in fact, shortly came in sight. The driver of this second train. a watchful and experienced hand, saw the carriages rushing towards him, and divined that they were on the same line. If he continued steaming on, of course, in a couple of minutes he would come into direct collision with them, while, on the other hand, if he ran back, the carriages would probably gather such way that they would leap from the bank. So, with great presence

of mind and wonderful judgment of speed, he ran back at
a pace not quite as fast as the carriages were approaching,
so that eventually they overtook him, and struck his moving
engine with a blow that was scarcely more perceptible than
the jar usually communicated by coupling on a fresh carriage. When this was done, all the rest was easy; he
resumed his down journey, and pushed the frightened
passengers safely before him until they reached their
destination, where the officials, as may readily be supposed,
were in a state of frantic despair at the loss of half the
train."

A SMUGGLING LOCOMOTIVE.

A singular adaptation of the locomotive has just been
made in Russia. Information having been given to the
authorities at Alexandrovo, on the Polish frontier, that the
locomotive of the express leaving that station for Warsaw
had been ingeniously converted into a receptacle for
smuggled goods, it was carefully examined during its
sojourn at the station. Though nothing was found wrong,
it was deemed advisable that a custom-house official should
accompany the train to its destination, when the engine
furnace and boiler were emptied and deliberately taken to
pieces. In the interior was discovered a secret compartment
containing one hundred and twenty-three pounds of foreign
cigars and several parcels of valuable silk. Several arrests
were made, including that of the driver; but his astonishment at finding the engine to which he had been so long
accustomed converted into a hardened offender against the
laws was so genuine that he was released and allowed to
return to his duties.

THE CUSTOM OF THE COUNTRY.

An English lady accustomed to travelling abroad, and
able to converse fluently in the languages of the countries
she visited, recently found herself alone in a railway
carriage in Germany, when two foreigners entered with
pipes in their mouths, smoking strong tobacco furiously.
She quietly told them in their own language that it was
not a smoking carriage, but they persisted in continuing to

smoke, remarking that it was "the custom of the country," upon which the lady took from her pocket a pair of gloves and commenced cleaning them with benzoline. Her fellow-passengers expressed their disgust at the nauseous effluvium, when she remarked that it was the custom of her country. She was soon left in the sole possession of the carriage.

—Truth.

AN INSULTED WOMAN.

Mark Twain in his interesting work "A Tramp Abroad," thus refers to a railroad incident:—"We left Turin at 10 the next morning by a railway, which was profusely decorated with tunnels. We forgot to take a lantern along, consequently we missed all the scenery. Our compartment was full. A ponderous, tow-headed, Swiss woman, who put on many fine-lady airs, but was evidently more used to washing linen than wearing it, sat in a corner seat and put her legs across into the opposite one, propping them inter-mediately with her up-ended valise. In the seat thus pirated sat two Americans, greatly incommoded by that woman's majestic coffin-clad feet. One of them begged her, politely, to remove them. She opened her wide eyes and gave him a stare, but answered nothing. By-and-by he preferred his request again, with great respectfulness. She said, in good English, and in a deeply offended tone, that she had paid her passage and was not going to be bullied out of her 'rights' by ill-bred foreigners, even if she *was* alone and unprotected.

"'But I have rights also, madam. My ticket entitles me to a seat, but you are occupying half of it.'

"'I will not talk with you, sir. What right have you to speak to me? I do not know you. One would know that you come from a land where there are no gentlemen. No *gentleman* would treat a lady as you have treated me.'

"'I come from a land where a lady would hardly give me the same provocation.'

"'You have insulted me, sir! You have intimated that I am not a lady—and I hope I am *not* one, after the pattern of your country.'

"'I beg that you will give yourself no alarm on that head, madam; but at the same time I must insist—always respectfully—that you let me have my seat.'

"Here the fragile laundress burst into tears and sobs.

"'I never was so insulted before! Never, never! It is shameful, it is brutal, it is base, to bully and abuse an unprotected lady who has lost the use of her limbs and cannot put her feet to the floor without agony!'

"'Good heavens, madam, why didn't you say that at first! I offer a thousand pardons. And I offer them most sincerely. I did not know—I *could* not know—that anything was the matter. You are most welcome to the seat, and would have been from the first if I had only known. I am truly sorry it all happened, I do assure you.'

"But he couldn't get a word of forgiveness out of her. She simply sobbed and snuffled in a subdued but wholly unappeasable way for two long hours, meantime crowding the man more than ever with her undertaker-furniture, and paying no sort of attention to his frequent and humble little efforts to do something for her comfort. Then the train halted at the Italian line, and she hopped up and marched out of the car with as firm a leg as any washerwoman of all her tribe! And how sick I was to see how she had fooled me!"

DISSATISFIED PASSENGERS.

Any one wanting a fair and yet amusing account of what really occurs to a person travelling in America should read G. A. Sala's book called *America Revisited.* He speaks of a gentleman from the Eastern States whom he met in the train across the continent, and who thus held forth upon the difference between reality and guide-books:—

"There ain't no bottling up of things about me. This overland journey's a fraud, and you oughter know it. Don't tell me. It's a fraud. This Ring must be busted up. Where are your buffalers? Perhaps you'll tell me that them cows is buffalers. They ain't. Where are your prairie dogs? They ain't dogs to begin with, they're squirrels. Ain't you ashamed to call the mean little cusses dogs? But where are they? There ain't none. Where are your grizzlies? You might have imported a few grizzlies to keep up the name of your railroad. Where are your herds of antelopes scudding before the advancing train? Nary an antelope have you got for to scud. Rocky Mountains, sir? They ain't rocky at all—they're as flat as my hand. Where are your savage gorges? I can't see none. Where are your wild injuns? Do you call them loafing tramps in dirty blankets, injuns? My belief is that they are greasers looking out for an engagement as song and dance men. They're 'beats,' sir, 'dead beats,' they're 'pudcocks,' and you oughter be told so."

Another passenger in the train with Mr. Sala was of a poetic mind, and he softly sang to himself during the whole journey over the Rocky Mountains the following effusion:—

> Beautiful snow,
> Beautiful snow,
> B-e-e-e-eautiful snow,
> How I'd like to have a revolver and go
> For the beast that wrote about beautiful snow.

COPY OF A NOTICE.

The following is a verbatim copy of a notice exhibited at a Welsh railway station. It is, perhaps, only a little more incomprehensible than Bradshaw. "List of Booking: You passengers must careful. For have them level money for ticket and to apply at once for asking tickets when will booking window open. No tickets to have after the departure of the trains."

SNOWED UP ON THE PACIFIC RAILWAY.

A writer in the *Leisure Hour* remarks:—"It is no joke when a town like New York or London is blocked up for a few hours by snow. Both labour and capital have then to submit to a strike from nature; but it is a more serious matter when a man is snowed up in the middle of the Pacific Railway. He is not then kept at home, but kept away from it; he is not in the midst of comforts, but most unpleasantly out of their reach. He may, too, have to endure his privations and annoyances for a week, or even a month. . . . Avalanches, in spite of snow-sheds and galleries, spring into ravines which the trains have to cross. . . . It was, however, with some little alarm

Q

that the writer found himself caverned for a considerable
time under one of these dark snow-sheds.   The difficulty
of running through the snow impediments had so exhausted
the fuel that it was necessary to go to a wood-station in the
mountains.   As it was the favourite resort of avalanches,
the prudent conductor of our train directed the pilot to back
the carriages into a snow-shed, and then be off the more
quickly with engine and tender for a supply of fuel.   It
was bitterly cold and in the dead of night.   The snow
was piled up around the gallery, and had in many places
penetrated through the crevices.   The silence was profound.
The sense of utter loneliness and desolation was complete.
The return of the engine after a lengthened absence was a
relief, like the spring sun following an arctic winter.

" The first parties snowed up were wholly unprepared.
They had had their dollar meal at the last station, and
were far enough from the next when fixed in the bank.   It
was, however, a rare harvest for the nearest store.   The
necessity of some was the opportunity of others.   Food of
inferior quality brought fabulous prices.   A dispute, involving a heavy wager, arose about one article of fare.
Was it antelope or not?   The vendor admitted that a very
lean old cow had been sacrificed on the pressing occasion.

" For a little while some fun was got-out of the trouble of
snowed-up trains.   Delicate attentions were tendered by
gentlemen as cooks' mates to the ladies.   Oyster-cans were
converted into culinary utensils, and telegraph wire proved
excellent material for gridirons.   Many a joke was passed
in the train kitchen, and hearty was the appetite for the
rude viands thus rudely dressed.   But when the food grew
more difficult to obtain, and the wood supply became less
and less, the mirth was considerably slackened.   It is true
that despatches were sent off for help, and cargoes of
provisions were steamed up as near as the snow would
permit; but it was hard work to carry over the snow, and
insufficient was the supply.   Frightful growlings arose
from the men and sad lamentations from the women.   Short
allowance of food, with intense cold, could not be positively
enjoyed any time; but to be cooped up within snow walls
in such a desolate region, far from expecting friends or
urgent business, was most annoying.   One spoke of absolute

necessity to be at his office within the week, as heavy bills had to be prepared for. Another was going about an important speculation, which would utterly break down if he were detained three days. Alas! he was there above three weeks.

The sorrows of the heart were worse. A mother was there hastening to nurse a sick daughter. A father had been summoned to the dying bed of his son. A husband was hoping to clasp again a wife from whom a long voyage had separated him. One poor fellow was an especial object of sympathy. He was hastening to an anxiously waiting bride. He had to cool the ardour of his passion in the snow-bound car, and pass the day appointed for his wedding in shivering reflections. In one of the snow depths was detained an interesting couple who had casually met on the western side and were obeying the mandate of the heart and of friends in proceeding to the east to effect their happy union. The three weeks they were compelled to pass together, under these cold and trying circumstances, must have given them a famous insight into each other's character, and this before the knot was tied.

"The story is told of one resolute man who, though but newly married, had been compelled to take a business journey. He was most impatient to return home, and was awhile confounded with his unfortunate imprisonment. When he found that little chance existed for an early escape, his heart prompted him to a bold enterprise. He was still two hundred miles from home. He had no guide before him but the telegraph posts. He could expect little provision on the way, as the stations were frozen up; but, sustained by conjugal affection, the good fellow set off on his lonely walk over the snow. Notwithstanding terrible sufferings, and some free fighting with wolves, he did his march in five days only. What a greeting he deserved!

"Those who had not his courage and strength were compelled to endure the cars. Americans are not folks to whine about a trouble; they succeed so often that their faith is strong. Though the most luxurious of people, the men—and the women too—can bear reverses nobly. But they never dream of Oriental submissiveness. They struggle hard to rise, and make the best of things till a change comes.

So with those in the cars. They soon found amusements; they chatted and laughed, played games and sang; the best jokes were recollected and repeated, and the liveliest tales were told; charades were acted; a judge and jury scene afforded much amusement; lectures were given to approving assemblies. The Sundays were decently observed, and services were held morning and evening; reading was dispensed with, and the sermons were extempore perforce.

" The worst part of their sufferings came when for forty-eight hours they were under a snow-shed without light, and with the stoves empty. As, for the maintenance of warmth, every crevice in the cars was stopped, the misery of close and unwholesome atmosphere was added to their sorrows. The writer, as an old traveller, has had some experience of odd sleeping dens, and has been obliged at times to inhale a pestiferous air, though he has never endured so much from this discomfort as in his winter passage on the Pacific Railway. For hours in the long nights, as well as in the day, he preferred standing outside on the platform, with the thermometer from fifteen to twenty-five below zero, rather than encounter the foul atmosphere and stifling heat within.

" Meanwhile the brave Chinamen were summoned to the rescue. They are capital fellows to withstand the cold, and work with a will to clear a passage. For a distance of two hundred miles the blockade existed, and several trains were thus caught on the way. Eight hundred freight wagons were detained at Cheyenne. At one period the cold was 30° below zero. The worst part of the road was toward Sherman, 8,252 feet above the sea. Wyoming and West Nebraska were the coldest regions.

" In this great blockade, strange to say, the mortality was but small. Three died during the imprisonment, and two in consequence of cold. But an interesting compensation was made, for five births took place in this season of trial. The principal sufferers were those in the second-class carriages. Room, however, was made for the more delicate in the already crowded first-class cars."

A SELL.

The *Indianapolis News* is responsible for the following story. A railroad official of Indianapolis had, among other passes, one purporting to carry him freely over the Warren and Tonawanda Narrow-Gauge Railway. Happening to be near Warren, he thought he would use this pass. Now, it appears that some enterprising citizens of Pennsylvania once proposed to lay a pipe-line for petroleum between Warren and Tonawanda. The Legislature having refused to sanction their scheme, they "engineered" a bill for building a narrow-gauge line, which passed, the oil capitalists not conceiving that they had any interest in opposing it. It is needless to say the narrow-gauge line was the "desiderated pipe-line." The enterprising citizens carried their joke so far as to issue annual passes over the road, receiving others in return. When the traveller sought for the Warren station on this line he found a chimney, and for the narrow-gauge an iron-lined hole in the ground. It is hardly surprising that now he is moved to anger at the slightest reference to the "Warren and Tonawanda Narrow Gauge."

AT FAULT.

It is rather a serious matter that our public companies, and especially our railway companies, are doing their best to degrade our language. I am not going to be squeamish and object strongly to the use of the word *Metropolitan*, though I think it indefensible. Still, it is too bad of them to persist in using the word *bye-laws* for *by-laws*—so establishing solidly a shocking error. The word *bye* has no existence in England except as short for *be with you*, in the phrase *Good-bye*. The so called by-laws are simple laws by the other laws, and have nothing to do with any form of salutation. In a bill of the Great Western Railway I find the announcement that tickets obtained in London on any day from December 20th to 24th will be available for use on *either* of those days—this *either* meaning the five days from the 20th December to the 24th inclusive. Either of five! After this I am not surprised that, in a contribution of my own to a daily paper, the editor gravely altered the phrase *the last-named*, applied to one of three people, to *latter*. In a railway advertisement I read a day or two ago, "From whence." Now, what is the good of such fine words as *whence* and *thence* if they are thus to be ill-used? Surely the railway companies might have some one capable of seeing that their grammar has some pretence to correctness.

—*Gentleman's Magazine.*

A WIDOW'S CLAIM FOR COMPENSATION.

Some time ago a railway collision on one of the roads leading out of New York killed, among others, a passenger living in an interior town. His remains were sent home, and a few days after the funeral the attorney of the road called upon the widow to effect a settlement. She placed her figures at twenty thousand dollars. "Oh! that sum is unreasonable," replied the attorney. "Your husband was nearly fifty years old." "Yes, sir." "And lame?" "Yes." "And his general health was poor?" "Quite poor." "And he probably would not have lived over five years?" "Probably not, sir." "Then it seems to me that two or three thousand dollars would be a fair compensation." "Two or three thousand!" she echoed. "Why, sir, I courted that man for ten years, run after him for ten more, and then had to chase him down with a shotgun to get him before a preacher! Do you suppose that I'm going to settle for the bare cost of shoe leather and ammunition?"

THE LADY AND HER LAP-DOG.

The following scene occurred at the high-level Crystal Palace line :—"A newspaper correspondent was amused at the indignation of a lady against the porters who interfered to prevent her taking her dog into the carriage. The lady argued that Parliament had compelled the companies to find separate carriages for smokers, and they ought to be further compelled to have a separate carriage for ladies with lap-dogs, and it was perfectly scandalous that they should be separated, and a valuable dog, worth perhaps thirty or forty guineas, should be put into a dog compartment.

I have some of the B stock of the railway, upon which not a penny has ever been paid, and I could not help comparing my experience of this particular line of railway with that of my fellow-traveller, and wondering what sort of a train that would be which would provide accommodation for all the wants and wishes of railway travellers."

WHAT IS PASSENGERS' LUGGAGE?

A gentleman removing took with him on the Great Western railway articles consisting of six pairs of blankets, six pairs of sheets, and six counterpanes, valued at £16, belonging to his household furniture. They were in a box, which was put in the luggage van and lost. The question at law was whether these articles came within the definition, "ordinary passengers' luggage," for which, if lost, the passenger could claim damages from the Company.

The judges of the Court of Queen's Bench sitting in Banco have decided that such is not personal luggage.

"Now (said the Lord Chief Justice) although we are far from saying that a pair of sheets or the like taken by a passenger for his use on a journey might not fairly be considered as personal luggage, it appears to us that a quantity of articles of that description intended, not for the use of the traveller on the journey, but for the use of his household, when permanently settled, cannot be held to be so.

—*Herepath's Railway Journal*, Jan. 10, 1871.

CONVERSION OF THE GAUGE.

The conversion of the guage on the South Wales section of the Great Western railway in 1872 was of the heaviest description, the period of labour lasting from seventeen to eighteen hours a day for several successive days. It was the greatest work of its kind, and nothing exactly like it will ever be done in England again. The lines of rail to be connected would have made about 400 miles in single length, the number of men employed was about 1500; and the time taken was two weeks nearly. Oatmeal and barley water was made into a thin gruel and given to the men as required. It was the only drink taken during the day. I had not a single case of drunkenness or illness. I have often heard these men speak with great approbation of the supporting power of oatmeal drink.

—*J. W. Armstrong, C.E.*

FOURTH-OF-JULY FACTS.

At a banquet in Paris attended by Americans in celebration of the late Fourth of July, Mr. Walker's speech in reply to the toast of the material prosperity of the United States and France, and the establishment of closer commercial relations between them, was especially striking and interesting. He remarked, "In 1870 the cost of transporting food and merchandise between the Western and Eastern States was from a cent-and-a-half to two cents a ton a mile. I well remember a conversation which I had in 1870 or 1871 with Mr. William B. Ogden, of Chicago, one of the modest railway kings of that primitive period. In a vein of sanguine prophecy, Mr. Ogden exclaimed to me, 'Mr. Walker, you will live to see freight brought from Chicago to New York at a cent a ton a mile!' 'Perhaps so,' I replied; 'but I fear this result will not be reached in my time.' In 1877 or 1878 the cost had fallen to three-eighths of a cent a ton a mile, and although this price was not remunerative, I was told by one of the highest authorities in railway matters that five-eighths of a cent would be perfectly satisfactory. The effect of this reduction in the cost of transportation is precisely as though the unexhaustible grain fields and pastures across the Mississippi had been moved bodily eastward to the longitude of Ohio and Western New York. It is estimated that it takes a quarter of a ton of bread and meat to feed a grown man in Massachusetts for a year. The bread and meat come to him from the far west, and I have no doubt that it will astonish you to be told, as it lately astonished me, that a single day of this man's labour, even if it be of the commonest sort, will pay for transporting his year's subsistence for a thousand miles."

TAY BRIDGE ACCIDENT.

Dec. 28, 1879.   A fearful disaster occurred in Scotland. As the train from Edinburgh to Dundee was crossing the bridge, two miles in length, which spans the mouth of the Tay, a terrible hurricane struck the bridge, about four hundred yards of which was, with the train, dashed into the sea below.   About seventy persons were in the train, of whom not one escaped, nor, when the divers were able to descend, could a single body be found in the carriages, or among the bridge girders, and some days elapsed before any were recovered.   No conclusive evidence could be produced to show whether the train was blown off the rails and so dragged the girders down, or whether the bridge was blown away and the train ran into the chasm thus made.   The night was intensely dark, and the wind more violent than had ever been known in the country.

Annual Register, 1879.

AN EXTRAORDINARY WAIF.

The following is a translation from the Norwegian newspaper *Morgenbladet*, dated Feb. 20th :—"By private letter from Utsue, an island on the western coast of Norway, is communicated to Dapposten the intelligence that on the 12th inst. some fishermen pulled on the Firth to haul their nets, and had hardly finished their labour when they sighted an extraordinary object some distance further out. The superstitious fears of sea monsters which have been written a good deal about lately held them back for some time, but their curiosity made them approach the supposed sea monster, and, to their great surprise, they found that it was something like a building.   As the sea was calm they immediately commenced to tow it to shore, where it was hauled up on the beach, and was then found to be a damaged railway wagon.   The wheels were off, the windows smashed, and one door hanging on its hinges. By the name on it, "Edinburgh and Glasgow Railway," it was at once surmised that it must have been one of the wagons separated from the train which met with the disaster on the Tay Bridge.   In the carriage was a portmanteau containing garments, some of them marked 'P.B.' The wagon was sent, on the 14th, to Hangesund, to be forwarded thence to Bergen."

A RAILWAY SLEEPER.

A railway pointsman, caught napping at his post and convicted of wilful negligence, said to the gaoler who was about to lock him up, " I always supposed that the safety of a railroad depended on the soundness of its sleepers?" " So it does," replied the gaoler, " but such sleepers are never safe unless they are bolted in."

NOT TO BE CAUGHT.

The following incident is said to have occurred on the North London Railway:—Some time ago a passenger remarked, in the hearing of one of the company's servants, how easy it was to "do" the company, and said, "I often travel from Broad Street to Dalston Junction without a ticket—anyone can do it—I did it yesterday." When he alighted he was followed by the official, who asked him how it was done. For a consideration he agreed to tell him. This being given. "Now," said the inquirer, "how did you go from Broad Street to Dalston Junction yesterday without a ticket?" " Oh," was the reply, "I walked."

THE DOCTOR AND THE OFFICERS.

The following is rather a good story from the Emerald Isle:—A doctor and his wife got into a train near—well. we will not say where. In the same carriage with the doctor were two strange officers. The doctor's wife got into another compartment of the same train, the doctor not having seen his wife in the hurry, neither knew that they were travelling by the same train until both had got into different carriages. Said one of the officers to his companion, "That is the ugliest woman I ever saw." "She is." replied the Son of Mars. "I should not like to be obliged to kiss her," responded the first speaker. "I should not mind doing it," sullenly said the doctor. "You never would, sir, think of such a thing," said the officer. "I'll bet you a sovereign I will," answered the man of "pills and potions." "Done," said the officer. So when they all got out at the station, the doctor went forward and kissed his wife, and won his sovereign—the easiest-earned fee he had ever received. The officers looked rather astonished when he presented his wife to them.

THE BOTHERED QUEEN'S COUNSEL.

Mr. Merewether, Q.C., got into the train one morning with a whole batch of briefs and a talkative companion. He wanted to go through his briefs, but his companion would not let him work. He tried silence, he tried grunting, he tried sarcasm. At length, when they came to Hanwell, the gossip hit upon the unfortunate remark, "How well the asylum looks from the railway!" "Pray, sir," replied Mr. Merewether, "how does the railway look from the asylum?" The man was silent.

A BRAVE ENGINE DRIVER.

An American contemporary says:—"John Bull, of Galion (Ohio), ought to have his name recorded in an enduring way, for few have ever behaved so nobly as that engine driver of the New York, Pennsylvania, and Ohio railroad. As he was driving a passenger train last month he found that, through somebody's blunder, a freight train was approaching on the same track, and a collision was inevitable. He could have saved his own life by leaping from the engine, but, dismissing all thoughts of himself, he resolved to try and save the passengers committed to his care. So he reversed the engine and set the air-brakes, and then put on full steam, started the locomotive ahead, broke the coupling attached to the train, and dashed on to receive the shock of the collision. The passengers escaped all injury, while the brave engineer was so badly hurt that he died in a few hours. Such heroism as this should not go unnoticed." The *Cincinnati Inquirer* says: "He remained in the car until the engine leaped into the air and was dashed into the ditch, when he attempted to spring to the ground, but had his foot caught between the frames of the engine and tender, striking his head on the ground and causing the fatal injuries. Railroad men say that the act of detaching the engine as he did, not even derailing the baggage car with his engine at the high rate of speed, and all in 150 feet, is without parallel in railroading. A purse of 500 dollars was raised by the grateful passengers. The body has been shipped to Galion for burial.

AN INDUSTRIOUS BISHOP.

In noticing the "Life of the Rt. Rev. Samuel Wilberforce, D.D., Lord Bishop of Oxford, and afterwards of Winchester," a writer in the *Athenæum* remarks:—"Busy he was, both in Oxford and in London, and his correspondence with all kinds of people was unusually large. A large proportion of his letters were written in the railway train, and dated from 'near' this town, or 'between' this and that. We remember to have heard from one who was his companion in a railway carriage that before the journey was half-finished the adjoining seat was littered with envelopes of letters which he had read, and with the answers he had written since he started. All this undeniably shows energy and determination, and power to work."

COOL IMPUDENCE AND DISHONESTY.

Some days since, the trains of the North London Railway were all late, and consequently every platform was crowded. At one of the stations an unfortunate passenger attempted to enter an already over-crowded first-class compartment, but one of the occupants stoutly resisted the intrusion. Thereupon, the unfortunate one said, "I will soon settle this," and called the guard to the carriage door. He then requested the official to ask two of the occupants to produce their tickets, which proved to be third-class ones. In spite of the delinquents protesting there was no room in the train elsewhere, they were ejected, and the unfortunate one took their place. The other passengers were naturally rather indignant; and, seeing this, the successful intruder quietly said, "I am very sorry to have had to turn those two gentlemen out, especially as I have heard them say they were already late for an important engagement in the city; and I am all the more sorry, seeing that I only hold a third-class ticket myself."

—Truth.

THE BOOKING-CLERK AND BUCKLAND.

Mr. Frank Buckland had been in France and was returning *via* Southampton, with an overcoat stuffed with natural history specimens of all sorts, dead and alive.

Among them was a monkey, which was domiciled in a large inside breast-pocket. As Buckland was taking his ticket, Jocko thrust up his head and attracted the attention of the booking-clerk, who immediately—and very properly—said, "You must take a ticket for that dog, if it's going with you." "Dog," said Buckland, "it's no dog, it's a monkey." "It is a dog," replied the clerk. "It's a monkey," retorted Buckland, and proceeded to show the whole animal, but without convincing the clerk, who insisted on five shillings for the dog-ticket to London. Nettled at this, Buckland plunged his hand into another pocket and produced a tortoise, and laying it on the sill of the ticket window said, "Perhaps you'll call that a dog too." The clerk inspected the tortoise. "No." said he, "we make no charge for them—they're insects."

REMARKABLE RESCUE OF A CHILD.

An engineer on a locomotive going across the western prairie day after day, saw a little child come out in front of a cabin and wave to him, so he got in the habit of waving back to the child, and it was the day's-joy to see this little one come out in front of the cabin door and wave to him while he answered back. One day the train was belated, and it came on to the dusk of the evening. As the engineer stood at his post he saw by the headlight that little girl on the track, wondering why the train did not come, looking for the train, knowing nothing of her peril. A great horror seized upon the engineer. He reversed the engine. He gave it in charge of the other man, and then he climbed over the engine, and he came down on the cowcatcher. He said though he had reversed the engine, it seemed as though it were going at lightning speed, faster and faster, though it was really slowing up, and with almost supernatural clutch he caught the child by the hair and lifted it up, and when the train stopped, and the passengers gathered around to see what was the matter, there the old engineer lay, fainted dead away, the little child alive and in his swarthy arms.

FEMALE FRAGILITY.

There was a time when American women prided themselves on their fragility. To be healthy strong, or plump was thought to be the height of vulgarity, and refinement was held to be inseparable from leanness and consumption. These views still obtain—so it is said—in Boston, and especially in Bostonian literary circles; but elsewhere the American woman is growing plump and healthy, and is actually proud of it. While wise men are heartily glad of this change in female sentiment and tissue, it must be admitted that there is one form of feminine fragility which has its value. There is a rare condition of the bony system in which the bones are so fragile that the slightest blow is sufficient to break them. A baby thus afflicted cannot be handled, even by the most experienced mother, without danger; and a man with fragile bones is so liable to be broken, that there is sometimes no safety for him outside of a glass case. The late Mrs. Baker—for that was her latest name—was not so fragile that she could not be handled by a careful man, but still a very light blow would usually break her. She did not share the Bostonian opinion of the vulgarity of strength, but she was, nevertheless, very proud of her fragility, and by its aid her husband managed to amass a comfortable fortune within three years after their marriage. She is perhaps the only fragile woman on record of whom it can be said that her whole value consisted in her fragility, but, as her story shows, her fragility was the sole capital invested in her husband's business. In January, 1870, Mrs. Baker—then a single woman, as to whose maiden name there is some uncertainty—was married to Mr. Wheelwright—James G. Wheelwright, of Worcester, Mass. Her husband married her on account of her well-known fragility, but he treated her with such kindness that in the whole course of their married life he never once broke her, even by accident. In February, 1870, the Wheelwrights removed to Utica, N.Y., and one day Mr. Wheelwright took his wife to the railway station, and had her break her leg in a small hole on the platform. He at once sued the railway company for 10,000 dols., being the value set by himself on his wife's leg, and ten days

afterwards accepted 5,000 dols. as a compromise, and withdrew the suit   The Wheelwrights left Utica in June, 1870,
and in the following August the dutiful Mrs. Wheelwright,
who now called herself Mrs. Thomas, broke her other leg in
a hole in the platform of the railway station at Pittsburg.
Again her husband sued the railway company for 15,000
dols., and compromised for 6,500 dols.   The leg was mended
successfully, and in July, 1871, we find the Thomases, now
passing under the name of Mr. and Mrs. Smiley, at Cincinnati,
where Mr. Smiley, after long searching, discovered a piece
of ragged and uneven sidewalk, upon which his wife made
a point of falling and breaking her right arm.   This
time the city was sued for 15,000 dols., and Mr. Smiley
proved that his wife was a school teacher by profession,
and that the breaking of her arm rendered it impossible
for her to teach, for there as on that she could not wield a
rod or even a slipper.   The city paid the 15,000 dols. and
the Smileys, having by honest industry thus made 26,500
dols., removed to Chicago, and entered their names on the
hotel register as Mr. and Mrs. McGinnis, of Portland, Me.
On the second day after their arrival at the hotel,
Mr. McGinnis found an eligible place on the piazza for
Mrs. McGinnis to break another leg, which that excellent
woman promptly did.   The usual suit of 15,000 dols. was
brought, and the hotel-keeper, fearing that the notoriety
of the suit would injure his hotel, was glad to compromise
by paying 8,000 dols.   By this time, it is understood,
Mrs. McGinnis was willing to retire from business, but her
husband had set his heart on making 50,000 dols., and like
a good wife she consented to break some more bones.   It
should be said that there was very little pain attending a
fracture of any one of the lady's bones, and that she did
not in the least mind the monotony of lying in bed while
the broken bones knitted themselves together.   There can,
therefore, be no charge of cruelty brought against her
husband.   Indeed, she herself entered with a hearty goodwill into the scheme of making a living with her bones, and
would go out to break a leg with as much cheerfulness as
if she was going to a theatre.   In March, 1872, Mrs. Wilkins
—hitherto known as Mr. McGinnis—walked into an open
trench in a street in St. Louis and broke another leg.   This

time the suit brought by Mr. Wilkins against the city did
not succeed, and the inquiries which were put on foot as to
the antecedents of the Wilkinses fairly frightened them out
of the city. They turned up a month later in Detroit,
where the weather was still cold, and much snow had
recently fallen. There were still 16,000 dollars to be made
before the industrious pair would have the whole of their
desired 50,000 dollars, and it was decided that Mrs. Wilkins
—who had changed her name to Mrs. Baker—should fall
on the icy pavement and break both arms. This, it was
estimated, would be worth at least 8,000 dols., and it was
hoped that the subsequent judicious breakage of two legs
on the premises of a Canadian railway would bring in
8,000 dols. more, after which the Bakers intended to retire
from business. Early one morning Mr. Baker took his
wife out and had her fall on a nice piece of ice, where she
broke both arms. Unfortunately, she fell more heavily
than was necessary, and, in addition, broke her neck and
instantly expired. The grief of Mr. Baker naturally knew
no bounds, and he sued for 25,000 dols., all of which he
recovered. He had thus made 59,500 dols. by the aid of
his fragile wife, and demonstrated that as a source of steady
income a woman who breaks easily is almost priceless.
Still, nothing could console him for the loss of his beloved
partner, and he is to-day a lonely and unhappy man.

—*New York Times.*

TAKING HIM DOWN A PEG.

A guard of a railway train, upon the late occasion of a
hitch, which detained the passengers for some time, gave
himself so much importance in commanding them, that one
old gentleman took the wind out of his sails by calling him
to the carriage door, and saying, "May I take the liberty,
sir, of asking you what occupation you filled previous to
being a railway guard?"

A REMARKABLE NOTICE.

On a certain railway, the following notice appeared:—
"Hereafter, when trains moving in opposite directions are
approaching each other on separate lines, conductors and

engineers will be required to bring their respective trains
to a dead halt before the point of meeting, and be very
careful not to proceed till each train has passed the other."

FLUTTER CAUSED BY THE MURDER OF MR. BRIGGS.

My vocations led me to travel almost daily on one of the
Great Eastern lines—the Woodford Branch. Every one
knows that Müller perpetrated his detestable act on the
North London Railway, close by. The English middle
class, of which I am myself a feeble unit, travel on the
Woodford branch in large numbers. Well, the demoralization of our class,—which (the newspapers are constantly
saying it, so I may repeat it without vanity) has done all
the great things which have ever been done in England,—
the demoralization of our class caused, I say, by the Bow
tragedy, was something bewildering. Myself a transcen-
dentalist (as the *Saturday Review* knows), I escaped the
infection; and day after day I used to ply my agitated
fellow-travellers with all the consolations which my tran-
scendentalism and my turn for French would naturally
suggest to me. I reminded them how Julius Cæsar refused
to take precautions against assassination, because life was
not worth having at the price of an ignoble solicitude for
it. I reminded them what insignificant atoms we all are in
the life of the world. Suppose the worse to happen, I
said, addressing a portly jeweller from Cheapside,—suppose
even yourself to be the victim, *il n'y a pas d'homme nécessaire.*
We should miss you for a day or two on the Woodford
Branch; but the great mundane movement would still go
on, the gravel walks of your villa would still be rolled,
dividends would still be paid at the bank, omnibuses would
still run, there would still be the old crush at the corner of
Fenchurch street. All was of no avail. Nothing could
moderate in the bosom of the great English middle class
their passionate, absorbing, almost blood-thirsty clinging
to life.

—Matthew Arnold's *Essays in Criticism.*

AN EXTRAORDINARY BLUNDER.

A correspondent, writing from Amélia les Bains, says :—A very singular blunder was committed the other day by the officials of a railway station between Prepignan and Toulon. A gentleman who had been spending the winter here with his family, left last week for Marseilles, taking with him the body of his mother-in-law, who died six weeks ago, and who had expressed a wish to be buried in the family vault at Marseilles. When he reached Marseilles and went with the commissioner of police—whose presence is required upon these occasions— to receive the body from the railway officials, he noticed to his great surprise that the coffin was of a different shape and construction from that which he had brought from here. It turned out upon further inquiry that a mistake had been committed by the officials, who had sent on to Toulon the coffin containing his mother-in-law's body, believing that it held the remains of a deceased admiral, which was to be embarked for interment in Algeria, while the coffin awaiting delivery was the one which should have been sent on. The gentleman who was placed in this awkward predicament, having requested the railway officials to communicate at once with Toulon by telegraph, proceeded thither himself with the coffin of the admiral, but the intimation had arrived too late. He ascertained when he got there that the first coffin had been duly received, taken on board, amid "the thunder of fort and of fleet," the state vessel which was waiting for it, and despatched to Algeria. He at once called upon the maritime prefect of Toulon, and explained the circumstances of the case, but though a despatch-boat was sent in pursuit, the other vessel was not overtaken. He is now at Toulon awaiting her return, and I believe that he declines to give up the coffin containing the deceased admiral until he regains possession of his mother-in-law's remains.

A CURIOUS RACE.

In July, 1877, a carrier-pigeon tried conclusions with a railway train. The bird was a Belgian voyageur, bred at Woolwich, and "homed" to a house in Cannon Street, City. The train was the Continental mail-express timed not to stop between Dover and Cannon Street Station. The pigeon, conveying an urgent message from the French police, was tossed through the railway carriage window as the train moved from the Admiralty Pier, the wind being west, the atmosphere hazy, but the sun shining. For more than a minute the bird circled round till it attained an altitude of about half-a-mile, and then it sailed away Londonwards. By this time the engine had got full steam on, and the train was tearing away at the rate of sixty miles an hour; but the carrier was more than a match for it. Taking a line midway between Maidstone and Sittingbourne, it reached home twenty minutes before the express dashed into the station; the train having accomplished seventy-six-and-a-half miles to the pigeon's seventy, but being badly beaten for all that.

—*All the Year Round.*

A GREENLANDER'S FIRST RAILWAY RIDE.

Hans Hendrik, a native of Greenland, thus describes his first journey by rail in America:—"Then our train arrived and we took seats in it. When we had started and looked at the ground, it appeared like a river, making us dizzy, and the trembling of the carriage might give you headache. In this way we proceeded, and whenever we approached houses they gave warning by making big whistle sound, and on arriving at the houses they rung a bell and we stopped for a little while. By the way we entered a long cave through the earth, used as a road, and soon after we emerged from it again. At length we reached our goal, and entered a large mansion, in which numbers of people crowded together." He likens the people going out of the railway-station to a "crowd of church-goers, on account of their number."

—*Good Words*, April, 1880.

A NOVEL ACTION.

Will bad table manners vitiate legal grounds of action? A collision recently occurred while an Italian commercial traveller was eating a Bologna sausage in a railway train. The shock of the collision drove the knife so violently against his mouth as to widen it. He brought suit for damages. The defence was that the injuries were caused by the knife; that the knife should never be carried to the mouth, and that the plaintiff, having injured himself by reason of his bad habit of eating. must take the consequences and pay his own doctor's bill. The case is not yet finally decided.

—Echo, Oct. 1st., 1880.

A KISS IN THE DARK.

On one of the seats in a railway train was a married lady with a little daughter; opposite, facing them, was another child, a son, and a coloured "lady" with a baby. The mother of these children was a beautiful matron with sparkling eyes, in exuberant health and vivacious spirits. Near her sat a young lieutenant, dressed to kill and seeking a victim. He scraped up an acquaintance with the mother by attentions to the children. It was not long before he was essaying to make himself very agreeable to her, and by the time the sun began to decline, one would have thought they were old familiar friends. The lieutenant felt that he had made an impression—his elation manifested it. The lady, dreaming of no wrong, suspecting no evil, was apparently pleased with her casual acquaintance. By-and-by the train approached a tunnel. The gay lieutenant leaned over and whispered something in the lady's ear. It was noticed that she appeared as thunderstruck, and her eyes immediately flamed with indignation. A moment more and a smile lighted up her features. What changes? That smile was not one of pleasure, but was sinister. It was unperceived by the lieutenant. She made him a reply which apparently rejoiced him very much. For the understanding properly this narrative, we must tell the reader what was whispered and what was replied. "I mean to kiss you when we get into the tunnel!" whispered the lieutenant. "It will be dark; who will see it?" replied the lady. Into earth's bowels—into the tunnel ran the train. Lady and coloured nurse quickly change seats. Gay lieutenant threw his arms around the lady sable, pressed her cheek to his, and fast and furious rained kisses on her lips. In a few moments the train came out into broad daylight. White lady looked amazed—coloured lady, bashful, blushing—gay lieutenant befogged. "Jane," said the white lady, "what have you been doing?" "Nothing!" responded the coloured lady. "Yes, you have," said the white lady, not in an undertone, but in a voice that attracted the attention of all in the carriage. "See how your collar is rumpled and your bonnet smashed." Jane, poor coloured beauty, hung her head for a moment, the "observed of all observers," and then, turning round to the lieutenant, replied: "*This man kissed me in the tunnel!*" Loud and long was the laugh that followed among the passengers. The white lady enjoyed the joke amazingly. Lieutenant looked like a sheep-stealing dog, left the carriage at the next station, and was seen no more.

—*Cape Argus.*

THE GRAVEDIGGER'S SUGGESTION.

The Midland Railway, on being extended to London, was the occasion of the removal of a vast amount of house property, also it interfered to a certain extent with the graveyard belonging to Old St. Pancras Church. The company had purchased a new piece of ground in which to re-inter the human remains discovered in the part they required. Amongst them was the corpse of a high dignitary of the French Romish Church. Orders were received for the transmission of the remains to his native land, and the delicate work of exhuming the corpse was entrusted to some clever gravediggers. On opening the ground they were surprised to find, not bones of one man, but of several. Three skulls and three sets of bones were yielded by the soil in which they had lain mouldering. The difficulty was how to identify the bones of a French ecclesiastic amid so many. After much discussion, the shrewdest gravedigger suggested that, being a Frenchman, the darkest coloured skull must be his. Acting upon this idea, the blackest bones were sorted and put together, until the requisite number of rights and lefts were obtained. These were reverently screwed up in a new coffin, conveyed to France, and buried with all the pomp and circumstance of the Roman Catholic Church.

AN AMUSING INCIDENT.

An American correspondent writes:—"I have just finished reading a most amusing incident, and, as it occurs in a book not likely to fall into the hands of many of the members, I am tempted to relate it, although it might prove to be 'stale.' Well, to begin: It tells of a maiden lady, who, having arrived at the mature age of 51 without ever having seen a railway train, decides to visit New York. The all-important day having arrived, she seats herself calmly on the platform of the country station, and gazes with amazement as the train draws up, takes on its passengers, and pursues its journey. As she stares after it the station-master asks her why she did not get on if she wishes to go to New York. 'Get on,' says Miss Polly, in surprise, 'get on! Why, bless me, if I didn't think this whole concern went!' Being placed on the next train, she proceeds on her way, when, finally, having seen so many wonderful things, she concluded not to be astonished, whatever may happen. A collision occurs and the gentleman next to her is thrown to the end of the car among a heap of broken seats. She supposes it to be the usual manner of stopping, and quietly remarks: 'Ye fetch up rather sudden, don't ye?'"

A LITTLE BOY'S COOLNESS.

The suit of William O'Connor against the Boston and Lowell Railroad at Lawrence has resulted in a verdict for the plaintiff in $10,000, one-half the amount sued for. This suit grew out of an accident which occurred August 27th, 1880. The plaintiff was the father of a child then between five and six years old. He and his brother, three years older, were crossing a private way maintained by the railroad for the Essex Company, and the younger boy, while walking backward, stepped between the rail and planking of the roadway inside and was unable to extricate his foot. At that moment the whistle of a train was heard within a few hundred feet and out of sight around a curve, and it appeared from the evidence that the older brother, finding himself unable to relieve his brother, ran down the track toward the train; but finding that he could not attract the attention of the trainmen to his brother's condition, and that he must be run over, ran back to him, and, telling him to lie down, pulled him outward and down and held him there until the train had passed. Both feet of the little fellow were cut off or mangled so that amputation was necessary. The theory of the defence was that the boy was not caught, but while running across the track, fell and was run over. But the testimony of the older brother was unshaken in every particular. It would be difficult to match the nerve, thoughtfulness, and disregard of self displayed by this boy, who at that time was less than nine years old.

PHOTOGRAPHING AN EXPRESS TRAIN.

An interesting application of the instantaneous method of photography was recently made by a firm of photographers at Henley-on-Thames. These artists were successful in photographing the Great Western Railway express train familiarly known as the "Flying Dutchman," while running through Twyford station at a speed of nearly sixty miles an hour. The definition of this lightning-like picture is truly wonderful, the details of the mechanism on the flying locomotive standing out as sharply as the immovable telegraph posts and palings beside the line. The photographers are now engaged, we believe, in constructing a swift shutter for their camera which will reduce the period of exposure of the photographic plate to 1-500th of a second. The same artists have also executed some charming pictures of the upper Thames, with floating swans and moving boats, which cannot but win the admiration of artists and all lovers of the picturesque.

—*Cassell's Family Magazine*, Nov. 1880.

NERVOUSNESS.

Surely people are far more *nervous* now than they used to be some generations back. The mental cultivation and the mental wear which we have to go through tends to make that strange and inexplicable portion of our physical construction a very great deal too sensitive for the work and trial of daily life. A few days ago I drove a friend who had been paying us a visit over to our railway station. He is a man of fifty, a remarkably able and accomplished man. Before the train started, the guard came round to look at the tickets. My friend could not find his; he searched his pockets everywhere, and although the entire evil consequence, had the ticket not turned up, could not possibly have been more than the payment a second time of four or five shillings, he got into a nervous tremor painful to see. He shook from head to foot; his hand trembled so that he could not prosecute his search rightly, and finally he found the missing ticket in a pocket which he had already searched half-a-dozen times. Now contrast the condition of this highly-civilized man, thrown into a painful flurry and confusion at the demand of a railway ticket, with the impassive coolness of a savage, who would not move a muscle if you hacked him in pieces.   —*Fraser's Magazine.*

A PROFITABLE RAILWAY.

The shortest and most profitable railway in the world is probably to be seen at Coney Island, the famous suburban summer resort of New York. This is the "Marine Railway," which connects the Manhattan Beach Hotel and the Brighton Beach Hotel. It is 2,000 feet in length, is laid with steel rails, and has a handsome little station at each end. Its equipment consists of two locomotives and four cars, open at the sides, and having reversible seats; and a train of two cars is run each way every five minutes. The cost of this miniature road, including stations and equipment, was 27,000 dols., and it paid for itself in a few weeks after it was opened for business. The operating expenses are 30 dols. a day, and the average receipts are 450 dols. a day the entire season, 900 dols. being sometime taken in. The fare charged is five cents. The property paid a profit last year of 500 dols. per cent on its cost.

THE POLITE BRAHMIN.

Owing to the various dialects in the South of India, as a matter of convenience the English language is much used for personal communication by the natives of different parts of the Presidency of Madras. Mr. Edward Lear, who has travelled much in that part of the country, gives the following interesting account of a journey:—"I was in a second-class railway carriage going from Madras to Bangalore. There was only one other passenger beside myself and servant, and he was a Brahmin, dressed all in white, with the string worn over the shoulder, by which you may always recognise a Brahmin. He had a great many boxes and small articles, which took up a great deal of room in the compartment, and when at the next station the door was opened for another passenger to get in, the guard said :—

" 'You cannot have all those boxes inside the carriage ; some of them must be taken out.'

" 'Oh, sir,' said the Brahmin in good English, 'I assure you these articles are by no means necessary to my comfort, and I hope you will not hesitate to dispose of them as you please.'

"Accordingly, therfore, the boxes were taken away. Then the newcomer stepped in ; he was also a native, but dressed in quite a different manner from the Brahmin, his clothing being blue, green, red, and all the colours of the rainbow, so that one saw at once the two persons were from different parts of India. Presently he surprised me by saying to the Brahmin,

" 'Pray, sir, excuse me for having given you the trouble of removing any part of your luggage ; I am really quite sorry to have given you any inconvenience whatever.'

"To which the Brahmin replied, 'I beg sir, you will make no apologies ; it is impossible you can have incommoded me by causing the removal of those trifling articles; and, even if you have done so, the pleasure of your society would afford me perfect compensation.' "

MR. FRANK BUCKLAND AND HIS BOOTS.

Mr. Spencer Walpole, furnishes some interesting and amusing gossip about the late Mr. Frank Buckland, describing some of his many eccentricities, and telling many stories relative to his peculiar habits. He had, it seems, a great objection to stockings and boots and coats, his favourite attire consisting of nothing else than trousers and a flannel shirt. Boots were his special aversion, and he never lost an opportunity of kicking them off his feet.

"On one occasion," we are told, "travelling alone in a railway carriage, he fell asleep with his feet resting on the window-sill. As usual, he kicked off his boots, and they fell outside the carriage on the line. When he reached his destination the boots could not, of course, be found, and he had to go without them to his hotel. The next morning a platelayer, examining the permanent way, came upon the boots, and reported to the traffic manager that he had found a pair of gentleman's boots, but that he could not find the gentleman. Some one connected with the railway recollected that Mr. Buckland had been seen in the neighbourhood, and, knowing his eccentricities, inferred that the boots must belong to him. They were accordingly sent to the Home Office, and were at once claimed."

DRINKING FROM THE WRONG BOTTLE.

An incident has occurred on one of the suburban lines which will certainly be supposed by many to be only *ben trovato*, but it is a real fact. A lady, who seemed perfectly well before the train entered a tunnel, suddenly alarmed her fellow-passengers during the temporary darkness by exclaiming, "I am poisoned!" On re-emerging into daylight, an awkward explanation ensued. The lady carried with her two bottles, one of methylated spirit, the other of cognac. Wishing, presumably, for a refresher on the sly, she took advantage of the gloom; but she applied the wrong bottle to her lips. Time pressed, and she took a good drain. The consequence was she was nearly poisoned, and had to apply herself honestly and openly to the brandy bottle as a corrective, amidst the ironical condolence of the passengers she had previously alarmed.

— *Once a Week*.

HORSES VERSUS RAILWAYS.

A horse for every mile of road was the allowance made by the best coachmasters on the great routes. On the corresponding portions of the railway system the great companies have put a locomotive engine per mile. If a horse earned a hundred guineas a year, out of which his cost had to be defrayed, he did well. A single locomotive on the Great Northern Railway (and that company has 611 engines for 659 miles of line) was stated by John Robinson, in 1873, to perform the work of 678 horses —work, that is, as measured by resistance overcome ; for the horses, whatever their number, could not have reached the speed of fifty miles an hour, at which the engines in questions whirled along a train of sixteen carriages, weighing in all 225 tons.   There are now upwards of 13,000 locomotives at work in the United Kingdom, each of them earning on the average, £4,750 per annum.   But we have at the same time more horses employed for the conveyance of passengers than we had in 1835.   In omnibus and station work—waiting upon the steam horse—there is more demand for horseflesh than was made by our entire coaching system in 1835.

—*Fraser's Magazine.*

A SLIGHT MISTAKE.

An Irish newspaper is responsible for the following:— "A deaf man named Taff was run down and killed by a passenger train on Wednesday morning.   He was injured in a similar way about a year ago."

EXPENSIVE CONTRACTS.

An interesting glimpse into the inner working of State, and especially Russian, Government railways was afforded in a recent discussion on railway management in Russia, published by the *Journal* of the German Railroad Union. During this debate it appears that the details were published of the famous contract of the late American Winans with the Government concerning the Nicholas Railroad.   By the use of considerable money, Winans succeeded in making a contract, to extend from July 1st, 1866, for eight years, by which the Government was to pay him for oiling cars and small car repairs at an agreed rate per passenger and per ton mile.   In addition to this he received a fixed sum of about £15,000 (78,000 dols.) per year for painting and maintaining the interior of the passenger cars ; £6,000 for keeping up the shops, and finally £8,000 yearly for renewing what rolling stock might be worn out.   The St. Nicholas line was eventually taken over by the Great Russian Company, which in 1872 succeeded in making the Government annul the contract by paying Winans a penalty of £750,000, which the Great Russian Company paid back with interest within four years. If the contract had been continued it would have cost the company more than one-third of its net earnings, since the saving amounts to nearly £523,000 per annum. Another contract which the Government had made for the same road with a sleeping-car company was settled shortly afterward by the Government taking from the company the few cars it had on hand, and paying £75,000 for them and £10,000 a year for the unexpired seven years of the contract.

MR. BRASSEY'S STRICT ADHERENCE TO HIS WORD.

The following is one of such stories, illustrative of one phase of Mr. Brassey's character—his strict adherence to his word, under all circumstances.

When the "Sambre and Meuse" was drawing towards completion. Mr. Brassey came along as usual with a staff of agents inspecting the progress of the work. Stopping at Olloy, a small place between Mariembourg and Vireux, near a large blacksmith's shop, the man, a Frenchman or Belgian, came out, and standing up on the bank, with much gesticulation and flourish, proceeded to make Mr. Brassey a grand oration. Anxious to proceed, Mr. Brassey paid him no particular attention, but good naturedly endeavoured to cut the matter short, with "Oui, oui, oui," and at length got away, the Frenchman apparently expressing great delight.

"Well, gentlemen, what are you laughing at, what is the joke?" said he to his staff as they went along.

"Why, sir, do you know what that fellow said, and for what he was asking?"

"No, indeed, I don't; I supposed he was complimenting me in some way, or thanking me for something."

"He *was* complimenting you, sir, to some tune, and asking, as a souvenir of his happy engagement under the Great Brassey, that you would of your goodness make him a present of the shop, iron, tools, and all belonging!"

"Did he, though! I did not understand that."

"No sir, but you kept on saying, 'Oui, oui, oui.' and the fellow's delighted, as he well may be, they're worth £50 or £60."

"Oh, but I didn't mean that, I didn't mean that. Well, never mind, if I said it, he must *have* them."

It must be borne in mind, that at that time, at best, Mr. Brassey knew very little French. and his staff were well aware of the fact."

Sep. 13, 1872.   S. S.

EXTRAORDINARY ACCIDENT.

In a leading article in the *Birmingham Post*, Nov. 12th, 1880, the writer remarks:—"The report of Major Marindin on the collision which took place between two Midland trains, in Leicestershire, about a month ago, has just been published, but it adds nothing to the information given at the time when the accident happened. The case was, as the report says, one of a remarkable, if not unprecedented nature, for the collision arose from a passenger train running backwards instead of forwards nearly half-a-mile, without either driver or stoker noticing that its movement was in the wrong direction. Shortly after the train had passed the village station of Kibworth, where it was not timed to stop, the driver observed a knocking sound on his engine. He pulled up the train in order to ascertain the cause of this, and finding that nothing serious was the matter, proceeded on his journey again, or rather intended to do so, for, by an extraordinary mistake, he turned the screw the wrong way, so as to reverse the action of the engine, and to direct the train back to Kibworth. There, a mineral train was making its way towards Leicester, and as the line was on a sharp incline the result might have been a most destructive collision. It was, however, reduced to one of a comparatively mild-description by the promptness and efficiency with which the brakes were applied to both the trains. Had not the mineral train been pulled up, and the passenger train lowered from a speed of twenty to three or four miles an hour, probably the whole of the passengers would have been crushed between the two engines. The

passengers, therefore, owed their safety to the excellent
brake-power which was at command.   The excuse offered
by the driver of the passenger train for turning the engine
backwards was the shape of the reversing screw, which was
of a construction not commonly used on the Midland line,
though many of the company's engines were so fitted.   The
fireman had also his apology for making the same oversight.
He said he was at the time stooping down to adjust the
injector.   Major Marindin, though admitting that the men
were experienced, careful, and sober, refuses to accept either
of these excuses; but he can supply no better reason himself
for the amazing oversight they committed.   The only satisfactory part of the report is that in which the working of
the brake mechanism is spoken of.   The passenger train had
the Westinghouse brake fitted to all the carriages, and such
was its efficiency that, had it extended to the engine and
tender as well, Major Marindin believes the accident would
have been entirely prevented."   .

REMARKABLE MEMORY FOR SOUNDS.

Among strange mental feats the strangest perhaps yet
recorded are the following singular feats of memory for
sound, related in the *Scientific American*.   In the city of
Rochester, N. Y., resides a boy named Hicks, who, though
he has only lately removed from Buffalo to Rochester, has
already learned to distinguish three hundred locomotive
engines by the sound of their bells.   During the day the
boy is employed so far from the railway that he seldom
hears a passing train; but at night he can hear every train,
his house being near the railroad.   To give an idea of his
wonderful memory for sounds (and his scarcely less wonderful memory for numbers also) take the following cases.
Not long ago young Hicks went to Syracuse, and while
there, he, hearing an engine coming out of the round-house,
remarked to a friend that he knew the bell, though he had
not heard it for five years: he gave the number of the
engine, which proved to be correct.   Again, not long since,
an old switch-engine, used in the yards at Buffalo, was
sent to Rochester for some special purpose.   It passed near
Hicks' house, and he remarked that the engine was number

so and so, and that he had not heard the bell for six years.
A boarder in the house ran to the railroad, and found the
number given by Hicks was the correct one.   To most
persons the bells on American locomotives seem all much
alike in sound and *timbre*, though, of course, a good ear
will readily distinguish differences, especially between bells
which are sounded within a short interval of time.   But
that anyone should be able in the first place to discriminate
between two or three hundred of these bells, and in the
second place to retain the recollection of the slight
peculiarities characterising each for several years, would
seem altogether incredible, had we not other instances—
such as Bidder's and Colburn's calculating feats, Morphy's
blindfold chess-play, etc.—of the amazing degree in which
one brain may surpass all others in some special quality,
though perhaps, in other respects, not exceptionally powerful, or even relatively deficient

—*Gentleman's Magazine*, March 1880.

A DISINGENUOUS BISHOP.

Max. O'Rell, the French author, in his book *John Bull at
Home*, writes English people are very great on words;
lying is unknown.   I was travelling by rail one day with
an English bishop.   There were five in our compartment.
On arriving at a station we heard a cry, "Five minutes
here!"   My lord bishop, with the greatest haste, set to
work to spread out travelling-bag, hat-box, rug, papers, &c.
A lady appeared at the door, and asked, "Is there room
here?"   "Madam," replied the bishop, "all the seats are
full."   When the poor lady had been sent about her
business, we called his lordship's attention to the fact that
there were only five of us in the carriage, and that, consequently all the seats were not taken.   "I did not say that
they were," answered my lord; "I said that they were *full*."

DROPPING THE LETTER "L."

In an advertisement by a railway company of some
unclaimed goods, the "l" dropped from the word "lawful,"
and it reads now, "People to whom these packages are
directed are requested to come forward and pay the *awful*
charges on the same."

THE SAFEST SEAT IN A RAILWAY CARRIAGE.

The *American Engineer*, as the result of scientific calculations and protracted experience, says the safest seat is in the middle of the last car but one. There are some chances of danger, which are the same everywhere in the train, but others are least at the above-named place.

RAILWAYS A JUDGMENT.

In *White's Warfare of Science* there is an account of a worthy French Archbishop who declared that railways were an evidence of the divine displeasure against innkeepers, inasmuch that they would be punished for supplying meat on fast days by seeing travellers carried by them past their doors.

CLAIM FOR GOODWILL FOR COW KILLED ON THE RAILWAY.

A farmer living near the New York Central lost a cow by a collision with a train on the line, anxious for compensation he waited upon the manager and after stating his case; the manager said, "I understand she was thin and sick." "Makes no difference," replied the farmer. "She was a cow, and I want pay for her." "How much?" asked the manager. "Two hundred dollars!" replied the farmer. "Now look here," said the manager, "how much did the cow weigh?" "About four hundred, I suppose," said the farmer. "And we will say that beef is worth ten cents a pound on the hoof." "It's worth a heap more than that on the cow-catcher!" replied the indignant farmer. "But we'll call it that, what then? That makes forty dollars, shall I give you a cheque for forty dollars?" "I tell you I want two hundred dollars," persisted the farmer. "But how do you make the difference? I'm willing to pay full value, forty dollars. How do you make one hundred and sixty dollars?" "Well, sir," replied the farmer, waxing wroth, "I want this railroad to understand that I'm going to have something special for the goodwill of that cow!"

THE INSURANCE AGENT.

An agent of an accident insurance company entered a smoking car on a western railroad train a few days ago, and, approaching an exceedingly gruff old man, asked him if he did not want to take out a policy. He was told to get out with his policy, and passed on. A few minutes afterwards an accident occurred to the train, causing a fearful shaking to the cars. The old man jumped up, and seizing a hook at the side of the car to steady himself, called out, "Where is that insurance man?" The question caused a roar of laughter among the passengers, who for the time forgot their dangers.

—*Harper's Weekly*, May 8th, 1880.

TOUTING FOR BUSINESS AND FRAUDS.

Sir Edward Watkin observed at the half-yearly meeting of the South Eastern Railway Company, January, 1881 :— "The result of this compensating law under which the slightest neglect makes the company liable, and the only thing to be considered is the amount of damages—the effect of this unjust law is to create a new profession compounded of the worst elements of the present professions— viz., expert doctors, expert attorneys, and expert witnesses. You will get a doctor to swear that a man who has a slight knock on the head to say that he has a diseased spine, and will never be fit for anything again, and never be capable of being a man of business or the father of a family. The result of that is all we can do is to get some other expert to say exactly the contrary. Then you have a class of attorneys who get up this business. We had an accident, I may tell you, at Forrest-hill two years ago. Well, there was a gentleman—an attorney in the train. He went round to all the people in the train and gave them his card ; and, having distributed all the cards in his card-case, he went round and expressed extreme regret to the others that he could not give them a card ; but he gave them his name as 'So and So,' his place was in 'Such a street,' and the 'No, So and So' in the City. That was touting for business. Now, there is a very admirable body called the "Law Association." Why does not the Law Association take hold

s

of cases of that kind? Well, you saw in the paper the case of Roper *v.* the South Eastern. Now that was a peculiar thing. Roper declared that from an injury he had received in a slight accident at the Stoney-street signal box, outside Cannon-street he was utterly incapacitated, and that, for I don't know how many weeks and months, he was in bed without ceasing. The doctors, I believe, put pins and needles into him, but he never flinched, and when the case came before the court we found that some of the medical experts declared that it was just within the order of Providence that in twenty years he might get better; but these witnesses thought that the chances were against it, and that he would be a hopeless cripple. So evidence was given as to his income; and the idea was to capitalise it at £8,000. That man had paid 4d. for his ticket I think—I forget the exact amount. Our counsel, the Attorney-General, went into the thing, with the very able assistance of Mr. Willis, who deserves every possible credit. We also had Mr. Le Gros Clarke, the eminent consulting surgeon of the company, and Dr. Arkwright from the north of England, and they told us that in their opinion it was a swindle. And it was a swindle. The result of it was, the Attorney-General put his foot down upon it, and declared that it was a swindle, and the jury unanimously non-suited Mr. Roper. Well, singularly enough, when I say he had paid 4d., I think it was not absolutely proved that he was in the train at all. But although this was a case in which the jury said there was no case, and where the Judge summed up strongly that it was a fraud, and where the most eminent surgeon said it was an absolute delusion altogether, and where, in point of fact, justice was done entirely to you as regards the verdict, you have £2,300 to pay for costs of one kind or another in defending a case of swindling, because when you try to recover the costs the man becomes bankrupt, and you won't get a farthing; and I do mean to say I have described a state of the law and practice that ought to excite the reprobation of every honest man in England."

HEROISM OF A DRIVER.

An engine-driver on the Pennsylvania Railway yesterday saved the lives of 600 passengers by an extraordinary act of heroism. The furnace door was opened by the fireman to replenish the fire while the train was going at thirty-five miles an hour. The back draught forced the flames out so that the car of the locomotive caught fire, and the engine-driver and the fireman were driven back over the tender into the passenger car, leaving the engine without control. The speed increased, and the volume of flame with it. There was imminent danger that all the carriages would take fire, and the whole be consumed. The passengers were panic-stricken. To jump off was certain death ; to remain was to be burned alive. The engine-driver saw that the only way to save the passengers was to return to the engine and stop the train. He plunged into the flames, climbed back over the tender, and reversed the engine. When the train came to a standstill, he was found in the water-tank, whither he had climbed, with his clothes entirely burnt off, his face disfigured, his hands shockingly burned, and his body blistered so badly that the flesh was stripped off in many places. Weak and half-conscious he was taken to the hospital, where his injuries were pronounced serious, with slight chance of recovery. As soon as the train stopped the flames were easily extinguished. The unanimous testimony of the passengers is that the engine-driver saved their lives. His name is Joseph A. Sieg.

—*Daily News*, Oct. 24th, 1882.

IT'S CROYDON.

As an early morning train drew up at a station, a pleasant looking gentleman stepped out on the platform, and, inhaling, the fresh air, enthusiastically observed to the guard, "Isn't this invigorating?" "No, sir, it's Croydon," replied the conscientious employé.

YOUR TICKET.

On a Georgia railroad there is a conductor named Snell, a very clever, sociable man, fond of a joke, quick at repartee, and faithful in the discharge of his duties. One day as his train well filled with passengers, was crossing a low bridge over a wide stream, some four or five feet deep, the bridge broke down, precipitating the two passenger cars into the stream. As the passengers emerged from the wreck they were borne away by the force of the current. Snell had succeeded in catching hold of some bushes that grew on the bank of the stream, to which he held for dear life. A passenger less fortunate came rushing by. Snell extended one hand, saying, "Your ticket, sir; give me your ticket!" The effect of such a dry joke in the midst of the water may be imagined.

—*Harper's Magazine.*

AN OLD SCOTCH LADY ON THE LOSS OF HER BOX.

Dean Ramsay in his *Reminiscences* remarks:—"Some curious stories are told of ladies of this class, as connected with the novelties and excitement of railway travelling. Missing their luggage, or finding that something has gone wrong about it, often causing very terrible distress, and might be amusing, were it not to the sufferer so severe a calamity. I was much entertained with the earnestness of this feeling, and the expression of it from an old Scottish lady, whose box was not forthcoming at the station where she was to stop. When urged to be patient, her indignant exclamation was, "I can bear ony pairtings that may be ca'ed for in God's providence; but I canna stan' pairtin' frae ma claes."

RAILWAY MANNERS.

A gentleman was travelling by rail from Breslau to Oppeln and found himself alone with a lady in a second-class compartment. He vainly endeavoured to enter into conversation with the other occupant of the carriage; her answers were invariably curt and snappish. Baffled in his attempts, he proceeded to light a cigar to while away the time. Then the lady said to him: "I suppose you have never travelled second-class before, else you would know better manners." Her travelling companion quietly rejoined: "It is true, I have hitherto only studied the manners of the first and third-classes. In the first-class the passengers are rude to the porters, in the third-class the porters are rude to the passengers. I now discover that in the second-class the passengers are rude to each other."

A BRAVE GIRL.

Kate Shelley, to whom the Iowa Legislature has just given a gold medal and $200, is fifteen years old. She lives near Des Moines, at a point where a railroad crosses a gorge at a great height. One night during a furious storm the bridge was carried away. The first the Shelleys knew of it was when they saw the headlight of a locomotive flash down into the chasm. Kate climbed to the remains of the bridge with great difficulty, using an improvised lantern. The engineer's voice answered her calls, but she could do nothing for him, and he was drowned. As an express train was almost due, she then started for the nearest station, a mile distant. A long, high bridge over the Des Moines River had to be crossed on the ties—a perilous thing in stormy darkness. Kate's light was blown out, and the wind was so violent that she could not stand, so she crawled across the bridge, from timber to timber, on her hands and knees. She got to the station exhausted, but in time to give the warning, though she fainted immediately.

—*Detroit Free Press*, May 13th, 1882.

SHUT UP IN A LARGE BOX.

The Merv correspondent of the *Daily News* in a letter dated the 30th of April, 1881, remarks, "I was very much amused by the description given me by some Tekkés of the Serdar's departure for Russia. It seems that my informants accompanied him up to the point where the trans-Caspian railway is in working order. "They shut Tockmé Serdar and two others in a large box (sanduk) and locked him in, and then dragged him away across the Sahara. And," added the speakers, "Allah only knows what will happen to them inside that box." The box, I need hardly say, was a railway carriage.

AWFUL DEATH ON A RAILROAD BRIDGE.

A man commonly known as "Billy" Cooper, of the town of Van Etten, was walking on the railroad track at a point not far distant from his home. In crossing the railroad bridge he made a miss-step, and, slipping, fell between the ties, but his position was so cramped that he was unable to get out of the way of danger. There, suspended in that awful manner, with the body dangling below the bridge, he heard a train thundering along in the distance, approaching every moment nearer and nearer. No one will ever know the struggles for life which the poor fellow made, but they were futile; with arms pinioned to his sides he was unable to signal the engineer. The train came sweeping on upon its helpless victim until within a few feet of the spot, when the engineer saw the man's head and endeavoured to stop his heavy train. But too late; the moving mass passed over, cutting his head from the shoulders as clean as it could have been done by the guillotine itself. Cooper was 60 years of age.

—*Ithaca* (N.Y.) *Journal.*

THAT ACCURSED DRINK.

. An English traveller in Ireland, greedy for information and always fingering the note-book in his breast pocket, got into the same railway carriage with a certain Roman Catholic archbishop. Ignorant of his rank, and only perceiving that he was a divine, he questioned him pretty closely about the state of the country, whisky drinking, etc. At last he said, "You are a parish priest, yourself, of course." His grace drew himself up. "I *was* one, sir," he answered, with icy gravity. "Dear, dear," was the sympathizing rejoinder. "That accursed drink, I suppose."

RAILWAY UP VESUVIUS.

This railway, the last new project in mountain-climbing, is now finished. It is 900 mètres in length, and will enable tourists to ascend by it to the very edge of the crater. The line has been constructed with great care upon a solid pavement, and it is believed to be perfectly secure from all incursions of lava. The mode of traction is by two steel ropes put in motion by a steam engine at the foot of the cone. The wheels of the carriages are so made as to be free from any danger of leaving the rails, besides which each carriage is furnished with an exceedingly powerful automatic brake, which, should the rope by any chance brake, will stop the train almost instantaneously. One of the chief difficulties of the undertaking was the water supply; but that has been obviated by the formation of two very large reservoirs, one at the station, the other near the observatory.

—*Railway Times*, 1879.

EXTRAORDINARY ESCAPE OF BALLOONISTS.

Yesterday evening, Aug. 6th, 1883, a special train of "empties," which left Charing-cross at 5.55 to pick up returning excursionists from Gravesend, had some extraordinary experiences, such as perhaps had hardly ever occurred on a single journey. On leaving Dartford, where some passengers were taken up, the train was proceeding towards Greenhithe, when the driver observed on the line a donkey, which had strayed from an adjoining field. An endeavour was made to stop the train before the animal was reached, but without success, and the poor beast was knocked down and dragged along by the firebox of the engine. The train was stopped, and with great difficulty the body of the animal, which was killed, was extricated from beneath the engine. While this was in progress, a balloon called the "Sunbeam," supposed to come either from Sydenham or Tunbridge Wells, passed over the line, going in the direction of Northfleet. The two aeronauts in the car were observed to be short of gas, and were throwing out ballast, but, notwithstanding this, the balloon descended slowly, and when some distance ahead of the train was, to the horror of the passengers, seen to drop suddenly into the railway cutting two or three hundred yards only in advance of the approaching train. The alarm whistle was sounded, and the brakes put on, and as the balloon dragged the car and its occupants over the down line there seemed nothing but certain death for them; but suddenly the inflated monster, now swaying about wildly, took a sudden upward flight, and, dragging the car clear of the line, fell into an adjoining field just when the train was within a hundred yards of the spot. The escape was marvellous.

PULLING A TOOTH BY STEAM.

"Dummy," is a deaf mute newsman on the Long Island Railroad. Lately he had suffered much in mind and body from an aching tooth. He did not like dentists, but he resolved that the tooth must go. He procured a piece of twine, and tied one end of it to the tooth and the other end to the rear of an express train. When the train started, Dummy ran along the platform a short distance, and then dropped suddenly on his knees. The engine whistled, and dummy cried, but the train took the tooth.

A HEAVY SLEEPER.

It happens, in numerous instances, that virtuous resolves are made overnight with respect to early rising, which resolves, when put to the test, are doomed only to be broken. Some years ago a clergyman, who had occasion to visit the West of England on very important business, took up his quarters, late at night, at a certain hotel adjacent to a railway, with a view of starting by the early train on the following morning. Previous to retiring to rest, he called the "boots" to him, told him that he wished to be called for the early train, and said that it was of the utmost importance that he should not oversleep himself. The reverend gentleman at the same time confessed that he was a very heavy sleeper, and as there would be probably the greatest difficulty in awakening him, he (the "boots") was to resort to any means he thought proper in order to effect his object. And, further, that if the business were effectually accomplished, the fee should be a liberal one. The preliminaries being thus settled, the clergyman sought his couch, and "boots" left the room with the air of a determined man. At a quarter to five on the following morning, "boots" walked straight to "No. twenty-three," and commenced a vigorous rattling and hammering at the door, but the only answer he received was "All right!" uttered in a very faint and drowsy tone. Five minutes later, "boots" approached the door, placing his ear at the keyhole, and detecting no other sound than a most unearthly snore, he unceremoniously entered the room, and laying his brawny hands upon the prostrate form of the sleeper, shook him violently and long. This attack was replied to by a testy observation that he "knew all about it, and there was not the least occasion to shake him so." "Boots" thereupon left the room, somewhat doubtingly, and only to return in a few minutes afterwards and find the Rev. Mr.—— as sound asleep as ever. This time the clothes were stripped off, and a species of baptismal process was adopted, familiarly known as "cold pig." At this assault the enraged gentleman sat bolt upright in bed, and with much other bitter remark, denounced "boots" as a barbarous fellow. An explanation was then come to, and the drowsy man professed he understood it all, and was *about* to arise. But the gentleman who officiated at the —— hotel, having had some experience in these matters, placed no reliance upon the promise he had just received, and shortly visited "No. twenty-three" again. There he found that the occupant certainly had got up, but it was only to replace the bedclothes and to lie down again. "Boots" now felt convinced that this was one of those cases which required prompt and vigorous handling, and without more ado, therefore, he again stripped off the upper clothing, and seizing hold of the under sheet, he dragged its depository bodily from off the bed. The sleeping man, sensible of the unusual motion, and dreamily beholding a stalwart form bent over him, became impressed with the idea that a personal attack was being made upon him, probably with a view to robbery and murder. Under this conviction, he, in his descent, grasped "boots" firmly by the throat, the result being that both bodies thus came to the floor with a crash. Here the two rolled about for some seconds in all the agonies of a death struggle, until the unwonted noise and the cries of the assailants brought several persons from all parts of the hotel, and they, seeing two men rolling frantically about in each other's arms, and with the hand of each grasping the other's throat, rushed in and separated them. An explanation was of course soon given. The son of the church was effectually awakened, he rewarded the "boots," and went off by the train.

Fortune subsequently smiled upon "boots," and in the course of time he became proprietor of a first-rate hotel. In the interval the Rev. Mr. —— had risen from a humble

curate to the grade of a dean. Having occasion to visit the town of ——, he put up at the house of the ex-boots. The two men saw and recognized each other, and the affair of the early train reverted to the mind of both. "It was a most fortunate circumstance," said the dean, "that I did not oversleep myself on that morning, for from the memorable journey that followed, I date my advancement in the Church. But," he continued, with an expression that betokened some tender recollection, "if I ever should require you to wake me for an early train again, would you mind placing a mattress or feather-bed on the floor?"
—*The Railway Traveller's Handy Book.*

A MAD ENGINE-DRIVER.

A startling event happened at an early hour yesterday morning (Jan. 8th, 1884), in connection with the mail train from Brest, which is due in Paris at ten minutes to five o'clock. Whilst proceeding at full speed the passengers observed the brakes to be put on with such suddenness that fears were entertained that a collision was imminent, especially as the spot at which the train was drawn up was in utter darkness. Upon the guard reaching the engine he found the stoker endeavouring to overpower the driver, who had evidently lost his reason. After blocking the line the guard joined the stoker, and succeeded in securing the unfortunate man, but not until he had offered a desperate resistance. The locomotive was then put in motion, the nearest station was reached without further misadventure, and the driver was placed in custody. The train ultimately arrived in Paris after two hours' delay.

A MEXICAN CHIEF'S RAILWAY IMPRESSIONS.

Steam and gunpowder have often proved the most eloquent apostles of civilization, but the impressiveness of their arguments was, perhaps, never more strikingly illustrated than at the little railway station of Gallegos, in Northern Mexico. When the first passenger train crossed the viaduct, and the Wizards of the North had covered the festive tables with the dainties of all zones, the governor of Durango was not the most distinguished visitor; for among the spectators on the platform the natives were surprised to recognise the Cabo Ventura, the senior chief of a hill-tribe, which had never formally recognised the sovereignty of the Mexican Republic. The Cabo, indeed, considered himself the lawful ruler of the entire *Comarca*, and preserved a document in which the Virey Gonzales, *en nombre del Rey*—in the name of the King—appointed him "Protector of all the loyal tribes of Castro and Sierra Mocha." His diploma had an archæological value, and several amateurs had made him a liberal offer, but the old chieftain would as soon have sold his scalp. His soul lived in the past. All the evils of the age he ascribed to the demerits of the traitors who had raised the banner of revolt against the lawful king; and as for the countrymen of Mr. Gould, the intrusive *Yangueses*, his vocabulary hardly approached the measure of his contempt when he called them *herexes y combusteros*—heretics and humbugs.

"But it cannot be denied," Yakoob Khan wrote to his father, "that it has pleased Allah to endow those sinners with a good deal of brains;" and the voice of nature gradually forced the Cabo to a similar conclusion, till he resolved to come and see for himself.

When the screech of the iron Behemoth at last resounded at the lower end of the valley, and the train swept visibly around the curve of the river-gap, the natives set up a yell that waked up the mountain echoes; men and boys waved their hats and jumped to and fro, in a state of the wildest excitement. Only the old Cabo stood stock-still. His gaze was rivetted upon the phenomenon that came thundering up the valley; his keen eye enabled him to estimate the rate of speed, the trend of the up-grade, the breadth, the length, the height of the car. When the train approached the station, the crowd surged back in affright, but the Cabo stood his ground, and as soon as the cars stopped he stepped down upon the track. He examined the wheels, tapped the axles, and tried to move the lever; and when the engine backed up for water, he closely watched the process of locomotion, and walked to the end of the last car to ascertain the length of the train. He then returned to the platform and sat down, covering his face with both hands.

Two hours later the Governor of Durango found him in still the same position.

"Hallo, Cabo," he called out, "how do you like this? What do you think now of America Nueva?" ("New America," a collective term for the republics of the American continent).

The chieftain looked up. "*Sabe Dios*—the gods know—Senor Commandante, but *I* know this much: With Old America it's all up."

"Is it? Well, look here: would you now like to sell that old diploma? I still offer you the same price."

The Cabo put his hand in his bosom, drew forth a leather-shrouded old parchment, and handed it to his interlocutor. "Vengale, Usted—it's worthless and you are welcome to keep it." Nevertheless, he connived when the Governor slipped a gold piece into the pouch and put it upon his knees, minus the document.

But just before the train started, the Governor heard his name called, and stepped out upon the platform of the palace-car, when he saw the old chieftain coming up the track.

"I owe you a debt, senor," said he, "*y le pagarè en consejo*, I want to pay it off in good advice : Beware of those strangers."

"What strangers?"

"The caballeros who invented this machine."

"Is that what you came to tell me?" laughed the Governor as the train started.

The old Cabo waved his hand in a military salute. "*Estamos ajustade*, Senor Commandante, this squares our account."

—*Atlantic Monthly*, Jan., 1884.

MY ORDERS.

"Ticket, sir!" said an inspector at a railway terminus in the City to a gentleman, who, having been a season ticket holder, for some time, believed his face was so well known that there was no need for him to show his ticket. "My face is my ticket," replied the gentleman a little annoyed. "Indeed!" said the inspector, rolling back his wristband, and displaying a most powerful wrist, "well, my orders are to punch all tickets passing on to this platform."

LUGGAGE IN RAILWAY CARRIAGES.

The question of the liability of railway companies in the event of personal accident through parcels falling from a rack in the compartments of passenger trains has been raised in the Midlands. In December last, a tailor named Round was travelling from Dudley to Stourbridge, and, on the train being drawn up at Round Oak Station, a hamper was jerked from the racks and fell with such force as to cause him serious injury. Certain medical charges were incurred, and Mr. Round alleged that he was unable to attend to his business for five weeks in consequence of the accident. He therefore claimed £50 by way of compensation. Sir Rupert Kettle, before whom the case was tried, decided that the company was not liable, and could not be held responsible for whatever happened in respect to luggage directly under the control of passengers. The case is one of some public interest, inasmuch as a parcel falling from a rack is not an uncommon incident in a railway journey. Moreover, the hamper in question belonged, not to the plaintiff, but to a glass engraver, and contained four empty bottles, two razors, and a couple of knives.

—*Daily News*, March 29th, 1884.

EFFECTS OF CONSTANT RAILWAY TRAVELLING.

A writer in *Cassell's Magazine* remarks:—"We hear individuals now and then talking of the ease with which the season-ticket holder journeys backwards and forwards daily from Brighton. By the young, healthy man, no doubt, the journey is done without fatigue; but, after a certain time of life, the process of being conveyed by express fifty miles night and morning is anything but refreshing. The shaking and jolting of the best constructed carriage is not such as we experience in a coach on an ordinary road; but is made up of an infinite series of slight concussions, which jar the spinal column and keep the muscles of the back and sides in continued action." Dr. Radcliff, who has witnessed many cases of serious injury to the nervous system from this cause, contributed the following conclusive case some years ago to the pages of the *Lancet*:—"A hale and stout gentleman, aged sixty-three, came to me complaining of inability to sleep, numbness in limbs, great depression, and all the symptoms of approaching paralytic seizure. He was very actively engaged in large monetary transactions, which were naturally a source of anxiety. He had a house in town; but, having been advised by the late Doctor Todd to live at Brighton, he had taken a house there, and travelled to and fro daily by the express train. The symptoms of which he complained began to appear about four months after taking up his residence at Brighton, and he had undergone a variety of treatment without benefit, and was just hesitating about trying homœopathy when I saw him. I advised him to give up the journey for a month, and make the experiment of living quietly in town. In a fortnight his rest was perfectly restored, and the other symptoms rapidly disappeared, so that at the end of the month he was as well as ever again. After three months, he was persuaded to join his family at Brighton, and resumed his daily journeys. In a few days his rest became broken and in two months all the old symptoms returned. By giving up the journeys and again residing in town, he was once more perfectly restored; but, it being the end of the season, when the house at Brighton could not readily be disposed of, and yielding to the wishes of his family, he again resumed his journeys. In a month's time he was rendered so seriously unwell that he hesitated no longer in taking up his permanent abode in town; and since that time—now more than two years ago—he has enjoyed perfect health."

AN ELECTRIC TRAMWAY INCIDENT.

The following appeared in the *Irish Times* (Dublin, 1884): "It is not generally known that the country people along the line of the electric railway make strange uses of the insulated rails, which are the medium of electricity on this tramway, in connection with one of which an extraordinary and very remarkable occurrence is reported. People have no objection to touch the rail and receive a smart shock, which is, however, harmless, at least so far. On Thursday evening a ploughman, returning from work, stood upon this rail in order to mount his horse. The rail is elevated on insulators 18 inches above the level of the tramway

As soon as the man placed his hands upon the back of tho animal it received a shock, which at once brought it down, and falling against the rail it died instantly. The remarkable part is, that the current of electricity which proved fatal to the brute must have passed through the body of the man and proved harmless to him."

DUTY IN DISGUISE.

A gate-keeper in the employ of the Hessian Railway Company was recently the hero of an amusing incident. His wife being ill, he went himself to milk the goat; but the stubborn creature would not let him come near it, as it had always been accustomed to have this operation performed by its mistress. After many fruitless efforts, he at length decided to put on his wife's clothes. The experiment succeeded admirably; but the man had not time to doff his disguise before a train approached, and the gate-keeper ran to his accustomed post. His appearance produced quite a sensation among the officials of the passing train. The case was reported and an inquiry instituted, which however resulted in his favour, as the railway authorities granted the honest gate-keeper a gratuity of ten marks for the faithful discharge of his duties.

THE MARQUIS OF HARTINGTON ON GEORGE STEPHENSON.

The Marquis of Hartington, when laying the foundation stone of a public hall to be erected in memory of the inventor and practical introducer of railway locomotion, expressed himself as follows:—"That almost all the progress which this country has made in tho last half-century is mainly due to the development of the railway system. All the other vast developments of the power of steam, all the developments of manufacturing and mining industry would have availed but little for the greatness and prosperity of this country—in fact they could hardly have existed at all if there had been wanting those internal communications which have been furnished by the locomotive engine to railways brought into use by Stephenson. The changes which have been wrought in the history of our country by the invention, the industry, and perseverance of one man

are something that we may call astounding. There are
some things which exceed the dreams of poetry and romance.
We are justly proud of our imperial possessions, but the
steam engine, and especially the locomotive steam-engine,
the invention of George Stephenson—has not only increased
the number of the Queen's subjects by millions, but has
added more millions to her Majesty's revenues than have
been produced by any tax ever invented by any statesman.
Comfort and happiness, prosperity and plenty, have been
brought to every one of her Majesty's subjects by this
invention in far greater abundance than has ever been produced by any law, the production of the wisest and most
patriotic Parliament. The results of the career of a man
who began life as a herd boy, and who up to eighteen did
not know how to read or write, and yet was able to confer
such vast benefits upon his country and mankind for all
time, is worthy of a national and noble memorial."

THE STEPHENSON CENTENARY.

Of all celebrations in the North of England there was
never the like of the centenary of the birth-day of George
Stephenson, June 9th, 1881. The enthusiastic crowds of
people assembled to honour the occasion were never before
so numerous on any public holiday. Sir William
Armstrong, C.B., in his speech at the great banquet
remarked :—"The memory of a great man now dead is a
solemn subject for a toast, and I approach the task of proposing it with a full sense of its gravity. We are met to
celebrate the birth of George Stephenson, which took place
just 100 years ago—a date which nearly coincides with that
at which the genius of Watt first gave practical importance
to the steam-engine. Up to that time the inventive faculties
of man had lain almost dormant, but with the advent of the
steam-engine there commenced that splendid series of dis-
coveries and inventions which have since, to use the words
of Dr. Bruce, revolutionised the state of the world. Amongst
these the most momentous in its consequences to the human
race is the railway system—(cheers)—and with that system
including the locomotive engine as its essential element,
the name of George Stephenson will ever be pre-eminently
associated. In saying this, I do not mean to ignore the

important parts played by others in the development of the railway system; but it is not my duty on this occasion to review the history of that system and to assign to each person concerned his proper share of the general credit. To do this would be an invidious task, and out of place at a festival held in honour of George Stephenson only. I shall, therefore, pass over all names but his, not even making an exception in favour of his distinguished son. (Cheers.) It seldom or never happens that any great invention can be exclusively attributed to any one man; but it is generally the case that amongst those who contribute to the ultimate success there is one conspicuous figure that towers above all the rest, and such is the figure which George Stephenson presents in relation to the railway system. (Cheers.) To be sensible of the benefits we have derived from railways and locomotives let us consider for a moment what would be our position if they were taken from us. The present business of the country could not be carried on, the present population could not be maintained, property would sink to half its value—(hear, hear)—and instead of prosperity and progress we should have collapse and retrogression on all sides. (Cheers.) What would Newcastle be if it ceased to be a focus of railways? How would London be supplied if it had to fall back upon turnpike roads and horse traffic? In short, England as it is could not exist without railways and locomotives; and it is only our familiarity with them that blunts our sense of their prodigious importance. As to the future effects of railways, it is easy to see that they are destined to diffuse industrial populations over those vast unoccupied areas of the globe that abound in natural resources, and only wait for facilities of access and transport to become available for the wants of man. There is yet scope for an enormous extension of railways all over the world, and the fame of Stephenson will continue to grow as railways continue to spread. (Loud cheers.) But I should do scant justice to the memory of George Stephenson if I dwelt only on the results of his achievements. Many a great reputation has been marred by faults of character, but this was not the case with George Stephenson. His manly simplicity and frankness, and his kindly nature won for him the respect and esteem of all who knew him both in the earlier and later periods of his career—(cheers)—but the prominent feature in his character was his indomitable perseverance, which broke down all obstacles, and converted even his failures and disappointments into stepping stones to success. It was not the desire for wealth that actuated him in the pursuit of his objects, but it was a noble enthusiasm, far more conducive to great ends than the hope of gain, that carried him forward to his goal. Unselfish enthusiasm such as his always gives a tone of heroism to a character, and heroism above all things commands the homage of mankind. Newcastle may well be proud of its connection with George Stephenson, and the proceedings of this day testify how much his memory is cherished in this his native district. Any memorial dedicated to him would be appropriate to this occasion, and if such memorial were connected with scientific instruction it would be in harmony with his well-known appreciation of the value of scientific education, and of the sacrifices he made to give his son the advantage of such an education. (Cheers.) I now, gentlemen, have to propose to you the toast which has been committed to me, and which is 'Honour to the memory of George Stephenson, and may the college to be erected to his memory prove worthy of his fame.' I must ask you to drink this toast standing; and consider that the birth of Stephenson is a subject of jubilation, I think that although he is dead we may drink that toast with hearty cheering. (Hear, hear, and loud cheers.)

Mr. George Robert Stephenson, who was warmly cheered on rising to respond to the toast, said: "Mr. Mayor and gentlemen,—Let me, in the first place thank Sir William Armstrong for the many kind words he has uttered in honour of the memory of George Stephenson. It is true that he was, as Sir William said, one of the most kind-hearted and unselfish men that ever lived; but I suppose that no man has had a more up-hill struggle during the present century. (Cheers). I have now in my possession documents that would show in his early life the extraordinary and peculiar nature of the opposition that was brought against him as a poor man. He was opposed by many of the leading engineers of the day; some of these men using

language which, it is not incorrect to say, was not only injurious but wicked. This is not the proper occasion to weary you with a long speech, but with the view of showing the peculiar mode of engineers reporting against each other, I could very much wish, with your permission, to read a few sentences from documents that I have in my possession, dating back to 1823. (Hear, hear). This, gentlemen, will clearly show the sort of opposition I have alluded to. It occurs at the end of a report by an opponent upon some projected work on which the four brothers were engaged:—
'But we cannot conclude without saying that such a mechanic as Mr. Stephenson, who can neither calculate, nor lay his designs on paper, or distinguish the effect from the cause, may do very well for repairing engines when they are constructed, but for building new ones, he must be at great loss to his employers, from the many alterations that will take place in engine-building, when he goes by what we call the rule of thumb.' In a preceding sentence he is taunted with being like the fly going round on a crank axle, and shouting 'What a dust I am kicking up.' Gentlemen, the dust that George Stephenson kicked up formed itself into a cloud, and in every part of the globe to which it reached it carried with it and planted the seeds of civilization and wealth. Notwithstanding the hard and illiberal treatment to which he was exposed, he was not beaten; on the contrary, by his genius and his never-failing spirit, he raised himself above the level of the very men who opposed every effort he made towards the advancement of engineering science— efforts which have resulted in a vast improvement of our means for extracting the valuable products of the earth, and also of our means of conveying them at a cheap rate to distant markets. It is not too much to say that George Stephenson headed a movement by which alone could employment have been found for an ever-increasing population."

In the town of Chesterfield the Centenary was celebrated most befittingly. It was there the father of railways spent his latter days, and there he died. Although there was not such a flood of oratory as at Newcastle-upon-Tyne, many interesting speeches were delivered in connection with the event. We give some extracts from an address delivered by the Rev. Samuel C. Sarjant, B.A., Curate-in-Charge at that time—delivered at Holy Trinity Church, Chesterfield. An address which, for ability, nice discrimination of thought, and true appreciation of the subject, would not disgrace any pulpit in Christendom :—

"We meet to-day for the highest of all purposes, the worship of Almighty God. But we also meet to show our regard for the memory of one of the great and gifted dead. It is no small distinction of this town that the last days of George Stephenson were spent in it. And it adds to the interest of this church that it contains his mortal remains. With little internally to appeal to the eye, or to gratify taste, this church has yet a spell which will draw visitors from every part of the world. Men will come hither from all lands to look with reverence upon the simple resting place of him who was the father of the Locomotive and of the Railway system. And perhaps the naked simplicity which marks that spot is in keeping with a life, the grandeur of which was due solely to the man himself, and not to outward helps and circumstances. . . . .

"Toil has its roll of heroes, but few, if any, of them are greater than he whose birth we commemorate to-day. He was pre-eminently a self-made man, one who 'achieved' greatness by his own exertions. Granting that he was gifted with powers of body and mind above the average, these were his only advantages. The rest was due to hard work, patient, persistent effort. He had neither wealth, schooling, patrons, nor favouring circumstances. He comes into the arena like a naked athlete to wrestle in his own strength with the difficulties before him. And these were many and great!

"I need not dwell upon the details of a life which is so well known to most, and to some present so vividly, from personal intercourse and friendship. We all know what a battle he fought, how nobly and well, first striving by patient plodding effort to remove his own ignorance, cheerfully bending himself to every kind of work that came in his way, and seeking to gain not only manual expertness, but a mastery of principles. We know how he went on toiling, observing, experimenting, saying little—for he was

never given to the 'talk of the lips'—but doing much,
letting slip no chance of getting knowledge, and of turning
it to practical account. He was one of those, who

> While his companions slept
> Was toiling upwards in the night.

And in due time his quiet work bore fruit. He invented a
safety-lamp which alone should have entitled him to the
gratitude of posterity. He then set himself to improve the
locomotive, and fit it for the future which his prescient mind
discerned, and on a fair field he vanquished all competitors.
He then sought to adapt the roadway to the engine and
make it fit for its new work. And then, hardest task of all,
he had to convince the public that railway travelling was
a possible thing; that it could be made safe, cheap, and
rapid. In doing this he was compelled to design, plan,
and execute almost everything with his own mind and hand.
All classes and interests were against him, the engineers,
the land owners, the legislature, and the public. He had
to encounter the phantoms of ignorance and fear, the solid
resistance of vested interests, and the bottomless quagmires
of Chat Moss. But he triumphed! And it was a well-
earned reward as he looked down from his pleasant retreat
at Tapton upon the iron bands which glistened below, to
know that they were part of a network which was spreading
over the whole land and becoming the one highway of
transit and commerce. Nor was this all his satisfaction.
He knew that Europe and America were welcoming the
railway, and that it was promising to link together the
whole civilized world.

"Of the 'profit' of his labours to humanity I scarcely
venture to speak, since it cannot possibly be told in a few
words. The railway system has revolutionised society. It
has powerfully affected every class, every interest and
department of life. It has given an incredible impulse to
commerce, quickened human thought, created a new
language, new habits, tastes and pleasures. It has opened
up fields of industry and enterprise inaccessible and unknown
before. It has cheapened the necessaries and comforts of
life, enhanced the value of property, promoted the fellow-
ship of class with class, and brought unnumbered benefits
and advantages within the reach of all. And it is yet, as
to the world at large, but in the infancy of its development.

"How much, then, do we owe, under God, to George Stephenson. How much, not merely to his energy and diligence, but to his courage, patience, and uprightness? For these qualities, quite as much as gifts of genius and insight, contributed to his final success. He was crowned because he strove 'lawfully.' His patience was as great in waiting as his energy in working. He did not work from greed or self-glorification; and therefore the hour of success, when it came, found him the same modest, self-restrained man as before. He neither overrated the value of the system which he had set up, nor made it a means of speculation and gambling. He was a man of sterling honesty and uprightness—of self-control, simple in his habits and tastes, given to plain living and high thinking. And yet he was most kindly, genial, and cheery, of strong affections, considerate of his workpeople, tender to his family, full of love to little children and pet animals, brimming with fun and good humour. He had the gentleness of all noble natures, the largeness of mind and heart which could recognise ability and worth in others, and give rivals their due. For the young inventor, or for such of his helpers as showed marked diligence or promise, he had ready sympathy and aid. Nor ought we to pass unnoticed his love of nature and of natural beauty. Strong throughout his whole life, this was especially conspicuous at its close. Such leisure as his last days brought was spent amidst flowers and fruits, gardens and greeneries which he had planned and filled, and from the midst of whose treasures he could look forth over venerable trees and green fields upon a wide and varied landscape. And yet, even in this relaxation, the old energy and earnestness of purpose asserted themselves. He toiled and experimented, watching the growth of his plants and flowers with more than professional pains. Nor is it improbable that the ardour which led him to confine himself for hours together in a heated and unhealthy atmosphere led to his fatal illness.

We are bound, then, to mark and admit how much the moral element in the worker contributed to his success, and to the freshness of the regard which is felt for his memory and name. England is proud of his works, but prouder still of the man who did them. Far different would have been the result if impatience, ungenerousness, and love of greed had marred his life and work. The tributes of respect which we gladly lay upon his tomb to-day, would probably have been placed elsewhere."

REMARKABLE COINCIDENCES.

Many years ago the editor of this book and an elderly lady, the widow of a well-known farmer, took tickets from Little Bytham for Edenham in Lincolnshire. They were the only passengers, and as the railway passed for nearly two miles through Grimsthorpe park, she asked the driver if he would stop at a certain spot which would have saved us both perhaps half-a-mile's walk. The request was politely refused. After going a good distance the train was suddenly pulled up. I opened the window and found it had stopped at the very spot we desired. The stoker came running by with a fine hare which the train had run over. I said we can get out now and he said, Oh yes. And so through this strange misadventure to poor pussy our walk was much shortened.

Some years before the above occurrence I was travelling by the early morning mail train from the Midlands to the West of England. At Taunton I perceived a crowd of persons gathered at the front of the train. I went forward and saw a corpse was being removed from the van to a hearse outside the station. On reading the inscription on the coffin plate I was somewhat taken aback to find my own name. So Richard Pike living and Richard Pike dead had been travelling by the same train. Perhaps rarely, if ever, have two more singular circumstances occurred in connection with railway travelling.

LOSS OF TASTE.

Serjeant Ballantine in his *Experiences of a Barrister's Life*, says:—"There was a singular physical fact connected with him (Sir Edward Belcher), he had entirely lost the sense of taste; this he frequently complained of, and could not account for. A friend of mine, an eminent member of the Bar, suffers in the same way, but is able to trace the phenomenon to the shock that he suffered in a railway collision."

INGENIOUS SWINDLING.

A party of gentlemen who had been to Doncaster to see the St. Leger run, came back to the station and secured a compartment. As the train was about to start, a well-dressed and respectable looking man entered and took the only vacant seat. Shortly after they had started, he said, "Well, gentlemen, I suppose you have all been to the races to-day?" They replied they had. "Well," said the stranger, "I have been, and have unfortunately lost every penny I had, and have nothing to pay my fare home, but if you promise not to split on me, I have a plan that I think will carry me through." They all consented. He then asked the gentleman that sat opposite him if he would kindly lend him his ticket for a moment; on its being handed to him he took it and wrote his own name and address on the back of the ticket and returned it to the owner. Nothing more was said until they arrived at the place where they collected tickets; being the races, the train was very crowded, and the ticket-collector was in a great hurry; the gentlemen all pushed their tickets into his hands. The collector then asked the gentleman without a ticket for his, who replied he had already given it him. The collector stoutly denied it. The gentleman protested he had, and, moreover, would not be insulted, and ordered him to call the station-master. On the station-master coming, he said he wished to report the collector for insulting him. "I make a practice to always write my name and address on the back of my ticket, and if your man looks at his tickets he will find one of that description." The man looked and, of course, found the ticket, whereupon he said he must have been mistaken, and both he and the station-master apologised, and asked him not to report the case further.

DANGEROUS LUGGAGE.

Complaints are sometimes made of the want of due respect paid on the part of porters to passengers' luggage. It appears that occasionally a like lack of caution is manifested by owners to their own property. It is said that on a train

lately on a western railway in America, some passengers
were discussing the carriage of explosives. One man contended that it was impossible to prevent or detect this; if
people were not allowed to ship nitro-glycerine or dynamite
legitimately, they'd smuggle it through their baggage.
This assertion was contradicted emphatically, and the
passenger was laughed at, flouted, and ignominiously put
to scorn. Rising up in his wrath, he produced a capacious
valise from under the seat, and, slapping it emphatically
on the cover, said, "Oh, you think they don't, eh? Don't
carry explosives in cars? What's this?" and he gave the
valise a resounding thump, "Thar's two hundred good
dynamite cartridges in that air valise; sixty pounds of
deadly material; enough to blow this yar train and the
whole township from Cook County to Chimborazo. Thar's
dynamite enough," he continued; but he was without an
auditor, for the passengers had fled incontinently, and he
could have sat down upon twenty-two seats if he had wanted
to. And the respectful way in which the baggage men on
the out-going trains in the evening handled the trunks,
and valises was pleasant to see.

The neglect of carefulness appears, in one instance at
least, to have involved inconvenience to the offending official.
"An unknown genius," says an American periodical, "the
other day entrusted a trunk, with a hive of bees in it, to
the tender mercies of a Syracuse 'baggage-smasher.' The
company will pay for the bees, and the doctor thinks his
patient will be round in a fortnight or so."

—Williams's *Our Iron Roads.*

STUMPED.

Several Sundays ago a Philadelphia gentleman took his
little son on a railway excursion. The little fellow was
looking out of the window, when his father slipped the hat
off the boy's head. The latter was much grieved at his
supposed loss, when papa consoled him by saying that he
would "whistle it back." A little later he whistled and
the hat reappeared. Not long after the little lad flung his
hat out of the window, shouting, "Now, papa, whistle it
back again!" A roar of laughter in the car served to
enhance the confusion of perplexed papa. Moral: Don't
attempt to deceive little boys with plausible stories.

EXCURSIONISTS PUT TO THE PROOF.

A good story is told of the Manchester, Sheffield, and Lincoln Railway Company. A week or two since, the company ran an excursion train to London and back, the excursion being intended for their workmen at Gorton and Manchester. There was an enormous demand for the tickets; so enormous that the officials began, to use an expressive term, "to smell a rat." But the sale of the tickets was allowed to proceed. The journey to London was made, and a considerable number of the passengers congratulated themselves upon the remarkably cheap outing they were having. But on the return journey they made a most unpleasant discovery. Their tickets were demanded at Retford, and then the ticket-collectors insisted upon the holder of every ticket proving that he was in the employ of the company. The result can be imagined. There were more persons in the train who had no connection with the company than there were of the company's employés; and the former had either to pay a full fare to and from London, or to give their names and addresses preparatory to being summoned. We hear, from a reliable source, that the fares thus obtained amount to about £300.—*Echo*, Sept. 23, 1880.

A MONKEY SIGNALMAN.

We learn from the *Colonies* that a monkey signalman manages the railway traffic at Witenhage, South Africa. The human signalman has had the misfortune to lose both his legs, and has trained a baboon to discharge his duties. Jacky pushes his master about on a trolly, and, under his directions, works the lever to set the signals with a most ludicrous imitation of humanity. He puts down the lever, looks round to see that the correct signal is up, and then gravely watches the approaching train, his master being at hand to correct any mistake.

A CURIOUS CLASSIFICATION.

The guard of an English railway carriage recently refused to allow a naturalist to carry a live hedgehog with him. The traveller, indignant, pulled a turtle from his wallet and said, " Take this too!" But the guard replied good naturedly, " Ho, no, sir. It's dogs you can't carry; and dogs is dogs, cats is dogs, and 'edge'ogs is dogs, but turtles is hinsects."

PULLMAN'S CARRIAGES.

In the discussion on Mr. C. Douglas Fox's recent paper on the Pennsylvania railway, Mr. Barlow, the engineer of the Midland, observed that there was a certain attractive power about a Pullman's carriage, which ought not to be overlooked, a power which brought passengers to it who would not otherwise travel by railway. A Pullman's carriage weighed somewhere about twenty tons. The cost of hauling that weight was about 1½d. per mile; that was the sum which the Midland Company proposed to charge for first-class passengers, so that one first-class passenger would pay the haulage of the carriage. If the attractive power of the carriage brought more than one first-class passenger it would of course pay itself.

Herepath's Railway Journal, Jan. 23, 1875.

PROFITABLE DAMAGES.

The Springfield *Republican*, of 1877, is responsible for the following story:—"The industry of railroading has developed some thrifty characters, among whom a former employé of the New York, New Haven, and Hartford road deserves high rank. He was at one time at work in the Springfield depôt, and while taking a trunk out of a baggage car from Boston he was thrown over and hurt, the baggage-smashing art being for a time reversed. The injured employé suffered terribly, and crawled around on crutches until the Boston and Albany and the New Haven roads united and gave him 6000 dollars. He was cured the next day. Shortly afterwards a man on the Boston and Albany road was killed, and the Company gave his widow 3,000 dollars. The former cripple, who had scored 6,000 dollars already, soon married her, and thus counted 9,000 dollars. He recovered his health so completely that he was able again to work on the railroad, but finally, not being hurt again within a reasonable time, he retired to a farm which he had bought with a part of the proceeds of his former calamities."

RAILWAY ENTERPRISE.

It would be difficult to close this series of Railway Anecdotes more appropriately than in the words of George Stephenson's celebrated son Robert at a banquet given to him at Newcastle-upon-Tyne, in August, 1850. "It was but as yesterday," he said, "that he was engaged as an assistant in tracing the line of the Stockton and Darlington Railway. Since that period, the Liverpool and Manchester, the London and Birmingham, and a hundred other great works had sprung into vigorous existence. So suddenly, so promptly had they been accomplished, that it appeared to him like the realization of fabled powers, or the magician's wand. Hills had been cut down, and valleys had been filled up; and where this simple expedient was inapplicable, high and magnificent viaducts had been erected; and where mountains intervened, tunnels of unexampled magnitude had been unhesitatingly undertaken. Works had been scattered over the face of our country, bearing testimony to the indomitable enterprise of the nation and the unrivalled skill of its artists. In referring thus to the railway works, he must refer also to the improvement of the locomotive engine. This was as remarkable as the other works were gigantic. They were, in fact, necessary to each other. The locomotive engine, independent of the railway, would be useless. They had gone on together, and they now realized all the expectations that were entertained of them. It would be unseemly, as it would be unjust, if he were to conceal the circumstances under which these works had been constructed. No engineer could succeed without having men about him as highly-gifted as himself. By such men he had been supported for many years past; and, though he might have added his mite, yet it was to their co-operation that all his success was owing."

THE END.

Printed by J. Derry, Albert Street and Hounds Gate, Nottingham.

www.ingramcontent.com/pod-product-compliance
Lightning Source LLC
Chambersburg PA
CBHW060601030726
47498CB00005B/1491